FOUR MINUTES

BOOKS BY
BRIAN ANDREWS
& JEFFREY WILSON

TIER ONE
Tier One
War Shadows
Crusader One
American Operator
Red Specter
Collateral
Dempsey

TIER ONE ORIGINS
Scars: John Dempsey

SONS OF VALOR
Sons of Valor
Sons of Valor II: Violence of Action
Sons of Valor III: War Machine

THE SHEPHERDS
Dark Intercept
Dark Angel
Dark Fall

W. E. B. GRIFFIN'S
PRESIDENTIAL AGENT
Rogue Asset

OTHER NOVELS
The Sandbox
Four Minutes

BOOKS BY
ANDREWS & WILSON
WRITING AS ALEX RYAN

NICK FOLEY
Beijing Red
Hong Kong Black

BOOKS BY
BRIAN ANDREWS
The Calypso Directive
The Infiltration Game
Reset

BOOKS BY
JEFFREY WILSON
The Traiteur's Ring
The Donors
Fade to Black
War Torn

FOUR MINUTES

A THRILLER

ANDREWS & WILSON

BLACK STONE
PUBLISHING

Printed in the United States of America

First edition: 2024
ISBN 978-1-6650-4195-9
Fiction / Science Fiction / Military

Version 2

Blackstone Publishing
31 Mistletoe Rd.
Ashland, OR 97520

www.BlackstonePublishing.com

For Peter and Marcus,
whose friendship and vision helped bring this story into existence . . .

AUTHORS' NOTE

For eight wonderful years, our readers have enthusiastically joined us on the adventures of John Dempsey, Keith "Chunk" Redman, Grimes, Munn, Whitney Watts, Jarvis, and all the others who live in the Tier One and Sons of Valor universes. You've told us that what you love the most is the characters, their relationships, their sacrifices, and how their lives bring an authentic voice and experience to the world of special warfare and covert operations. We receive regular emails from fans asking if we are going to continue writing those series and the answer is YES—as long as you keep reading them, we'll keep writing them. The next Tier One and Sons of Valor books are in production as we pen this authors' note.

With *The Sandbox* and now *Four Minutes*, we are not making a pivot toward sci-fi. Rather, we are expanding our work and attempting to bring the same gritty, grounded, real-world storytelling to topics of emerging technology. Artificial intelligence and other breakthrough technologies will dramatically impact the human condition—how we perceive and interact with the world around us and with each other. In our new line of techno-thrillers, we'll pose questions to you, the reader, and offer our take on what the near future "could be." Despite falling outside the Tier One universe, these tales feature military and veteran characters with the same real-world problems, relationships, lives, and sacrifices our readers love in our military thrillers. We hope you'll be not only willing but *excited* to join us on these new adventures in between installments of our legacy characters.

So, thank you! Thank you for coming along with us on the journey into the great unknown.

A&W

PROLOGUE

Pat Moody sighed as he trudged down the wet grass between the long rows of perfectly symmetrical grave markers toward the lone figure standing in front of the headstones, head bowed as usual.

Of course the grave has to be at the end of the damn row.

It was a hike to Section 60 from the visitor's center, and he felt more than annoyed at having to be here at all. His irritation was driven partly by his exhaustion: he'd landed back in DC from his trip to the aircraft carrier only hours ago and he had way too much shit to do, including getting a few hours of sleep. But he found meetings annoying on his best day. First, he was perfectly capable of sending update reports as events warranted, so being called out for an update was irritating at best, if not downright insulting. And second, they were well into the twenty-first century now, with myriads of encryption capabilities for voice and other forms of communications.

But the man Moody was meeting, Brigadier General Travis Waltrip, still insisted on Cold War–era cloak-and-dagger meetings at the most

inconvenient place in all of the Beltway. Despite Waltrip's trim athlet-
icism and reputation for a sharp mind, such requests showed him for
what he was—a friggin' dinosaur nearing extinction. Ironic that this
man was the person in charge of America's most advanced technology-
based task force.

The gray sky let loose a few early dribbles of rain from the thicken-
ing clouds—the gods laughing at his situation, Moody decided.

He stepped up beside General Waltrip, his boss and the head
of Task Force Omega, a man who answered only to the Director of
National Intelligence and the President. Moody imagined the number
of people read even superficially into the program could be counted on
one hand—if there were any more at all.

I wonder just how much the President knows, Moody thought, studying the warrior beside him, head bowed and hands clasped, holding
his blue Air Force cap against his military-issue trench coat. Whatever
Moody thought about these asinine covert meetings, he knew it was
folly to underestimate the intelligence and cunning of the man praying
at the foot of the grave.

Moody glanced at the headstone:

AARON LOUIS WALTRIP
CAPT USMC
FALLUJAH, IRAQ
OCT 3 1979
APR 19 2005
LOVING HUSBAND AND SON

The general let out a long, slow breath and opened his eyes. Without looking up, eyes on the headstone marking the grave of his son, he
spoke. "Do you ever wonder how the world would be different if we'd
had this technology twenty-five years ago—how many lives could have
been saved?"

Moody nodded. "All the time, sir," he said, as empathy for the man
knocked the edge off his irritation.

The general looked over at him, his steel-blue eyes sharp and clear.

"I was commanding a fighter squadron of F-15 Strike Eagles when I was notified that Aaron had died. I'd already lost a man and this was when things were heating up in Iraq, but we had scores of dead in Afghanistan as well. I'm not the only one who lost a child or a friend over there. Almost all of America has only one degree of separation from loss in war. You see, it's not the moment alone that matters, Pat. It's the ripple of time. In the case of 9/11, that ripple spread out over decades. What we're trying to do here is stop things that can affect good people for generations. That ripple of time . . ." Waltrip glanced again at his son's headstone, then gave it a slight nod.

"I know that, sir," Moody said.

"Good," Waltrip said, and Moody witnessed the man's instant transformation from sad old father to razor-sharp head of a program designed to stop future attacks and to win future wars. Moody followed as General Waltrip began a slow walk between the headstones, back toward the main path. "You know, I don't bring you out here for security reasons. I bring you out here because I want the intimacy of in-person meetings. It keeps us bonded in purpose and in responsibility for what we're doing. I imagine you can guess my second reason for choosing this place in particular."

"To remind us both of the purpose for the program, but also the cost of our failures," Moody offered. The general was overly philosophical for Moody's taste, but he had no choice but to play along.

"Well done. Nice to see a heart still beats beneath that hard and cynical mind of yours," Waltrip said with a patronizing smile as he resumed his stroll. "You of all people, Pat, don't need reminding that the clock is ticking. How is candidate selection and recruiting coming along?"

"We've identified the last two candidates, both members of the Joint Special Operations Command. They're deployed, so I'll be traveling to them in short order. We know they'll say yes, so we'll begin testing and evaluation, establish our baselines, and then get back to fulfilling our charter."

"Good. I can't overemphasize how important it is that we get Omega back up and running. We're blind until you do."

"Yes, sir."

"And the bugs in our tech? Have you worked those out?"

"We believe so, sir."

"I hope so, Pat," Waltrip said. "We need this team to last. People with these *attributes* don't just grow on trees, so we can't treat them as expendable, you understand?"

Moody met the general's eyes—eyes that almost seemed to stare into his soul. He wanted to blurt out that what happened to the last team wasn't his fault. That they were still learning the rules and figuring things out as they went along, that the first team would have aged out soon anyway. In fact, one could argue that it was their degraded and slow combat skills—rather than the fact that Moody had put them at the wrong place and the wrong time—that had gotten them killed. But he didn't dare say such a thing. Waltrip was not a man who tolerated excuses.

He buried the thoughts and simply said, "Yes, sir. I understand, which is why I brought in a new medical director, Claire Donahue. She's got the knowledge and fresh approach we need to get this thing sustainable."

"That's good, Pat, because it's not just our losses that have me pressing the timeline."

Moody stopped in surprise, and the general took an additional step or two before stopping and turning to him. "Is there some imminent threat I should be aware of, sir?"

"Scores of them, son. America is under assault from all sides and within. Everyone wants to see us fall," Waltrip said with vitriol. "But that's not the only thing that keeps me up at night. Let me ask you something, Pat. When you look at the latest generation of Chinese fighter jets, drones, and submarines, what do you see?"

Moody shook his head, confused. "I'm sorry, sir, I'm not following you."

"What I see is the F-35. I see the Predator. I see the Virginia class submarine."

"Okay . . ."

"Pat, if you believe that this project will tilt the scales permanently toward us gaining and maintaining an asymmetrical tactical and strategic advantage over our enemies, then you are not as smart as I thought, and maybe not the right pick to head up this project."

"Again, sir, is there something actionable I should know about?" Moody said, feeling irritated again.

Just get to the point, old man.

"Look, it is only a matter of time before the Chinese, or the Russians, or—God help us—the North Koreans steal this technology and start operating. In fact, I'm of the mind that using Omega is the *only* way to stop that from happening."

Moody nodded as they made it to the asphalt pathway.

"I'll have them trained and traveling within a week, sir. I promise you that."

"It's only a matter of time, Pat," Waltrip repeated and turned to face him. "If it hasn't happened already."

A chill ran down Moody's spine. What if Waltrip was right? What if there was already another team out there? He'd been so focused on counterterrorism and intelligence collection that he'd not even contemplated such a wrinkle.

It might explain . . .

"Get back to work, Pat," Waltrip said, turning away from the long hike back to the visitor's center. "I have a few more friends to visit."

PART I

"Time is the wisest counselor of all."

—Pericles

CHAPTER 1

LEAD VEHICLE

SPECIAL OPERATIONS THREE-VEHICLE CONVOY

ONE AND A HALF MILES WEST OF GOUNDAM

SOUTH OF LAC TÉLÉ, MALI

PRESENT DAY

0215 LOCAL TIME

Special Operations Chief Tyler Brooks shifted in the front passenger seat of the Hyundai H200 SUV, but it didn't help. He was wedged in tight, and no amount of squirming could fix that. The vehicle certainly had plenty of room for a Sunday family drive to Cracker Barrel but was clearly not designed with fully kitted-up special operators in mind. Navy SEALs weren't compact dudes by "normal" standards, but add sixty pounds of body armor and gear and you got yourself the Special Operations equivalent of a clown car.

And I'm the ringleader of this circus, he thought with a chuckle.

Despite uncomfortable moments like this, Tyler loved being on mission. He loved serving his country, sure, but most of all, he loved the brotherhood that was US Naval Special Warfare. He'd die for his country, but he'd die for his brothers first . . . if that made sense.

He used a gloved hand to scratch at his beard and then adjusted the FN SCAR-L assault rifle in his lap. Tonight, their X was a walled compound housing two two-story buildings just outside Goundam, which was every bit of three hundred miles northeast of Bamako. According to Farley, their 18 Delta Special Operations combat medic whose real name was Warren Perry, the run-down metropolis of Bamako was the only "real" city in Mali. Of course, Farley hailed from some tiny ass town outside of Mobile, Alabama, so Tyler wasn't sure how much of an expert on "real" cities that made him. Tyler made a mental note to ask Farley what was the biggest city the kid had ever actually visited. If New Orleans was the answer, then he was going to haze the shit out of him.

"Reaper One, Mother—I show you one mile from the turn," Zee called in his ear from her duty station in the TOC, or Tactical Operations Center.

Tyler smiled. Always a step ahead, planning the next move and anticipating fires—that was Lieutenant Zee Williams. She'd already been the intel lead when he'd arrived at the Tier One unit as a second-class petty officer. Zee wasn't just the smartest person in every room, but she was also a total badass. As an intel officer, she wasn't required to fully qualify on Green Team—the JSOC SEAL Team training-and-selection course—but she'd completed the course anyway on her arrival to the unit. The Green Team instructors had used her success to browbeat seasoned SEALs who came after and found themselves struggling. In Tyler's Green Team class, the instructor had pulled Zee out of a meeting to run the ropes course and "show these frogmen how to do it." As it turned out, there's no better way to motivate a bunch of SEALs than forcing them to congratulate a female intelligence officer after she'd run the course they'd failed to satisfactorily execute.

Everyone in the command had mad respect for Zee, and that included Tyler.

"Reaper One, roger," he finally answered. "Time to next overflight pass?"

"Pass coming in two mikes," Zee said in his ear. Her voice took on a cautious slowness that gave Tyler pause.

Brooks double-clicked his mike in response. Something had Zee's antennae up, but he couldn't tell what. Tonight's op was a straight-forward snatch-and-grab. Resistance would be light because AQIZ believed no one was working this deep into Mali anymore. They felt safe because they believed Americans had lost their stomach for hunting down terrorists. The Ethiopian bomb maker they were hunting tonight was, according to HUMINT, living at the target compound full time with limited security. Tonight's op should be a milk run. But Brooks also knew, after almost a decade of combat operations hunting down terror-ists and other threats, that the key to staying alive was always assuming the shit could hit the fan at any moment. Nevertheless, that mantra didn't explain what had Lieutenant Zee Williams on edge.

"There it is," Tyler said to Skip Harrison, who was behind the wheel of the Hyundai.

"I got it," Harrison said and made the sharp turn off the shitty, pothole-covered "highway" and onto the dirt road that somehow seemed to ride smoother.

Harrison killed the headlights, and Tyler immediately pulled down the NVGs on the front of his helmet. The pitch-black road came alive in incredibly sharp greens and grays.

"Two, the turn is fifty yards short of where it shows on the GPS," Harrison said, giving the driver of their second vehicle—which was three-quarters of a mile in trail—a heads-up.

That vehicle, a Hilux pickup truck, carried Max Keaton, the driver and number two on the op, and Curt Lehmann, who would man the Mastova M02 Coyote heavy machine gun in the bed of their truck should the need arise. It still felt weird to Tyler, grandson of a preacher from Tampa, just how many countries there were in the world where a 12.7 mm machine gun in the bed of a pickup truck was so common that no one would even pay attention when it passed.

"You're two miles out," Zee said, her voice still not the normal singsong cadence it carried on most ops. "Can you slow a minute? I want to check something out."

"Is there a problem, Mother?" Tyler asked.

"I don't think so," she said after a beat. "We just had a pass over the X. There are five confirmed heat signatures on-site in Building One where we know one of them is Lotto," she said, referring to the call sign for their target, notorious bomb maker Fawaz al-Hamdi. "One is a sentry who is taking a smoke break beside the rear wall. Three others are inside with him. And Building Two has four thermals that all appear to be sleeping. If you're quiet, you could be in and out without waking them . . ."

She let that hang in the air for a minute.

"So what's the problem, Mother?" Tyler asked.

Another pause.

"I've got a pickup heading north on the exfil road," she said.

"Is it heading toward the compound?"

"Can't tell yet, but I don't like it," Zee said. "Recommend hold."

Tyler considered a moment. There was no question that Zee was overly cautious at times. He got it; that was her job. She was like their mother hen, the reason the call sign for the TOC was so often *Mother*. But she also had incredible instincts.

"How many thermals?"

"Two in the cab, one in the bed," she said.

"Let's just say it is heading to the X. What's their ETA?"

"Fifteen to twenty mikes," she said.

Tyler clenched his jaw. It would be tight, but if the op went smoothly his team could *be the night* by then. Besides it was only three dudes in a pickup. He chopped a hand forward and Skip Harrison pressed the gas. "Two, we're going to accelerate things a bit. Set up at where the compound drive intersects the exfil road, just in case, to watch our six. We're going to be in and out in under ten."

"Two," came Keaton's reply, acknowledging the adjustment.

"Mother, we're still green," Tyler said. "We'll compress the timeline and be ghosts before they arrive."

"Roger all," Zee said.

He wasn't sure if her flat voice meant she didn't like his call or if she was glad to be unburdened of the decision. She was an officer and he was enlisted, having just put on Chief at the young age of twenty-seven. But he was the senior NCO in the field and "One" for this op. At the end of the day, it was his call to make, and they'd been waiting on an opportunity to black bag this HVT for months.

He wasn't prepared to abort the op based on a maybe.

Sometimes, you just gotta go all in.

"Reaper One is Mako," he said when they made the next turn. Stick, who sat in the rear seat beside Farley, had begged for tonight's checkpoint call signs to be shark names, announcing he was sick of the beer brands, whiskeys, and sports cars they typically used.

"Roger, we show you at Mako," Zee said. "Two is a half mile in trail."

Tomorrow they'd be out again, no doubt. Maybe they could do skateboard brands . . .

The road transitioned to a hill, and Tyler clutched his SCAR as the SUV rocked side to side. Skip and Farley preferred their H models, with the more powerful 7.62 mm rounds, but for Tyler, it was about dexterity these days. The L model SCAR fired a smaller 5.56 mm round, but the magazine held ten more rounds than the H, and in a less bulky package. The 5.56 was ideal for close-quarters combat, which is what he constantly found himself in these days.

"Two is Mako," Keaton announced in Tyler's ear.

Harrison slowed the SUV as they approached the crest of the hill and then came to a stop. "Is this it?"

Tyler checked the GPS on his wrist and then said, "Should be. Mother, Reaper One is Tiger."

"Roger One," Zee came back. "I show you Tiger. Call Great White."

"One," he said in acknowledgment. He opened the door and climbed out, adjusting his gear and rolling his head until he got a satisfying crack from his neck. "Let's go to work, boys," he said, then waved a hand over his head.

Tyler led his squad toward the east corner of the medium-sized compound at the bottom of the hill, but halfway down, Harrison vectored left toward the west corner.

"Sentry from the rear of Building One has circled the structure and is moving east, Reaper," Zee said softly in Tyler's ear.

Tyler double-clicked his mike in acknowledgment instead of talking. He moved swiftly in the lead, with Stick offset on his left side. He kept low, in a combat crouch, his upper body practically floating as he scanned over his rifle, the green IR designator cutting the night in a horizontal pattern under his NVGs—but invisible to the naked eye.

After a few minutes, he felt the familiar burn as lactate built up in his thighs, but he ignored the pain. As they approached the wall, he saw the glow on night vision of a cigarette flare, followed by the outline of a roving sentry rounding the corner of Building One. Tyler raised a closed fist over his head and took a knee. The sentry moved to the northeast corner of the compound, where he stopped to smoke.

Tyler glanced over at Stick, who was call sign Reaper Six, and communicated with a series of hand gestures his plan to ambush the sentry from behind.

The SEAL nodded, then crossed behind Tyler, staying low and moving swiftly to the southeast side of the wall. Tyler crawled along the wall northeast, silent as a slithering serpent. He looked back at Stick who nodded, then rose slowly until just the top of his helmet and his NVGs cleared the four-foot-tall stucco. The sentry leaned his back against the wall, smoking and oblivious to Tyler's presence behind him. Heart beating like a metronome, steady and unflappable, Tyler lowered himself into a squatting crouch and withdrew the SOG bowie knife from the horizontal sheath on his kit.

"Not yet," came Stick's almost-silent whisper, magnified in Tyler's earpiece. "Hold . . ."

He let Stick be his eyes, every muscle tense and ready to pounce.

"Go."

Tyler vaulted over the wall and took the sentry, wrapping an arm around the man's neck and crushing his throat tight enough to prevent even a puff of air, much less a scream, from escaping. Tyler fell backward, pulling the man down on top of him, feeling the sentry's windpipe fracture under his forearm. He wrapped both legs around the man's upper thighs as he landed, then squeezed harder, cutting off blood flow to the man's brain.

The sentry squirmed, rolling back and forth and flailing his arms uselessly in front of him. He tried to kick but he was locked in place.

The squirming slowed.

Then stopped.

Tyler smelled the stank of urine, and he pushed the man away, over onto his face. Kneeling beside the motionless body, he drove his knife swiftly up into the space at the base of the skull, moving it back and forth once and then pulling it out of the man's brain stem. All connection between brain and body severed, the sentry was now out of the fight.

Permanently.

Tyler sheathed his knife and brought up his SCAR for a fresh scan of the rear of the compound.

"Tango down," he reported.

"Four is Great White," Harrison said from his ready position on the other side of the compound.

"Go," Tyler said.

Harrison and Farley, call signs Reaper Four and Reaper Five, would now hop the wall, make sure there were no booby traps or shooters, then converge to breach the front of Building One while Tyler and Stick entered the rear.

"Position," Harrison announced in Tyler's ear just moments later.

"Reaper is Great White," Tyler said, signifying they were in position to breach. "Sitrep, Mother."

"The back room, where One and Six will enter, has one tango who is pacing. The front room, where Four and Five will breach, has two shooters side by side—they appear to be sitting on a couch and watching TV or playing a video game. They'll have their backs to you on entry."

"What about Lotto?" Harrison asked, seeking clarification on the HVT they planned to grab.

"Lotto is in a middle room, alone and seated at a table, working."

"Copy all," Tyler said. "Four, breach on my mark . . ." Tyler flipped up his NVGs and then nodded at Stick. His teammate checked the doorknob and nodded back to confirm it wasn't locked. The plan was to avoid flash-bangs which would wake the three sleeping terrorists in Building Two more easily than gunfire from their heavily suppressed rifles. It might not work, but it was worth a try. Tyler nodded back and counted them down.

"Three . . . two . . . one . . ."

On *zero* Stick pulled the door open and Tyler darted through the gap.

Tyler cleared left then swiveled to center and put the red dot from his holographic sight onto the first target's forehead—a man drinking tea at a table. The terrorist lunged for his rifle propped against the table, but too late. Tyler's SCAR burped and the 5.56 mm round tore off the top of the man's head. The terrorist pitched backward, the chair toppling with him and crashing onto the floor.

Tyler cringed at the racket the kill had made, but he advanced to fall in beside Stick who was moving toward a cased opening separating the back and middle room. He heard three burps from Farley and Harrison's rifles as they breached the front. Four pops confirmed his teammates had dispatched the two shooters on the sofa as they all converged on the bomb maker in the middle room in perfect unison.

Four red dots hovered on the chest of Fawaz al-Hamdi.

The man's eyes, set deep in the lined and weathered face, glared hatred at them, but his hands went up in surrender. Tyler centered his red dot on the target's face as Stick moved in to run his hands over the man's body and reach under the terrorist's long, gray tunic, checking for weapons, but more importantly, any explosives or a suicide vest that could take the op sideways really fast.

Tyler signaled Harrison and Farley to hold sentry in case they'd awoken the sleeping fighters in Building Two.

So far so good . . .

"Reaper is Lotto. Say again—Lotto," Tyler reported, letting the TOC know they had achieved their mission objective and captured Fawaz al-Hamdi.

"Understand Lotto," Zee said in his ear. "You need to get moving. The pickup is still inbound."

Stick had forced the bomb maker onto the floor and had a knee on al-Hamdi's neck while Tyler kept his red dot on the man's temple. After binding the terrorist's hands behind his back, Stick jerked the man roughly to his feet and forced him back into the chair he'd been sitting in.

"Copy, Mother. Two mikes," Tyler said, notifying his teammates how much time they had left for housekeeping before the exfil.

Farley held watch on the other building while Tyler and Harrison managed the dead bodies, taking quick pics of faces and scanning handprints onto specialized tablets they carried for this purpose. Next, they tossed cell phones into a coyote-tan bag along with al-Hamdi's laptop and paper notes from the table.

"Reaper, we may have a problem," said Zee's suddenly tense voice. "The inbound truck is hauling ass toward your position on the exfil road."

"Copy. Two, did you hear that? You've got incoming," Tyler said.

"One, Two—'I'm your huckleberry,'" Keaton said in Tyler's ear, his voice full of swagger.

Tyler spun a hand over his head, and his three fellow SEALs formed up on him, Stick guiding al-Hamdi by his flex-cuffed wrists toward the back door. Tyler led them out, clearing left as Harrison followed clearing right. The compound still sat empty and quiet—no new fighters pouring out of the second building. They slipped over the wall, Stick lifting the terrorist up and over where he landed in a heap, and together they sprinted up the hill to where their vehicle waited.

"Inbound vehicle is almost on you, Two," Zee said.

"We don't see them yet—must still be around the bend," Keaton said from the other vehicle stationed between the compound's dirt entrance and the exfil road.

Tyler could picture Curt Lehmann already in the bed of the truck, both hands on the mounted heavy machine gun, ready to light up the approaching threat.

"They stopped," Zee said. "I think they're going to try to sneak up and engage you on foot."

Tyler and his party, for their part, had just arrived at their Hyundai. Stick shoved the bound al-Hamdi into the back seat and then slid in beside him. Tyler stood in the open door on the front passenger side, looking down the long approach road as Farley climbed in the rear seat, sandwiching the terrorist between the two SEALs.

"Sitrep, Mother?" Keaton pressed.

"I got two heat sigs moving as a pair and one doing something in the bed of the truck." Then abruptly, she said, "Wait . . . hold on. Scratch that, now I've got seven."

"You said there were only three in the truck," Keaton came back. "Where did the other four come from?"

"I don't know," Zee said, her voice electric with tension, "but I'm staring at them on my feed."

"Shit," Tyler said and turned to Harrison. "They're going to get overrun. We gotta help them. Go, go, go!"

Gunfire erupted in the near distance as their brother SEALs engaged the enemy QRF that had somehow just magically doubled in size.

Harrison started the Hyundai's engine, slammed the transmission into gear, and stomped on the gas. The SUV fishtailed wildly in the dusty gravel, then went barreling down the drive toward their team-mates.

"Heavy fire," Keaton reported. "We're taking heavy fire."

"Two, look out, I think they have an RPG!" Zee called.

Tyler, who was standing on the running board, half out of the truck, saw an orange-yellow streak ahead, followed by an explosion that rocked the night a heartbeat later. A fireball rose in a mushroom cloud of dark smoke where Keaton's pickup was positioned. With his left hand holding onto the doorframe, Tyler snapped his NVGs into place, lighting up the world again in gray-green monochrome. Then, he brought his rifle up. Stick popped out from the rear passenger compartment, steadying his own rifle on the roof as the SUV screamed down the road, a hundred-yard-long plume of dust in their wake.

As Keaton's pickup came into view, a shadow of a body hung limp, draped over the mounted machine gun with flames dancing around it. *Lehmann.* Next, Tyler watched tracers of machine-gun fire riddle

Keaton's body as the SEAL crawled out of the driver's seat, trying to escape the burning wreckage that had once been their vehicle.

Tyler couldn't see the enemy shooters, but he guessed they were spread out and concealed just beyond the turn at the crossroads, obstructed by a medium-sized Joshua tree. He opened up with his SCAR in that direction, and Stick did the same. Harrison veered their SUV hard right to provide blocking cover with their vehicle. Stick, who was on the wrong side of the SUV for the evasive maneuver, was launched into the air as if from a catapult. Tyler watched his teammate hit the dirt, roll, and scramble for cover.

Harrison ducked low in his seat as incoming machine-gun fire exploded the driver's-side windows. Tyler jumped off the sideboard and ducked low into cover as his teammate belly-crawled across to the passenger side and out the door. At the same time, he felt burning pain rip through his shoulder at the base of his neck, then felt warm wet pour down his chest and back. He dropped onto the ground beside Harrison, cursing at having been shot as they pressed their backs into the side of the Hyundai.

"Shit, shit, shit," he heard Farley call from behind him.

"Are you hit?" Tyler called.

"I'm shot, but in the fight," Farley said, pain in his voice.

"Al-Hamdi?" Tyler asked.

"Dead," came the reply.

The enemy fire went quiet a moment, indicating the shooters were reloading or repositioning.

"Where's Stick?" Harrison said.

"Here," Stick called between bursts of renewed gunfire from behind a rock. "I'm intact."

Tyler nodded, then looked over to see Harrison holding a hand to the side of his face, blood streaming between his gloved fingers. "You hit?"

"Just grazed me, I think," Harrison said.

"Dropped the RPG guy," Stick shouted.

"Mother, how many tango thermals have you got now?" Tyler asked.

"Six," she said in his ear. "Be advised, they're setting up a heavy gun."

Shit . . . if they get that up, we're done for.

"Stick, you're with me. If we don't take out that heavy gun, we're hamburger," Tyler said, then turned to Harrison and Farley. "Covering fire."

"Check," Farley said, repositioning to do just that.

Staying low, Tyler moved behind Farley, who climbed onto the running board and began firing his rifle at the Joshua tree and the four new assholes who'd somehow ambushed them. A second later, Harrison opened fire, alternating with his teammate, giving Tyler and Stick the cover they needed to sweep left. Tyler's plan was to flank the pair of shooters setting up the heavy gun, kill them from behind, and turn the machine gun on the four magical arrivals.

Tyler and Stick moved swiftly as a pair, circling wide in low crouches, rifles up and scanning. As they reached the bottom of the little hill, Tyler saw one tango pressed against the side of a Joshua tree, shooting at Harrison and Farley while just beyond, another shooter was stepping up to man a heavy machine gun—a Kalishnikov PKC on a tripod. It must have taken both of them to carry the damn thing.

Tyler took a knee and so did Stick beside him.

"We cap these guys, and I'm gonna man that heavy gun," Tyler said.

"You'll be completely exposed to the east. The four assholes over there will have a line on you," Stick said.

"Yeah, but I'll have a line on them and the bigger gun. I just need you to keep them busy long enough to go to work."

"You're a crazy motherfucker, Brooks. You know that?"

Tyler flashed his brother a fatalistic grin. "Hooyah, frogman."

The plan set, Tyler raised his weapon and placed his green infrared beam on the head of the terrorist manning the heavy gun. He squeezed twice and the dead shooter collapsed into the dirt. At the same time, Stick dropped the jihadi crouching by the Joshua tree who they'd flanked.

"On your mark," Stick said, shifting his aim toward the cluster of brush and trees where the four remaining shooters were dug in.

But before Tyler could respond, Zee said, "Be advised—you've got two tangos repositioning northwest, and the other pair is sweeping south. Four, you're going to lose your cover."

"I see the southern pair," Harrison said. "Mother, these guys ain't al-Hamdi's men. They're kitted-up and wearing blacked-out BDUs."

Tyler screwed up his face at Stick.

What the hell?

Gunfire erupted as everyone engaged simultaneously, tracers criss-crossing from multiple locations like a laser light show.

Feeling the opportunity slipping away, Tyler said, "I'm going now. Cover me."

"Go," Stick said, swiveled, and started shooting.

Tyler sprinted—head down and quads on fire—toward the Kalishnikov PKC. Tracers zipped past him as he skidded to a stop behind the weapon and went to work strafing where he saw movement. The first volley evaporated the lead shooter in a cloud of blood and gore. His teammate dropped and rolled into cover behind the trunk of a stout tree. Unlike the other jihadis they'd been fighting, this guy was a pro—he moved like an operator and was kitted-up in tactical gear. Tyler shifted the muzzle to target the tree and squeezed the trigger, sending a barrage of bullets into the trunk.

Then, the heavy gun jammed.

What unfolded next happened in a blur.

The pro behind the boulder rolled west to take a prone kill shot at the wide-open and unprotected Tyler. But Stick, who had eyes on the shooter, fired a three-round burst—compromising the shot and giving Tyler a split second to dive for cover. From his belly, Tyler swept his target designator, looking for the bearded enemy operator who'd since shifted aim to Stick. Tyler saw the muzzle flash before he could squeeze the trigger and send his own round toward the target. But instead of Tyler's round slamming into the shooter's unprotected face, the bullet kicked up a puff of dirt.

Confused, he scanned left then right for the blacked-out operator.

"Where the hell did he go?" he murmured. "Mother, do you have eyes on the northwest shooter I'm engaging?"

"Negative, One," Zee came back. "He's gone. In fact, all four of them have disappeared."

"What?"

"I'm serious, even the heat sigs of the two bodies you dropped are gone. Just . . . gone."

Tyler whirled right to look at the spot where he'd shredded the first shooter with the PKC and he saw nothing. Nothing . . . The body was gone.

"Stick, talk to me," Tyler said, scanning the ground for blood and body parts that couldn't get up and walk away but somehow had done just that. "Please tell me you have eyes on these guys?"

When no answer came, he turned and sprinted to where Stick had been covering him, only to find his brother SEAL sprawled on his back with a black hole in his forehead. Finding Stick down was a punch to the gut. Tyler could barely get the next words out of his mouth.

"Four, sitrep?"

"Four and Five are in the fight, but barely," came Harrison's voice, "but the guys we were trading bullets with are gone, just like Mother said. We dropped one before they disappeared."

"Check. Mother, report all threats?" he asked, his mind unsure about the tactical picture for the first time in his career as a SEAL.

"One, all immediate threats appear neutralized. No sign of the four ambush shooters who disappeared. Maybe they have a tunnel system or something there. But, Reaper, you need to get out of there. Everyone is awake in Building Two and you're going to have fresh guns heading your way any second."

"Load up the wounded," Tyler barked as he hoisted Stick's lifeless body into a fireman's carry.

Hardly able to bear the weight, he ran to the Hyundai and dropped Stick with Farley. Then he sprinted to the burning Hilux to retrieve his other fallen brothers.

No man left behind.

Tyler's stomach turned at the sight. Lehmann had fallen off the back of the truck now, the flames out but the charred remains of his friend and teammate still smoking. To his left, Keaton lay dead, his body riddled with machine-gun fire. Tyler squeezed his eyes shut, knowing that this image would visit him again and again for the rest of his life, and slung his rifle on his chest. Despite the incoming threat, he refused to leave a brother behind. He grabbed Lehmann by an arm, but when he pulled, char came off in his hand—burnt clothing and flesh slipping from bone underneath. Tyler bent over and vomited, then grabbed Lehmann by the straps of his kit. He dragged his brother to where Keaton's body lay. Then, he grabbed Keaton by the kit with his other hand and grunted. It took every ounce of strength in his body, but Tyler pulled the two fallen SEALs up the hill to their SUV.

"Oh, dear God," Harrison said, choking and gagging as he ran over to help Tyler lift the bodies into the vehicle's rear cargo hold, where Stick's body had already been loaded.

"We gotta go, bro," Tyler said, squeezing his teammate's shoulder.

"You're bleeding," Harrison said.

"I know. Later," Tyler said.

With Harrison behind the wheel and Farley sobbing in the back, Tyler steadied himself with the dashboard to climb into the front passenger seat. Harrison maneuvered onto the exfil road. His head swimmy, Tyler looked over his shoulder at Farley. The SEAL medic had dirt and blood caked on the left side of his face and it looked like a significant amount of his left ear was missing.

"You good to drive?" Tyler asked.

"Five by," Harrison said, eyes on the road.

"Pack this on your neck, boss," Farley said from the back seat, his voice mushy.

Tyler turned around to see Farley holding out a trauma dressing from his own blowout kit. Only now did Tyler realize that the SEAL had taken two rounds—one a grazing laceration that ended where the top of his ear should have been, but the other a penetrating wound on the side of his jaw, which was now swollen to twice normal size. Tyler reached for the dressing with tingling left-hand fingers and pressed it tight to the wound burning at the base of his neck. He secured it under the shoulder of his kit, blinking sweat and tears out of his eyes.

"Thanks, brother."

Farley nodded with his jacked-up face.

"I think you're clear, Reaper," Zee said. "No pursuit from the compound."

"Copy, Mother . . ." he said, closing his eyes to stem off a wave of dizziness that engulfed him—physical or emotional, he wasn't sure. "Mother, Reaper needs urgent surgical evacuation. We're . . . we're . . ." His voice cracked and he swallowed hard. "Mother, Reaper is three angels and three wounded, with at least one urgent surgical."

"Roger, Reaper. Stalker One and Two are already airborne and headed to you. Will coordinate exact rendezvous point as they get closer. I show you still moving west. Are you able to continue heading west?"

He looked over at Harrison who nodded, growing concern in his eyes.

"Affirmative, Mother," Tyler said and realized he was sobbing. "Tell them to hurry."

A pause hung on the line while Zee did the mental math. "ETA for pickup is fifteen mikes," she said, her voice tight. "Hang on, Reaper."

He tried to say "Roger," but the word didn't come out. So instead, he let his eyes drift shut, feeling warm tears on his cheeks while cold darkness engulfed the rest of him.

CHAPTER 2

Protect your brother . . .

Those were the last words Lin Jun's father had spoken to him fifteen years ago. In the time since, Jun had made good on his promise to do just that, but Guo didn't make it easy. His little brother had a knack for finding trouble disguised as opportunity, and this gig had turned out to be the most troublesome of all. But the pay was insane and jumping was an adrenaline rush the likes of which Jun had not found elsewhere. He'd tasted the forbidden fruit and, despite the toll his body had to pay, the not knowing was intolerable.

It's like a drug, he mused, lying reclined on his mattress and staring up at a picture of Sisley Choi that he'd taped to the bottom of the bunk above him. *Just like your beauty.*

"Where's your brother?" the Frenchman, Damien Rolle, said, sticking his head inside the open door to the Lin brothers' bunk room.

"Probably with Garth at the range," Jun replied in heavily accented English, which was the common tongue used by the multinational cadre of contractors who worked for *Die Ursache* as well as a prerequisite for employment.

"We jump in fifteen minutes, *mon ami*. Get your ass out of bed *maintenant*."

"English, French guy. Speak English," Jun said, blew a kiss at the most beautiful woman in the world whom he was certain to never meet, and gingerly swung his legs off the bed.

"I'm talking to you in English every time, Chinese guy."

"No, you switch to French at the end. You do this all the time."

"No, you imagine this. I'm speaking *Anglais seulement*."

"There, you just did it again," Jun said as he grabbed his kit off a wall hook beside his bunk.

Damien flashed him a grin and tapped his temple. "No, man, I think you're just getting senile."

They both laughed. There was truth in the jab, and laughing about it was better than the alternative. Besides, trading barbs was the conversational currency in Field Ops division. Most of the guys on the team were assholes, especially the organic Germans who kept to themselves, but Jun liked Damien. They'd gotten on since day one. The same had been true for Guo and the American operator, Garth.

Hired guns of a feather, flock together, the strange American shooter was fond of saying.

At first, Jun didn't know what that meant, but now he thought he understood. Since the day his father left, Jun and his brother had done everything together—enlisting in the Army, joining the elite Snow Leopard counterterrorism unit, and most recently, leaving China to work in the private sector. Since age fifteen, the Lin brothers had *flocked* together, and this stint working at *Die Ursache* was just the latest chapter in their shared lives.

"See you in the pit," Damien said and left.

After adjusting the cummerbund on his vest and checking his load out, Jun holstered a pistol and grabbed his rifle from the rack. He slipped the sling over his head and walked out of the room into the hallway. Pistol reports echoed from the indoor range at the far end of the passage. Guo had always been a good marksman, but Garth operated at a different level. Jun had never seen anyone who could move and shoot with the precision of the soft-spoken, bearded American. Garth might be a man of few words, but he sure knew how to let the bullets fly. On reaching the range, Jun grabbed a pair of muffs from a cubby and popped them over his ears. He pulled the heavy steel-and-glass door open and stepped inside as Guo was taking his turn in a shoot-and-move drill while Garth repositioned the target with a joystick at the control station. Jun nodded at his brother's performance, which was more impressive than Jun had expected. Apparently, the hours of training with Garth were paying dividends.

As soon as Guo finished emptying his magazine, Jun clapped his hands. "Impressive, little brother. You killed it."

Guo flashed him a cocky smile. "Do you want to go next?"

Jun checked his watch. "The jump is in ten minutes, guys."

"As you can see, I'm ready to go," Guo said, gesturing to his fully kitted-up self. "We got time for one more."

Jun shook his head. "You know how Hoffman is about punctuality. We need to go now."

Guo pursed his lips and looked at Garth for support, but the American set down the target controller and picked up his kit in silent agreement with Jun. "Okay, okay, you guys win. Let's go."

Jun returned his hearing protection to the cubby on the way out and walked with his brother and Garth down the corridor to the windowless, underground pit of a room where the machine was kept. Damien and two German operators from Viper Squad were standing outside the reactor waiting for them, along with Mission Director Hoffman.

I wonder what those guys are doing here? My team doesn't need an augment.

Jun didn't know Hoffman's first name and frankly didn't care to. The man made Chinese military officers look soft and cuddly, and that was saying something.

"You're late," Hoffman said, glaring at Jun.

Jun, who was team leader, said, "Apologies, my teammates were fine-tuning their weapons in preparation for the mission."

"That should have been done hours in advance," Hoffman said with a grim expression. "Time is uncompromising. As you know, the window to affect change in our business is very limited."

There was no point in arguing with the man. "Understood. Apologies, Herr Hoffman."

Hoffman said nothing for a moment then shifted his gaze to the two German operators who nodded in silent consensus of superiority and judgment. Then, he spoke to the group.

"The location is Mali. The scout team has identified a suitable event for an intervention . . ." Hoffman held up a picture of a bearded operator dressed in unmarked fatigues. "This American is your target . . ."

Jun committed the target's face to memory. Since he was a young boy, he'd had a very good mind for detail. He never forgot a face or a place, and he knew that Hoffman was aware of this skill. In fact, he suspected having a strong memory was an important recruiting criterion for *Die Ursache*. Hoffman never revealed the mission parameters, offsets, or location details until moments before the jump. Being able to quickly and effectively memorize these details was critical to success.

". . . he and his Navy SEAL unit will be engaged in a capture/kill operation against a local warlord who is housing an Islamic bomb maker. You'll be jumping into the middle of a firefight," Hoffman continued. "As always, we want the target's death to appear organic and not look like an assassination. The scout team reports this is a highly kinetic engagement, so take that into consideration. We're dropping you in the middle of the main action where you will be able to capitalize on the confusion. According to the scouting report, the target will run from a covered position behind a burning truck to take control of a heavy machine gun on a tripod at an open and uncovered position. This is your opportunity. Does anyone have questions?"

When no one spoke, Hoffman fixed his steely gaze on Jun. "You and Rolle will not be traveling for this op. Jurgen and Kaspar will be going in your place."

"Why?" Jun asked, irritation blooming in his chest.

"Doctor's orders," Hoffman said.

Jun looked at Damien, who shrugged with indifference, then at his brother, Guo.

"Don't worry about me, big brother," Guo said and clapped his hand on Garth's shoulder. "We'll be fine."

This wasn't the first time Hoffman had shuffled the teams. Jun could think of two other times he'd jumped without Guo, but never the other way around. Hoffman was clearly trying to even the jump count among the operators, but Jun didn't care. Looking out for Guo was his job, and if that meant paying a toll, he'd gladly pay it.

His father's words echoed in his mind: *Protect your brother . . .*

"Sir, I really think I should—" he started to say.

"It's not your decision to make, Lin Jun," Hoffman said, using his full name, which the German only did when he was exerting his dominance. Hoffman turned to Guo, Garth, and the two Germans. "Remember the rules. You have four minutes and any injury you sustain on the jump comes back with you."

"Thanks for the reminder, asshole," Garth murmured under his breath as he shuffled toward the machine.

Guo, who was bringing up the rear of the group, paused at the threshold of the reactor door, looked over his shoulder, and flashed Jun a wide, toothy grin. He flashed a *hang-loose* sign and disappeared inside the machine. Teeth clenched, Jun watched the heavy steel door to the reactor swing shut and the locking mechanism clank. A computer voice commenced a sixty-second countdown while he and Damien looked on, rifles hanging uselessly across their chests.

"Everything is going to be okay. *Fais-moi confiance*," the French mercenary said.

Jun nodded, but his gut was in knots. He had a bad feeling about this . . . a really bad feeling.

At T-minus ten seconds, the hum of the reactor reverberated loudly in the pit and a faint golden glow emanated from the porthole window.

At T-minus five seconds, Jun shouted at Hoffman to stop the launch.

The German shot Jun a look that a father might give a misbehaving child in a restaurant, but he did not abort the launch.

At T-minus zero, the team was gone, and Hoffman headed for the door.

"Where the fuck are you going?" Jun called after him.

"To get a coffee," Hoffman said without a backward glance.

The next three minutes and forty-five seconds would last an eternity for Jun. His brain told him his anxiety and worry were entirely irrational, but his heart knew otherwise. Dread powered his nervous feet and he paced a loop around the pit.

"Stop that and have a seat," Damien said, from where he sat cross-legged on the concrete floor of the pit, his rifle unslung and leaning against a steel I-beam pillar.

"No . . ."

"*Personne ne m'écoute jamais,*" Damien mumbled.

"What did you say?" Jun said, casting a sideways glance at his friend.

"I *said* nobody ever listens to me."

"That's because you're French," Jun said, finally managing a smile.

The computer voice on the loudspeaker drowned out the Frenchman's retort as it commenced the return countdown.

At T-minus ten seconds, Hoffman returned to the pit with his coffee.

At T-minus five seconds, Damien got to his feet and walked to stand beside Jun.

And at T-minus zero seconds, the whir of the reactor stopped.

The chamber shuddered as the jumpers returned. A moment later, the access hatch hissed as pressure equalized and opened via a mechanical actuator. Jun, who expected to see Guo's smiling face in the doorway, was instead greeted by Kaspar.

The distressed look on the German's face said it all.

Jun shoved past Damien and Hoffman and sprinted to the machine. He ducked under the low hatch doorframe and stepped inside the toroidal chamber. Two bodies were upright. Two bodies were down.

Jun scrambled to where Garth was blocking a bloody and sprawled mess of a figure.

"No," Garth said, blocking his path and pressing a gloved hand to Jun's chest. "You don't want to see this."

Jun swatted the American's hand away and dropped to his knees beside the body. What was left of his brother's head was . . . *unrecognizable.*

He vomited.

He trembled, briefly lost in some psychological state of disconnected dissonance, until rage seized control. He turned away from his brother's ruined corpse and looked at Hoffman.

"Tell me the man's name who did this."

"You know it doesn't work that way, Jun," Hoffman said, his face a pitiless mask.

Jun sprung to his feet and, in a flash, had Hoffman pinned against the reactor wall with his combat blade pressed to the German's neck. "Either you tell me the American's name, or I open your throat."

Hoffman, who seemed unfazed by Jun's swift and impulsive threat of mortal violence, stared unblinking into Jun's eyes. Then, as if completing a cost-benefit calculation, in a flat and perfectly calm voice, the German said, "His name is Tyler Brooks. And until you kill him, our mission will fail again, and again, and again . . ."

CHAPTER 3

SICK BAY

USS *GERALD R. FORD* (CVN-78)

THE ATLANTIC OCEAN

SEVENTY-TWO MILES SOUTHWEST OF MONROVIA, LIBERIA

0925 LOCAL TIME

Navy Lieutenant Xiang "Zee" Williams peered around the curtain that stretched across the barrier between the main sick bay and the area labeled Surgery. The room had a half dozen beds, but only one held an occupant. She could see Tyler on the middle bed, a Navy corpsman in scrubs taking his vitals and writing something into a tablet she held. Tyler's eyes were closed, his breathing slow and relaxed. She thought he might be awake but wasn't sure. There was a bulky dressing on his right shoulder, extending well onto the right side of his neck and down onto his chest. The massive bone frog tattoo the SEAL sported on his left chest was covered by dressings, save a frog tibia extending from below the bandage.

"How is he?" a baritone voice asked from behind, giving her a start.

Zee turned, her hand pressed to her heart.

"Sorry," Commander Maddox "Dax" Carroll mumbled. He stood with his thick forearms across his chest, the embroidered trident over his left breast pocket just visible. "Didn't mean to startle you."

"No, it's okay, sir," she said. "And you didn't. I was just . . ."

"Thinking?"

"Yes, sir."

The SEAL commander nodded, his dark eyes set in his chiseled granite face, giving away nothing.

"So," he said, his voice soft, leading her back into the empty preop area with the gesture of one powerful arm. "What happened out there, Williams?"

She looked at the head of the squadron, confused.

"I mean, well, they were ambushed, sir," she said, hoping her voice reflected her confusion and not sarcasm. She had a hard time keeping sarcasm out of her voice on a good day.

"Yeah, I know," he said, crossing his arms again. "But I'm asking for a hot wash from my intel lead. That okay with you, Lieutenant?"

"Of course . . . I mean, yes, yes, sir," she said, fumbling with her words and aware how childlike she sounded. "What can I tell you?"

"What the hell happened out there?" he said, his voice softening only slightly.

"I don't know, sir. There's a lot of nighttime activity in Goundam. I wasn't concerned until the pickup was well out of the city proper and headed west on the highway. I couldn't tell whether they would continue west or head north at the last roundabout. Once they turned north I thought I should give Reaper a heads-up."

"And you did."

"Yes, sir, I made them aware that there could be a problem."

"And your instinct was right?"

She pursed her lips.

"Well, yeah . . . I mean, yes, sir, I suppose in hindsight."

"Your instinct was that the inbound vehicle could be a QRF. And Chief Brooks—he disagreed?"

She felt her stomach churn. What happened was horrible. Beyond horrible; it would haunt her maybe her entire life. But they weren't really trying to blame Tyler, right?

"I don't think I'd say that. It was a single vehicle, so I would not classify it as QRF. But I did give him a heads-up on a potential threat."

"Did you ask him to pause or to slow the infil?"

"I offered that as an option."

"He disagreed?"

"Sir, he asked for information on the size of the force and on timing. Based on that, he elected to accelerate the hit and get in and out before they could become a potential threat."

"But it was a QRF, wasn't it?"

"It was three guys in a pickup," she said, hugging her chest.

"But it turned out to be more than three guys, didn't it, Lieutenant?"

"Yes, sir . . . I mean, well, not exactly. There were only three heat sigs in that truck all the way from Goundam. I don't know where the other four came from. We think, maybe, there was an underground bunker or hidden compartment in the bed of the pickup . . ." She sighed and closed her eyes a moment. "Whatever the reason, I missed them."

"But it was Tyler's call to go ahead with the op, not yours."

She turned to meet his gaze. "What are you trying to get me to say, Commander?"

Carroll gave her a soft smile. "We're not trying to hang Tyler out to dry here, Zee. This is a dangerous job and shit happens sometimes. No one is trying to blame anyone, I promise. But the nature of our business is to ask these hard questions, no matter what the outcome, to arm ourselves from the lessons learned and minimize the risks next time. Understand?"

"Yes, of course, sir. I just . . ." She looked down at her feet.

"And no one is blaming you either, Zee. We're all watching the same screens. We all saw what happened and nobody that I've talked to has a good explanation for it. This is not your fault."

"Thank you, sir," she said, but wasn't sure she believed him—it absolutely felt like her fault. "How are Farley and Harrison, sir?"

"Both doing well. Farley has a fractured jaw and they said maybe some minor nerve damage in his face—that the side of his face will be numb, but that will improve with time. Lost the top of his ear but they cleaned up the deep scalp laceration and closed both wounds. It'll all heal. Harrison is fine—just a few stitches in his cheek. He said it'll make him look more like a pirate."

She nodded and chuckled softly.

"And Tyler?"

"Haven't spoken to him yet," Carroll said, looking at where the SEAL lay, fresh out of surgery. They watched Tyler stir, then pull himself up to a sitting position, grimacing and touching the bulky dressing on his neck, glancing around to see if anyone was watching him. "The bullet tore through the muscle at the base of his neck but didn't hit anything with a Latin name. He suffered a large hematoma, that collected down deep, but they say no nerve damage. As I understand it, he should fully recover. I predict he'll be back in the fight in no time."

She nodded, unsure what to say.

He squeezed her arm and then slipped into the ward where Tyler lay.

She sat on the edge of the last bed in the row, watching through the break in the curtain, as Carroll talked with Tyler. She heard the murmur of conversation but couldn't make out the words as they spoke. She imagined he was getting a pep talk, but maybe also a short hot wash like she'd had.

"No, sir," she heard Tyler say more loudly, and looked up again to where the SEAL straightened himself in the narrow, and no doubt uncomfortable, bed. "Zee is the best. I don't know where the hell those shooters came from, but if they could be seen, she would have found them. And then . . . I don't know where . . ." His voice trailed off with a strange timbre she'd not heard—something odd in his voice. Maybe it was just the meds he must be on. "Look, if she could have predicted what would happen, she would have. There's no magic crystal ball in these things. She gave us all the information she had, and in the end, scrubbing the op or proceeding was my call to make and I made it."

She saw Carroll put a hand on Tyler's shoulder and then voices went soft again.

A few moments later, they shook hands, and the SEAL commander came back through the curtain. She smiled at him awkwardly, and he gave her a tight smile and curt nod, then headed through the sick bay and out into the passageway beyond.

Zee took a deep, steeling breath, then she pushed through the curtain and walked to Tyler's bed. He met her eyes as she approached. She didn't know what she expected—sadness, a bonding look of shared suffering, guilt.

What she didn't expect was rage.

"Come to gloat, Lieutenant?" he said, his voice a growl.

"What are you talking about?" she asked, shocked and confused.

"Oh, come on," he said, rolling his eyes and then raising himself up, the move making him grimace with pain. "We all know how you pride yourself in your perfect record of being right. Go ahead—say it."

"Say what?" she asked, hands on hips, feeling her own rage rising now. What the hell was wrong with him? She knew he was hurting, but so was she. She was part of this unit. She'd lost teammates too—no, *friends* . . . "What the hell is wrong with you?"

"Nothing's wrong with me except for my bullet wound and the brothers I lost. So just say it and be on your way. SAY IT!" he demanded, his voice loud enough that the Navy corpsman over at the desk on the far side of the ward noticed and rose, heading their way. She had a scowl on her face.

He backs me with Carroll but tries to assassinate me in person. What the hell?

"What the hell do you want me to say, Tyler?"

"Say what you're dying to say, Zee. Say 'I told you so.' Say 'I was right, and you were wrong.' Say whatever it is you came here to say so you can get back to your day."

She thought of a dozen things she wanted to say in that moment, but she settled on only one. "Fuck you, *Chief.*"

"Everything okay over here? You okay, Chief?" the corpsman said, stepping between them.

Tyler ignored the woman. "Is that it, LT? Anything else?"

"I asked you to pause," Zee blurted, "to slow down."

"And there it is," Tyler said, a smug look on his face. "You were right, and I was wrong."

She struggled for emotional control, her rage wrestling with her grief, and both winning over reason. She let out a long breath.

"I told Commander Carroll I thought you made the right call, with the information you had . . ."

"Well, that's the issue, isn't it? Once again, SEALs die from an intelligence failure . . ."

"What? Are you friggin' kidding me?"

"Ma'am," the corpsman said, actively separating them. "Ma'am, can I ask you to give the chief a little time? He just came out of anesthesia. He doesn't know what he's saying . . ."

"Oh, he knows what he's saying," she growled, feeling her eyes rim with tears, which made her even more angry.

"Damn right I do," he said, spittle flying from his lips.

Zee spun on a heel and headed toward the main area of the sick bay. As she left he called after her.

"Zee, wait. Hold on, I just . . . Just wait."

"And to think I came to check on you," Zee shouted over her shoulder, then under her breath added, "asshole."

Fists clenched, she stormed down the passageway and ascended the ladder, heading to her quarters. Hopefully, Lieutenant Bradshaw, the intelligence officer and her roommate, would be in the TOC because the last thing Zee needed was to talk.

She needed to be alone.

CHAPTER 4

JUNIOR OFFICER QUARTERS
USS *GERALD R. FORD* (CVN-78)
THE ATLANTIC OCEAN
SEVENTY-TWO MILES SOUTHWEST OF MONROVIA, LIBERIA

Still fuming, Zee pushed open the door to her stateroom to be greeted by both good and bad news. The good news—that Zee's roommate, the *Ford*'s intelligence officer, Lieutenant Bradshaw was not in the stateroom—was far outweighed by the bad: a man she didn't recognize was sitting at her desk.

"Can I help you with something?" she asked the stranger, her voice every bit as sharp as she intended. Not only had this a-hole invaded her private space, but he was a civilian and a dude at that. She didn't care what GS level this guy rated, he had no business being in a female officer's stateroom.

"Lieutenant Williams," the man said, looking up, "I can't tell you what a pleasure it is to meet you."

"How did you get in here?" she said from the doorway, uncertain whether going in was a good idea or not.

"Lieutenant Bradshaw let me in," the man said with a sheepish, apologetic smile. He stood, awkwardly, beside her desk. "I hope you don't mind. I asked her to give us some privacy. I'm Pat Moody, by the way." The man held out a hand to her, but she ignored it.

"Don't care," she said.

Despite her directness, the aw-shucks look on his face didn't go away as he fished out his ID case and presented it to her. The identification suggested he was with the Defense Intelligence Agency, but spooks lied for a living, and this guy, she suspected, was a professional liar. She shrugged her indifference. Three-letter acronym IDs stopped impressing her thirty days into her stint at JSOC.

"Still don't care," she said. "I'd like you to leave, Mr. Moody. Right now."

"What the ID doesn't tell you is that I'm the codirector of a joint interagency black-ops task force," he said, undeterred. "The nature of our work is highly classified."

"Then we should be having this conversation in the SCIF instead of my stateroom," she said, with judgment.

But Moody just kept smiling—his confident eyes both charming and disarming. "Pffft . . ." he said with a chuckle and a dismissive wave of his hand. "Your stateroom isn't bugged—I checked—so you can sleep better with that knowledge."

She laughed out loud.

Who the hell is this guy?

She crossed her arms, aware of how much the gesture echoed Commander Carroll. "Enough with the games, Mr. Moody. If you're read in on what I do and who I work for, then you know I've had a very bad day. I'm only going to ask politely one more time—please leave."

"Not without having a conversation first. I have express *written* permission to talk to you from Admiral Reeves. All I ask is that you hear what I have to say before kicking me out."

"Admiral Reeves? The head of JSOC?" she asked, cocking an eyebrow at him.

The only thing harder to believe than the fact that this guy got Admiral Reeves's permission was that Reeves had any idea who she—a lowly O-3 serving at the squadron level—was.

A written, by-name request from Reeves . . . I'll believe that when I see it.

As if reading her thoughts, Moody unfolded a TS/SCI classified letter and handed it to her. She skimmed the paper, and the gist was permission for Patrick Moody, from an unnamed joint interagency special task force, to speak privately with one United States Navy Lieutenant Xiang Williams.

What in the hell is going on?

"Lieutenant, have you heard of DARPA?" he asked, taking the paper back from her.

"Everyone's heard of DARPA."

"See, the thing is," he said and lowered himself back into her desk chair, "they're busy, busy beavers over there. Inventing all kinds of crazy things. Most of the stuff they invent has no immediate tactical value. But every once in a while, those crazy engineers come up with something truly amazing—I'm talking earth-shattering, paradigm-shifting, change-the-face-of-covert-operations-forever kind of amazing."

"Okay, you piqued my interest. Tell me."

"I'll need you to sign an NDA, of course."

"Fine, I'll sign it, but why me?"

"Because you have a unique and particular set of skills that make you an ideal candidate to become a senior member of our team."

"Yeah, right," she scoffed, then did a double take at his smiling face. The man, it would seem, was not kidding.

Her throat tightened at the thought, and she felt the weight of the man's stare.

"And if I say no?"

"Then we shake hands and you send me on my way, or . . ." he said, pausing for effect. "You can say yes and I can answer the question that's driving you mad right now."

"And what question is that?"

"How did those four enemy shooters magically appear and then disappear during your op?"

Her heart skipped a beat as she processed the words.

"Yes, Lieutenant, I know all about that . . ."

At this, she finally stepped out of the doorway and shut the door to the stateroom.

"I take that as a yes?" he said with a smile.

She nodded and cautiously took a seat in Bradshaw's desk chair while Moody reached for his leather satchel.

"Let me just find the NDA here," he said, shuffling about in the bag.

While she waited, her mind drifted back to the op and the four heat signatures that appeared and disappeared from her satellite feed.

"Is this real?" she asked, feeling a sudden wave of paranoia. "Because if this is some sort of postcasualty event counseling or psychological fitness-for-duty screening, I'm going to be a very, very angry woman."

The charming smile was back as he glanced at her.

"Oh, this is for real, Lieutenant," he said and handed her a simple, one-page nondisclosure form. "Sign this and I will tell you things that will completely rock your world, Xiang. Can I call you Xiang?"

"Everyone calls me Zee," she said, which was the compromise reached between her Taiwanese mother and African American father when the kids in elementary school couldn't pronounce Xiang.

"Zee it is."

She skimmed the insanely simple NDA, which threatened imprisonment should she reveal to any living soul the contents of the brief from one Patrick Moody, of an unnamed combined joint task force, contents of which she freely agreed to receive. With an eye roll, she signed the document and handed it back. He slipped the NDA into a brown legal envelope and then pulled out a tablet computer. He typed his passcode to open a program, but before turning it to her so she could see the screen, he met her eyes.

"Zee, what DARPA discovered is that if you want to make a change in the present, you're much better off looking to the future than the past."

"What does that even mean?" she said, her head spinning. "And more importantly, what the hell does it have to do with our failed op?"

He smiled at her and said, "Nothing . . . and everything."

CHAPTER 5

It wasn't even about being confined to bed. Tyler needed to *pace*. He was a pacer—his default state whenever he had things on his mind. He paced when he talked on his phone. He paced while they put together an op, and he paced while they debriefed it. But most of all, he needed to pace when he was alone with his thoughts.

Right now, his head was full of turmoil—thoughts and raw emotions running wild. On top of his grief and guilt for the deaths of his brother SEALs, he felt like a total asshole for how he'd treated Zee. He knew she hadn't come to gloat. She was not that kind of person. She'd come to check on him—her teammate—and he'd shit all over her for it. Truth was, he believed everything he'd said to Commander Carroll. Zee was the best intel officer he'd ever worked with. It wasn't her fault.

In combat, sometimes bad things happened, and no one was to blame.

But still, that didn't explain what had happened, or *how* it had happened.

I saw a dead terrorist disappear into thin air . . . I must be losing my mind.

He chased the thought away because he wasn't the only one. Harrison and Farley had traded bullets with those shooters. Zee and Carroll and everyone in the TOC had seen the heat signatures appear and disappear. Whatever had happened, it had a logical explanation. Someone smarter than him would figure it out.

It's not my job to go down that bunny hole. It's for the spooks to figure out.

Pain burned in Tyler's neck and chest, growing in intensity, but he couldn't bring himself to press the damn morphine button. The idea he might be even minimally impaired felt unbearable. He was a weapon, and he treated himself like one, especially downrange. He tried to treat his body like a temple, eating clean and living substance-free when he was deployed. His brothers gave him shit for it sometimes, calling him Mother Teresa, but he didn't care and laughed along with them.

It had driven Nikki crazy too, he thought with a sad smile.

Only then did it occur to him that his ex-wife, and his little girl, Harper, had no idea he was in the hospital recovering from being shot. Even if he was still married, he probably wouldn't have told them until he'd recovered. In his mind, he'd rationalize that he was trying not to worry them, but the truth was more complicated than that. He'd done a lot of things to shield his family from his professional choices while he'd been married, and in doing so he'd only ended up driving them away. The wedge he'd put between himself and his girls had been entirely of his own making.

Time passed . . . each second a physical and emotional agony.

The morphine button beckoned, offering to numb his mind and his pain, but he refused to press it. Guilt over Nikki and Harper soon gave way to guilt over the deaths of his teammates. But he didn't deserve relief, lying in a warm bed in medical, while three of his teammates were in aluminum coffins down in the hangar . . .

"Everything okay, Chief?" the nurse asked, walking up to the bedside. "Do you need something for pain? I can call Doc Weatherby for a bolus if . . ." He stopped, leaning in to look more closely at the machine attached to the IV bag beside the bed. "Chief, you haven't used your PCA at all. Did HM1 explain how to . . ."

"The corpsman explained everything," Tyler said, waving his left hand as if shooing away a bug. "I'm not in pain."

"Well, your pulse rate says otherwise, Chief," the nurse—Lieutenant Romero, according to his name tape and rank insignia—said. "Your pulse rate is eighty-eight. My guess is the resting heart rate is around fifty for a SEAL like you. Why aren't you using your pain meds?"

"Cuz I'm not having much pain, Lieutenant," Tyler lied.

"Okay, well, do you need to pee? I can bring you a urinal."

Tyler shook his head, although now that Romero mentioned it maybe he did need to pee.

"I'm good," he said. He didn't need to whiz in some bedpan or bottle or whatever. He was a friggin' operator, not some old man. "My teammate is in the ICU after his facial surgery. HM1 Perkins said I could go and visit him once he was awake. If he's awake, I'd like to go check on him."

"Okay, well how about I take you over there in a wheelchair after you're done talking with your visitor?"

Tyler screwed up his face in confusion.

Visitor?

"First off, I don't need a damn wheelchair. And second, I don't know anything about any visitor."

Lieutenant Romero pursed his lips, then scowled. "The guy told me you'd want to talk to him, so I assumed you knew him. I'll send him packing and tell him next time to go through your chain of command."

"Who is he?" Tyler asked, curiosity now getting the better of him.

Romero shrugged.

"Some civilian. A spook is my guess, from the look. We don't get a lot of 'em aboard the *Ford*, but I know a Smith when I see one. He had some letter from Admiral Reeves at JSOC to talk to you specifically, so I just assumed . . ."

"You can let him in," Tyler said, straightening up. A civilian sent from the flag officer in charge of JSOC . . . that was different.

"Okay, I'll give you guys the room."

Romero disappeared around the nurse's station, and Tyler puzzled over just what was going on. A spook with a by-name request from the head of JSOC didn't appear in the last few hours without a lot of planning. The *Ford* was forward deployed thousands of miles from CONUS off the coast of Africa. It would take practically a full day in the air to make that trip, so what the hell was going on? It certainly couldn't have anything to do with what happened in Mali, right?

A man appeared from past the nurse's station dressed in cargo pants and a black unbranded golf shirt. He carried a leather satchel over his shoulder and glanced around with keen eyes beneath unkempt hair. As soon as he spied Tyler, he smiled and hustled over.

Yep, dude's a Smith all right.

"Special Operations Chief Tyler Brooks, I assume?" he said, extending a hand.

Tyler shook it, pain shooting through his chest and neck as he sat up slightly in the reclined hospital bed. "Yeah, I'm Brooks. Who the hell are you?"

"I'm Pat Moody," the spook replied with an easy confidence. At the Tier One, they worked with tons of OGA, or "other government agency" guys—most from the CIA but some from more highly classified, joint task force entities. They came in two varieties—bureaucrats and direct-action guys, the latter mostly veterans of military Special Operations. This guy looked bureaucrat, but there was something in his eyes. A confidence, but also something else. In any case, just not introducing himself with the last name Jones or Smith made his stock go up.

"What can I do for the CIA today, Mr. Moody?" Tyler asked, probing.

"Once upon a time you'd have been right," Moody said. "Spent enough time in the suck with guys like you to have my own share of stories and lies to swap. Got a little long in the tooth, so now I'm with a joint interagency task force."

"Mm-hmm, but you still didn't answer my question."

"I can see you're in pain, so how about I cut to the chase? I'm here to recruit you." The man let the statement hang out there, but Tyler resisted the urge to bite at that bait.

"I have Admiral Reeves's blessing to invite you to our party, Chief.

I'm the project manager for a DARPA program driven by advanced next-generation technology that makes us the most lethal and capable direct-action unit in the world."

"You're recruiting me?" Tyler said, and at that he had to laugh. "Mr. Moody, I don't know you, but you obviously don't know me either. I'm a pretty simple guy—a door-kicker—and I'm already in my dream job. I can't imagine anything you or DARPA could have that would tempt me away from that."

The glimmer in Moody's eyes became a sparkle.

"Look, Chief, I know what happened in Mali. I also know the hell your head and your heart are going through right now—hell, I've been there many times myself—but here's the thing, Tyler . . . what happened to you and your team is yesterday's problem. At Omega, we have technology that makes us immune to intelligence failures—technology that can remove intelligence gaps altogether."

It wasn't lost on Tyler that Moody had dropped the task force name as a golden nugget of trust and respect. The man understood the currency that special operators traded in, and it had just won him a point.

"In real time?" Tyler asked, suddenly intrigued.

"*Ahead* of time," Moody said, and there it was again, that sparkle of something in his eyes.

Tyler laughed. "If I didn't know better, it almost sounds like you're saying DARPA developed a crystal ball."

Moody leaned in, smiled, and said in a low voice, "That, Chief Brooks, is exactly what they've done. We're talking about technology that makes tragedies like what you and your team experienced in Mali a thing of the past." The man grinned mysteriously. "So to speak."

Tyler raised his eyebrows in surprise, unsure what exactly the spook was hinting at, but the reference to his lost teammates was more than enough to suck him in.

"You have some very unique skills, Chief—as an operator, of course, but also other skills as well. Taken together, those skills make you a perfect fit for the direct-action component at Omega." Moody glanced around, then leaned in even closer, close enough for Tyler to smell the man's aftershave. "Want to sign an NDA and HALO jump with me through this looking glass?"

"What if I don't like what's on the other side?" Tyler asked, but he already knew damn well he would sign. Whatever the hell this guy was talking about, he couldn't resist at least a peek behind the curtain. Especially if it meant no more Malis ever again. The pain in his neck and shoulder was barely even background noise now.

Moody straightened up and shrugged.

"If you don't like it, then I release you back to leading your fellow SEALs the old-fashioned way, and we both pretend this conversation never happened. But I know that ain't gonna happen, Tyler . . . because we found a way to eliminate the one variable that every operator despises."

"And what is that?" Tyler said, accepting the NDA paperwork from Moody's outstretched hand.

"Uncertainty . . ."

CHAPTER 6

HAWKER 900 AT TWELVE THOUSAND FEET
EN ROUTE TO PHILLIPS ARMY AIRFIELD, ABERDEEN PROVING GROUND
NINE MILES SOUTHWEST OF HAVRE DE GRACE, MARYLAND
SEVEN DAYS LATER
0746 LOCAL TIME

Tyler shifted in his seat, wishing he could pace. He hated traveling by plane.

Also, his stitches itched.

It took all his willpower not to scratch them out.

He glanced over his shoulder at the only other passenger on the bizjet, a guy about the same age as Tyler who was sipping a latte while chowing down a massive plate of breakfast. The dude was clean-shaven and wore his hair closely cropped, but that didn't necessarily mean he wasn't an operator. Even Tyler had shaved his downrange beard and given his shaggy mop a trim for this gig. But this guy didn't give off an operator vibe. He looked like a government consultant.

Or a middle school chemistry teacher, Tyler thought with a silent chuckle.

"'Sup?" Tyler said when the guy looked up and made eye contact.

"Dude, you gotta try the eggs Benedict. It's to die for, man. I'm talking real ham steak—none of that Canadian bacon garbage."

"But aren't Canadian bacon and ham just different names for the same thing, like pancakes and flapjacks?"

"Actually, that's not true. They're different cuts of meat with different preparations. Ham comes from the hind legs, specifically the thighs and pork butt, while Canadian bacon is rendered from back meat. Canadian bacon is typically cured, smoked, and cut into round thin slices. Ham, on the other hand, has no standard preparation and tends to have a higher fat content. Whoever made this eggs Benedict knows the difference, and that's something I appreciate."

"Okaaaaay," Tyler said, making a mental note not to bring up anything else that might get the guy talking. The dude was weird.

Tyler passed on food. He wasn't an eggs Benedict guy, ham or no ham.

Even if he had been, there was practically no time to eat it. The flight from Norfolk International Airport to Aberdeen, Maryland, was the briefest of hops, and before he knew it, they were landing. He barely had time to yearn for his little girl, whom he had yet to see since returning from the *USS Ford*, and the jet was descending. He wasn't ready to face Harper's mom, his ex-wife, just yet. The brothers he'd lost had been *their* friends, before the divorce. As the plane broke through the scattered clouds, he shifted his thoughts back to the present. In the days since Moody had recruited him for this gig, he'd yet to learn anything substantive about his new assignment or the spooky task force he'd be working for. In the days since he'd signed on the dotted line, Moody's tease had played on a loop in his head.

"We found a way to eliminate the one variable that every operator despises . . . uncertainty."

Tyler blew air through his teeth as he turned to look out the window as they landed.

If this turns out to be just some lame computer program calling the shots, I'm outta here.

Once on the ground, the jet taxied toward a hangar located by itself at the relatively empty airfield. A lone Suburban SUV was parked on the ramp with a G-man wearing a dark suit standing beside it, his

hands folded in front of him. The dude was a total caricature, reminding Tyler of a Secret Service agent from some B-level action movie.
After the jet came to a stop, Tyler slung his duffel bag over his left
shoulder while the flight attendant opened the cabin door.

As they waited for the airstair, Tyler turned over his shoulder to his
fellow passenger, "Nice to meet you."

"Well, we didn't actually meet," the other guy said. "I'm Stan."

"Tyler. Nice flying with you."

"You too," Stan said.

And with that, Tyler headed down the steps to the tarmac and
walked over to where the G-man in the suit waited with a rear door
open and ready. Without a word, the G-man took Tyler's duffel and
loaded it into the back. He climbed inside the air-conditioned middle
row of the blacked-out Suburban and was turning to shut the door
when Stan got in behind him.

"I got the door," Stan said, pausing for Tyler to move across the aisle
into the passenger-side bucket seat so he could take the one behind the
driver.

"Where are you headed?"

"Same place as you, I presume."

"Oh," was all Tyler could manage, feeling slightly more uncertain
about his decision to transfer from the Tier One than before.

As the big SUV got underway, Stan pulled a book from his backpack, crossed his legs, and began to read. Tyler stole a glance at the title:
Quantum Mechanics For Dummies.

Oh my God, who the hell is this guy?

He was about to point out the humor of the oxymoronic title but
stopped himself because that would probably just get Stan talking
about quantum mechanics, a subject which Tyler had neither the intellect nor interest to discuss.

For the rest of the drive, he stared out the window and thought
about Nikki and Harper, whom he'd still not informed of either his
injury or his change of commands. It had only been seven months
since he'd signed the divorce paperwork, but it felt like so much longer.

He'd balked when she'd given him the ultimatum, not really believing that she'd go through with it. But she had, and he gave Nikki credit for sticking to her guns. They'd still been living together when she presented him with the papers. He'd signed on the line right in front of her without a second's hesitation. He didn't even read the damn thing. He'd been so proud of himself for that at the time. He'd wanted to show her that she couldn't wound him, to demonstrate, with one callous stroke of the pen, that he didn't need her. The irony was, he'd already done that in spades, which was why she was divorcing him in the first place, and now he'd only proven her point. He couldn't claim she hadn't supported his career; she'd been the perfect SEAL wife. Harper had been born while Tyler was deployed.

He'd missed the birth.

The SUV began to slow, and Stan snapped his book shut, rousing Tyler from his melancholy rumination. A rusty eight-foot chain-link fence topped with barbed wire surrounded a humdrum series of red brick buildings that looked like they had been built in the '80s. The grass outside the fence along the road needed a serious mow, and the security shack beside the main gate looked like it could use a paint job. The sign at the property entrance read: Wilson Spice Company— Because Taste Matters.

Tyler chuckled to himself and watched the driver present his ID to the rent-a-cop at the guard shack . . . except the guy scanning the driver's badge was *definitely* not a rent-a-cop, no matter what the Walmart uniform was meant to convey. Tyler knew a pro when he saw one. The EGA tat on the guard's muscular forearm, the Wiley X sunglasses, and the SIG Sauer M17 on his hip erased any doubt about whether this dude was a shooter. The driver and guard exchanged wordless nods and the rinky-dink chain-link roller gate began to rattle open. He turned to Stan who shrugged and flashed Tyler a *this ought to be interesting* look.

Instead of parking in the lot, their driver pulled inside a warehouse with a roll-up door that closed behind them. Looking out the passenger-side window, Tyler scanned the building and instantly concluded that— no surprise—it was *not* a spice factory. From the outside, the place looked run-down, but the inside told a different story. The space looked like the inside of a Boeing or Lockheed Martin testing facility—with electrical control cabinets, server racks, and industrial air handlers. Heavy, thick, black cables snaked across the floor from the electrical cabinets and connected to a massive stainless steel ring positioned in the middle of the room. The walls and ceilings appeared insulated for both thermal and EMF, and the concrete floor had a smooth epoxy finish that looked clean enough to eat off of. Instead of factory workers in coveralls, the people milling about were either dressed in lab coats or business attire.

"Chief Brooks, Master Sergeant Abernathy, welcome," Pat Moody said with a smile while shuffling down a flight of metal stairs from a midlevel mezzanine to greet them as soon as Tyler and Stan stepped out of the SUV. "How was your flight in? Do you fellas need any coffee before we get started?"

"No thanks," Stan said. "I'm fed and caffeinated."

"I'm five by, thanks for offering," Tyler said.

"I've only seen these in pictures," Stan said, awe in his voice as he walked toward the giant stainless steel structure in the middle of the warehouse. "Looks like a tokamak . . ."

Tyler had no idea what the hell a *tokamak* was, but he followed behind the man he now had pegged as Army and stared up at the donut-shaped device towering above them. It reminded him of a CT scanner, only this one was the size of a studio apartment, upended, and wrapped in cooling coils with tubing and wires connected everywhere.

"*That* is the world's first and only transdimensional field reactor, or as everyone around here likes to call it—the Donut," Moody said, hands on hips.

"When you say *transdimensional*, which dimensions does it translate across?" Stan asked with his back to Moody as he gawked at the machine.

"We'll get into that later during the indoctrination brief," Moody said with a self-satisfied grin. "For now, let me simply say that the TFR is the reason you're here."

Tyler didn't know what the hell was going on, but he suspected that Stan just might.

"This way," Moody said, with a wave. When Stan didn't budge, he added, "That means you, Master Sergeant. I promise to answer all of your questions."

Stan mumbled something Tyler couldn't make out, then grudgingly followed as Moody climbed back up the same set of metal stairs he'd descended only moments earlier. The steps led to a balcony with a metal floor and a simple metal railing separating it from the open warehouse floor below, overlooking the machine. Tyler assumed it was an observation and control mezzanine and counted a half dozen workstations with multiple monitors and keyboards, all of which were presently empty except for one. A woman in a lab coat, her red hair pulled back in a stubby ponytail, smiled up at them from where she stared at a monitor showing several graphs that populated in real time.

"Hey, Becca," Moody said as he walked past.

"Hiya, Pat," the woman said. "This must be Tyler and Stan."

"Nice to meet you, Becca," Tyler said, shaking her hand.

"You too," she said with a warm smile. "Thank you both for your service and your sacrifices."

"Thanks," Tyler said awkwardly. He never knew what to say when people said that to him.

"We'll be talking with Becca more later," Moody said. "Come on, follow me. The rest of the team is waiting."

Tyler followed Moody as they exited the control mezzanine via a steel door and entered a hallway with white walls and ceiling and a gray tile floor. Tyler noted name placards beside what he took to be office doors on each side of the hall. Moody stopped at the fourth door on the left beside a placard that read Conference Room A, opened the door, and held it for them to enter.

When Tyler looked inside, his heart skipped a beat. Zee was one of four people sitting at the conference table. He couldn't decide whether her presence was a relief or an unpleasant surprise. The last time he'd seen her had been in the sick bay on the *Ford* when he'd been a total asshole.

He nodded at her, and she gave him nothing more than a tight smile before looking down at her hands as Stan and Tyler took their seats.

"Always best to start with introductions," Moody said as he walked to the head of the table, where he remained standing. "You've all met me, but what you don't know is that I'm the program director here at Task Force Omega—which is a TS/SCI code word classified operation. Going around the table, we've got Chief Tyler Brooks from the JSOC Naval Special Warfare side of the house."

Tyler nodded with a closed-lip smile to the group. To his right sat a fit-looking dude wearing a black polo shirt with no logo. Tyler pegged him for an operator and turned out to be right.

"Next is Technical Sergeant Ben Driscoll from the Air Force's 24th Special Tactics Squadron, an 18 Delta Special Operations combat medic. Beside Ben is Lieutenant Zee Williams, intelligence analyst also from the NSW side of the JSOC house. Thanks for joining us, Zee . . ."

Tyler's eyes indexed to the next person, a woman who made and held eye contact with him. She appeared to be in her late thirties to early forties and her confident demeanor said she was no rookie. This, along with her squared shoulders and lean frame, made him peg her for either DIA or CIA.

"After Zee, we have Adela Khoury, who's worked with a number of our most elite agencies including stints at CIA and, most recently, DIA," Moody continued. "Seated beside Adela is Martin Back, who joins us from The Lamb Institute for Defense Policy where he works in the Quantitative Analysis and Predictive Warfare Division."

Tyler nodded at Adela before shifting his gaze to the other civilian, a skinny kid who looked sixteen, but Tyler knew had to be at least a decade older. Martin went to great lengths *not* to make eye contact, instead looking down at the table while tucking a strand of his straight, chin-length, black hair behind his ear.

"And last, but not least, Stan Abernathy, who is here on loan from the Army's Delta Force, also a JSOC element also known as Task Force Green."

"Nice to meet you guys," Stan said with a smile.

There was a flurry of handshakes and nods as Moody teed up a slide showing a bird's-eye view of the massive TFR machine in the warehouse. Instead of talking about the machine, he just stared at it—almost in reverence—for a long moment before advancing the slide. The next showed a picture of an outdoor track-and-field facility.

"Before I blow your minds with what we've accomplished here, I want to introduce you to our primary limitation because it becomes a major factor in how we can apply this technology. Have you ever considered what can be accomplished in four minutes or less? I know, it's a strange question, but around here it's all we think about."

When no one said anything, he gestured to the screen and continued.

"In 1954 Roger Bannister ran the world's first documented four-minute mile at Oxford University's Iffley Road Track. He finished the race in 3 minutes 59.4 seconds. By the latest count, 1,663 athletes have broken the four-minute barrier since . . ."

He advanced the slide to a picture of a rocket on a launch pad.

"This the SpaceX Falcon Heavy rocket. From blastoff, it takes three and half minutes to reach the Kármán line—one hundred kilometers above sea level and considered by most people to be the start of space . . ."

Moody clicked the remote in his hand and a new slide appeared, this one showing a picture of a tea kettle.

"A good electric tea kettle can bring a liter of water to a boil in under four minutes . . ."

Click.

A picture of the thriller novel *The Sandbox* appeared.

"The average American adult with a college education reads between two hundred and fifty and three hundred words per minute, which means in four minutes most people can comfortably read and comprehend four pages of a novel. Page a minute is a good rule of thumb . . ."

Click.

A picture of a band that Tyler recognized as Glass Animals appeared on the screen.

"According to Billboard Music, the average duration of hit songs across all genres in the Top 100 is three minutes and thirty seconds long," Moody said.

"As much as I'm loving learning all these little factoids, Mr. Moody," Adela said, interrupting with a polite, but exasperated, smile, "is there a point to all this that I've somehow missed?"

"The point is, in fact, a question—a question I'd like each of you to ponder for a moment. What can *you* accomplish in four minutes?" Moody asked, with the self-satisfied expression of a teacher who'd just announced a pop quiz to his class. Then, he clicked a button and started a four-minute countdown timer on the screen.

Ben Driscoll leaned over toward Tyler and whispered, "Speaking of doing things in under four minutes, the average male orgasms in three minutes while most women cannot break the four-minute barrier."

"I assume you're speaking from experience," Tyler whispered back with a wry grin.

"Not me, bro," Ben said with feigned indignation. "I pace myself."

Tyler shook his head. Despite a part of him not wanting to play along, he couldn't help himself. The SEAL inside immediately went to work answering the question.

In four minutes, a squad can fast rope out of a Blackhawk and breach a target compound. We can board a cargo ship and start to take out an entire crew of bad guys.

We can load into an SDV and be underway from a submarine . . .

Strangely, his mind suddenly flipped the script and thought about all the stuff they could *not* do in four minutes. Infils and exfils often took hours not minutes. ISR and mission prep might take days. And locating, prosecuting, and bagging an HVT often took months from the time the target warranted a package. In the context of fulfilling a complete mission, four minutes was nothing.

"Mr. Moody, I still—" Adela started.

"Just humor me, okay?" Moody said, cutting her off and pointing to the timer, which read 2:44.

Everyone stayed silent for the remainder of the countdown. When the timer hit 0:00, Moody said, "Time's up."

Like a kid in class, Driscoll raised his hand. He was the only one.

"Ben," Moody said with a little chuckle. "Your thoughts?"

"Well, it's interesting. At first, I started thinking about everyday stuff—like taking a shower or shaving—but then my mind went to how short the time is that muscles can produce energy efficiently using aerobic metabolism—like your Bannister reference. In the Special Operations world, the metabolic burn rate is extreme, and we use up our ATP stores in way less than four minutes . . ."

Tyler shot a surprised look at the AFSOC operator and pursed his lips.

Great, Ben's another closet genius like Stan. Don't tell me I'm the only dumbass in the room.

"Again, as much as I'm loving these little science lessons, can we please get to the point," Adela said, her patience exhausted. "When you recruited me, you hinted that DARPA had figured out a way to let you see into the future. How exactly does that machine work and why the fixation on four minutes?"

Moody flashed her a Cheshire cat grin. "The TFR doesn't just let you *see* into the future, it lets you go there. What you saw in the warehouse is the world's first fully functioning time machine . . ."

The room fell instantly silent, and Tyler found himself resisting the urge to laugh. This had to be bullshit, right? There was no such thing as time travel.

Stan was the first to speak, saying simply, "I knew it!" and slamming a hand on the table. Before the room exploded with questions, Moody reigned them in with his sobering caveat.

"But there is a catch," he said, folding his arms across his chest. "You can only stay for four minutes . . ."

CHAPTER 7

Tyler laughed.

Time travel . . . seriously?

"That's impossible," Adela said simply, folding her arms across her chest. "I don't believe you. And even if it were possible, it would be impossible to keep it secret."

"It's not impossible," Moody said. "I know because we've done it. *I've* done it."

"So, we're not the first?" Stan asked, seeming genuinely disappointed. Unlike Adela, Stan had blown right past skeptic to true believer in ten seconds flat. "I assumed this was, you know, a *Right Stuff* moment. That you had recruited us to be America's first time travelers."

"Dude, I didn't even think about that," Ben said with the deflated expression of a kid who'd just been told he was too short to ride Space Mountain. "That would have been so cool."

"You guys are idiots," Adela said. "He's fucking with us. You've been watching too much science fiction. Like I said, time travel is *impossible*. It violates the laws of physics."

"Actually, that's not true," Stan said, tapping the table with his index finger. "We're time traveling into the near future right now—at a velocity of one second per second. Just like we travel in space, we also travel in time. Accelerating the rate of temporal travel is theoretically possible and would feel like traveling into the future."

Tyler couldn't believe what he was hearing.

Is this real life?

An argument broke out with everyone talking at once until Moody shouted for them to stop. "Everyone needs to just settle down. It's a lot to take in, I know. But I can assure you that I am not bullshitting you. What we've achieved here is mind-boggling, but it is *real.*"

"But we have questions," Stan said.

"Yeah, lots of them," Adela added.

"I know, and I'll answer every single one of them, but let's talk shop *in* the shop," Moody said and headed toward the door. "I think it would be best to let our subject matter experts field your questions."

Tyler and the rest of the gang scooted their chairs back from the conference table and filed out of the room, each lost in thought. Moody retraced the path they'd walked earlier, exiting the admin building on the second level and stepping out onto the mezzanine where the control room was located, overlooking the Donut on the warehouse floor below. The woman who'd been working before turned in her task chair to face them and smiled. Beside her now, another tech had joined and turned as well, an expectant grin on his face.

"Everyone, this is Jimmy, one of our senior jump technicians," Moody said. "Not only is he, along with Becca here, a systems expert, but he's also the head of our TFR maintenance team. I've asked him to sit in on our Q&A and help field any technical questions you folks might have."

Jimmy, who was dressed in khaki slacks and a wrinkled button-down shirt, nodded and said, "Nice to meet you, folks."

Stan and Adela both spoke at the time with Stan blurting, "How does it work?" and Adela asking, "How far into the future can you travel?"

"Both great questions," Jimmy said. "First, as to how it works, the short answer is we don't know—or don't fully understand it, anyway—though we have some theories."

"You don't know?" Stan said, his expression incredulous. "How can you not know?"

"The TFR was not built to be a time machine," Moody said. "This facility was originally built to test an experimental fusion reactor."

"I thought that looked like a tokamak," Stan mumbled.

"A *toka*-what?" Tyler said, cocking his head.

"*Tokamak* is a Russian word for a donut-shaped field generator, Tyler. Based on the work by Nobel Prize winners Sakharov and Tamm, almost every experimental fusion reactor in operation today is a tokamak," Jimmy said.

"Actually, that's not true," Stan said. "The term *tokamak* was coined by Igor Golovin, not Igor Tamm, in 1957. Also, it's not a word, it's an acronym from the Russian: *toroidal'naya kamera s magnitnymi katushkami*—which roughly translates to *toroidal chamber with magnetic coils*."

"Thank you, Stan, for clearing that up for everyone," Moody said with a patient smile.

"Just a moment," Martin Back said, speaking for the very first time. "This machine is a functioning fusion reactor?"

"No," Jimmy said. "We never got that far. It was conceived as an advanced prototype field generator. A traditional tokamak has multiple magnetic fields which are managed simultaneously—toroidal, inner poloidal, outer poloidal, and helical. Particle drift and banana orbits are two of the major problems all tokamak reactors face when trying to achieve prolonged plasma stability. To address these problems, we thought—"

"Hey, Jimmy, you're getting into the weeds a little bit. Maybe just stick to the higher-level stuff," Moody said, interrupting.

"Sure, no problem, boss. Long story short, we invented time travel by accident. We were investigating phased fields for enhancing fusion stability but we pivoted the moment we recognized it had a temporal effect none of us imagined. We don't fully understand how it works— how the overlapping phased fields can accelerate objects forward in time—but we know for sure it *does* work. We've tested it extensively."

"That thing can travel into the future?" Adela said, pointing at the massive structure on the warehouse floor below.

"No," Jimmy said, "whatever is *inside* the ring travels to the future. The TFR doesn't travel. It stays right here in the present."

"I see," Ben said, "so when the field is active, everything inside the field is sent into the future and when you turn the machine off, the field collapses, and whatever you sent to the future is sucked back to the present."

"Well, a little more mathematically challenging, but yeah, that's correct."

"So, how far into the future can you go?" Zee said, repeating the exact question on Tyler's mind.

Tyler tried to imagine traveling a hundred years into the future. What would the world look like? Would it be a bastion of technological wonder or a dystopian hellscape? This opportunity, which had seemingly dropped out of the sky and into his lap, was the coolest thing that had ever happened to him.

I'm going to get to friggin' time travel to the future. How badass is that?

"Twenty-eight days," Jimmy said, the words a cold wet blanket that instantly smothered Tyler's fiery enthusiasm.

"I'm sorry, did you say twenty-eight days?" Tyler said, certain he must have misheard the man.

"That's right, we can select any time between the present and 28.135 days in the future."

"But no further?"

"That's correct."

"What about the past?" Zee asked, which was Tyler's next question. "Can you travel to the past?"

"No, just the future."

"Why not?" she pressed.

"This is more Becca's area, as a theoretical mathematician. Dr. Rosen?"

Tyler raised an eyebrow. He'd assumed her to be a technician, but it turned out she was yet another person whose intellect eclipsed his.

"Have any of you heard of the flowing river metaphor of time?" Becca asked.

Stan raised his hand.

Of course he has, Tyler thought with an eye roll.

"There are some mathematical issues with this metaphor, but in its simplest form, it stands up," Becca said. "Imagine time is a river, flowing in one direction, and we're all on a riverboat. The riverboat is the present. The water behind us is the past and the uncharted water ahead is the future . . ."

Tyler did—simple enough, so far so good.

"Everyone standing on the riverboat is moving at the same velocity of one second per second into the future. If our Navy SEAL, Tyler, jumps off the front of the boat, then he momentarily accelerates beyond the velocity of the present and lands in the future. Once he lands in the river, he'll be swept up by the current—a.k.a. time—and if he swims to match the boat's velocity he will continue traveling ahead of us in the future indefinitely. From his new vantage point, when he looks back at us, he sees our present as the past. If he decelerates, the riverboat will catch up and we can pull him back aboard into the present. But if he jumps off the back of the boat . . ."

"Then he lands in the past," Zee said, and she seemed mesmerized.

"Correct."

"And for him to get back to the present, it would take far more energy for him to catch up. Because he couldn't just slow down a little and wait for us," Zee concluded, looking quite impressed with herself.

Becca nodded. "Exactly."

"But," Stan interjected, "if your metaphor really holds true, then travel into the past *is* possible? The problem is getting back . . ."

"The energy required to do so, yes. Traveling to the past is theoretically possible, but not practical because of the way the TFR works," Jimmy said.

"And maybe not advisable. There are potential time paradoxes involved in going to the past," Becca said, and her face conveyed concern as she glanced at Moody.

"None of which are germane to this brief," Moody said. "Our capabilities are our capabilities, and our limits are our limits, but the implications of what we can do are astounding."

Tyler, who could barely wrap his head around any of this, nodded in awe.

"Back to the twenty-eight day future travel limit . . . Is that a design or energy limitation of the machine?" Stan asked.

"We're still not sure why we can't accelerate a payload beyond 28.135 days into the future," Becca said, "but that seems to be the limit—for now at least."

"You said the loiter time in the future is limited to four minutes? If you send a payload twenty-eight days in the future, shouldn't it take twenty-eight days for the present to catch up?" Ben asked.

"One has nothing to do with the other," Martin said, with a hint of superiority in his voice. "Time distance traveled into the future and loiter time are independent variables."

"That's correct," Jimmy said. "The TFR is the mechanism that accelerates the payload into the future and holds it there. The flux vortex dictates the loiter time. The second we turn off the reactor, the payload decelerates and returns to the present. Currently, four minutes is the longest we can maintain a stable flux vortex in the reactor. The moment we start to detect field degradation we have to shut it down."

"What happens if you leave it on?" Ben asked.

"Well, an unstable field creates distortions, which we imagine would be bad for the travelers."

"Bad in what way?" Ben pressed, clearly bent on going down this particular rabbit hole.

"We don't know, but we'd prefer not to find out."

Moody's eyes went dark for a moment, and Becca looked at her hands.

Tyler suspected that they did know—perhaps during animal testing or something—and didn't want to scare the shit out of the team with the details of whatever happened.

"We don't exceed four minutes—not ever. Safety is our paramount concern here," Moody said, taking control of the conversation back. "We were all disappointed to discover we couldn't go millions of years back in time to see the dinosaurs or centuries into the future to see the wonders of what lies ahead, but what we have created is a device with game-changing strategic—and dare I say, tactical—implications. The TFR is a crystal ball that allows us to look up to four weeks into the future anytime we want."

"Which gives us four weeks in the present to change that future, if we don't like what we see," Zee said, in a dubious tone Tyler had never heard her use before.

Is that awe or dread in her voice?

"Precisely," Moody said with the flair of a ringmaster announcing the next act under the big top. "Imagine if we'd known about the 9/11 attacks twenty-eight days before they happened. We would have hunted down Bin Laden's operatives before they boarded those planes. The towers would never have fallen, and the world would be a different place. All those people wouldn't have died. The war on terror would have unfolded completely differently . . ."

Tyler felt like an idiot for not seeing the forest for the trees. Countless movies and novels had explored the time paradoxes and implications of traveling into the past. A hero goes back in time to right a wrong, undo a mistake, or save a life, and in doing so changes the present. And in these stories, unintended consequences always reared their ugly head. But this was different. With this technology, they wouldn't be meddling with the past and constantly worried if their actions were monkeying up the present. Moody's plan was clean and straightforward: identify which threats succeed in the future, then stop them in the present.

An unexpected wave of guilt washed over him as his mind revisited his last and fateful JSOC op in Africa.

If I'd only had access to this technology before Mali, we would have known about the ambush. Zee and I would have changed the plan, and my SEAL brothers would still be alive.

He looked over at Zee. The truth was he regretted the things he'd said on the carrier that day. He had just wanted anything or anyone to blame, to lash out at, to make the loss less his own.

"... I don't have all the answers, which is why I recruited the six of you," Moody was saying, still in full ringmaster mode. "Together, your job is to begin to imagine how best we can utilize this technology. In a nutshell, the charter of this task force is to collect intelligence from the future and develop mission packages to neutralize the deadliest threats in the present. It is not hyperbole when I say that what we're about to undertake, if properly executed, will become the foundation of the nation's defense policy and Special Operations tasking. The President has given us a tall order, but he put it in simple terms that even a dense old bureaucrat like me could understand. He said, 'Pat, I want you to protect America, but you have to do it without screwing up the rest of the world. Can you do that for me?'" Moody let the words sink in for a moment before adding, "So, what do you think? Are you up to the challenge? Do you think this team can safeguard our nation, but do it without screwing up the rest of the world like the President said?"

When no one spoke, Tyler did what came naturally to him.

He led.

"Hooyah," he said to his new boss, then turned to the group. "Now, who's ready to get to work?"

CHAPTER 8

DIE URSACHE UNDERGROUND COMPOUND

SZCZECIN, POLAND

1915 LOCAL TIME

Jun tossed his ruck on the bottom bunk. It landed with a dull thud and made the springs creak twice as it bounced and settled. His gaze ticked up to the empty upper rack, perfectly made, with the bedsheets and top blanket pulled taut—no visual evidence that anyone had ever slept in it. Even before they'd joined the Army, his brother had been a stickler for tidiness and order.

Jun lowered his gaze to his own bunk.

The room felt different now. Sterile. Lifeless. He wasn't sure if he'd be able to sleep in here going forward and briefly considered asking Hoffman for a new room assignment.

No . . . this is your new reality, a voice said in his head. *You broke your promise, now this is your penance. This is your fate.*

"You're back. How was the funeral?" Damien said from the doorway behind.

Jun turned to face his teammate and friend. Hoffman had authorized and arranged Jun's trip home to Chengdu to bury Guo's ashes.

"It was small and private. Very sad . . . my mother had not seen him for ten years and she had to say goodbye to an urn."

"It pains me to say it, but it is better that way. The condition of the body was . . ."

Jun nodded and a flashbulb memory of his brother's unrecognizable face prompted a fresh wave of fury that made him ball his fists. "I'm going to make the American pay for this. It's my only mission."

"Don't let Hoffman hear you say that. He is German. Mission. Milestones. This is all he cares about."

"I know, but Tyler Brooks is the mission. So, our objectives are in alignment. The trick is getting Hoffman to let me do it my way."

The Frenchman considered this a moment then nodded. "Whatever your plan is, I will help you. And so will Garth. Your brother was a friend to everyone *ici.*"

"Thank you."

"*C'est ainsi que.*"

"I've decided it's not enough for him to die. I want him to feel like I do. I want him to know this kind of pain," Jun said and tapped his closed right fist against his chest over his aching heart.

Damien said nothing but he nodded in agreement or solidarity, either of which sufficed as far as Jun was concerned.

"Any developments while I was gone?" he asked, his mind already working the problem. All intelligence collected was highly compartmentalized at *Die Ursache.* Hoffman's grip on details, operations, and agendas was virtually ironclad, but operators were a brotherhood in and of themselves, and that meant keeping eyes and ears open at all times.

"Hoffman has been running two scout teams the entire time you've been gone. Six jumps a day."

"Are you serious?"

"*Oui* . . . he's burning them up like jet fuel."

"Do you know if—"

The radio, which sat in its charging cradle on top of the room's simple wooden desk, crackled to life, cutting him off midsentence. "Lin Jun, Op Center—over."

Jun stretched for the radio, keyed it, and said, "Go for Lin."

"Report to the director's office," came the reply.

"Roger," he said and looked at the Frenchman.

"Lucky you," Damien said with a smirk that Jun had come to think of as very French.

"Yeah, lucky me."

Jun left Damien and his vacant room behind and made his way to Hoffman's office. When he arrived, the German waved him inside the partially open door before he could knock. Jun shut it behind him.

"Take a seat," Hoffman said.

Jun lowered into the hard plastic chair across from the director's desk.

"Everything is settled at home with your mother and the funeral?" Hoffman asked, staring at Jun from behind a pair of silver-framed, rectangular eyeglasses.

"Yes."

The German used the nail on his pinky finger to try to free something between his upper canine and incisor. "Good."

"Have you found an opportunity for an intervention on Brooks?" Jun said, getting straight to the point.

"Not yet."

"But I heard the advance teams have been very active while I was gone," he said, his irritation at the lack of progress stoking his anger.

Hoffman looked at the nail of his littlest finger then wiped whatever the offending piece of food was on his trouser leg. "The new Omega team is not operational yet."

"So . . ."

Hoffman lowered his eyeglasses and looked at Jun as if he were the world's stupidest person. "There are an infinite number of locations in space-time where the team can jump. Without knowing their jump schedule, it is virtually impossible to intercept them."

"But we have future knowledge."

Hoffman laughed. "All we can see are the aftereffects of what they are going to change. Until we know, in the present, when and where they are going to jump, we can't plot a match."

Jun blinked, trying to decipher what Hoffman had just said. Time travel and future interdiction were confusing. Every time he thought he understood it, he'd soon find himself more bewildered than before he'd tried to work out what was cause and what was effect.

"Simply put, we know they are foiling our plans but we don't know how because they haven't started yet," Hoffman said, as if talking to a child. "Unless we get lucky, we have to wait until the present catches up with their first jump outside the Omega Room. Once we know those details, we should be able to stay one step ahead."

"But what about Brooks?" Jun said through clenched teeth.

"You're just going to have to wait until the right time comes. An intervention at the facility now is too dangerous. It would fail." The German stared at him a moment, his face a mask. "I assume your urgency is driven by my assertion that the Navy SEAL and his team are a major impediment to our success. I hope you would not let *personal* reasons drive your actions. Such things are dangerous."

"Of course," Jun said, feeling his blood boil. "Until we eliminate the threat that Brooks and the Omega team represent, we cannot hope to succeed in our mission."

The German gave a curt nod and looked down at his computer, signaling the meeting was over.

"There is another option, however," Jun said, an audacious idea coming to him. "One that might expedite satisfying both our objectives."

Hoffman looked up. "I'm listening . . ."

"They think they're hiding in plain sight, but we know where they operate from. What if we hit them when and where they least expect it," Jun said, leaning in and meeting the German's eyes.

Hoffman reclined in his chair and clasped his fingers together. "Tell me . . . what exactly do you have in mind?"

CHAPTER 9

CREW QUARTERS—WAREHOUSE A
WILSON SPICE FACTORY / TOP SECRET DEFENSE TECHNOLOGY PROVING
GROUND
HAVRE DE GRACE, MARYLAND
1248 LOCAL TIME

Tyler paced his stateroom, or whatever they were calling the individual living quarters they'd been assigned in a shared hallway. Yesterday had left his mind reeling as the details of what they were attempting were filled in with the predictable, bureaucratic PowerPoint briefings. He'd lay in bed staring at the ceiling in awe at the impossibility of the whole thing. But, today was a new day. He'd worked through the wonder and emotions of the thing and now saw its tactical value.

He was ready to roll. Ready to jump. Ready to friggin' time travel. But as was so often the case in the military, bureaucracy had thrown a cold wet blanket on his fire.

The morning had been consumed with medical exams, blood draws, CT scans, and other tests he didn't even understand. They'd met with a woman named Dr. Donahue, who explained the need to have a baseline for various parameters—which she'd named and he'd not understood at all—as they prepared for their first jump. His questions about the actual missions they would be sent on had been answered with vague descriptions of intelligence gathering to stop emerging threats. After that, he'd been given a personality assessment and asked to complete a questionnaire on each of his teammates. There was some bureaucratic BS at the Tier One, but nothing like this. At JSOC, at least you knew that on any given day odds were good you'd be in the fight, taking it to an enemy intent on destroying America. He hoped very much that would be true here as well. The tour through Warehouse C had been encouraging, since it held a team room, weapons lockers, and a very sophisticated kill house for training.

"You wanna walk with me over to the Pepper Grinder?" a familiar male voice said.

Tyler looked up to see Stan standing in his doorway, leaning against the doorframe with his arms crossed. The Delta operator had a thin and wiry build, which might have been why Tyler misjudged the possibility he was a SOF guy at first, but he could see now the powerful, sinewy muscles of the Army operator's forearms. There were plenty of guys at the Navy's JSOC unit who looked more like bankers than SEALs, but Tyler rationalized that it was the guy's *personality* more than his appearance that had caused his initial misjudgment.

"What the hell is the Pepper Grinder?" Tyler asked grudgingly, knowing he would no doubt regret the question, as he pulled an Under Armour quarter-zip top over his SEAL Legacy Foundation T-shirt. He slipped his folding knife into the right pocket of his cargo pants out of habit, then looked expectantly at Stan.

"Glad you asked," Stan said, excited.

I'm sure . . .

"As you know, the NOC for this super-secret defense research facility is the Wilson Spice Factory."

"Right," Tyler said, sighing. He squeezed past his new teammate and closed the door behind them.

"So," Stan continued as they headed down the second-floor hallway, past the men's showers and restrooms, to the stairwell, "I thought it would be fun to give the buildings names based on that. They call this building Warehouse A, but since it's kind of where we do the pleasant stuff—you know, private time in our rooms, hanging out in the rec room, the chow hall downstairs and all—that's like the good stuff, the stuff that gives a nice *taste* to the work, so I named it the Salt Shaker."

"Uh-huh," Tyler said, wondering how long this explanation would take.

A normal person would make the joke in a single sentence and get on with their day . . .

"And Warehouse B is where the work happens. So, it's an important flavor to our job here, but not like salty fun flavor, so I call it the Pepper Grinder."

"Oh God, is he telling you his spice names for the buildings?" Ben said, intercepting them on the stairs. The combat medic operator's eyes twinkled with impish amusement. "Hey, Stan, tell him what you call Warehouse C."

"Oh, yeah," Stan said. "So, I call Warehouse C, the Poblano."

Tyler stopped, turning to the man who, impossibly, was a Tier One Delta Force operator. "You named the training and shooting range, the best part of this whole damn facility, after a spicy pepper?"

Stan nodded enthusiastically, his face suggesting he expected to be congratulated on his brilliant insight.

"That's the dumbest thing I ever heard," Tyler said instead, shaking his head and resuming their walk toward Warehouse B, which his damn brain was already calling the Pepper Grinder. "First of all, that's not a spice, so you broke your own naming convention. Second, the range and kill house are where we shine, where we have our best fun while honing our skills for combat. Hell, that's the salt. But you named it after a pepper that burns your mouth?"

"Actually . . ."

Please don't say, "That's not true."

". . . that's not true."

Here we go.

"The poblano is a very tasty, and in fact, very mild pepper. The poblano is only one thousand to fifteen hundred on the Scoville scale—way less than even, say, the jalapeño, which is at least twenty-five hundred even at its most mild. Now if I had named Warehouse C the Ghost Pepper, well, sure"—the man chuckled as if anyone could possibly still be listening to his rant, which of course Tyler reluctantly was—"then I would see your point. I mean, forget about the Carolina Reaper."

"How many Scoville units is a Reaper, Stan?" Ben asked, staring at Tyler. He got it now—Ben Driscoll was totally screwing with him, and now he had to laugh at himself a bit.

"Oh, the Carolina Reaper is at *least* 1.4 million. It can get up to 2.5 million! Better have a gallon of whole milk ready for that one."

Ben laughed and, in spite of himself, Tyler did now too.

"Your teammates must have loved you over at Delta, Stan," Tyler said, patting the man on the shoulder.

"They loved me outside the wire, that's for sure," Stan said, and his voice changed timbre enough to make Tyler glance over. The man's face had switched in a blink from the smiling, goofy one Tyler'd come to know the last twenty-four hours to an emotionless mask that made Tyler raise an eyebrow.

"Why's that?" Ben asked in a low, soft voice, perhaps seeing the change as well.

"Because outside the wire, I'm a killing machine," he said in an even, almost monotone voice. "It's the thing I'm the very best at."

From anyone else, the operator bravado would have brought a chuckle and more Team guy ass-grabbing, but the dark, haunted look in Stan's eyes left Tyler speechless for a moment.

"It's the one thing I've always had a gift for."

The words, the tone, and the look on Stan's face made a chill run up Tyler's spine and he felt gooseflesh rise on his arms.

Then, pressing his hand onto the palm scanner that would unlock the main door to the Pepper Grinder, he said, "Well, we're lucky you're on our team, Stan," and realized he maybe even meant it.

"Yes," Stan said, looking away now, his eyes still haunted by something. "You are."

"You're a walking encyclopedia, Stan," Ben said.

"I just remember everything I read," Stan said with a shrug.

"Seriously?" Tyler asked, turning to his fellow operators, but he smiled, already starting to feel a weird, brotherly affection for the strange Delta shooter.

"Yeah," he said. "Remembering stuff is the *second* thing I'm really good at."

They arrived at Warehouse B and minutes later peered through the door into Conference Room A. Zee sat at the table next to Adela, and Marty was at the front, chatting with Moody about something Tyler guessed he wouldn't understand. Zee looked up and gave him a tight smile.

"How was lunch?" Moody asked the room as they entered and took their seats.

"Fantastic, actually," Ben answered, and it was true—they were going to be well-fed in this assignment, it seemed.

"I still have some questions about the medical testing," Stan said, and Moody held up a hand.

"I get it, Stan. But I would ask that you wait and ask Dr. Donahue when you see her. You can swing by anytime. I don't wanna just give you some half-baked, layman's answer when she's the medical expert here."

Stan nodded but seemed less than impressed.

"This afternoon, I want to go over my vision for how a tactical application of the technology looks from my perspective, but I want you guys to weigh in with any ideas you may have. We're designing this together, so I want your thoughts on how to make it the most effective use of the tech. After, I'll have you guys go over to Warehouse C . . ."

"The Poblano," Ben whispered, still staring straight ahead, grinning.

"Stop it," Tyler said, smiling as well, especially when Stan gave them both a thumbs-up.

". . . where you'll choose and familiarize yourselves with the weapons available, get issued other gear you'll need, and set up your equipment cages. Then, I think it would be good for Tyler to take you onto the indoor range for at least a fam fire before he gets you started on training tactical scenarios as a team . . ."

"Why Tyler?" Ben said, but he was still smiling. "Is there some preference for Navy SEALs? I mean, sure, they write books . . ."

Everyone laughed except Martin, who didn't seem to get the dig.

"Special Operations Chief Brooks is the team leader . . ."

Tyler looked up, eyes wide in surprise. "What?"

"Chief Brooks, this isn't a science experiment anymore. The TFR is a tool that will bring a new level of asymmetry to the world of covert and Special Operations. It's more than a tool, in fact—it's a weapon that will allow us to foil attacks by our enemies. To do that, we need to be able to do far more than just jump a few weeks into the future. We need to be able to harvest actionable intelligence while we're there and then use that intelligence to plan short-fuse operations to defeat our enemies in the window of time available to us before they happen. You were selected, after very careful screening, as the best person to lead this unit."

Tyler's mind ran through a litany of reasons why he was *not* the best person to lead a team of brainiac shooters and spies, not the least of which was how he'd been proven yesterday, in his mind at least, to be the dumbest guy in the room. Before he could voice his concerns, Zee shocked him.

"Chief Brooks is not only a gifted operator and natural leader," she said, addressing the room but not looking at him, "but also has an uncanny ability to read a tactical scenario with lightning speed and intuitively come up with the correct tactical response."

"Which is, I assume, why you suggested that I recruit him when we met," Moody said, and Tyler felt the blood drain from his face.

Zee nodded.

Tyler found himself speechless.

"I know everyone here, with the exception of Marty, has some level of weapons-and-tactics training, but we come from different backgrounds and need to operate as a unit. So, Chief Brooks, let's get everyone comfortable with the gear and weapons, do some time on the range, or evolutions in the kill house—whatever you think best to kick off the process of making this unit come together tactically," Moody said.

"Will do," Tyler said. He glanced over at Martin Back and wondered just how far down that road he could get with the kid. Marty was not and never would be an operator. Tyler'd see how it went, then have a conversation with Moody if needed. "It will help to know what kind of operations and mission parameters we're working with here," he said.

"Today is about getting baselines—medically, cognitively, and tactically. Then, we'll brief in detail what I expect a typical mission might look like and discuss information gathering. After, we can begin to formulate a training program—together—that will get you ready for those challenges. Sound good?"

Everyone nodded.

"All right," Moody said. "Because we need to move fast and get this team up and operational as quickly as possible."

"That's not the first time you've mentioned needing to spin up quickly. Is there some threat on the horizon that is pushing us to move fast?" Adela asked, taking the thought literally right from Tyler's mind.

Moody's face darkened only a moment, and then he smiled. But in that moment, Tyler thought he saw a different side of the project director.

"A huge amount of money has been poured into this program. I have milestones to meet. I need to demonstrate progress to the people holding the purse strings—my bureaucratic problems, not yours, but a reality nonetheless . . . All right, shall we move on?"

"I have a question. I get the medical exam, but what was up with all the brain teasers and puzzles after?" Ben asked. "Are you checking to make sure we're smart enough to be on this team?"

"I didn't do any puzzles," Stan said. "I like puzzles, but that's not what my tests involved."

"Oh, I just assumed we all had the same tests," Ben said. "What kinda tests did they give you?"

"Reading comprehension and timed recall accuracy," Stan said.

"I didn't have any of those kinds of tests," Ben came back.

"Are you kidding me?" Adela said, looking at them like they were a bunch of idiots. "I can't believe you guys haven't figured it out yet."

"Figured what out?" Ben said, turning to look at her.

"That everyone on this team is a savant," Adela said. "It's so obvious."

"And what's your gift, Adela—knowing how to push people's buttons?" Ben quipped.

"That's one of them," she said, crossing her arms and grinning.

Moody held up a hand. "You guys make me laugh, you really do. And you bicker like a bunch of kids. But that's okay, it's to be expected, I guess," he said with a paternalistic chuckle. "Adela's right, by the way. Each of you possesses a remarkable gift—an ability so rare that less than one-tenth of one percent of the people on the planet are eligible to be members of your club. About two percent of the population claims to have an eidetic memory, but there are degrees. The team I've assembled is the top gun of memory savants. Adela, would you like to take a crack at identifying each team member's specific memory gift?"

"Sure," she said, sitting up in her chair. "Stan is the easiest: he remembers everything he reads, which he shows off at every damn opportunity he can. Ben is a Gestalt guy—pattern recognition. Give Ben a *Where's Waldo?* book and he'll find where that little freak is hiding on every page in milliseconds."

"Hey, I loved those books as a kid," Ben said.

"See, told you," Adela said and shifted her gaze to Zee. "Zee doesn't take notes, but her ears are always on. She doesn't forget anything she hears. And Martin is a quant. He perceives qualitative information in quantitative terms. His brain can perform calculations and store numbers like a computer. Am I right, Martin? You're a human spreadsheet, aren't you?"

"Yes, that is an accurate summation of my capability," Martin said with flat affect. "What about you? What is your gift, Adela?"

The right corner of her mouth curled up a pinch at the question. "I have what most people call a *photographic* memory. Why do you think the CIA recruited me? They used me as their human camera for all the places you can't have a camera or observe with a drone," she said, tapping the side of her head.

"You left out Tyler," Ben said. "What is his memory gift?"

"Oh, yeah, as far as I can tell, he doesn't have one," she said and looked at Moody. "I just assumed he's here because he's a demon on the trigger and great at kicking down doors."

Tyler bristled. Normally, a comment like that would roll off him like water off a duck's back, but coming from Adela it stung.

"He's here to lead," Stan said, with a defensive edge to his voice. "I think that's pretty obvious."

"Every member of this team was carefully screened and selected out of hundreds of candidates to fulfill a unique and specific role. I'm confident everyone's talents and contributions will make an impact and lead to mission success," Moody said. "Now, I'm sure the next question on everyone's mind is *why* did I recruit a team of memory savants? The answer is simple: I didn't really have a choice. We can't bring digital data back from jumps to the future. We've tried, but the magnetic fields are too powerful. Even shielded drives come back wiped. I have people working on some ideas, but for now, human memory is the only thing that survives the trip. And as we've already discussed, the loiter time in the future is limited to four minutes. You've got four minutes to collect and memorize as much information as possible. Today, we're going to do our first training jump."

"Ah, I see. You wanted to make sure you had enough 'devices' to capture every modality of information," Stan said, using finger quotes on the word *devices*.

"That's right," Moody said and powered on his projector. The screen in front of them displayed a picture of a room that reminded Tyler of a typical TOC—a command center with computer terminals and lots of monitors displaying satellite feeds, data streams, and live news broadcasts. Only this room appeared to be round. "This is the Omega Room, and it's where you will be traveling to on every jump. It's a fully automated data processing facility conceived and designed by me and fed information by the NSA. As far as the NSA is concerned, they are simply supplying real-time data to secure terminals in a secure location. Nothing earth-shattering there. No one at NSA, even the director, is read in on this project because they don't need to be. As far as they're concerned, the Omega Room exists only in the present. But you'll be traveling to it in the future and mining NSA data. Pretty cool, huh?"

"Very cool," Stan said. "Are you going to give us a tour before our first jump?"

"No," Moody said, taking Tyler by surprise. "The Omega Room's location is compartmentalized. It's imperative that nobody with access to the TFR knows where it is. In fact, I don't even know where it is."

"I call bullshit," Ben said with a chuckle. "You said you designed it."

"Yeah, it was my idea, and it was also my idea that it be built in a location already redacted on all the paperwork. I swear, I don't know where it is, and I don't want to know," he said. "It's not just for security purposes either; there's a practical reason as well."

"So we don't run into our future selves," Zee said, and Tyler was pretty sure he saw her shiver at the thought.

"Precisely," Moody said. "In fact, the Omega Room has no operable doors. We cannot risk anybody being inside that room when you travel. Inside the Donut, there are six Xs painted on the floor. Each of those Xs is mapped to a safe drop location in the Omega Room. Each of you will have your own designated mark that you launch from and land on, for both directions of travel."

The idea Moody suggested—meeting oneself in the future, but also not landing where someone or something else might be in the future—had not occurred to Tyler, but now the protocol made perfect sense.

"What *would* happen if the machine sent us into the future and I wasn't standing on my X?" Zee asked. "What if I was standing in a place that mapped to where a computer terminal is located? Would our atoms get mixed together? Would I have a computer terminal stuck out of my torso?"

Moody's face lit up at the question, and she sensed he'd been waiting for someone to ask it. "A great question, and one that all of the science and engineering folks here, including myself, have spent quite a lot of time worrying about and validating through testing. As it turns out, the adage that two things can't occupy the same space at the same time turns out to be true. In the case of time travel, the incoming matter gets priority and moves the existing matter out of the way. When you land in the future, even the air molecules are dispersed to make room for your body. That's not a problem because the air moves easily and happily. As for solids, um, not so much. If you were to land in the same location as a computer terminal, its molecules are ripped apart to accommodate your arrival."

"In other words, it blows up?" Tyler asked.

"Yes. Pretty much."

"Note to team, make sure everyone stands on their X," Tyler said, sweeping his gaze across the group.

"The Omega Room is unmanned at all times, except for those four-minute windows when we jump into it to collect future data?" Stan asked.

"That's correct."

"Okay, Pat, so to summarize," Adela said with her no-nonsense swagger, "our job is to stand on the X in the Donut, Jimmy zaps us into the future, we drink from the data fire hose in a room without any doors or windows, and after four minutes we get sucked back to the present where we barf up all the stuff we learned . . . for you."

Moody made a finger pistol and pointed it at her, "Winner, winner, chicken dinner."

"In that case, I'm out," Adela said.

"What do you mean you're out?" Tyler said, shocked and confused by the comment.

"Sounds friggin' lame," she said, crossing her arms.

"You think time traveling to the future is lame?" Stan said, his expression incredulous.

"Like that, yes," she said. "My days of being somebody else's human camera are over. I'm tired of being treated like a tool in a toolbox. It's why I left CIA for DIA. You can find someone else."

Tyler let the discussion unfold, but he felt himself leaning toward Adela here. He was an operator—a door-kicking, direct-action, Tier One SEAL. Intelligence collection wasn't the mission set he had in mind. He wondered just why the hell he'd been selected in the first place.

Moody pursed his lips. "Adela, the data collection trips are only a small part of executing the task force's charter. Knowing what happens in the future is not the same thing as knowing how and why it happened. I recruited you specifically because of your CIA and DIA operational pedigree, not in spite of it. Yes, your visual photographic memory is a huge bonus, but what this team needs is your two decades of experience tracking down HVTs and foiling terrorist attacks. Ninety percent of the work we're going to be doing here is between the jumps. It's the data analysis—a process we call *reconstruction*. Then it's using that data to find the how and why. Lastly," he looked at Tyler and gave a small nod, "it's using all of the information to put together a mission to stop something horrible before it happens. All of that happens in the *now*. If you stay, you'll be helping to plan and execute the most important mission packages in the history of this nation. But, if you want to leave, I can prep the paperwork and get the green light to return you to your previous billet at DIA."

"All right, I'll give it two weeks," she said, arms still folded. "Two weeks, Moody, and if it sucks, I'm gone."

"That's fair," he said and swept his gaze across the rest of the faces. "Does anybody else have reservations or want to leave the team? Speak now, because this is the time to do it."

"I have something," Ben said, his voice tinged with excitement.

"Go ahead, Ben," Moody said, smiling.

"Okay, I can't believe I'm the only one seeing this." He looked around the room, going from face to face. "No one?" He turned back to Moody. "If the Omega Room is in a secure location—a location *not* here—then what you've created here is not just a time machine . . . but a machine that can travel in three-dimensional space as well."

"Oh, shit. He's right," Tyler said, the epiphany hitting him like a slap to the face. "The TFR is a time *and* teleportation machine."

"That's right," Moody said; his voice sounded far less enthusiastic than Tyler would have expected. "But for now, I'm afraid, completely impractical. We can safely jump into the Omega Room because we have it mapped geospatially to the micrometer. Jumping anywhere else would incur incredible risk—as we just talked about regarding your marks on the floor when jumping. The calculations for traversing three-dimensional space and time are difficult and complex—"

"Yeah, but totally worth it," Ben interrupted and turned to Tyler with a wide-eyed expression. "We could jump into the bedroom of the head of ISIS and cap him in his sleep tomorrow night. The tactical implications are *huge!*"

"That's true, but also not," Moody said. "The problem with Ben's hypothetical is that when you jump into the future to kill a terrorist, or do anything to try to change the future, you return to the present in four minutes. And once you do, that event has not yet happened, so . . ."

"You're saying any changes made in the future reset or something?"

"Yes, that's exactly what I'm saying."

"Well, that sucks," Tyler said, deflating.

"Look, we're as interested in this kind of application as you are, I promise," Moody said with a professorial grin. "But this program is still in its infancy. We need to walk before we run. You're going to be pioneers, and I expect you'll devise tactics, methods, and uses the science team here has not even contemplated yet. But as far as this task force is concerned, reconnaissance happens in the future, direct action happens in the present. Are we all on the same page?"

Tyler nodded and so did the others.

"Last but not least, there's something else very important I need to discuss with all of you before we brief your first jump and the techniques we've developed for data collection in the future—and that's my zero-tolerance position around the collection of unauthorized information, or UNAUTH for short. In the future, you will have access to information about future events that you might be tempted to exploit for financial or personal benefit. The winning Powerball numbers, for example, come to mind. Such knowledge is not part of the parameters set into our searches, but trust me, you will be tempted. And even if you don't actively query such data, there might be *inadvertent* exposure to future knowledge that could be exploited for personal gain or advantage. To be clear, this is a direct and criminal violation of the NDA you signed but also it is a moral violation . . ."

Tyler tried to stop his mind wandering as Moody lectured the team about the UNAUTH protocols and the dangers of violating them, but he couldn't help himself. Moody's sales pitch about removing uncertainty on the *USS Ford* finally made sense.

We're gonna know exactly what the bad guys do before they have a chance to do it, he thought, leaning back in his chair with a satisfied smile. *We're going to kick a lot of ass and save a ton of lives. If only Moody had recruited me before Mali, then my brothers would still be alive . . .*

CHAPTER 10

Zee scooted her chair away from the conference table and stretched her back as everyone filed out of the room for the fifteen-minute break between sessions.

"Got a second?" Tyler said, hanging back from the others.

"Sure," she said and forced a tight-lipped smile onto her face.

"Look, I owe you an apology for how I treated you in sick bay. I said some things I shouldn't have."

"You were in pain and on morphine at the time. I know you didn't mean it," she said—but the truth was that his selfish words that day had wounded her.

"That's nice of you to say, but I don't deserve a free pass. I was an asshole, and you didn't deserve that."

"Thank you," she said and held his eyes for the first time since they'd arrived.

"Did you really recommend me to Moody when he recruited you on the *Ford*?" he asked.

"Yeah, about that. I know I should have checked with you before floating your name. I just . . ."

He held up a hand. "Actually, Zee, I appreciate that you thought I'd be a good fit. The truth is, I feel a little out of my league here. I don't have an uber intellect or a photographic memory like the rest of you do. The fact that you thought I was worthy of this means a lot."

She gave him an awkward smile. "I meant what I said earlier. You're a gifted operator and team leader. But most importantly, you have integrity. That's rare these days."

He nodded. "I feel the same way about you. You know I trust you, right? My decision to proceed with the op that night wasn't about not trusting you. I conducted a risk-reward calculation on the spot. If it had been two trucks with seven dudes I would have held. But that's not what you saw."

"I know," she said, feeling a sudden pang of guilt in her abdomen as the memory of that night came rushing back. "And Commander Carroll agreed with your call. What happened will haunt me for the rest of my life. It's the reason I agreed to join this task force."

"Me too," he said, looking down for a moment, before putting on a smile. "So, are we good?"

"We're good," she said, smiling back.

"Cool. Wanna go grab a coffee with me? We still have ten minutes."

"Sounds great," she said, but when they stepped out into the corridor Moody stuck his head out of his office and beckoned her.

"Lieutenant Williams, do you have a moment?"

"Sure," she said, then turned to Tyler. "Looks like I'm gonna have to take a rain check on that coffee."

"No worries," Tyler said and departed with a two-finger salute.

On entering Moody's office, the director said, "Close the door behind you, please, and have a seat, Lieutenant."

"Is something wrong, Mr. Moody?" she said, suddenly feeling a *called to the principal's office* vibe.

He waved a hand dismissively and settled back comfortably into his chair. "Absolutely not, Lieutenant. I called you in because I wanted to get your feedback on how you think things are going."

The question most definitely felt like a curveball she'd not expected. "My feedback?"

"Yes, you're the senior ranking member of the task force," he said.

"You must have some observations you can share. It's really important to me that everyone is feeling confident and informed . . . and, you know, *heard*. This is not your typical task force, obviously, and things are moving fast. As program director, the last thing I want is for you guys to feel like mushrooms—you know, kept in the dark and fed a steady diet of bullshit."

She couldn't help but smile at the line, which was the same one her Air Force colonel father loved to use. Moody and her dad were probably about the same age, both DoD establishment lifers, so they were cut from the same cloth.

"In that case, I appreciate the opportunity . . ." she said, answering him while racing to collect her thoughts. She'd been so inwardly focused, she'd not really given much thought to the rest of the team, which instantly made her feel like a crappy officer. "First, let me say that I don't believe any of us feel like mushrooms. You've made it clear on multiple occasions that you have an open-door policy, and you've also been very forthcoming about the technology and answering everyone's questions . . ."

"I sense a *but* coming," he said with a chuckle.

"Well, the *but* is that you've told us we're going to travel to the future, Director Moody," she said with a chuckle of her own. "Do you know how insane that is? I think most of us are still trying to wrap our heads around *that*."

He nodded and met her eyes, his smile slowly evaporating as his expression turned serious. "There is something important pertaining to future knowledge that I do need to talk to you about, Zee. A burden that, unfortunately, is going to fall primarily on you, and one that I need to know if you're willing to shoulder."

"Okaaaay," she said, drawing out the word as the butterflies assaulted her stomach.

"When the team travels to the future, you're going to have access to a wealth of information about future events, and not just those pertaining to national security. To use a biblical analogy, the temptation to taste the forbidden fruit is going to be both strong and omnipresent," he said and leaned in to rest his elbows on the desk.

"You're referring to UNAUTH—the policy you briefed us on earlier?"

"That's right. In the near future, for example, the World Series has already been decided. Hypothetically speaking, if a particular team member had a history of sports gambling, the temptation to find out which team won the series and make a sizable bet in the present might be too irresistible to pass up."

And there it was . . . *the blindside*.

"Are you asking me to be your spy on my team?" she said, stiffening in her chair.

"No, no," he said. "Of course not. I'm not asking you to be a spy; I'm asking you to be an officer with integrity. Your billet here is to lead and oversee our intelligence collection activities. Just like at your last command, you're responsible for maintaining the sanctity of all the data we collect and enforcing this operation's most important data collection tenet."

"Which is?"

"That the gathering and application of UNAUTH by members of the task force is strictly and unequivocally forbidden," he said. "You're a brilliant young woman, Zee, so I don't have to explain how violating this protocol has the potential for disastrous consequences."

Her mind raced ahead, imagining a half dozen scenarios, and in doing so she understood the gravity of the situation. "Election results, stock market movements, scientific breakthroughs, a preventable plane crash, a school shooting . . ." she said, and her voice trailed off.

"Precisely."

"Have you talked to Tyler about this?" she asked.

"Not yet, I wanted to talk to you first . . ."

"With all due respect, Director, as a Navy lieutenant I might be the highest-ranking member on the team, but this is a joint task force with both military and civilian members. Rank doesn't take precedence in the task force hierarchy as you've organized it. You made Tyler the team leader, so I think you should be having this conversation with him, not me."

"Yes, Tyler is team leader, but during jumps, you will be running the show for intelligence gathering. And after, you're in charge of data reconstruction, analysis, and policing our UNAUTH policy."

"In other words, I'm internal affairs now," she said, not loving this new collateral duty he'd sprung on her.

"No, no, nothing of the sort," he said, shooing away the characterization. "I'd take the duty on myself, but I'm not going to be traveling. I really do need someone to run point on this, and the person I trust most with this responsibility is you."

"Mm-hmm . . ."

"Certainly you can see how potentially corrosive and destabilizing future knowledge could be. We can't risk having our team members distracted from the mission by temptations that might lead to pursuing personal agendas off the books, so to speak."

"Like personal enrichment . . ."

"Right. Or," he hesitated, "attempting to prevent an undesirable future event that might impact a team member, friend, or loved one, for example."

Ah, so there it is . . .

She fixed him with a tight-lipped smile. "So, hypothetically speaking, if I were to discover that my parents will have a fatal car accident driving to Costco next weekend, your expectation is that I will not act on that information and simply let them die because, you know, OPSEC."

Moody fixed her with a tight-lipped smile of his own. "My expectation is that you will never find yourself in such a morally compromising situation because during jumps to the future, you will not be actively seeking out information concerning the fates of friends, colleagues, and loved ones. This, Lieutenant, is the heart and soul of the UNAUTH policy."

"A funny choice of words . . . to describe a policy *without* heart or soul."

Moody leaned in, his patience now seemingly on the verge of failing. "Until this machine was invented, the future was unwritten. Not knowing how or when we die, or how or when our loved ones die, makes living in the present psychologically viable. I, for one, am glad I don't know the details of my death. The anxiety that would create would make doing my job and living my life joyless, and probably unbearable. When it comes to certain things, not knowing is best."

She was tempted to point out the absurd hypocrisy of his argument given his job as program director of a task force created to do the very thing he was arguing against, but doing so would be pointless. And a part of her actually agreed with him on this last point. He was giving them the power to play God, but only as unbiased arbiters of fate. Using the technology in a self-serving capacity was wrong. A line had to be drawn somewhere, and he'd just drawn it.

"I understand," she said after a beat. "And you're right."

"Okay, good," he said, leaning back into his chair. "I'm glad to hear you agree with me. That said, this is not something you have to do alone. I fully expect your entire team to back you up when it comes to policing UNAUTH, and that holds true for your team leader. You and Tyler will share the burden, okay? Speaking of Tyler, aboard the *Ford* I heard rumors there were some words exchanged between the two of you . . ."

She shook her head. "Things get said in the heat of the moment. We talked it out. Chief Brooks and I are good to go."

"Great," Moody said. "I feel much better hearing that, thank you."

"Copy that," she said. "Is there anything else you wanted to talk about?"

"Nope," he said, but she sensed this wouldn't be their last one-on-one meeting.

"Okay, well, I'll see you back in the conference room," she said, getting to her feet.

"Yep, see you in a few. Oh, and you can leave the door open on your way out."

Before turning to leave, she took a moment to scan Moody's office with an intelligence officer's eye for details, her curiosity strangely piqued.

"Something else I can do for you, Lieutenant?" he said, narrowing his eyes.

"No, I just noticed you don't have any family pictures up. You seem like a family man to me, Pat. Kinda remind me of my dad sometimes," she said, trying for a friendly probe.

"Ah, well, unfortunately having a family wasn't in the cards for me. It's ironic," he said with a wan smile, "the guy they put in charge of time travel ran out of time. Go figure."

"Yeah, go figure," she said and walked out of his office wondering, not for the first time, if he was telling her the truth.

CHAPTER 11

As a Navy SEAL, Tyler knew that he never rose to the occasion but rather fell to the level of his training and mental toughness, so *worry* wasn't something he did. But today he felt amped and, if he was honest, a little nervous. It wasn't that he was afraid of dying. He'd tangoed with the Grim Reaper enough times to appreciate what it meant to gamble with his life. Mortality wasn't the issue. It was facing the unknown that really got under his skin. Every mission had unknowns—variables that couldn't be predicted, intelligence gaps that couldn't be filled—but this was different. What he and his team were about to do was something that defied all convention and logic. They were traveling in time via a magnetic vortex created by a fusion reactor, and even the scientists who invented it couldn't explain how or why it worked. Helicopters didn't look like they should be able to fly, but at least the pilots could explain the physics.

Not the case with these yahoos.

"You nervous?" Zee asked as Tyler pressed his palm on the scanner and punched in his code to open the door.

"Nah," he lied and shot her his best Team-guy grin. "Easy day."

A moment later they emerged onto the metal mezzanine control center overlooking the TFR, which everyone here called the Donut. The room was packed with technicians, both at the consoles and standing around chatting in hushed tones. The room was buzzing with energy and anticipation that something big was about to happen. Martin stood beside Stan and Ben, who made him look even smaller than he was, and Adela stood chatting with Becca and one of the techs at a console.

"Good afternoon, Tyler," Becca said, smiling at him behind large glasses. "Did you get your CrossFit workout in? Standing in a room for four minutes is hard work."

"I'm ready to go, Becca," he said through a laugh, grateful to her for teasing because it broke his serious mood.

"Don't forget to pay homage at the shrine," Jimmy added with a grin. "For good luck and a safe return."

Tyler nodded. "Thanks for the heads-up."

"All right, boys and girls—it's show time," Moody said, clapping his hands together with enthusiastic flair. He led the team down the metal stairs to the warehouse floor and the staging area in front of the time machine. "This jump is your first and it's going to feel weird. You heard this morning from one of our early test pilots about what it feels like to travel through time and the déjà vu that will hit you on the return . . ."

As Moody talked, Tyler's eyes drifted to "the shrine" of the Father of Time Travel. According to Jimmy, time travel was discovered entirely by accident when one of the cleaning staff fell asleep on the job and was inside the Donut when the reactor fired up for a four-minute test of the flux vortex. At that time, the Donut didn't have any windows and nobody knew that Facilities Technician Roberto Lopez was in there. If you believed the tale—and Tyler had no reason not to, because who the hell would make such a crazy story up—Lopez woke up two days in the future on the floor of the control room. During that first four-minute jump, Lopez had seen pink balloons celebrating the birth of Jimmy's daughter who'd arrived two weeks early, information which the janitor brought back with him. In accordance with the rules of time travel, none of the control room staff remembered seeing Lopez blink in and out of existence, but the future knowledge the man obtained astounded everyone and was the spark that "birthed" the Omega program.

In typical science nerd fashion, a hilarious little shrine had since been made with a goofy picture of a grinning Lopez holding a mop handle in one hand and giving a thumbs-up with the other. The inscription on the plaque read: The Father of Time Travel. Tyler was dying to meet and talk to the guy, but apparently the dude took a ginormous hush money payment and retired to the Caribbean, legally bound to keep his experience a secret until the day of his death.

Moody continued. "Keep in mind, you're only gone four minutes. It goes fast, people . . . faster than you think it will. We've issued each of you a custom Swiss watch with a self-winding precision movement and mechanical countdown timer window. Push the button on the left side of the crown and a four-minute timer starts with two preset alarms that chime at thirty seconds and ten seconds remaining. As team leader, Tyler is the assigned timekeeper, but any of you are welcome to back him up. This is a training jump, so your only objective is to familiarize yourself with the Omega Room and try to collect as much current event data as possible from the feeds. To facilitate data collection and efficient presentation of that information, we utilize an algorithm that continuously scans and collates information in the background. It flags, prioritizes, and validates events in advance. That way, when you're trying to devour information, it's a bit more manageable. It'll still feel like drinking from a fire hydrant at first, I imagine, but at least not like trying to slurp up the whole ocean. Questions?"

Tyler scanned his team, who looked at one another and then shook their heads.

"Should be super easy, folks," Moody said. "It's T-minus five minutes, so go ahead and roll your left sleeve up for your prejump injection from our med tech Julie."

Tyler did as instructed and was the first one to get the jab. It burned at the injection site, but nothing outrageous. He rolled his sleeve down as Julie moved through the team.

"Remind me, Mr. Moody. What's in this cocktail you're injecting us with?" Stan asked after both Adela and Marty had received their shots. "I know you told us, but I forgot."

"Somehow, Stan, I find that difficult to believe," Moody came back, "given the fact that you have one of the most robust eidetic memories ever tested. I imagine you could repeat the information verbatim with 99.5 percent accuracy."

"It's a proprietary antioxidant cocktail, rich in vitamins B6, B12, D3, and essential amino acids to minimize cell oxidation from the magnetic vortex," Adela said. "It also has an anti-inflammatory compound and zinc, which are designed to—"

"Okay, okay," Stan said. "You're just showing off."

"You don't have to take it, Stan, but I think that you'll feel much better an hour from now if you do," Moody said. "At least if the docs are to be believed."

Tyler watched Stan press his lips together and then give the nurse his shoulder for the stick. Stan wasn't the squeamish type, but something clearly bothered him about the shot. Maybe he just hated shots. Tyler knew a burly, fast-roping, door-kicking breacher back at JSOC who passed out every time he had to have blood drawn, so you never knew.

Once everyone had been "antioxidized," Moody gestured at the Father of Time Travel shrine. "If any of you are superstitious . . . now's your chance."

Grinning, Tyler walked over to the goofy picture and gave Lopez a matching thumbs-up. Stan followed, but he nodded his head in deference for a moment. Ben crossed himself and said a little prayer—to the real God, not Lopez, Tyler figured. Zee blew the legendary janitor a kiss. And Martin ran his index finger over the engraved brass placard. When it was Adela's turn, everyone turned to look at her.

"You guys are idiots," she said with her trademark exasperated face. "I'm not friggin' doing that."

"It's bad luck if you don't. Come on, Adela," Ben said.

"Don't care; ain't doing it," she said and turned to Moody.

"All right then, time to get this show on the road," the program director said with a paternal grin and walked to the access door for the TFR, where he entered his security code via keypad and gave the scanner his thumbprint. An LED light flashed green, the heavy metal door clicked loose the magnetic locks, and there was a hiss of air. Tyler looked up and could see again why they called the machine *the Donut*. In the middle of the room, which Tyler recalled measured thirty-three and a third feet wide, sat a cylindrical fusion reactor. Every square inch of the curved interior surface was lined with graphite-colored metallic heat tiles.

With a deep, steeling breath, Tyler led the team inside. He walked to his assigned *X* on the floor and watched his five teammates each do the same, stepping onto their spots marked with colored duct tape. Tyler chuckled. Funny, he thought, that at a facility with so much money and so much technical acumen relied on literal red tape to mark the spots.

"I think you'll find that four minutes goes by really fast. Your goal on this jump is simple: familiarize yourselves with the Omega Room and commit as much information as possible to memory. This will be a good test of what this team is capable of, and we'll be able to optimize and tailor how the AI presents data to best accommodate your individual eidetic modalities," Moody said from the doorway as Tyler let out a slow breath. "Godspeed and good luck."

Stan waved goodbye to Moody with just his fingers, like a parent waves to a little kid. Tyler saw Moody roll his eyes but he watched the man's shoulders shaking with laughter as he shut the hatch. A heavy metallic clunk followed as the hatch door contacted the frame, followed by the click of magnetic locks engaging that made Zee jump. Tyler watched her scan the chamber, her nerves quite apparent, and she let out a slow, trembling breath.

I get it, he thought. *Me too, sister.*

"Do you think this is going to hurt?" Ben asked, addressing no one in particular.

"Nobody told us it would hurt," Tyler said, pretty confident that if time travel was excruciatingly painful, Moody or one of the science team would have said so. "I think they would have mentioned that, if only to prepare us."

"Yeah, well, I have a feeling there's lots of stuff they haven't *mentioned*," Stan came back.

"Like what?" Ben said.

"If I knew that, then we wouldn't be having this conversation," Stan said.

"I'm working with children," Adela murmured under her breath.

"I think I might be sick," Marty said and looked over at Tyler. "Is it too late to . . . to . . ."

"You're okay, Marty. We're all in this together, bud. Team before self. You got this, bro."

The young man nodded, but his face seemed unconvinced.

"Alpha Team, this is Control," Moody's voice said over a speaker somewhere, shutting down the banter. "Sound check?"

Tyler gave a thumbs-up and said, "Alpha copies Lima Charlie."

"Checks are complete and Control is ready to commence countdown. Alpha sitrep?"

Tyler looked at each of his teammates in turn and got positive confirmation before replying, waiting an extra beat for Marty to shoot him a weak thumbs-up. "Alpha is set and ready to travel on your mark."

"Copy, Alpha, starting the reactor. It will take a few moments for the field to come up and become stable."

Tyler heard a whirring sound, like a clothes dryer coming up to speed, and felt a tingle in his extremities. When he looked down, all the fine hairs were standing up on his forearms.

"Dude, Zee, check out your hair," Ben said.

Tyler looked up to see Zee's fine ebony locks waving in the air like a sea anemone's arms.

"It's like we're touching one of those static electricity lightning balls," Ben said.

"More like standing inside one," Stan said.

"We're such idiots," Adela said, her hair swaying like those funky, inflatable air dancers that car dealerships have. "I can't believe I agreed to do this . . ."

"If I get turned inside out," Ben said, turning to face Tyler, "I want you to shoot me, Ty. Do you understand? Put me out of my misery, bro."

"Actually . . ." Stan began.

"Shut up, Stan," Zee, Adela, and Ben snapped in unison.

"You have my word," Tyler said, "unless I get turned inside out too."

"That was my point," Stan said and clapped a hand on Tyler's shoulder.

"Dude, Stan, you probably shouldn't be touching Ty. When this thing goes, you don't want your bodies to be combined or some shit," Ben said. "Remember the movie *The Fly*?"

Stan jerked his hand away as if Tyler's shoulder were a hot frying pan. "Oh my God, you're right."

Marty looked around, scanning up toward the ceiling. "There better not be a fly in here with us."

"No one is going to be rendered inside out or turned into a fly," Moody's voice said reassuringly over the speaker. "All your molecules travel together. Stand by for the countdown—Alpha is traveling to Omega in five . . . four . . . three . . . two . . . one . . ."

Moody's voice cut off.

Tyler blinked, felt a sudden breeze, then he was somewhere else.

The Omega facility, his brain reminded him.

"Shit, this is weird," Ben said.

"I feel like I do after a vivid dream—like my brain is stuck in two realities at once," Marty said. "Is anyone else experiencing something similar?"

"Oh, yeah," Zee said, rubbing her temples.

The SEAL in Tyler's brain reminded him that they were on the clock and that he was in charge and needed to validate his team's health and readiness. He pressed the four-minute countdown button on his watch—something he'd planned to press at the instant of travel. *Oh well, I'll subtract five seconds,* he decided. This was his first trip time traveling so he could probably cut himself some slack.

"Alpha, sitrep?" he said, scanning the room and trying to wrestle his mind out of the past and into the present.

Or is it out of the present and into the future?

"Two," Zee said, "is intact and alert."

"Three is intact and still processing this shit," Stan said, giving himself a pat down.

"Four is intact and five by," Ben said.

"Five is good," Adela said, then added, "and so is Six."

Tyler glanced over to find Martin staring at his hands, turning them over and really studying them.

"Anybody inside out?" Tyler said with a shit-eating grin as he looked his teammates over for visible signs of trauma.

"That's a negative, Chief," Ben said, grinning back. "But Stan does have antennae now."

"I've always had those," Stan quipped. Everyone laughed, even Adela.

"Does it feel like there's enough air in here to you guys?" Zee asked. He glanced over at her, surprised to see her still looking anxious.

"Seems fine to me," Stan said. "It's a secure room with no access, so I imagine it's sealed up pretty good, but the air feels like it's circulating—"

"All right, Alpha Team," Tyler interrupted. "Let's get to work. We've got three minutes and forty seconds to check this place out and drink from the current events fire hose."

Having been briefed on the facility in detail, the Omega Room felt instantly familiar to Tyler. Truth be told, it wasn't anything jaw-dropping—just a windowless room with lots of flat-screen televisions and computer workstations. The location, however, was TS/SCI and kept compartmentalized even from the team. They could right now be in the Pentagon, some bunker at Area 51, or on the moon for all they knew . . . The point was to keep it secret and secure. And anyway, as incredible as the *where* might be, it was the *when* that blew his mind. They'd just jumped four days into the future.

To Tyler, the Omega Room looked basically like a TOC, or Tactical

Operations Center, and not much different than the ones utilized on bases around the world to coordinate spec ops. Only in this case, instead of being staffed 24-7 by an army of analysts, cyber geeks, and Head Shed bosses, Omega was vacant and unmanned. Data was flowing but nobody was present to collect it . . . until now.

The first thing Tyler did was check the date and time projected prominently on a dedicated display above the TVs. "Hey guys, looks like we traveled four days, eighteen hours, and fifty-one minutes into the future," he said, doing quick mental math.

"Apparently, the world still exists," Stan said, dryly, "so we've got *that* going for us."

Live news feeds from CNN, NBC, BBC, Al Jazeera, Israel's i24news, as well as Korean, Japanese, and Chinese channels were streaming on the wall of monitors. Ben immediately fixed his attention on the world's news while Zee walked to the giant touchscreen workstation in the middle of the room. The interactive surface, essentially an iPad the size of a dining-room table, was a prototype that aggregated, summarized, and prioritized current events and intelligence collected over the period since the last logged visit or the last seven days, whichever was shorter. The goal of the interface was to optimize how the team utilized their precious seconds by serving up the "greatest hits" from the future.

Leisurely browsing was a luxury they didn't have.

"I'll take this side of the table and you take that side," Zee said, walking to the right side of the surface and entering her four-digit PIN into the pop-up window for TS access.

"Check," Tyler said, stepping up beside her. He watched Marty take a seat at a workstation and immediately start typing.

Adela and Stan both grabbed chairs at computer terminals and opened windows on the screens with their access codes.

The interface on the giant surface accepted Zee's PIN and divided the screen into two virtual workspaces, one for Tyler and one for her. Feeling the press of time, Tyler scanned a list of curated one-liners prepared by a data bot. The no-frills interface reminded him of Reddit. Entries were presented in a vertical scroll, ranked by perceived importance with the headline in bold, a trending rank, an icon to click if he wanted to expand the entry, and a link button if he wanted to be redirected to the source material. He hyperfocused and began to parse the entries, starting at the top and quickly working his way down.

> 1↑ Magnitude 7.1 earthquake in Chile
> kills 372, hundreds more missing. ↲ ∞
> 2↓ White House hit by cyberattack.
> Website offline for two hours. ↲ ∞
> 3↑ Chinese PM warns US not to meddle
> in Taiwan or face repercussions. ↲ ∞
> 4↑ SpaceX rocket suffers failure during reentry,
> crashes into Atlantic. ↲ ∞
> 5↓ Salmonella outbreak in Midwest
> traced to peanut supplier. ↲ ∞

"Nothing earth-shattering on domestic news," Ben called out.

"Same for international," Zee said.

"Cyberattack on the White House could be a big deal," Tyler said. "Happened yesterday—or I guess three and a half days from now . . . You know what I mean."

"I'm scrolling through the TS daily briefs from various intelligence agencies and see nothing of crushing concern," Stan said. "I mean, the world is an evil, violent mess, but that's nothing new . . ."

"Check," Tyler acknowledged, then asked, "What have you got, Adela?"

She ignored him. He glanced over and saw her eyeballs indexing with machinelike precision as she scanned her feed. He didn't ask again because the message was loud and clear: *Don't waste my time; I'll tell you when we get back.*

Tyler shifted his attention back to the unclassified feed and devoted the time left to committing information to memory. His watch chimed, announcing thirty seconds remaining after correcting for his slow start of the timer.

"Twenty-five seconds," he announced, feeling frantic as he tried to speed up his reading pace.

His watch chimed again.

"Everyone on your X," he said, and the team hustled to their assigned spots, Adela lagging a moment behind as she scanned a few extra lines of whatever she had been reading.

He turned to say something but then blinked once and he was standing in the Donut. A powerful wave of déjà vu hit him, the likes of which he'd never experienced before.

"Holy déjà vu, Batman," Ben said, clutching the sides of his head. "This is messed up."

"It's normal," Moody's voice said over the intercom. "The déjà vu you're feeling is a by-product of the return trip to the present. Your brain is reconciling the state change of your reality. The feeling will slowly subside over the next ten minutes."

"Thank God," Martin said, expressing the sentiment of the entire group, Tyler guessed.

"I'm heading down to let you out," Moody said and the intercom static disappeared.

Thirty seconds later the steel access door hissed open.

"Welcome back, intrepid time travelers," Moody said, blocking the doorway and grinning from ear to ear, hands on hips. "How was your jump?"

"Freaky," Ben said. "But good freaky."

"Excellent," Moody said. "And as promised, no one turned inside out or became a human-fly hybrid. As it turns out, time travel is a walk in the park, other than the déjà vu you're feeling. I promise it goes away."

"It better, because I hate this feeling," Adela said.

"Me too," Stan said and beside him, Martin was shaking his head like a puppy when someone blows air in their face.

"A small price to pay for a glimpse into the future," Moody replied. "Based on your reactions and the fact that none of you are hyperventilating or sobbing, I gather that Armageddon does not happen in the next four days?"

"Lots of dysfunction and saber-rattling, but that's business as usual in the world," Tyler said. "Nothing requiring urgent action, right, guys?"

"Adela, the look on your face suggests you might not entirely agree with Chief Brooks's assessment," Moody said.

"While these guys mostly scoured TS feeds and breaking news, I was scanning regional media," she said, her expression dour. "And I found something."

Moody folded his arms and looked at her expectantly.

"There's a mass shooting tomorrow night, and we might be the only ones who can stop it."

CHAPTER 12

THE DONUT—WAREHOUSE B

STILL STANDING INSIDE THE DONUT

Zee's hands were trembling, and her mouth tasted like metal. She decided to chalk both physical reactions up to an adrenaline dump. After all, she'd just traveled into the future and back . . . and there was the *other* thing. She'd never told the Navy—or anyone for that matter—that she was moderately claustrophobic. It was an embarrassing and irrational fear that people who didn't experience it didn't understand or appreciate. If her secret came out, the hard-core operators like Tyler, Stan, Ben, and maybe even Adela, would rib her mercilessly about it and maybe even silently judge her as weak.

The problem was, the feeling was getting worse, not better, the older she got.

If being locked inside the Donut wasn't bad enough, knowing that the machine was originally designed to be a fusion reactor only made it worse. The polished graphite heat tiles covering every surface inside the Donut really freaked her out. She felt like she was standing inside a blast furnace that could turn on and incinerate her at any moment. On top of that, the travel destination was no better. The Omega Room was equally disconcerting—another completely enclosed, windowless space, with the doors welded shut. Making matters worse, Moody wouldn't tell them the Omega Room's location. Her mind automatically conjured the worst possible scenarios.

It's probably buried one hundred feet underground, she thought. *Or, God forbid, what if it's underwater?*

A mechanical whirring sound made her flinch.

She felt a powerful compulsion to shove Stan—who was blocking the exit to inspect how the heat tiles fit against the doorframe—out of the way so she could exfil the friggin' Donut.

"Stan, can you please go," she said, barely reining in her stupid limbic brain.

"Oh, yeah, sorry," he said. "It's just interesting how they—"

"Don't care. Please go," she snapped.

"Yeah, yeah, I heard you the first time," he said and ducked out the hatch.

Stepping out of the Donut and into the wide-open warehouse, she finally felt like she could breathe again. With her claustrophobia subsiding, the strange déjà vu effect kicked in and she felt like she'd done all of this before: her hair standing up, scanning the data feed on the giant iPad table in the Omega Room, Stan blocking the door . . .

So weird.

Everyone formed up in a semicircle around Moody. She scanned her teammates' faces and no one else looked like they were recovering from a panic attack, which meant she must be the only claustrophobic.

"Normally we'd take our time to debrief and compare notes but, Adela, you said you saw something concerning," Moody said, his expression all business. "Why don't you read us in on the event before we head over to the Reconstruct Room."

She nodded. "Temple Beth El, a synagogue in Buffalo, New York, was—or, I guess, *is*—targeted in a mass shooting attack. Nine people die, including two middle schoolers and an off-duty Buffalo cop moonlighting as security at the temple. Eleven are wounded, including two teenage girls who are—or will be—in the ICU. It happens tomorrow night at 1937 hours during an event called Women Emerging: the Pentateuch, Midrash, and Modernity."

"Are there any other details you can share?" Moody said.

"Two shooters, both male, a father-son team armed with long guns. Walter and Jason Odeh, both Syracuse residents."

"What else do you know about them?"

She gritted her teeth and shook her head. "Not much, which is how they slipped through the cracks, I guess. Not on any watch lists. No criminal activity or records. No activity found on social media that seemed anti-Semitic—at least according to what I read. No ties to any domestic terror groups had been found. They're of Yemeni descent, but the son is third-generation American. The intel stream I checked found little to connect them to anything specific."

Moody patted Adela's shoulder. "Strong work. This is exactly how this is supposed to work. The next step is for us to reconstruct, expeditiously build a case file, and forward details through the appropriate channels so we can get local law enforcement and the FBI involved to subvert the threat."

"Now hold on a second," Tyler said, speaking up. "You could do that, or we could look at this as an opportunity. It's a short-fuse situation. Why risk FBI and local law enforcement dropping the ball? Not that they're not up to the task, but with zero footprint being reported in retrospect, how likely are they to uncover something that will motivate them? The best chance of stopping this is for us to intercede and neutralize the threat ourselves. This may not be a 9/11-level event, but people's lives are at stake, and this seems like a perfect opportunity to put our charter to the test. It's close, it's domestic, and it's an easily manageable threat. It proves our concept works, if we're successful, and allows us to operate as a team."

Moody seemed to consider the request for a moment before shaking his head. "Let's talk about our charter for a moment because I think there still might be some confusion on that front. The charter for this task force initially is to collect future ISR, assess that data, identify gaps where additional intelligence is needed, and then put together a mission package that makes it easy for partner entities to prosecute. Ninety-five percent of the time, we do the heavy lifting up front and send a well-developed package to JSOC, FBI HRT, CIA ground branch—or which-ever direct-action entity is best suited—and they neutralize the threat."

"Then why bring me in? Why have a direct-action component to this team if you're never going to use it?" Tyler said.

"For two reasons. First, to complete our charter of generating a mission package worth its salt, I needed experienced operators, intelligence officers, and field agents. With the exception of Martin, the five of you have over sixty years of field and joint operations experience. I need people who can see, but also evaluate and reconstruct, the future intel from an operational lens. Also, for this task force to remain anonymous and be effective, the mission packages we create need to look organic. We can't be raising eyebrows across IC because we appear one hundred percent prescient. Our intel needs to look, smell, and feel like it was generated organically in the present. You guys, as a team, can do that."

Tyler nodded. "And the second reason?"

Moody grinned. "The second reason is the other five percent. There will be times—and this is where you have to trust me—when this team needs to be at the pointy tip of the spear to neutralize the threat. Most of the time, you'll be augmenting a ground branch team, but in rare circumstances the information could be so sensitive that only the smallest possible footprint will serve. In those cases, this team will be the alpha-to-omega solution—pun intended."

"Makes sense," Tyler said, seemingly satisfied, but Zee could tell he wasn't—not entirely.

"Maybe," Zee said, glancing at Adela who shook her head and looked at her feet. "But I believe that this one falls in that five percent category. Maybe it doesn't measure up to a 9/11 event, like Ty said, but there are innocent young lives about to be wiped out in just twenty-four hours. We can stop it, and I don't believe some anonymous tip routed up to FBI on a short fuse has anywhere near the likelihood of preventing this attack. This one is for us, and like Ty said, it will prove the concept, make us a team, and save lives."

She watched Moody carefully as he checked his watch and pursed his lips. "We've got a little over twenty-four hours until the attack. Tell you what, Chief. Let's hit the reconstruct hard, and I'll consider it for direct action."

"Rock on," Ben said, clearly excited by the possibility of getting to operate.

"Follow me, everyone," Moody said and led them to the Reconstruct Room located directly below the mezzanine control room.

Inside, the space looked like a cross between a TOC and a lounge. The front half of the room had flat-screen monitors, computer workstations, printers, and videoconferencing equipment like a TOC. A rectangular counter-height worktable with stools in lieu of chairs dominated the middle of the room. Zee immediately gravitated to the standing workspace, feeling its energy as a place for the team to caucus and share what they'd learned, like how everyone gravitates to high-top tables in a bar. The far end of the room had a more relaxed feel with a four-person leather sofa, club chairs, and a kitchenette with a double refrigerator, a range and microwave combo, a countertop espresso machine, and a soft-serve ice cream maker.

Moody waited while everyone but Stan, who was helping himself to a generous serving of soft-serve, grabbed bottles of water. Then the director summoned the group over to the tall rectangular table in the center of the room. Everyone gathered around, some people taking stools while Zee and Marty remained standing. She still had far too much adrenaline coursing through her to sit. She guessed that for the operators, the Off switch after a big op came naturally. Not for her— not yet anyway.

"You've seen this place on the tour, but this will be your first time working in the Reconstruct Room. The basic idea is to have a place to gather after traveling, to data dump, and then collaborate on *reconstructing* the events you learned about in the future while they are fresh in your minds," Moody said. He pointed to the far wall, which Zee now noticed was faced entirely with square cork panels. "That's your case wall where you can pin anything and everything you want, if that's helpful to you. It's old school, but sometimes there's just no substitute for getting to step back and look at the big picture. Don't feel obligated to use it. If you guys prefer to do everything digitally, no problem, we've got plenty of workstations and tablets."

Zee glanced at the cork wall, noting many small chunks missing and a mishmash of thumbtacks in an irregular line at the bottom. Clearly, during the testing phase, before they had arrived, this room had been used for something else because the cork wall was well worn.

"Full disclosure, everything you do and say in this room is being recorded. We've got cameras and mikes all over the place covering every angle. It's not because we don't trust you or that we're trying to make things weird, it's simply that, unlike you guys, nobody here has an eidetic memory. Consequently, we want to have a record of your data dumps and revelations, especially in those cases where things don't unfold as we expect them to . . ."

Zee didn't love the idea of being recorded but she wasn't surprised by the protocol. At least Moody was honest about it.

". . . we tried our best to anticipate how this team might work and how to leverage your gifts in both the Omega Room and the Reconstruct Room. We want the future data collection and reconstruction processes to be as efficient and streamlined as possible. As you work the kinks out, any process improvements or hardware that you identify needing . . . just ask, and I'll make it happen."

"Hold on," Martin said with a quizzical expression. "I'd like to go back to something you said a moment ago."

"Sure," Moody said.

"You seemed to imply that the future might not unfold as observed during a jump. How is that possible?"

"That's the whole point of the program, Martin," Adela said before Moody could answer. "To change the future by acting on information in the present."

"You misunderstand me, Adela," Martin said. "I think Director Moody was implying that the actual future might deviate from the observed future, even without intervention by us?"

"No, I was referring to hypothetical situations when the data you retrieve from the Omega Room might be insufficient or lacking. In those cases, even with reconstruction and additional intelligence collected in the present, I could imagine scenarios when we simply aren't able to put all the puzzle pieces together in time to mount an effective intervention. If or when that happens, I predict we'd all like to look back through the reconstructed materials and figure out what we missed," Moody said.

Martin nodded. "Understood, but what about my question? Without intervention, do future events unfold *exactly* as observed in the Omega Room, or is there the possibility of deviation on account of entropic factors?"

Moody chuckled. "I don't mean to laugh, but no one on the science team has ever broached that subject, and the thought never occurred to me. I'll talk to Jimmy and Becca, but I think the short answer is we don't know. That's a very powerful question, Martin, and we've all been operating under the presumption—or assumption, not sure which term is correct here—that without intervention the future would unfold as observed. In fact, it's why we contain you in the Omega Room, so as not to introduce any confounding factors, if that makes sense."

Zee noticed that everyone was staring at Martin, and she sensed that this was just the tip of the iceberg regarding the man's intellect.

"Any other questions?" Moody asked.

"Yeah, I got one," Ben said. "Let's say that Stan suffers cardiac arrest in the Omega Room and dies in the future. What happens to him? Does he return dead to the present with the rest of the team, or does the future reset and he'll be alive upon returning?"

"Why'd you use me for the example?" Stan said, with feigned indignation. "Why not Tyler?"

Ben shot Stan a grin.

"Another great question," Moody said, crossing his arms. "Based on the limited number of test jumps that we've run, as far as we can tell, anything you change in the future gets reset when the present catches up to that moment. On one of the test jumps, I moved multiple items in the

Omega Room—a binder, a headset, a tablet computer—but none of them moved in the present on the real-time video feed. Also, when the present caught up to the future time stamp where I had moved them during the jump, they didn't shift positions. It was as if I never moved them."

"Interesting," Stan said.

"And expected," Martin added. "The change made in the future hasn't happened yet, so once the traveler returns to the present, time progresses without knowledge of that change, so . . ." The young genius screwed up his face and Zee watched him silently working something out in his head. Then he nodded. "Yes, that makes sense."

"With respect to the *traveler*, however, the rules are different. On one of the test jumps, I cut my finger in the Omega Room and when I came back the cut was still there. So, to answer Ben's original question, if Stan has a heart attack and dies in the future, on return to the present he'll be dead," Moody explained.

"Okay, hold on," Tyler said. "Let me get this straight. Anything we change in the future resets when we come back to the present, but whatever happens to *us* in the future is permanent?"

"That's correct, and if you think about it, it makes sense. Each of us only has one timeline. When you travel, the four minutes you would have spent in the present instead transpires in the future. For those four minutes, our future is your present. When you return, you don't lose those minutes, but you don't relive them either. Four minutes passes for the control team here while we're waiting for you to return. Think of it as a conservation of time. From time's perspective, what happens to you during those four minutes—regardless of whether you experience them in the present or the future—is written in stone."

"What about if I tried to bring something back from the future?" Zee asked. "You know, like, one of the tablets or pens from the Omega Room."

"It won't come back with you," Moody said. "Only the matter sent forward returns when the field is shut down."

"Even if I'm holding it in my hands?"

"Even if you're holding it," Moody said. "Maybe you didn't realize this, but all the air in the Donut travels with you when you jump. The

FOUR MINUTES
chamber stays a vacuum until you come back. We had to reinforce the structure to withstand the vacuum force transitions."

"I noticed a breeze when we jumped into the Omega Room," Tyler said. "I thought it was my imagination."

"No, that was the air you brought with you making room for itself, pushing the static molecules out of the way."

"That's so freaking cool," Stan said.

"It's physics," Martin said. "These are the principles of the conservation of matter and conservation of energy at work. All of the empirical observations you've described are perfectly logical and expected."

"Maybe for you," Ben said, slapping Martin on the back, "but I'm just the *Where's Waldo?* guy."

"As fascinating as the physics of time travel might be, we are literally on the clock," Zee said, bringing the group back to the urgent matter at hand. "We need to focus and come up with a plan."

Moody nodded. "All right, here's what we're going to do. First, we notify FBI that we have credible intelligence that a shooting is planned for tomorrow night with the shooters' identities and the target location. I will route the action request through my boss, who will ensure the FBI director is personally read in on the threat, while not compromising Omega as the source. At the very least, we need to give FBI and local law enforcement the *opportunity* to stop this. However, Tyler, I want you to plan an intervention op for tomorrow night in Buffalo. Four-shooter team—you, Stan, Ben, and Adela—with Zee and Martin running support. We'll give the FBI the first shot, but if the shooters aren't in custody by 1600 tomorrow, we jump to the future to see if FBI and local law enforcement are successful in stopping the attack. If not, we hop on the jet and intervene in real time. Comments? Questions?"

Zee nodded. It was a good plan with a primary and contingency component. Moody wasn't willing to let innocents die, and that mattered—a lot, in fact.

"All right, everybody, you heard the boss," Tyler said, rolling up his sleeves. "We have a mass shooting to stop. It's time to get to work."

CHAPTER 13

Hiding inside one of the wrecked vehicles in the repair center parking lot, Jun sat in silence as Garth scanned the grounds of the Wilson Spice Factory with a thermal imaging scope. It had taken several days for them to pinpoint the location of Task Force Omega's top secret facility. The first hurdle had been obtaining a special magnetometer to detect the magnetic flux signature created by the time machine. The second had been waiting for the newly assembled American team to make their first jump, which had finally happened today.

One step at a time, Jun reminded himself.

Jun waited patiently for Garth to finish his assessment, not interrupting the former American military man with questions or demands to hurry. If there was one thing Jun had learned during his years as a Snow Leopard conducting counterterrorism operations, it was that the only person who benefited from rushed ISR was the enemy. A very long time passed before Garth finally lowered the scope.

"What do you think?" Jun asked.

Garth didn't answer the question immediately. Instead, he retrieved a round plastic container of chewing tobacco and pressed a large wad of the stuff into his lower lip before saying, "Well, I don't think it can be done, at least not with the team we have. We'd need double our number and even if we had that, most of us wouldn't make it out. I know it don't look like it, but that shoddy-looking place is formidable."

"Explain what you mean by this, please," Jun said.

Garth dribbled brown saliva into an empty water bottle. "Well, remember these people are highly trained professionals. During the day, the facility presents a minimal overt security footprint, but that's by design. It's supposed to be a spice factory, and from a petty criminal point of view, there ain't much that would need protecting. They got one rent-a-cop walking around with a dog. That's all you see, but that's exactly what they want you to see. At night, with the thermal imager, you get a different picture altogether. They got two sniper nests, plus the gate guard, and three rovers walking the perimeter—which makes a total of six on alert. I reckon they got six more off watch who are on standby for head calls and breaks until they rotate back on duty twelve hours later. But don't forget about the jump team, half of which are Tier One operators. So, all total, we're looking at having to defeat a defending force of at least eighteen shooters . . . with *defending* being the critical word in that sentence. As you well know, buddy, breaching a fortified position is a helluva lot harder than defending one."

Jun wasn't surprised by Garth's assessment, but that didn't make the news any less frustrating to hear. He'd imagined killing Tyler Brooks a dozen different ways—each more brutal and painful than the last—since he'd buried his brother. But he also knew it went beyond that—eliminating the American SEAL was mission critical. Now that Omega was jumping, things would get complicated and his *Die Ursache* team's odds of completing the primary tasking would fall dramatically.

"I know you want to get this guy, and so do I, but we can't rush it," Garth said. "If we try to force it, we're the ones who are going to be dancing with Death. I was there in Mali . . . I saw how he moves. How he shoots. This dude is one badass, kinetic motherfucker. Plus, he ain't been jumping like we have. He don't have a stiff back and bad knees and need reading glasses. It ain't apples to apples between us and them. What's the harm in letting the playing field get a little more level?"

"The problem is Hoffman," Jun said, turning to meet Garth's eyes. "What if he calls us back to Poland to start jumping again? The DC mission is his priority."

Garth laughed. "Yeah, that's true, but like you said the other day, for the time being, Brooks is also the mission. And Hoffman knows it too, or we wouldn't be here. So long as that dumbass SEAL keeps fucking up our future, then Hoffman ain't gonna pull us back."

"Maybe we should go back to Poland," Jun said, returning his gaze to the complex across the street. "Maybe jumping in there is the solution."

"Didn't work in Mali. We'd only get one swing at him and four minutes to do it." Garth spit into his bottle again. "I think our best shot is to take him in the present. We need Father Time working for us, not against us, you know what I'm sayin'?"

Jun nodded. "Then I need to think of something to lure him out . . . something he can't ignore. Something he's willing to risk his life and career for."

"Or *someone*," Garth said.

He looked at the American mercenary and a grin curled Jun's lips. "Yes, or someone . . ."

CHAPTER 14

Zee watched Tyler pace in front of the case wall where pictures of Temple Beth El, a synagogue in Buffalo, had been tacked to the floor-to-ceiling corkboard along with photos of the father-son shooter duo. Everyone was on edge, and Tyler's pacing was driving everyone crazy. But this bad habit was written in his DNA and no amount of badgering him was going to change that. Zee checked her watch: fifteen minutes from Omega's self-imposed deadline, and still no word that FBI or local law enforcement had arrested the future suspects.

"Anything?" Tyler said to Adela, who was sitting at a terminal in the Reconstruct Room scanning the high side.

"Nothing," Adela said without turning to look at him.

"All right, I'm going to talk to Moody," Tyler said.

"I think Martin already did," Ben said.

"Excuse me. Martin did what?" Tyler said, a screwed-up look on his face.

Just then, the double doors leading to the warehouse floor flung open.

"I'm sick of waiting," Moody said, barreling into the room with Martin in trail clutching a laptop to his chest. "Let's jump."

"Thank God," Ben muttered from the high-top worktable where he'd been looking over satellite imagery of the neighborhood where the synagogue was located.

"Are we going to jump seven days again?" Stan asked.

"No," Moody said. "We're going to jump out to the limit of twenty-eight days. I want to maximize the amount of additional intelligence we can collect while still getting a resolution on the synagogue shooting. That's a data point you can collect quickly: Did our partner agencies stop it or not? It would be a waste to send you and not take advantage of the trip to scan for other future events."

"Makes sense," Tyler said, and Zee saw his gaze tick to Martin.

She knew Tyler better than anyone here, and she suspected that look was his *de-escalated* attempt to signal to Moody his irritation that Martin had leapfrogged the chain of command and not come to Tyler first. The young genius coming in with Moody and his new eagerness to travel back to the Omega Room seemed too much of a coincidence to her as well.

But, apparently, whatever Marty said to Moody had worked.

"Ah, yes, there's one other thing worth noting," Moody said. "Martin came to me with a suggestion this morning, which he offered to implement, and after speaking with the technical team, I gave him the green light."

"Oh really, what was that?" Tyler said. It wasn't lost on Zee how Moody had subtly dodged the issue by signaling that the suggestion in question fell outside Tyler's purview.

"I hinted at this, but we utilize artificial intelligence—an AI steward program, if you will—to aggregate, sift, and prioritize the information provided in the Omega Room when you travel. To use a SEAL metaphor," Moody said, talking mostly to Tyler, "it preps the battlefield in advance so that when the six of you show up on the *X* and kick down the door, you can *pop, pop, pop,* take care of business. The software is always running in the present, preparing information to serve up in the future to maximize your efficiency. You already experienced the power of this system on your first jump but might not have been aware of it."

"*Actually*, I was aware of it," Stan said. "And I shall dub this program HAL."

"HAL?" Ben said, shooting Stan a quizzical look.

Stan's eyes went wide. "Dude, seriously? *2001: A Space Odyssey* . . . Moody, how can you recruit a time traveler who doesn't know the foundations of modern science fiction?"

Zee watched Moody chuckle, and she smiled herself as the director steered them back on course. "HAL is the perfect moniker for the AI steward program, and now Martin has made HAL even better by adding a subroutine that allows us to key in specific events and prompts *before* a jump that we know we want prioritized for future collection. That way, you guys aren't forced to do what Adela did yesterday and manually scan events that are not prioritized as significant or don't appear on the hierarchical or breaking news feeds. We've entered the shooters' names and any keywords relevant to the attack so the program—err, I mean HAL—will know to prioritize finding them for this event and any others we flag in advance. Adela's terminal will now feature this customized search stream . . . Assuming you're okay with that, Adela?"

"Sure," Adela said with a smile. She looked impressed, which Zee imagined happened with the frequency of a solar eclipse.

"Strong work, Marty," Tyler said, nodding at the kid. "This could be a game changer for us."

Martin nodded and his cheeks went instantly red from Tyler's shout-out.

"So," Moody said, clapping his hands and rubbing his palms together. "Unless there are any other questions, let's do this."

Tyler nodded. "You heard the man, Alpha, let's rock and roll."

Zee put on a brave face as Stan and Ben led the charge to the Donut. The thought of going back inside the machine was about as appealing as being told that she needed a root canal, but she followed, with Adela, Martin, and Tyler falling in behind her.

One by one, they stepped through the open hatch. Once inside,

Tyler grabbed the heavy door and pulled it shut. The locking mechanism engaged with a definitive metallic clank. Zee ground her teeth and shuffled to her *X* on the floor as the rest of the team assumed their own positions.

"Anybody wanna bet on whether FBI snags these guys?" Stan asked, his voice reverberating off the circular donut geometry inside the TRF. "I got fifty buck that says we're on the jet to Buffalo in half an hour to—"

Moody's voice on the loudspeaker cut him off. "Alpha Team, this is Control. Sound check?"

"Alpha copies Lima Charlie," Tyler announced.

Zee noticed Tyler had taken a knee and appeared to be inspecting his red tape *X* on the floor.

She closed her eyes and forced four long, slow breaths as Moody counted down. Then she heard the whirring sound of the magnetic field generators and, as before, felt her skin tingle as the little hairs on her forearms and back of her neck stood up and began to sway. She pulled a hair tie from her wrist and worked her hair into a tight ponytail so it wouldn't stand on end like last time, then closed her eyes.

She felt the rush of air and opened her eyes.

And found herself in absolute darkness.

She blinked, but the blackness persisted. *What the hell is going on?* A wave of panic hit her, and her pulse rate shot up. She'd expected to land in the Omega Room, surrounded by glowing computer monitors and televisions live streaming the news. But she couldn't see or hear anything.

Where had Moody sent them? Did the technicians screw up the calculations and send her and the rest of the team into the black void of deep space?

No, I'm not floating. And there's air . . . I can breathe.

She reached up to touch her face, to make sure she still had one . . .

"Omega, sound off," Tyler called.

Hearing his voice, his confidence, instantly quenched her fear like water dousing a fire. She quickly patted herself down for injuries and missing parts. Finding herself whole and intact, she called in. "Two is intact."

"Three is intact," Stan said.

"Four intact, but a little freaked out," Ben called.

"Five sat," Adela said, cool as a cucumber.

"Six intact," Martin said, his voice robotic but with a hint of fear.

A white light flicked on from Stan's position, the beam cutting through the pitch-blackness like a lighthouse beacon on a moonless night. A second flashlight joined the fray, Tyler's, followed by a third from Ben's position a moment later.

Operators—gotta love 'em.

"Okay, we're in the Omega Room, but it appears we've lost all power," Stan announced.

"Why isn't the battery backup powering the emergency systems?" Adela asked as she clicked on her flashlight and trotted over to a terminal.

"The UPS is rated to last up to six days, depending on the load," Stan said, rattling off details he'd undoubtedly researched because that's the kind of thing Stan did for fun. "In theory, during a power outage, the system should automatically shut down nonessential loads and transition to an emergency lineup, but who knows what happened here."

"Or how long ago it happened," Ben said.

She watched Tyler walk over to Stan who was looking at the UPS panel. She stayed frozen on her *X*, fighting the feeling that the Omega Room was swallowing her whole . . .

"Okay," Tyler said calmly, "let's figure this out. Our last jump was seven days into the future, but one full day in the present passed since then. Which means this could have happened anytime between six and twenty-two days in the future."

"Exactly," Stan said as he turned to Tyler. "The batteries are completely drained. The control panel won't even power on for me to check the charge."

"What do we do now?" Adela asked.

Tyler turned from Stan to Adela. "There's nothing we can do here without power."

"Will the power outage affect our ability to go home?" Ben asked, and Zee could hear his voice tight with tension at the thought.

The question made her begin to panic. How long could they survive if they were trapped here? Moody had said the Omega Room was sealed. How long would the air last without power to refresh it with six of them in here?

"It shouldn't," Tyler said. "The machine that's keeping us here is in the past and powered on. And anyway, they told us that when the field collapses we get sucked back to the present. Any loss of power in the past would automatically return us home regardless of the machine's status in the future."

"Good point."

"Unless the scientists' best theories prove to be bullshit," Adela said, her voice eerily calm and fatalistic. "How many times during the brief did they admit they didn't fully understand the science."

"I've got a bad feeling about this," Ben said. "Do you think the spice factory lost power?"

"We're twenty-eight days in the future," Stan said, "and Moody was adamant that the Omega Room is not located on the premises. For the sake of security and redundancy, I bet that the spice factory and the Omega Room are served by completely different power grids."

Tyler's watch pinged and he glanced at his wrist. "In thirty seconds, we'll have our answer. But in the time we have left, Stan, Martin . . . is there anything else we need to check before we leave?"

Stan laughed. "We could go outside and inspect the electrical control cabinets and breakers, but obviously that's a nonstarter since there's no doors."

Zee blinked, wishing the time would tick down quicker and they could go home. There was nothing she could do here but wait, which made the seconds crawl by. She felt herself begin to hyperventilate and tried to concentrate on slowing her breathing.

"Unless there's another way out Moody hasn't told us about," Adela said.

Tyler nodded and looked like he was about to say something, but his watch pinged. "Ten seconds. Everybody on your marks."

Zee opened her eyes and looked at her feet—still on the *X* she had never left. Everyone else jogged to their *X*s on the floor in the darkened room lit only by flashlight. A moment later, Tyler was counting down.

"Returning in three . . . two . . . one."

With a whoosh Zee was back, standing inside the massive graphite-tiled-fusion-reactor-turned-time machine. She inhaled as the déjà vu hit her like a freight train.

This was not the first time she'd jumped to a pitch-black Omega Room. She was certain of it.

Absolutely certain.

I've seen all of this before . . . I know I have.

"Damn, I hate this part," Ben said. "It's super bad this time."

"For me too," Adela said, rubbing her temples. "It really feels like that's happened before."

"Omega One, sitrep?" Moody's voice said on the speaker inside the Donut.

"Omega Team is five by, but we've got a problem, boss," Tyler said, marching toward the door.

"Copy, unlocking and opening the door."

Zee heard the exterior locking mechanism retract and a loud hiss as pressure equalized across the hatch. Zee helped Tyler give the heavy slab a shove open. She followed him, glad to be out of the damn Donut and able to breathe fresh air.

"Talk to me," Moody called as he hustled down the metal stairs from the control mezzanine, his footsteps echoing loudly in the cavernous warehouse. "What's happened?"

"The Omega Room was dark," Tyler said. "As in *completely* dark. No power. Even the battery backups were drained."

Moody's brow furrowed. "That's never happened before. Had the room been breached? Was there anything damaged or missing?"

"No. It looked exactly the same as it always does, just without power."

"Power outage is the most logical explanation, except . . ."

"It has a battery backup that lasts six days," Stan said.

"Yeah." Moody ran his fingers through his hair, and Zee wondered what he was thinking but not sharing. "And, of course, this means you weren't able to get future intel on the synagogue shooting."

"I say we jump again," Tyler said, a suggestion that made Zee's chest tighten. "We can land an hour before our test jump. We know the Omega Room had power then because we were there. Let's reconcile Buffalo first, then we can get to the bottom of the future power failure."

Moody hesitated a long moment, then said, "We normally don't like to jump back-to-back like this, but I think Tyler is right. I'm willing to make an exception in this case. I'll get Jimmy to reset the TFR and prep for a second jump. Use the facilities, grab a drink or a snack, and I'll see you back inside the Donut in ten."

CHAPTER 15

The second jump had been a success, and Tyler's suggestion to jump to a time when they knew the Omega Room had power had proven to be a good one. Now, hours later, he was lying on his back in his bunk, fingers knitted together behind his head, listening to his stomach gurgle and wishing for sleep. Moody had ordered beer and pizza for everyone, and they'd had a little party in the team room over in the Poblano—*damn you, Stan*—to celebrate their first successful intervention of future tragedy.

The indigestion he was suffering now was the result of that party.

They'd learned that the home of the domestic terrorists had been successfully raided one hour before the synagogue shooting in a joint operation by the FBI and local SWAT. The father-son pair had been caught with enough ammunition and weapons to equip a small army, and enough damning material to put them away for a while.

Or so Moody said.

As much as Tyler lamented the fact that his team hadn't personally conducted the raid, he still felt pride and a sense of accomplishment. From the perspective of Task Force Omega's charter, today's outcome was Mike Charlie—mission complete—because this was exactly how things were *supposed* to work. Collect future intel, identify the incident, help plan a mission package, and send it off for disposition without taking an ounce of the credit. At the Tier One, it was the same deal. JSOC operations were executed with absolute secrecy. If credit needed to be given, it was given to someone else.

But something still felt off. He'd begun to worry that maybe Moody wasn't telling them everything. He had no idea what it was he didn't know, but he couldn't shake the feeling. While he liked the guy well enough, he still felt, well, managed somehow. And his experience with spooks while at JSOC was that they only told you what they wanted you to know.

And he was disappointed that they'd lost out on the opportunity for direct action.

Traveling to the future was certainly cool and all, but Tyler suspected that once the novelty wore off, he'd quickly grow bored. Was leaving Task Force Omega and going back to the Tier One even an option? He couldn't help but wonder if Moody's promise that they could walk away any time had been little more than a sales pitch that he would renege on now that Tyler had peeked behind the curtain.

At JSOC, I'm an operator. Here, I might be nothing more than a time-traveling spook . . .

A quiet knock on his door shook him from his thoughts. He reached over and turned on the desk lamp, then swung his legs out of bed and padded across the room with bare feet. With a twist of the handle, he opened the door a crack to find Zee's worried face staring back at him.

"Everything okay?" he asked.

"There's something bothering me that I'd like to talk to you about."

"Well, there's something I'd like to talk to you about too," he said, letting her in. He nodded at the door. "Open or shut?"

"Definitely shut."

He closed it quietly. "Have a seat wherever you want."

There weren't a lot of options, just his desk chair, a reading chair in the corner, and his mattress. She chose the reading chair, so he pulled out the desk chair, angled it the wrong way, and sat in it backward so he could face her. Something was definitely up with her today. He could tell from her body language pre- and postjump that she did *not* like the Donut. And the déjà vu seemed to hit her harder than the rest of them—or maybe she was more sensitive to it. But something told him that wasn't the whole story. He decided to give her time to bring it up on her own before broaching the subject himself—provided whatever *it* was didn't impact the team's ability to conduct its mission. Maybe she was here to do just that.

When Zee didn't say anything, Tyler asked, "Do you want to go first, or should I?"

"Why don't you start?" she said.

"All right . . ." He gathered his thoughts. "I wasn't actually quite ready to bring this up yet, since I'm not sure anything I'm about to say holds water, but screw it, I'll just say it—I don't think Moody has been entirely honest with us. I've noticed some things that seem to contradict the narrative he's spun about Omega and us being the first operational team and all that."

"Like what?" she said, but he saw she already nodded in agreement.

"Well, for starters, the facility is new, but not brand spanking new. You know what I mean? That's not a virgin range in the Poblano. There are scars all over the place. I'm pretty sure I'm not the first tenant to live in this stateroom either. The paint is fresh and the carpet's clean, but there are faint wear tracks in a line from the door. Scuffs on the chair legs. The case wall in the Reconstruct Room had a haphazard row of thumbtacks at the bottom and the cork is marred from use. Even the *X*s on the floor of the Donut are taped over."

"I wondered what you were doing when you took a knee before that jump."

"The duct tape on my *X* was peeling up in one corner. When I knelt to smooth it back down, I noticed it was covering an old well-worn piece of tape. I even noticed that some of the keys on the keyboard Adela likes to use in the Reconstruct Room are faded from fingertip wear. My point is: there's empirical evidence everywhere I look that tells me we're not the first team to operate here."

"You're right," she said, and he could see her mind working the problem. "Just the flow in general supports your theory."

"What do you mean by *the flow*?"

"The workflow. You know . . . the jump procedures, the Omega Room protocols, the AI data-harvesting program that Stan named HAL, the antioxidant shots before we jump, even the way Moody coordinates with the staff and interacts with us. It's too smooth and logical and efficient to be something that's happened organically and on the fly since our arrival."

Tyler felt his pulse tick up as she talked. "You're totally right. From the day we showed up, it felt like arriving at a new command where we're the ones who have to quickly get up to speed. Since that's what I'm used to, it felt normal, but if we were really the first operational class, then it shouldn't have felt like that at all. There should have been kinks, friction points, and unexpected complications to figure out."

"Exactly," she said. "And Moody is such a smooth operator that he made it all feel expected and normal. It's kind of like the Wizard of Oz—look at me and don't pay attention to the man behind the curtain."

They both sat in silence for a long moment, trying to wrap their heads around the revelation. When Tyler spoke, Zee did at the same time.

"Do you think— Sorry, go ahead," he said.

"No, you go, but I suspect we're about to say the same thing," she said with a hint of a smile.

"Okay, well, I was going to ask you if you thought Moody showing up on the *Ford* and recruiting both of us right after what happened in Mali might not be a coincidence."

"Yep, that's what I was going to ask you."

"Did you really recommend me for the program after he recruited you?"

She nodded. "I did, but I can't help but wonder if he didn't set me up for it. He's good at steering a conversation exactly where he wants it to go—you know what I mean?"

Tyler nodded.

"There is another possible explanation," Zee said, locking eyes with him. "What if we're not the only team in play? What if there's another team out there?"

Tyler considered that a moment. Again, he'd been played by spooks plenty of times, telling operators just what they needed to.

Tyler stood up and began to pace. "That seems like a better explanation, but if you're right, what do we do about it?"

"I don't know. I just—I just feel like he's keeping us in the dark. It's scary to not know what it is we don't know."

She leaned forward in her chair and looked anxious. "What do we do now? Do we confront Moody? Do we tell the others?"

Tyler sighed. "I don't know. But we sure as hell have to do something, Zee. I'm not happy being in the dark."

He watched as she scrunched up her face like she did when working a problem. It always looked to Tyler like she was doing math in her head. After a beat, she refocused and stared at him.

"I think we need to stew on it for a bit and see what other information or evidence we can find—something that might show us what it is he's hiding. If we're wrong and we make an accusation, it hurts the team and the mission. Hopefully, with a little time, the right answer will come to us."

As much as the operator in him needed to act, he suspected she was right.

"I'm okay with that . . . for now." He stopped pacing and turned to face her. "Is this what you came to talk to me about?"

"No," she said, "but compared to this, what I wanted to discuss feels like small potatoes."

"Might as well get it off your chest," he said.

"Okay," she said. "Do you remember a couple days ago, when Moody called me into his office?"

"Yeah, I remember."

"Well, he basically ordered me to spy on the team during our jumps to make sure people weren't violating his UNAUTH policy." As she spoke, she massaged the base of her skull, rubbing her neck with her left hand.

"Hold on. Are you saying he doesn't trust us and wants you to be his snitch?"

"If I had to distill the entire conversation down into a single sentence then yes, that's pretty much the gist of it."

Tyler shook his head. He sure didn't like the sound of that. He'd judged Moody as a slick spook but a straight shooter. And it was rare for his instincts about people to be wrong.

First time for everything, I guess . . .

"I'm not going to lie, Zee, that's disappointing to hear. We're all professionals who he recruited from the tops of our fields. I can't believe Moody thinks any of us would conspire to sneak the winning Powerball numbers. Besides, it's not like we could get away with it even if we wanted to. It would be pretty obvious if millions of dollars started appearing in our bank accounts."

"I don't think it's money he's worried about."

"What then?" Tyler said, but his brain was already ahead of his mouth.

"I think he doesn't want us running our own reconnaissance programs. He doesn't want us monitoring for outcomes that affect us personally."

"Or maybe he's terrified we're going to go off book and use Omega to investigate him and all the shit he's hiding from us," Tyler said, well aware of the fresh venom in his voice.

"That too," she said.

"Zee, I'm glad we talked, and that we're on the same page. Thank you for trusting me," he said. He realized just how much he meant it—especially after he'd been such an asshole to her on the *Ford*.

"Ditto for me."

"Are you still of the opinion that we keep this to ourselves for the time being and not confront Moody?" he asked.

She nodded. "I think confronting him now would be a mistake. And, as you well know, compartmentalizing information in our line of work is pretty common and doesn't mean much on its own. If we play our cards right, we have a window of opportunity—a honeymoon period we can exploit—to ask probing questions and snoop around a little without tipping our hand. Moody is super smart; the longer we're here, the more likely he is to figure out we're onto him."

"Good point. The moment that happens, who knows what he'll do."

"Exactly. Business as usual for a little while, but we both agree to keep our eyes and ears open and take every opportunity to collect intel," she said and caught him grinning at her. "What?"

"You must love this . . ."

"Love what?"

"Love the fact that our spooky task force is up to spooky shit, that we have to use spooky tactics and methods to figure it all out. It's like your dream job," he said.

"I wouldn't go *that* far," she said, getting up from her chair. "But I will say one thing . . ."

"And what's that?"

"If there was one person I had to team up with to figure this all out, I'm glad that person is you."

CHAPTER 16

THE TEAM ROOM

THE PEPPER GRINDER—WAREHOUSE B

THE NEXT DAY

0749 LOCAL TIME

Still bleary-eyed from a night of tossing and turning and staring at the ceiling, Tyler made his way to the team room for coffee. When he arrived, he found Stan and Adela already up and arguing about something. His natural inclination was to let grown adults sort out their own disagreements, but from what he was learning about these two, he suspected without intervention even a small skirmish could quickly escalate into thermonuclear war.

They're like gladiators those two, he thought with a chuckle, *each always trying to slay the other.*

". . . you're not wrong, Stan, but I do think you're missing the point," Adela said, tapping the countertop with her right index finger for effect. "We still have the four-minute time limit to contend with. A collective twenty-four minutes of investigative time is far more likely to bear fruit than twelve minutes."

Stan exhaled with annoyance. "But that's assuming each of us is completely and independently productively engaged. The truth is that only Martin and I have the technical expertise to assess the probable modes of electrical failure. The rest of you would simply be watching us."

"Okay, now that's just rude, Stan."

Tyler wandered over to the kitchenette where they were arguing. "What are you guys talking about?"

Stan looked up and said, "We're discussing whether or not everyone should travel on the next jump—assuming Moody gives the authorization for a jump outside the Omega Room."

"Whoa, whoa, whoa," Tyler said, holding up both hands. "Who said anything about a jump *outside* the Omega Room?"

Stan and Adela both looked at each other and then back at Tyler.

"Well, how else are we going to figure out why the Omega Room is dark twenty-seven days from now?" Stan asked. "It doesn't have any doors. We can't keep jumping inside; we'll never learn anything."

"And Stan thinks we should split the team to mitigate risk. He thinks only three of us should travel, but I think we should all go," Adela said.

"I think we might be putting the cart before the horse. We haven't even talked about a jump outside, and I suspect the answer is going to be a big fat no," Tyler said.

"We'll see," Stan said with a smug little smile. "Ten bucks says he authorizes a jump outside the room and agrees with me to split the team."

"Whatever, Stan," Adela said through a squint. "Does money have to change hands for something to count?"

"Guys, please," Tyler said, gesturing like a conductor for them to take things down a notch. "We're briefing a plan with Moody in nine minutes. Let's table this discussion, grab some coffee, maybe a blueberry muffin, and head over to the conference room. Cool?"

Stan nodded. Adela turned and walked away without saying a word.

I'll call that a win, he thought with a chuckle.

Tyler didn't see Zee or Martin, but Ben was sitting on the sofa, listening to something on headphones and sipping coffee. Tyler fixed himself a coffee, grabbed a cranberry-orange muffin, since Stan had taken the last blueberry, and tapped Ben on the shoulder on his way to the door.

"Morning," he said to the AFSOC shooter.

"Mornin'," Ben echoed. He popped up to walk with Stan and Tyler to the Pepper Grinder.

Moments later, they arrived in the conference room, and Tyler saw the rest of the team was present and seated. Moody greeted them with a nod as they found their seats, and Tyler struggled not to let his face reveal his new concern about their director. One thing was for sure, he'd be reading between the lines more than ever now. The truth was, while Moody hiding shit from them changed his opinion of the man drastically, it didn't change Tyler's passion for the mission. This wouldn't be the first spook or bureaucrat who only told the operators half the truth. Tyler had dealt with it since joining the Teams, and more than ever once at JSOC.

"With the Buffalo event behind us, it's time to focus on why the Omega Room lost power. If the battery backup was drained as you described, that means it's been without power for up to as many as six days," Moody said, then sighed and ran his fingers through his hair. "I've given this considerable thought, and instead of trying to jump you to different times and hope we get lucky, I'm going to send you to the same day as your last jump, but five minutes before your previous arrival. That way, there's no risk of running into yourselves from the previous jump. Becca claims that scenario is impossible because the laws of physics prevent the same matter from existing in the same place at the same time, but we've never tested it. I want to minimize as many confounding variables as I can."

"Why would we jump back to the Omega Room on the same day? Everything will be the same as our last jump. We'll be stuck inside without power and learn nothing new," Ben said.

Moody grimaced. "I'm afraid I haven't been entirely honest with you about the Omega Room."

Tyler felt himself bristle.

Yeah, no shit . . .

"It's true it doesn't have any functional doors, but for maintenance and safety purposes there's an escape hatch in the ceiling. It's hidden above one of the drop ceiling tiles in the middle of the room. On arrival, you'll egress via that escape hatch and use the external staircase to descend to where the electrical switchgear room is located. You'll have to move fast, but theoretically, it can be done."

Tyler looked at Zee and knew she was thinking the same thing.

First lie he's confessed to . . .

"What do you mean *descend*? Is the Omega Room located on a rooftop somewhere?" Ben asked.

"The Omega Room is hidden inside a dry water tower outside of the Beltway, west of DC. It's in Copley, just north of the Potomac on the Maryland side." Moody pulled a simple map from his back pocket, spread it out on the long table, and pointed to a spot along the north bank of the Potomac. "It's located here."

"I thought you didn't know where it was located," Tyler said with a fresh flash of anger.

"I didn't, but after what happened, I had to break my own rule and order Jimmy reveal the location. The jump technicians were the only team members allowed to know."

"Mm-hmm," he said, narrowing his eyes at Moody.

I'm going to have to start keeping a ledger.

"Location aside, time is going to be a problem," Zee said. "How can we possibly make it from the top of the tower to the electrical switchgear on ground level, then back up and inside to our *X*s in four minutes?"

"First, the electrical boxes are on the catwalk of the tower, so you don't have to go to the ground. But second, you don't have to be on your *X* for the return," Moody said. "Wherever you are when time's up, you'll return to the exact spot you left from in the Donut. We mapped the landing spots in the Omega Room for arrival, but it's not necessary for the return. Heck, we couldn't locate you in the future even if we wanted to. The only purpose of your marks is to keep you separated to minimize the risk of two bodies trying to occupy the same space at the same time during a jump, which is something the math geeks are still trying to figure out."

"I don't think any of us realized that," Zee said.

"Actually, I figured that was the case," Stan said.

Tyler saw Zee roll her eyes at that.

"So, to summarize: The plan is to jump to the Omega Room five minutes before our previous blackout jump. We'll egress through the emergency escape hatch in the roof, double-time it down the stairs to the electrical switchgear, and try to determine what happened," Tyler said.

"Yes," Moody said.

"Do we really need to send everyone on this jump?" Zee asked. "It seems redundant, possibly even less efficient for all of us to jump."

"I agree," Moody said. "Any volunteers to sit this one out?"

Zee and Martin raised their hands.

Adele smacked Stan on the shoulder with a victory grin. "I'm going. How do you like them apples?"

Stan smiled back, conceding she'd won this round.

"I'll have Jimmy brief the jump team on the switchgear and electrical backup system while Becca programs the jump. Since you will be exiting the safety and anonymity of the Omega Room, Chief Brooks, what's your opinion on kitting up for this jump?"

"I think that's not a bad idea," he said and swept his gaze across Stan, Ben, and Adela. "What about you guys?"

They nodded their agreement.

"All right, let's kit up. We'll get briefed by Jimmy on the electrical stuff, and then do this thing," Tyler said, sliding his chair back from the table.

CHAPTER 17

Tyler looked over to where Stan, Ben, and Adela stood on their respective *X*s inside the Donut, fully kitted-up and ready to jump. He felt guilty leaving Zee and Martin behind, but they had volunteered after all. It was obvious to Tyler that Zee didn't like traveling. She'd not said as much, but he could tell. In fact, he even suspected she might be claustrophobic—she made a beeline to the hatch after every jump, hands trembling while they waited to exit. For this afternoon's jump, she and Martin would get to watch from the control room on the mezzanine, an opportunity that Marty seemed almost giddy for.

Nerds—you gotta love 'em.

Tyler could feel that his pulse rate was slightly elevated for this jump. Whatever had caused the Omega Room to lose power had happened at least six days before the time they jumped to. They were kitted-up out of an abundance of caution, but Tyler felt confident this jump would turn out to be nothing more than a fact-finding mission.

"Y'all ready for our first look outside?" Tyler asked, turning to his teammates as Moody began the final countdown.

"'Yippee-ki-yay . . .'" Ben said with *Die Hard* enthusiasm.

"Flashlights on," Tyler said and powered on the flashlight in his right hand. Three clicks followed in rapid succession as his teammates did the same.

His attention shifted back to Moody's voice, which echoed over the loudspeakers: "Traveling in four . . . three . . . two . . . one . . ."

Tyler blinked, felt the whoosh, and was standing in the blacked-out Omega Room. Flashlights in hand, the team worked swiftly. Ben jumped onto the digital workstation table in the middle of the room while Stan snatched a chair for him to stand on. Tyler and Adela illuminated the drop ceiling panels for him. Ben slid the centermost tile out of the way, then shined his own light into the void above.

"I see the escape hatch, right where Moody said it would be. Just two feet up."

Ben stepped up on the chair, his upper torso disappeared into the ceiling, and Tyler looked at his watch—only nine seconds had passed. A heartbeat later, Ty heard the AFSOC shooter grunt, followed by the squeal of a geared metal mechanism being worked.

"Got it open," Ben called down and his booted feet disappeared into the gap in the ceiling as he hauled himself up and out.

Stan went next, followed by Adela, and finally Tyler.

He grunted as he hauled his weight up. The pull-up felt more difficult than usual, but maybe he'd just spent too much time without his full combat kit the few last weeks.

Damn pizza and autodog soft-serve machine. I must have packed on more pounds than I realized.

The instant his head broke the plane, Tyler knew something was wrong. His teammates stood motionless on the flat roof of the water tower, staring east in silence. Tyler got to his feet and stared east with them, his jaw dropping open and a wave of nausea sweeping over him at what he saw.

"My God . . ." he mumbled.

They stood in silence, surveying devastation like he'd never seen. There was a horrible sulfur stench mixed with smoke and char, and as far as he could see to the east he saw nothing but smoldering destruction, the scorched earth tapering to brown just a mile or so from the tower they stood on.

"That's the Potomac," Stan said, the first to speak, pointing south. "Right where Pat said."

Adela pointed to their right. "And so that's DC . . . or, what's left of it."

"What the hell happened?" Ben asked, his voice barely above a whisper. "What could do such a thing?"

"A nuke," Stan said.

"You mean, like, a dirty bomb?"

"No. This was no dirty bomb. To do this," Stan said with a sweeping gesture, "would require a yield in the megatons. What we're looking at here is the aftermath of a nuclear strike on Washington, DC."

"Oh my God," Adela murmured.

Tyler had never seen her so visibly shaken. He felt it too, a surreal and dystopian cloud of emotion as he looked out at the charred remains of the nation's proud and mighty capital.

"Guys, we need to head back inside," Stan said. "Who knows how much radiation and contamination we're being exposed to up here. From the looks of it, we're not far from ground zero and maybe inside the blast radius, which means this area is still hot."

"Agreed," Adela said. "We'll need to bag our clothes and gear when we get back, as well as decontaminate our bodies."

Tyler glanced at his watch countdown timer: 97 seconds. "Back inside, everyone. There's no point in further investigating why the facility lost power. The answer is obvious."

In morbid silence, the four operators lowered themselves through the hatch and into the Omega Room. Tyler dropped through the hatch last, closing and dogging it behind him before getting down and finding his mark on the floor, out of habit rather than necessity.

"Twenty seconds," he said, glancing at his watch.

"What are we going to do?" Ben asked. "I mean, holy shit, somebody nuked DC."

On hearing those words, the unsettling despair Tyler had been feeling suddenly evaporated, replaced by hot, defiant anger as he remembered that they had the ultimate intelligence-gathering tool ever invented at their disposal.

"I'll tell you exactly what we're going to do," he said, balling his fists, his mind filling with images of his young daughter and what her future would be like if they failed. "We're going to figure out who did this, and then we're going to stop it before it fucking happens." He clenched his jaw. "And then make those responsible pay . . ."

PART II

"I look to the future because that's where
I'm going to spend the rest of my life."

–George Burns

CHAPTER 18

"We have a serious fucking problem," Moody said on the satellite phone, pressing it tight to his ear as he paced his office.

"Take a deep breath, Pat, and tell me what's going on," General Waltrip said. From the background noise, Moody could tell the man was outside somewhere with people and traffic.

"Sometime in the next three weeks Washington, DC, gets nuked," he said. The silence on the line lasted so long that Moody actually pulled the phone from his ear to make sure the general hadn't hung up on him. "Did you hear what I just said?"

"Are you certain of this?" the general came back, his voice as grave as ever.

"One hundred percent. The Omega Room was dark on the team's last jump, so I jumped them back to the same day and authorized a look outside. They saw the city in smoldering ruins. The Omega Room, fortunately, was outside the blast radius, but not by much."

"Do you know the precise date and time the bomb detonates?"

"No, sir."

"Obviously, obtaining that information is priority one as well as determining if this was an isolated attack or part of a broader nuclear exchange."

"I understand." Moody ran his fingers through his hair. He was just barely keeping it together as a dozen scenarios—all of them bad—ran through his mind. "Are you going to tell the President?"

"Of course. What kind of a question is that?" Waltrip said, his tone just short of accusatory outrage. But something about the general's response made Moody question if it was earnest. The rebuff had come a split second too soon and felt defensive.

As someone who engaged in subterfuge for a living, Moody was a man capable of both recognizing and appreciating a properly executed lie. Deception was performance art—theater to keep middle management and the soldiering class toeing the line.

And then it clicked. Moody realized that the thought exercise he'd contemplated more than once was, in fact, possible. The President of the United States might have no knowledge at all of Task Force Omega. And if that was the case then neither, Moody presumed, did the Director of National Intelligence. That likely meant that the highest-ranking official in the United States government and defense industrial complex who knew about the discovery of time travel might well be General Travis Waltrip.

That wily, self-important sonuvabitch.

"I have another question," Moody said, "and it's one that I'm praying you'll be forthright about with me."

"What is that supposed to mean?"

"It means we are about to start the most important investigation this task force has ever undertaken, but we can't afford to waste any time chasing our tails. If there is something you've kept compartmentalized from me that might be relevant to our investigation, I am begging you to share it with me now."

Waltrip paused. "You have my word. Ask your question."

"Do you know who does this to us? Do you know who's responsible?"

"No, I do not."

It's been a while since he's told me the whole truth, Moody thought. He felt certain, deep in his bones, that the general was being honest . . . *About this one thing, at least.*

"Is there precursory activity with Russian, Chinese, or North Korean forces that could presage a potential attack on the United States?"

"Not that I'm aware of. Everyone is behaving themselves in the South China Sea at the moment. Neither Russia nor China has mobilized elements of their respective naval fleets or missile corps in a manner that would raise eyebrows or concerns. And North Korea . . . well, is acting like North Korea always does," Waltrip said. "From a status of forces and geopolitical perspective, DC getting nuked in three weeks is an absolute blindside."

"That's what I needed to know. Thank you, sir," Moody said.

"What are your next steps?" Waltrip asked. "The President is going to want to know."

Is he?

Moody wasn't yet sure, but he strongly suspected that his chain of command ended with General Waltrip.

"We're still working on that, sir. I called you minutes after the team landed. We're going to regroup and come up with a plan."

"I want regular updates, Pat. That means three times a day until we have a handle on this. Is that understood?"

"Yes, sir," Moody said.

"One more thing, Pat . . ."

"Sir?"

"I have faith in you, son," the general said, his voice even and ardent. "I can't think of anyone I'd want running the show to foil this attack other than you."

Moody hesitated, wondering if this was performance art or a compliment born of candor. Given the circumstances, did it really matter? It was what he needed to hear.

"Thank you, sir. I promise I won't let you down."

CHAPTER 19

Feeling like she'd stolen a page out of Tyler's playbook, Zee couldn't stop pacing a racetrack around the center table. Her parents lived in DC. Her father worked at the Pentagon and their family home was in Alexandria. The temptation to pick up the phone and call her dad and tell him to get the hell out of town was powerful, but she tabled that option for later. Because they still had time . . .

No matter the cost, no matter the toll, Task Force Omega would stop it.

Claustrophobia be damned, she told herself with gritted teeth. *Even if it takes a hundred jumps to figure this out, I will not quit until we rewrite the future.*

The moment Tyler and the others had returned to the Donut and reported that DC had been nuked, all hell had broken loose at Omega. Even the normally unflappable and all-knowing Moody had reacted to the news with shell-shocked disbelief. While the medical staff swooped in to evaluate and decontaminate the jumpers, Moody had run off to inform his boss—a high-ranking official whom he'd yet to formally identify by name or title—of the new intelligence. With only one option available to them, Zee and Martin had retreated to the Reconstruct Room to start working the problem.

Martin typed away at a lunatic pace, his hands flying between the workstation keyboard and a notebook computer he had set up beside it. When she'd asked him what he was doing he'd rattled off an answer, but he might as well have been speaking Chinese. She knew she should be working—researching *something*—but she felt too antsy to sit at a computer. Instead, her brain was prepping the discussion she planned to lead when the rest of the team returned from medical.

As luck would have it, the facility had two different handheld radiation monitoring units—a detector for determining ambient radiation and measuring point source emitters, as well as a frisker for quantifying contamination. The frisker employed a Geiger–Müller tube to detect alpha, beta, and gamma emissions. Moody said he'd procured both devices during the early days of testing to validate whether the machine or time travel itself might expose the travelers to radiation. Time travel, it turns out, was radiation-free—but the future Washington, DC, that Tyler, Stan, Ben, and Adela had visited was not.

Just thinking about the nuclear hellscape they'd seen made Zee feel physically ill.

Don't think about it.

Don't imagine it . . .

The door to the Reconstruct Room flung open so hard it slammed into the doorstop and vibrated on its hinges, giving Zee a start. The expression on Tyler's face as he led the others into the room said everything she needed to know. He was a man on a mission. The others looked equally determined and pissed off.

"What's the verdict?" she asked. "Did they have to wash you down with a fire hose?"

"Zero contamination," Ben said. "We're completely clean."

"How's that possible?" Zee asked, but she felt a huge sense of relief that her teammates were intact and healthy—for now at least.

"Actually," Stan said, "it validates everything Moody told us about how time travel works. Only the atoms that travel to the future return to the present. Whatever radioactive particulate contaminated our skin and clothes in the future *stayed* in the future."

"That's good news," she said.

"The bad news is whatever cellular damage we suffered from the few minutes we were standing in radiation is ours to keep," Adela added. "Which is the other law of time travel—if you get damaged in the future, you return damaged to the present."

"How bad is it?" Zee asked.

"Based on Stan's calculations, that damage should be minimal," Ben said with a tight smile.

"Thank God," she mumbled.

"Enough about that. We've got work to do," Tyler said, facing everyone. "The way I see it, we've traded one unknown for a dozen. We know that DC gets nuked, but what about the rest of the country? Was what we witnessed the aftermath of a global thermonuclear war with Russia or China, or was it the result of a terrorist attack? Before we do anything else, we need to understand the nature and magnitude of the threat we're dealing with—and the only way to do that is to start planning our next jump."

"Jumping to the Omega Room after the attack is pointless," Adela said. "And jumping before the attack—provided we figure out when it happens—is only going to provide us with limited information. Sure, we can program HAL to look for precursor activity that might give us clues to narrow the search, but jumping after the attack—when the world already knows what happened and we can read the headlines like we normally do—would be way more efficient and effective."

"But the fucking Omega Room is useless after the attack," Stan said.

"I know that, Stan," Adela snapped.

Zee watched the exchange, her own mind reeling. They needed to do something, but what?

Tyler shook his head. "The hell with protocol. A nuclear bomb annihilated the nation's capital. It's time for big-boy rules."

"And by *big-boy rules*," Moody said from behind them as he walked into the room, "what exactly are you proposing, Chief?"

"I'm proposing we jump to somewhere other than the Omega Room. We jump to Chicago or Los Angeles, or maybe both—somewhere we can get another data point. Hell, maybe we jump to Moscow or Beijing to see if there was a counterstrike. We can debate the where and when, but Adela is right—jumping to the Omega Room doesn't cut it in this scenario. We're going to have to break protocol and jump to outside locations."

"I agree with Tyler," Zee said. The thought of jumping still filled her with anxiety, but anywhere other than the small airtight space of the Omega Room would be better, right?

"So do I," Ben added.

Moody inhaled, then exhaled loudly. "Okay . . ."

"*Okay* you heard us, or *okay* you agree that we need to break protocol?" Tyler said, crossing his arms.

"Both," Moody said. "I understand and agree with the logic, but we need to maximize the value of the jump. What if Chicago was also targeted and you arrive to find it a wasteland? Then do I authorize you to jump to another city and another and another until we find one intact?"

"What we really need is another Omega Room in another location," Zee said, the idea hitting her like a lightning bolt. "Tell us the truth, Pat: Is there another Omega Room out there?"

"Unfortunately, no," Moody said. She studied his face for one of the typical tells that he might be lying, but his expression seemed unflinching.

"Then why don't we make one?" Tyler said.

"It took months to build the current facility. Even if I had a site, materials, and a dedicated crew working 24-7, we couldn't get it done in time."

"We don't need you to build us a new one," Zee said, having an epiphany, "we've got an Omega Room on practically every major base in CONUS. They're called SCIFs. We won't have HAL curating the data for us, but we'll have everything else we'll need—security, anonymity, and access to the classified intelligence network."

"That's a great idea, but it comes with its own set of complications and risks," Moody said.

"Complications and risks aside, I don't see a better alternative," Tyler said.

Moody took a step backward toward the door. "I need to get authorization for this and select and prep the site. The SCIF we choose needs to be operational, unoccupied, and secured when you arrive . . ."

"And somewhere least likely to have been destroyed in a wider nuclear exchange," Tyler said.

"Agreed," Moody said.

Zee watched the director's gaze go to the middle distance—his mental gears turning now, she supposed—and wondered if he'd learned any additional intel from other sources he was keeping hidden from them.

"The clock is ticking. As soon as you've made the arrangements, I want to jump. We should go today," Tyler said.

"You're not going to back down, are you?"

"No, sir."

"All right," Moody said with a nod. "The big question now is where I send you."

Zee had a second epiphany in as many minutes and smiled.

"I think I know just the place, but it'll be up to you to find a SCIF inside that you can guarantee will be empty." She felt Tyler's eyes on her, then realized the entire team was staring at her. "What if we jump to NORAD, inside the Cheyenne Mountain Complex outside Colorado Springs?"

"Wait— What?" Stan stuttered. "NORAD is built inside a mountain. It's under two thousand feet of granite."

Zee nodded. "But it is arguably the most secure and fortified bunker on the planet. If there's one facility that will still be operational after a global nuclear event, it's NORAD. The engineers designed it to survive a thirty-megaton nuclear strike. Even if the rest of the United

States was destroyed by a Russian or Chinese ICBM attack, NORAD would survive."

"Yeah," Stan said, "but, again, inside a mountain, dude."

"If the calculations are off even a little . . ." Adela said, shaking her head with an emphatic no.

"We could wind up materializing inside solid rock," Ben said, finishing the thought.

Moody had his hands behind his back now, pacing. "On paper, jumping to NORAD makes sense," he said, after a long beat, "but there are other complications in addition to geolocating, which you all have rightly expressed trepidations about."

"Such as?" Ben said.

"For starters, NORAD is a strategic nerve center jammed packed with staff and security. Arriving undetected would be nearly impossible."

"There's a solution for that," Zee said, strangely finding herself fighting for an idea that scared the crap out of her. "You get a DNI order to secure a room, empty it of everything but a few computer terminals against the walls, and leave it that way until after our jump."

"Yeah, that could work," Tyler said, apparently warming to the idea.

"Getting that authority might be easy but getting them to hold a SCIF in NORAD vacant after a nuclear attack on DC and wherever else seems unlikely," Adela said, but she, too, seemed to be coming around.

"I hear what you're saying, but what you're proposing isn't without personal risk," Moody said, holding her gaze. "Remember, any injuries you suffer in the future do not reset."

"The stakes are a nuclear attack on DC. I think we're willing to take that risk," Tyler said, speaking for the group.

"Okay, I'll make it happen. Give me some time to make a few calls, and I'll get back to you to brief the jump."

She watched Moody stride with purpose out the door. While the others began to talk excitedly about the mission, she leaned in close to Tyler.

Keeping her voice low and in a soft whisper, she said, "We can't put it off forever. We have to confront him about the thing we talked about in your stateroom."

"I know, but we have more pressing concerns at the moment," he whispered back, "and it would be nice to have proof."

She looked at her teammates, who were all mentally and emotionally charged, at the table.

Soon or later, we're going to have to read the others in . . . whether we have that proof or not.

CHAPTER 20

THE DONUT

THE PEPPER GRINDER—WAREHOUSE B

1832 LOCAL TIME

Even though Zee was standing three feet away from him on her *X*, Tyler could practically feel her anxiety. And honestly, he couldn't blame her. She was worried about what would happen if Jimmy made a miscalculation and jumped them into the middle of those two thousand feet of granite . . . he knew this because the grisly thought had crossed his mind more than once.

He made a *pssst* sound at her.

When she turned to look at him, he mouthed the words *It's going to be okay.*

She fixed him with a brave smile and mouthed, *I know.*

Moody's voice reverberated over the loudspeaker, interrupting their silent dialogue.

"I need everyone to listen to me very carefully. This is your first time landing outside the Omega Room. We've done this before during early testing, but only a couple of times. The team here in control have quadruple-checked their calculations, but you're jumping inside a mountain. It's a hollow mountain, but a mountain, nonetheless. If something goes wrong, you only have to last four minutes and you'll be back here. Dr. Donahue and her medical team will be standing by, ready to administer emergency care if anything happens to you."

"Very comforting," Adela said under her breath. "Great pep talk, Moody."

Tyler donned his Wiley X safety glasses and ordered the team to do the same. Given the possible risks associated with "free jumping," Moody had insisted everyone kit up for safety—which included wearing Kevlar vests, helmets, eye protection, and gloves. They were not, to Tyler's annoyance, permitted to bring weapons. The argument against traveling armed into Cheyenne Mountain made sense, but still.

If you're gonna kit up, then kit up all the way.

"Alpha, sitrep?" Moody announced, double-checking one last time.

The team sounded off with their numerical call signs, then Tyler made his standard report: "Alpha is ready to travel."

"Roger. All prejump checks are sat . . . but before I start the countdown, I just wanted to say that what the six of you are doing today is both admirable and incredibly brave," Moody's voice echoed. "I'm proud of this team. Good luck and Godspeed."

Tyler nodded at the team and then felt all the hair on his body stand up as the magnetic flux whirred to life. While the field spun up, he took a moment to say a short prayer for his team's safety but also that the jump would be fruitful. Millions of innocent lives were hanging in the balance.

He opened his eyes just as Moody's voice announced: "Traveling in five . . . four . . . three . . . two . . . one . . ."

Tyler pressed the timer button on the zero beat and felt the typical whoosh, but the transition was accompanied by something new—an eardrum-splitting *crack.*

On landing, something hard and heavy slammed into the meat of his right thigh while something else hit the back of his left wrist. Reflexively, he dropped into a combat crouch and performed a rapid threat assessment followed by a quick self-check. His thigh and wrist both throbbed like hell, but he confirmed that he'd *not* been shot. Visually, he verified they'd landed in a room that certainly looked like a SCIF, but there were *complications*.

"Moody, you bastard!" Stan shouted from where he was lying on his back on the floor. "So much for an empty room . . ."

"What happened?" Tyler called.

"I friggin' landed in the middle of a table and it exploded, that's what happened," Adela said, wide-eyed as she patted her midsection.

"Remember when Moody said that two sets of matter can't occupy the same space at the same time?" Stan said, sitting up. "Well, Adela appears to be living proof of that fact."

Tyler scanned the SCIF and saw that table shrapnel was everywhere. Most of his team were down on the ground. "Omega, sound off!"

"Two is intact, but I took a blow to the chest," Zee said. "Think I might have a broken rib."

"Three took a chunk to the head, but the helmet saved me," Stan growled. Tyler felt immediate relief that they'd decided to fully kit up.

Ben answered next. "Four is on his ass, but intact."

"Five is freaking out, but somehow uninjured," Adela said, standing in the middle of the remains of a conference table.

When Marty didn't answer, Ty prompted him. "Six? Marty, where are you?"

"He's behind that big chunk of table over there," Zee said. "I can see his boot."

Ben, the team's only medic, rushed to check on Martin. In his peripheral vision, Tyler saw a tuft of brown hair stick up above a different chunk of toppled table on the other side of the room. The hair became a forehead, then a pair of bespeckled eyes.

"Guys, we're not alone," Tyler said and rose to his full height to face the room's other occupant. "Hey, you, stand up!"

"What the hell just happened . . . and who the hell are you guys?" a trembling staff sergeant asked, getting to his feet. The man's Space Force uniform was doused with coffee, but Tyler didn't see any blood on the sergeant, nor was the man armed.

"We're a red team conducting an infiltration security drill," Tyler said without missing a beat, pulling the idea completely out of his ass. "There were orders in place that this room was to be unoccupied . . ."

"I don't know anything about that. It's kinda crazy here after . . . you know . . ." The man narrowed his eyes at them. "A Red Cell event inside Cheyenne Mountain . . . the most secure bunker on earth?"

"That's right," Tyler said. "In light of the attack on DC, it seemed imperative that we confirm security here at Cheyenne. Are you hurt, Staff Sergeant Bloom?" Tyler asked, reading the man's name tape.

"I . . . I . . . don't think so."

"Good. Red Team—resume exercise," Tyler said, playing out the only script he could think of.

"Why did you blow up the conference table?" Bloom asked, scanning the destruction.

"Shock and awe. It's kind of our trademark," Stan deadpanned. Then he looked at Tyler and tapped his watch. "We're on the clock, boss."

"Six is coming to," Ben hollered. "Must have been knocked out or fainted. I don't find any notable trauma."

Tyler checked his watch timer. "We've only got three minutes, people. Go, go, go! You too, Four."

"Roger that," Ben said. After helping Marty into a sitting position, he ran to the terminal beside Adela.

"I'm really starting to freak out now," Staff Sergeant Bloom said, crossing his arms. "I know you guys didn't come in the door because I was walking toward it when the table blew up. Oh my God—you're from the future, aren't you? You traveled back in time to try to stop World War III. Was it Russia? China? Do we launch a counterstrike? Tell me what happens. It's bad, isn't it? That's why you came . . ."

"Good news," Zee announced. "Looks like DC was the only target. I find no reports listing other cities getting nuked."

"Same here," Stan said.

"Is that true?" Tyler said, taking a chance and asking Bloom the question point-blank. "Was Washington, DC, the only city that got hit?"

"Yes, but," Bloom said, narrowing his eyes, "if you're from the future, you would already know that."

"We're *not* from the future," Tyler said, shifting his gaze from Bloom to check on Marty who looked dazed and confused.

"In that case, I'm calling security," Bloom said.

"Shut him up, One," Adela snapped from her terminal. "I can't concentrate with that jackass babbling."

"Listen, Staff Sergeant, it doesn't matter where we're from," Tyler said, putting a hand on the man's shoulder. "All that matters is that we're on the same team. We both want the same thing, which is to prevent World War III, okay? Now I'm going to need you to sit down against the wall over there and be quiet until my team finishes what we came here to do. Can you do that for me, Bloom?"

The sergeant glanced at the door to the SCIF, and Tyler could see he was calculating whether he should try to make a break for it. Tyler narrowed his eyes and squeezed the top of Bloom's shoulder hard enough to make the man wince.

"Okay, I can do that," Bloom said and moved to the corner, taking a seat on the floor as directed.

"I think I got something," Stan said.

"Me too," Zee chimed in.

Tyler's watch tolled. "Thirty seconds, people . . ."

"What happened?" Marty said, standing up on unsteady legs and walking toward Tyler.

"I'll explain when we get back," Tyler said. "Are you all right, buddy?"

"Yeah," Marty said, "but I think I'm concussed."

"You're definitely concussed," Ben said without taking his eyes off the terminal screen.

Tyler turned back to Bloom and thought, *What the hell, I might as well ask.* "Bloom, do you know who nuked the capital?"

"No. In fact, I was ordered to prep this SCIF for a briefing with the President in an hour," Bloom said.

"Where is the President?" Tyler asked, wondering if the President had somehow survived or if there was a new chief executive in the wake of the attack.

"She's here, of course," Bloom said, as if Tyler was a moron.

Tyler cocked an eyebrow. "*She?*"

"Yes, based on the presidential line of succession, Attorney General Elizabeth Prelogar is now the acting President. She designated Cheyenne Mountain Complex as the emergency capital."

His watch chimed a second time. "Ten seconds, people."

"Ten seconds until what?" Bloom asked.

"Until we say goodbye," Tyler said, then with a crooked grin added, "Oh, and Bloom, I know everyone's under a lot of stress, but you need to get some sleep, bro. You're starting to have hallucinations."

Bloom shot him a confused look.

The air shimmered.

Tyler blinked once, felt the whoosh, and he was home.

CHAPTER 21

Zee's right chest throbbed with every breath. She'd never had a broken rib before, but she'd definitely felt the *crack* when the chunk of conference table hit her during the jump to Cheyenne Mountain. She probably should have gone to medical with Martin for an X-ray, but that would have to wait. They had work to do, which meant she'd just have to suck it up—like she'd watched JSOC SEALs do countless times.

Power through it, girl. Just power through it.

"All right, team, let's get to it," she said walking to a giant digital whiteboard assigned to this, their most important case. "Adela, you're up."

The landing complications had resulted in only the former DIA officer and Stan collecting much information, despite Ben's attempts to help. Zee hoped the duo had gotten everything they needed. They were about to find out.

"First and most importantly, the only city that got nuked was DC, and we now know the exact time and date of the incident—November 11 at 1215 hours," Adela said, talking in the clipped no-nonsense voice she defaulted to in every operational setting. "The working theory is this was a terrorist attack, but the brass hasn't ruled out a Russian, Chinese, or North Korean false flag attack. What we do know is that whoever is behind it chose 1215 hours intentionally to maximize casualties. The bomb was detonated in the middle of the workday after everyone who commutes inside the Beltway was at work, but during lunch when the maximum number of government employees would have left hardened structures for dining out or running errands. Truly diabolical if you ask me."

"Bastards," Ben murmured.

"Next, I looked for the culprit. No nation or terror group has claimed responsibility for the attack. The media is reporting the strike as a terrorist attack, but USSTRATCOM and the NSA are not convinced. I spent the remaining time investigating the most plausible scenarios for how the bomb was deployed."

"Well done," Zee said with a nod to Adela, then picked up the stylus pen for the digital whiteboard. "Let's map out possible scenarios for the bomb deployment. What's case one?"

"Case one is the nuke was smuggled into the country via an aircraft and detonated at Reagan or Dulles. Case two, the bomb was smuggled into the city by truck, rail, or ship. And finally, case three, we were hit by a new and previously unidentified class of nuclear-tipped missile with stealth capabilities."

"Does such a missile even exist?" Tyler asked.

"Not to our knowledge," Adela said, "but we didn't know the Chinese had hypersonic missiles until twelve months ago. Who knows what else they've developed that we don't know about."

"We have constant satellite surveillance in place. If it had been some new hypersonic missile, wouldn't there be some evidence of that, in retrospect at least?" Ben said.

"That sounds right to me, too, but if the IC still has it on their list, it must be possible," Tyler said.

"Which case is the IC focusing on?" Zee asked, using the shorthand term for the intelligence community.

"Don't you mean what's *left* of it?" Adela said, her face grave.

"The Pentagon was inside the fireball radius," Stan said, jumping in. "It was completely vaporized, and so was DIA HQ at Joint Base Anacostia–Bolling on the other side of the river. CIA headquarters and the National Counterterrorism Center in McLean were outside the heavy blast radius and lethal radiation zones at eight miles away, but anyone not sheltering would have third-degree burns over their entire body from the thermal radiation. Half the people who survived the blast will be dead within a week of the event, their organs annihilated from the inside out. In a single strike, they decapitated our intelligence apparatus. Only the NSA and The Activity at Fort Meade survived unscathed."

"Well, not to mention the rest of the government. Both the White House and Capitol Hill were completely destroyed with a ninety-five percent mortality rate," Adela said. "The government as we know it is gone. Just gone . . ."

"*Will* be gone," Tyler corrected with the Navy SEAL, no-bullshit, mission-before-self ethos Zee loved about him. "If we fail—which we won't." She watched his face, wondering if it was team, country, or just his little girl, Harper, and her mom that drove him. Knowing Tyler, she imagined it was equal parts of all three.

Adela's expression was stone-cold, but Zee could see the angst and pain the woman was feeling. Moody had recruited her from DIA and before that she'd spent a dozen years with CIA. Zee could only guess how many of the woman's friends and mentors worked in those buildings . . .

If anyone here can empathize and relate to what she's feeling, it's me.

Her own thoughts went to her parents. Macabre imagery flashed before her mind's eye: The Pentagon incinerated with her dad inside working at his desk. Her mom sitting on the front porch, reading a book, with their sweet little Cavapoo, Sadie, in her lap, only to have her flesh burned off her bones a heartbeat later. She shuddered at the horrific thought and forced the vile mental movie to stop playing.

"What size nuke are we talking about here?" Tyler asked, snapping Zee from her thoughts.

Zee turned to Stan, who looked like he was about to explode if she made him wait any longer to share what he'd found. "Stan, what did you find?"

"Consensus is that it was big. One- to three-megaton yield," Stan said.

Ben shook his head. "Dear God, that's, like, ICBM territory."

Stan nodded. "That's exactly right. We're not talking about some dirty bomb or suitcase nuke. A nuke with that sort of yield is big and weighs a metric ton or more."

"Moreover, there are only a handful of countries on earth that have the know-how, facilities, and fissile material to build a weapon like this, and half of them are our allies. Russia, China, Israel, the UK, France, India, Pakistan, and North Korea," Adela said. "It's a very short list."

"Unless some zealot was able to steal or purchase a weapon," Tyler pointed out. "We've all seen the evolution of the jihadists firsthand. They're not the 9/11 terrorists. They're educated, tech-savvy, multilingual . . ."

"Yeah, but dude—a full-sized nuke? They ain't nuclear physicists," Ben said.

"Some might well be," Moody said. Zee knew he was right, from serving firsthand as intel for the top counterterrorism unit in the world. The new breed of terrorist came in all shapes and sizes—and levels of education. "And, with the aid of someone who hates us enough . . ." Moody added and let it hang out there.

"The enemy of my enemy," Stan said.

Zee jotted these notes on the digital whiteboard. "That may be true, but we know it's going to happen. Our job is to start ruling things out and prosecuting leads. We now know the exact moment of detonation, which anchors us in time. If we work backward, we should be able to figure out how it was deployed and plan an intervention."

All eyes turned to Program Director Moody who pressed his lips together in a thin line and nodded. "That's right," Moody said. "Which means we're going to have to solve this case using a combination of traditional ISR methods and free jumping into the preblast timeline to investigate the leads we generate."

"That's exactly what I was going to propose," Adela said, and Zee couldn't tell if she was being sarcastic or not. Apparently, nobody else, including Moody, was sure either, because everyone just stared at her. "I'm not being a jerk; I actually agree with him."

Tyler laughed first, which opened the door for everyone to join him. There was nothing funny about their situation, nothing at all, but emotionally they all needed the release. It felt cathartic for Zee—if only for a minute.

"All right," Zee said, setting her stylus down. "Let's start building out these cases and trying to assign persons of interest and time-stamped locations we want to investigate. Once we have a short list, we'll start jumping."

CHAPTER 22

THE RECONSTRUCT ROOM
THE PEPPER GRINDER—WAREHOUSE B
THE NEXT MORNING
0747 LOCAL TIME

Fueled by adrenaline rather than caffeine this morning, Tyler strode into the Reconstruct Room to find Zee, Adela, and Martin already working. Of the three, only Zee looked up from her work to acknowledge his arrival with a nod. He hated not being the first one in the room, but everything that had happened—everything he'd seen—had left him pacing his stateroom, obsessing about something else. He needed, almost desperately, to hear his little girl's voice. If she were a teenager, he would have called her a dozen times by now. But she was three years old. That meant he had to call her by calling Nikki, his ex. After everything that happened in Mali—and she would know all about it by now—he dreaded that call. Of course, the longer he waited the worse it was, but in the end, he rationalized that he needed a clear head this morning and kicked the can down the road again.

Tyler wandered over to where Zee was standing at the giant corkboard. She had cleared off all the notes, photos, and items pertaining to the Buffalo synagogue shooting and readied it for the new case, which she'd code-named Operation Ares. She'd positioned both of the large digital whiteboards on wheels so that they flanked the case wall. The one on the left had their brainstorming notes from yesterday and the other was filled with a giant map of DC centered on the White House.

"The god of war," Tyler said with a nod to the case name Zee had added to the top of the left-hand whiteboard. "Fitting."

"I thought so," Zee said. "How did you sleep?"

"I didn't . . . You?"

"Not a wink," she said with a weary smile.

He scratched at the stubble on his neck. "I've been thinking. Maybe we should jump back to the SCIF in Cheyenne Mountain today. We can have Jimmy adjust Adela's jump coordinates so she doesn't end up in the conference table this time."

"We certainly could do that, but what additional intel do you want to try to get from there?"

"We know *when* the bomb went off, but we also need to narrow down the *where*. DC metro is a huge and very busy place, with thousands of miles of roads, multiple airports, maritime traffic, and a million people. If our goal is to work backward from the detonation to try to track the bomb and find the people who positioned it, we have to narrow the search area. The blast zone is simply too big to search without a starting point. Maybe NORAD has a team of nerds who already did the calculations and figured it out." He saw that she was smiling at him. "What's that look for?"

"We can definitely do that, but go talk to Martin first. I think you'll be impressed."

He nodded and wandered over to where the kid was crushing the keyboard at the terminal he habitually sat at. "What are you working on, Marty?"

Martin finished typing whatever code or command he was in the middle of and looked up, flustered. "There is, I mean, I can . . . I've been writing a program to identify the detonation epicenter using preblast security camera footage recorded of the area. There's a camera on top of the tower and all the data is archived. I'm tasking a generative graphics AI to simulate the destruction based on two-, three-, four-, and five-megaton yield nuclear bombs detonated at a dozen different possible locations in the DC metro area. I would like Ben—on account of his eidetic visual memory and pattern recognition skills—to look at the simulation and tell me which landscape reconstruct most closely matches what he saw from on top of the Omega Room tower. If it works, we can narrow our search parameters by an order of magnitude and identify the bomb's detonation location with a high confidence interval."

While Marty had been talking, Ben and Stan had arrived and wandered over to catch the tail end of the conversation.

"That's brilliant, Marty," Tyler said and turned to Driscoll. "Ben, are you on board with the plan?"

"Absolutely," Ben said, tapping his temple with an index finger. "I'm ready to get my Gestalt on."

Stan laughed at the comment, but Tyler didn't know what *Gestalt psychology* meant, so he just smiled.

"Have you got any fresh ideas in that database you call a brain that you want to share?" Tyler asked, turning to Stan.

"Remember what I said yesterday about the nuke's yield?" Stan said.

"Yeah, that it was big—one- to three-megaton I think you said."

"That's right, but I also said that to achieve that kind of yield it would have to be physically big as well. For example, the warhead on the Chinese Dong Feng 4 missile has a three-megaton yield and is estimated to weigh nearly five thousand pounds."

"Dude, to move something like that requires serious load-handling equipment," Tyler said.

"Exactly. Early US nuclear warheads had similar yield-to-weight ratios, but the designers at Los Alamos worked on this problem over the decades. For both tactical and practical reasons, warhead miniaturization is highly advantageous. There are physical limits, of course, because the higher the yield the more fissile material is required, and uranium is dense and heavy, but one way the US solved the problem was by developing MIRVs."

Tyler was no munitions expert, but he knew this one. "Multiple Independently Targetable Reentry Vehicles."

"That's right. So, for example, the Trident D5 missile that our Ohio class ballistic missile submarines carry is fitted with up to eight W88 warheads. Each W88 is rated at half a megaton and weighs around four hundred pounds. It's sixty inches long and eighteen inches in diameter . . . Do you see where I'm going with this?"

"You're looking at the problem logistically," Tyler said. "If the package is too big and heavy for practical transport, then break it up. Instead of sneaking one massive bomb into the country, sneak in three or four smaller ones and daisy-chain them together."

"Exactly," Stan said, nodding.

"Well, damn it. That sucks, Stan. If you're right, that means this thing doesn't have to be moved by train or in some CONEX box on a boat. They could have loaded warheads into the back of a Ryder truck or into the cargo hold of a biz jet. Four hundred pounds per bomb is very manageable."

"If DC got hit by a missile, then this is all a moot point, but if this was an act of terrorism or a false flag, then it matters immensely. I was lying in bed thinking about this all night. If it's terrorism, we can't risk limiting our search to heavy haul transport scenarios because we could easily waste all our time chasing red herrings."

"It's strong work, Stan," Tyler said and clapped him on the shoulder. "Why don't you and Zee build this out."

"Will do."

Zee gave him a nod from where she sat nearby at the conference table.

The morning seemed to evaporate, and the next thing Tyler knew his stomach was rumbling. On checking his watch, he saw that it was already quarter to noon. He was about to suggest breaking for lunch when Moody arrived carrying six boxes of pizza. Tyler wasn't sure where the program director had been all morning but decided not to confront him about it. He had some serious questions about what information Moody might be keeping from them, but waist-deep in intel analysis didn't seem like the time to open Pandora's box. A part of him worried it might even get them shut down, if the worst of their suspicions proved true, and the team had plenty to do.

"I ordered the gambit," Moody said as he set the boxes on the big worktable in the center of the room and started flipping open lids. "I got plain cheese, a meat lover's, a vegetarian, a buffalo chicken and blue cheese, a pepperoni and mushroom, and my personal favorite—pizza Margherita."

"I've never met a slice of pizza I didn't like," Tyler said as he grabbed a slice of meat lover's and took his first bite.

For fifteen wonderful minutes, he didn't think about the impending nuclear attack, the ghosts of his fallen SEAL brothers in Mali, or the fact that he'd *still* not called Nikki to tell her that he was back in CONUS and had taken a job at a new command. Instead, he ate pizza, drank sweet tea, and bantered with his new team—his new *family*—and he was grateful to Moody for the moment.

As soon as everyone had finished eating and the break had run its course, Ben spoke up.

"Guys, Marty and I have some news. Thanks to his blast simulation generator—"

"And your remarkable visual memory and gift for pattern recognition," Martin interrupted.

Ben chuckled, "Thanks, Marty. Anyway, by putting our two heads together we determined with ninety-five percent confidence that ground zero for the attack is approximately 38.86 minutes north by 77.03 minutes west which—not surprisingly—is where the Potomac runs smack dab through the heart of DC. High-probability epicenter locations include Ronald Reagan National Airport to the southwest, Joint Base Anacostia–Bolling to the southeast, the National War College at Fort McNair to the northeast, and the Pentagon to the northwest."

"Now we're talking," Stan said.

"Great job guys," Moody said. "That really narrows the field."

Zee scooted herself back from the table and walked over to the digital whiteboard with the giant map of DC. She recentered the image over the lat-long that Ben had rattled off, just north of the confluence where the Potomac and the Anacostia Rivers merged. She zoomed in so the four high-probability epicenter targets—which essentially formed a box—were roughly positioned at the corners of the frame. Next, she used a digital distance tool to measure the sides of the box. Two miles between each landmark.

"This is the region we're going to focus our investigation," Zee said. "Martin and Ben have dramatically shrunk the search area, but this box still spans four square miles. Where do we start, and how can we shrink the cone of uncertainty even further?"

"What we need is satellite imagery of this area at the time the nuke goes off," Adela said. "I'm no expert on the subject, but I would imagine at one or two milliseconds after detonation we'd have a compact, bright sphere of thermal energy we can pinpoint."

"I can put in a request to have a dedicated satellite watching this exact location on D-Day and have the imagery aggregated and waiting for you, but the Omega Room will be dark," Moody said.

"Then why don't we jump back to NORAD?" Tyler asked.

"Uh-uh, no fucking way," Adela blurted. "My table-exploding days are over."

"Easily solvable," Stan said. "The rest of us landed without intersecting furniture. All our positions can stay the same, only yours needs to be adjusted. Ben can do his thing and reproduce a map of where everyone landed and where the table is. Then, all Jimmy has to do is shift you."

"Fine," Adela said, but her face said otherwise.

"Sounds like a plan," Moody said. "Zee, if you could generate a list of all the data you want me to requisition in the next hour, I'll route the requests. Ben, please get with Jimmy to revise the jump landing coordinates. Let's shoot for a 1600 jump time, and we'll see what the future holds."

Tyler watched Moody head out of the room and felt himself purse his lips. He had a lot to figure out about their director but now was simply not the time. He felt a hand on his shoulder and turned to see Zee giving him a tight smile.

"You good?" she asked simply.

"Five by," he assured her. "What about you? You must be worried about your parents . . ."

"Yeah, but not just that. I mean, I also care about the million other people who live there too."

"Of course, I didn't mean to imply . . ."

"I know you didn't," she said, "but you can't tell me you haven't thought about Nikki and Harper and what will happen to them if we fail."

He nodded and a guilty pang made his throat feel tight.

"How are they doing, Ty?"

He shook his head, feeling like he'd been caught.

"I still haven't called Nik to tell her I'm back in town."

She turned to look at him. "Wait, what? Does she know about what happened in Mali?"

"Not from me . . . but there's no question the news has made it to her. You know how it is—tight community and all. We lost SEALs, so the network of spouses will all be circling the wagons," he said and exhaled loudly. "I'm such an asshole. I should have called her as soon as I got stateside."

"Probably."

"But we got here and the OPSEC is off the charts, and then we hit the ground running and things happened so fast . . ."

"I know, Ty. Believe me, I get it. It's been a whirlwind," she said. "Even though you're divorced, I'm sure she's worried about you. It probably wouldn't be a bad idea to give her a call. She might be angry, but speaking as a woman, I can promise you that the longer you wait, the worse it's going to get."

"I know," he said and checked his watch. "Maybe I should give her a call now, catch her over lunch."

"I think that's a good idea. Now's a good time to slip out for a bit."

Feeling both anxious and strangely excited, he drained the rest of his tea and said, "Thanks, Zee."

"Anytime."

He made the short trek to the Salt Shaker, a.k.a. Warehouse A, and to his stateroom in the crew quarters where he kept his mobile phone in its charging cradle. He took a deep breath, exhaled through pursed lips, and called Nikki from his *Favorites* list.

She picked up on the second ring. "Hello?"

"Nik, it's Tyler," he said.

"Tyler? What the hell! Are you okay? I heard you got shot." Her voice sounded more relieved than angry, thank God.

"Yeah, I'm fine. It was just a graze," he said and hesitated before adding, "I'm sorry it's taken me this long to check in."

"Ty, I don't want to fight about this . . . I know we're not husband and wife anymore," she said, and he could hear the tight chord in her voice as she tried to keep the emotions she was clearly feeling under control, "but after what happened, I can't believe you didn't call."

"I know and I'm sorry."

"Sarah Keaton and the kids . . . and Liz . . . It's terrible, Ty. Terrible."

"I know . . ."

He listened to her unsteady breathing as the dam of pent-up emotions broke.

"I'm sorry, Nik, but I haven't been in a position to call until now. After the incident, I was . . ."

"You were what?"

"I was transferred to another unit," he said, which was a white lie, but a white lie that would be impossible for her to disprove.

"What kind of unit?"

"A special counterterrorism task force. There's a major threat to the country we're prosecuting," he explained. The narrative he was spinning now felt closer to the truth than he should be sharing. "That's all I can say for now. If I could have read you in sooner I would have."

She didn't say anything for a long moment. "So, this thing you're doing—is it out of . . ." He could picture her pacing the kitchen, trying to decide which questions to ask first. "Virginia Beach? And what's the deployment schedule gonna be like?"

"Well, actually, that's the good news," he said. "There won't be any real deployments. I mean, there will, but they'll be measured in days instead of months."

"Can you tell me where you are?"

"I'll be working out of Maryland . . . mostly."

"Maryland? That's like five or six hours away."

"More like four and a half," he said, "and with a lighter deployment schedule . . ."

"I promised to stay in Virginia Beach so you could spend time with Harper," she said, anger rising in her voice, "and now you tell me you're moving to Maryland?"

He sighed. The truth was, regardless of where he lived, Nikki wasn't leaving Virginia Beach. Yes, her work had offered her a job in Houston, but even if Tyler weren't in the picture, she was a Virginia Beach girl, born and raised. Her parents lived only five minutes from her new house near Sixty-Sixth at the oceanfront, and her mom watched Harper five days a week. But he knew better than to point any of this out at this particular moment.

"I know, Nik, but hear me out. It's Maryland, not California. The commute is totally doable. I was thinking I could keep the place in Chic's Beach and come home at least every other weekend to spend time with Harper," he said, a plan he was making up on the fly.

"Tyler," she said, using his full name as she did only when she was disappointed in him. "As much as I like the sound of that, your track record would suggest this is nothing more than wishful thinking."

I deserve that . . .

"Can I at least talk to Harper?" he asked, pivoting. "I miss her."

"I dropped her off at my mom's early today because I'm meeting Sarah Keaton for coffee before work. She's a mess, Ty, as you can imagine. But . . ." She sighed. He could imagine the stress she was under with the loss of her best friend's husband, worrying about her ex-husband, keeping things steady for Harper . . .

I'm such a dick.

"Call back this evening, or tomorrow morning if that's better, and you can talk to her."

"That's fair," he said, feeling like the shittiest dad in the entire world.

"But when you do, please don't tell Harper you're coming to visit until you know with one hundred percent certainty that you're going to make it. I refuse to put her through that kind of disappointment."

"I understand."

There was an awkward pause.

"Well, goodbye, Ty," she said.

"Please tell her I called for her and I love her."

Another long sigh.

"I always do, Tyler. Even when it's a lie."

He closed his eyes, unsure what to say to that.

"Well . . . Bye."

And she was gone.

He frowned at the phone. When he rose from the chair, he got a sharp twinge in his lower back. He arched and immediately massaged the spot, barely dodging what felt like a muscle spasm brewing.

That's weird.

He stretched his back, getting a satisfying crack, then felt another twinge in his hip as he headed for the door to get back to work.

Good God, I'm falling apart . . .

CHAPTER 23

Jun raised the pair of compact binoculars to his eyes and focused on the young mother as she strapped her daughter into a car seat in the back of a white Nissan Rogue parked in the driveway of a modestly sized, upscale two-story house.

"Is that them?" Damien asked from the driver's seat of their rental car.

"Yes," Jun said, guessing the American SEAL's little girl to be three or four years old at the most.

"What's the plan?

"Kill the wife and kidnap the daughter. Then, we use the child as bait and lure the SEAL—and hopefully his companions—into a kill box to eliminate them just like we did the other team. Garth is scouting locations as we speak," Jun said, watching the woman give the child butterfly kisses, to the toddler's delight, before closing the door and climbing into the driver's seat.

"You're cold as ice, *mon ami*. I hope I never piss you off."

Jun ignored the comment and lowered the binoculars. "Follow them."

The Frenchman put the transmission in Drive, spun the wheel, and pulled away from the curb. Ten seconds later, they were tailing the Nissan through the streets of Virginia Beach with a proper offset. He did not expect the woman to notice she was being surveilled, but Damien was a pro and well-versed in tradecraft.

"When do you want to do it?"

"As soon as we get the green light from Hoffman," Jun said, shifting uncomfortably in his seat.

The work was taking a toll. Despite not having jumped for almost two weeks, his hips really bothered him today. He pulled a foil pill pack from his left front pocket, tore it open, and popped two hospital-strength anti-inflammatory painkillers into his mouth.

"And in the meantime?" Damien asked, glancing at him sideways.

Jun dry-swallowed the pills with the saliva he had in his mouth, then said, "We learn her routine and identify the perfect place to take them."

CHAPTER 24

Tyler grinned as he watched Adela and Stan bicker in front of the Father of Time Travel shrine. Stupid shit like this was why he loved being an operator.

"Last time you were the only one who didn't pay homage at the shrine and looked what happened," Stan said, standing with hands on hips beside the display with the framed picture of Roberto Lopez. "You landed in the middle of a table. Just sayin'."

"It's stupid, and I'm not kissing that thing," she said, crossing her arms.

"Then give the plaque below a little belly rub."

"No!" she said with theatrical outrage.

"At least give him a thumbs-up," Ben said, joining the fun. He mimicked Lopez's goofy smile and thumbs-up in the picture.

Adela rolled her eyes, turned on a heel, and walked toward the Donut.

"The Father of Time Travel does not take kindly to being slighted," Stan said to her back.

"You're playing with fire, girl," Ben called.

"You're a man-child, Stan, you know that? And so are you, Ben," Zee said as she walked by, but she kissed her fingertips and pressed them to the glass on Lopez's cheek as she did.

Laughing, Tyler gave Lopez a thumbs-up and headed into the Donut, enjoying the moment of respite from the seriousness of what they were doing and the global stakes if they failed. Once everyone stepped onto their *Xs*, he ordered goggles on. They were kitted-up like last time, which Tyler had decided would be the protocol for all free jumps going forward. The team sounded off.

"Prechecks are complete. Control is ready to commence countdown," Moody said.

Tyler shifted to a balanced stance, with his feet shoulder-width apart and his weight divided evenly between the balls of his feet and his heels. He donned his safety googles, then said, "Control, Alpha—commence the count. Alpha is ready to travel."

"Copy, Alpha, commencing reactor start-up sequence . . ."

"Roger that, Control."

Tyler heard the familiar whirring of the magnetic field generators powering up, and a moment later felt the tingle on his skin as the little hairs on his forearms stood up.

Moody's voice reverberated inside the Donut as he counted them down: "Stand by to travel in five . . . four . . . three . . . two . . . one . . ."

Tyler started the timer, felt the whoosh, and heard something disconcerting—a strange, mushy pop. Warm red spatter sprayed his cheeks, goggles, and kit. Someone let out a bloodcurdling scream, which sent his heart rate skyrocketing.

Oh, dear God, he thought as he scanned the room for carnage and casualties. The SEAL in him performed a rapid head count and threat assessment.

Two through Six are upright and intact, no visible threats . . .

The scream came from Adela. She turned in a slow circle looking at her teammates, who were all covered in blood spatter and other bits. Tyler rushed over and grabbed her by the shoulders. She locked eyes with him and only then did she stop screaming.

"Adela, are you okay? Are you hurt?"

She was hyperventilating, her complexion had gone ghostly pale, and her entire body was trembling. He looked her up and down, just to confirm all her body parts were intact. Unlike the rest of them, Adela didn't have a drop of blood or spatter on her person.

"What . . . the fuck . . . just happened?" she said between gasps, her eyes as wide as dinner plates.

"I think you landed in the exact place that Staff Sergeant Bloom happened to be standing," Tyler said gently. "I think you're going into shock. How about we get you into a sitting position . . ."

"You mean the Space Force guy who was in here last time?" she asked, letting Tyler help lower her to the ground.

"Yeah."

"I just murdered a man by exploding his molecules . . ." she said. Once on the floor, she immediately hugged her knees to her chest.

"I told you not to diss the Father of Time Travel," Stan murmured, tossing his filthy goggles aside as he walked toward one of the open terminals.

"Shut the fuck up, Stan," Tyler snapped, then took Adela's gloved hand in his own and gave it a squeeze. "This all resets when we land back in the present, remember? Bloom is going to be fine because none of this is going to happen."

She nodded, and Tyler could see she was trying to pull herself together.

"That's one of the rules," she said. "The shit we change gets reset."

"That's right; everything's going to be fine," he said and turned his attention from Adela to the rest of the team who, to his surprise and despite their gruesome appearance, were all sitting at computer workstations harvesting critical data in the precious time they had left.

"Got it!" Ben shouted from his console.

"You found the epicenter?" Tyler asked.

"I froze the sat feed with the fireball at five meter's width. It detonates on a boat in the middle of the Potomac, which it looks like is practically on top of the lat-long that Marty's algorithm predicted."

"Get every visual detail you can on that boat," Zee called.

"I'm all over it," Ben fired back.

Tyler's watch chimed. "Thirty seconds."

Adela took a deep, cleansing breath and got to a knee.

"Are you okay to stand?" Tyler asked. When she nodded, he helped her to her feet.

"Thanks, Tyler," she said, fixing him with a tight smile. "I'm not normally . . . you know, like that."

"There's no *normal* in combat. What just happened is called trauma. Your reaction was justified," he said with a respectful nod. "I want you to know I'm here for you if you need me."

She nodded, exhaled, and started to make her way to an open terminal when his watch chimed a second time.

"Don't worry about that now," he said, stopping her with a hand and flashing her an easy smile. "We got what we came for."

CHAPTER 25

THE DONUT

THE PEPPER GRINDER—WAREHOUSE B

1605 LOCAL TIME

The first thing Zee noticed on landing was that the blood spatter on her goggles was gone. She examined herself. Her kit and uniform were clean and unmarred.

Only the atoms that travel to the future return from the future, she reminded herself. *Thank God for that.*

Would Staff Sergeant Bloom really be okay, like Tyler said? Or would he be exploded by Adela in that SCIF weeks from now when the future became the present? What was the proof that the future actually resets like Moody had told them?

When that time comes, we'll still arrive . . . Won't we?

Was this another case—like the Omega Room not having any doors—where Moody hadn't been entirely honest with them? Was he telling them what he thought they needed to hear to ease their minds, to prevent them from overthinking their actions? It made her brain swim. She decided to table it and talk to Tyler—or maybe Stan—about it later.

She let out a long raspy sigh and forced her shoulders to untighten as she rolled her head on her aching neck. She hated being in the Donut. Friggin' hated it. The curved walls played tricks on the mind and made her feel like they were closing in, like one of those optical illusions where a drawing on a piece of paper seems to distort and move. The lines formed by the seams of the tiles seemed to constrict and coil around her like a giant metal serpent.

The door hissed as the locking ring disengaged. As the pressure equalized, the door popped open a few inches but the inertial mass stopped it like always. She slammed her shoulder into the heavy door and shoved.

"Looks like somebody wants out," Stan said with a chuckle behind her, as he lent a hand to push the massive slab open wide enough for them both to fit through.

Once Zee stood in the wide-open, cavernous space of Warehouse A, she felt better. As the compulsions induced by her claustrophobia began to wane, her mind reset. She stopped thinking about herself and suddenly remembered that Adela was the one who'd experienced trauma.

Well, I suppose we all did, she thought with an involuntary shiver at the memory of being covered head to toe in bits of Bloom.

In that moment, Tyler had handled the situation with the professional compassion of a trauma counselor combined with the triage instincts of a surgeon. Watching him lead Omega under stress and duress reminded her of a hostage negotiator working under pressure—he had to manage the clock, diverse personalities, and team members with different strengths and weaknesses, all the while trying to save lives and keep the bosses happy. As an operator the SEAL was impressive, but as a leader he was phenomenal. Thinking about her own reaction to the event, she felt guilty and a little ashamed that she'd not rushed to support Adela.

Zee walked over to her teammate to check on her, but the former superspy acted as if nothing had happened. She decided to try anyway. "Adela, are you—"

Adela cut her off. "I'm fine. It's over. I don't want to talk about it."

"Well?" Moody asked, jogging up to where the team was clustered. "Did you ID ground zero?"

"Yes. The future satellite you tasked to watch ground zero

happened," Tyler said and threw an arm around Ben's shoulder. "Ben got everything we need."

"The nuke is on a boat," Ben said. "It's a yacht cruising north in the middle of the Potomac when the bomb goes off—smack dab in the heart of DC where we predicted."

"Excellent, this is very good news," Moody said, grinning like a kid. "We use the data to build a case file, NCTC gets involved, a future intervention will happen, and the nuke will be intercepted before it ever reaches the Potomac."

"Same as what we did for the Buffalo mass shooting," Ben said. "Lay the groundwork in the present so the proper agencies can intervene in the future for a threat they otherwise would have missed."

Zee liked the way that sounded, but there might be one more thing they could do first.

"Hold on a second," Zee said, hating herself for what she was about to propose because it would involve an extra jump, if not multiple jumps. But the intelligence officer in her couldn't keep quiet. "Yes, we need to do all that, but I think it would be a missed opportunity not to jump to that boat in the minutes before detonation. Think of the intelligence we can collect to help with the data package. We can identify the exact model and configuration of the bomb. We can identify the crew and captain and look for clues that might help us find the group behind the attack."

"She's right," Tyler said, backing her up. "Assuming NCTC stops the attack, the mastermind responsible for it will be in the wind. We need clues from the boat to help us ID the Head Shed the bombers are working for. It would allow us to start working the problem from Omega predetonation."

"Agreed. We're already kitted-up. I say we go now," Stan said. "Who else is game?"

Five hands went up, Martin being the only one who opted out.

"Hold on, let's everybody take a breath and talk about it," Moody said, raising a hand to settle them down.

Zee tried to read his expression. She hated that her suspicions made her look at every exchange with the man as another potential deception. He was keeping secrets from them, and she resented him for it. But as an intelligence officer she understood the purpose behind, and necessity of, compartmentalized information. This wasn't the first time a leader put the greater good of the country ahead of the needs of the individuals fighting to safeguard it.

"That's exactly what we're doing here, Pat," Tyler said with a hint of annoyance in his voice. "*Talking.*"

"NCTC doesn't have a four-minute time limit. I'm not convinced of the value of this jump when they can task an FBI tactical squad to hit the boat and take everything."

"It's no different than what we do every time we jump. We harvest details from the future and feed it into the IC data stream. Every detail we collect gives them a head start, intelligence that increases their probability of success."

"It *is* different, Chief. You're jumping into a tactical operation in progress, which introduces risk for you and every team member," Moody said and turned to Martin. "Is that why you didn't raise your hand, Marty. Are you a dissenting vote?"

"No, I think jumping to the boat is a good idea," Martin said, "but it's not an op I will add value to. If there is an armed presence onboard, I would probably be a liability. My time would be better spent here populating the case file with data."

Tyler nodded. "It's true, everything has happened so fast and furious since we got here, I haven't been able to spend nearly enough time with Marty on the range and in the kill house to prepare him for this kind of fieldwork. He would be a liability on a maritime mission with the possibility of close-quarters combat. And, Zee, no offense, but you might be too."

"None taken," she said and breathed a sigh of relief.

Moody let out defeated exhale then fixed his attention on the four experienced operators. "This is really something you guys want to do?"

They all nodded.

"All right, you've got the green light," Moody said.

"Hooyah," Tyler said with fire in his voice. "For this jump, I'd go with two teams of two. Drop a pair of us on the bow, a pair on the stern, and we clear to the middle." She watched Tyler turn to Moody. "Is that doable?"

Moody nodded. "It's possible, but more complicated. We're relying on Ben's eidetic memory to give us a tremendous amount of detail here. I'd hate to drop half of you into the Potomac."

"Or into a bad guy," Adela said, and Zee watched the spook cross her arms and shudder.

Ben tapped his temple. "I looked at satellite stills of the boat at T-minus one minute, five minutes, and fifteen minutes before detonation so I'd understand its position in relation to landmarks on the shore. I know exactly where it is at those timestamps."

"Did you see armed personnel topside?" Moody asked.

"No. As far as I could tell, the decks were clear."

"They could have a small militia of armed martyrs inside guarding the bomb," Moody said. "It could be dangerous."

"No more dangerous than what the four of us did for a living before coming here," Tyler said.

"Okay. Ben, get with Martin and Jimmy to plan the jump based on imagery of the boat moving up the Potomac, but five minutes before detonation. That will put you close enough to the epicenter without any risk of you being . . . er . . . *present* during the event."

"It's okay to say it, Moody. The word is *vaporized*," Stan said. "And yes, we'll want some time to spare . . . Unless, of course, they decide to detonate early when we show up."

Zee felt her chest go tight on hearing that. Stan was right. A trigger-happy martyr would probably not hesitate to push the button early if four commandoes appeared out of nowhere topside.

Moody smiled awkwardly. "Well, if that's the case, let's hope you're faster on the trigger than they are."

Zee began to speak but Tyler beat her to it with the same thought, apparently.

"Adela," he said, and the DIA officer turned his way. "Are you sure you're five by? We can decompress for a short time to let you collect—"

"I'm fine, Chief," Adela snapped. "It's over, and I'm in the fight."

Zee watched Tyler purse his lips, but he nodded.

"Hooyah," he said. "Two sticks, then, if Jimmy thinks we can pull off a split landing. Adela and I land up front on the bow, and Ben and Stan aft at the stern."

Zee watched Adela for a moment. Her teammate was still rattled, but she decided the woman was tough as nails and if Adela said she was good to go, then, hopefully, she was.

CHAPTER 26

THE POTOMAC RIVER

THE FUTURE

T-MINUS 5 MINUTES TO DETONATION

Tyler blinked.

One second he was crouching inside the Donut and the next he was on the triangular bow deck of the Ocean Alexander 100 Skylounge yacht cruising in the middle of the Potomac. He scanned over his Wilson Combat 300 Blackout SBR for threats, while Adela did the same beside him. The tinted reflective glass surrounding the pilot house directly in front of them made it impossible to see inside. If there were shooters in there, then he and Adela were fish in a barrel—which meant they needed to move fast. With the bow clear, he hand-signaled for Adela to move aft along the port rail, while he did the same on the starboard side. He could tell that Zee had been worried about Adela's emotional state after the trauma of the last jump, but as an operator, he knew what Zee couldn't possibly understand about the human mind's ability to put trauma in a box and continue to function until the time to deal with it was right.

Been there many times . . .

Stan and Ben were supposed to have landed on the upper-level aft deck and clear forward while he and Adela did the opposite on the main deck, clearing bow to stern. If this had been a JSOC op, he'd be wired up with radio and mike, but electronics did not function properly or reliably after traveling through the flux vortex. They knew that memory cards and hard drives were wiped clean after travel, but other electronics such as comms went wonky as well, apparently, so he couldn't check in with Ben and Stan. But they were pros and he had no worries that they would execute as planned. In the few hours between jumps, they'd studied the yacht's design and conducted a virtual walkthrough before the jump. One of the benefits of hitting a ten-million-dollar yacht is that capitalism provides great intel. Yacht brokers spend big bucks putting together HD virtual walkthroughs of their inventory, so Tyler felt like he knew this model inside and out without ever having stepped aboard.

Tyler moved low and fast aft, ducking below the row of windows that extended the entire length of the salon. He'd yet to hear a gunshot—either from above where Ben and Stan were clearing the skylounge or from inside the salon. The next ten seconds would decide whether that was a good or bad thing . . .

He buttonhooked around the corner and moved centerline toward the automatic slider doors leading to the salon, Adela moving in mirror image until she fell in beside him on his left shoulder with perfect synchronicity. She squeezed his shoulder, and they surged toward the motion-activated double glass doors.

With a whoosh, the doors slid open and he and Adela crossed the threshold. A blast of warm air hit him as they transitioned from the cool midafternoon November air to the heated main cabin. He cleared right as she cleared left, dragging his laser target designator over and around the luxury furniture in the exquisitely appointed salon.

"Clear," he said, charging through the living room toward the bridge up front, knowing Adela would be in position, clearing her sectors.

"Clear," she said, falling in behind him to cover his six.

He moved fast through the vacant dining area, scanning left and

right, then the cabin necked down to a narrow passage. He cleared the
small kitchen on the left, knowing Adela would clear the bathroom on
the right, then continued forward to the pilot house. Heart pounding,
mind focused, and thighs on fire from the prolonged quickstepping
in a deep combat crouch, he surged into the pilot house ready to slay.
Seeing no one at the controls directly ahead, he had to choose which
side to clear. The passage was too narrow to allow him and Adela to
breach the pilot house shoulder to shoulder. If a shooter was hiding
against the back wall and Tyler chose wrong, he was dead.

Operating entirely on instinct, Tyler rounded the corner and
cleared right. Behind him, he felt Adela breach and clear left.

"Clear," he barked, finding his corner vacant.

"Clear," she echoed.

Above, he heard footsteps through the deck in the skylounge cabin.
He sidestepped left and sighted up the stairwell that led from the pilot
house to the upper level.

"Upper level, clear," Ben shouted, his voice reverberating down the
narrow staircase.

Only then did Tyler give his burning quads a respite and allow
himself to straighten as he turned to scan the yacht's control panel.

"What the fuck?" Adela asked, glancing at him before taking a
knee to cover their six and sight down the main passage they'd just
traversed. "Is the boat on automatic pilot?"

"Looks that way," Tyler said, scanning the fancy, high-tech control
station.

"We still need to clear the engine room," she said. It was located on
the deck below them.

"I know," he said. "Maybe our martyrs are down there with the
bomb?"

Tyler checked the countdown timer on his watch: 01:32

Shit, we've burned a ton of time.

"Five, sitrep?" he shouted up the stairs.

"Think I found the nukes," Ben called back. "You might want to
get your ass up here."

"Want me to clear the engine room?" Adela said.

"Not alone," Tyler said and headed for the stairs. "I think it's empty, but in case I'm wrong, stay right where you are. Access is via that closed door on the starboard side. To get to us, they'll have to come through you."

"Check," she said.

He took the stairs two at a time to the skylounge level, which was comprised of a master bedroom suite forward and a partially covered, open-air party deck aft. Ben stood next to the king bed in the suite. He'd taken the mattress off and propped it against the bulkhead. Inside the bed frame were three conical-shaped warheads that appeared to be daisy-chained together. A wire led from the last in line to a detonator box that displayed a countdown in a red LED window: 01:57

Tyler checked his watch, confirming they were one minute offset from the bomb's countdown timer.

00:56

"Looks like Stan's MIRV theory was right. Those look similar to the pictures he showed us of the W88—" Tyler said, then abruptly looked up from the cone-shaped nukes to scan the bedroom. "Where is Stan, by the way?"

"He landed in the water," Ben said with a chuckle. "Figured there was no point in trying to fish him out. When I looked back, he was already five yards in our wake."

Tyler shook his head. "Nice one, Jimmy."

Ben stepped inside the bed frame and took a knee beside the hardware.

"Careful, dude, we don't want to set this thing off early," Tyler said, resisting the instinctive but pointless compulsion to take a step backward.

"Don't worry, I ain't touching shit."

"Did you do your thing and get mental images of all this?" Tyler said, gesturing to the setup.

"I got the layout and the wiring, but I'm the pattern guy, remember? The writing is all in Russian. I could really use Adela to back me up. She's the human camera."

"Adela, get your ass up here ASAP!" Tyler shouted.

His watch chimed with the thirty-second alert.

Footsteps pounded in the stairway as she sprinted up to join them. "Where's Stan?" she said.

"No time. We need you to take mental snapshots of all this. Especially the Russian," Tyler said.

"On it." She stepped inside the bed frame to get a better look.

Tyler's watch chimed again. "Ten seconds."

She ignored him and craned her neck to look at the underside of one of the MIRVs. As Tyler watched her work, he said a little prayer they got what they needed while his subconscious silently counted down the final seconds.

Five . . . four . . . three . . . two . . . one.

CHAPTER 27

"How was your swim?" Tyler asked, clapping a hand on Stan's completely dry shoulder as they walked from their duct tape *X*s to the door.

"As much as I want to be pissed off about getting cheated out of the op," Stan said through a chuckle, "I can now say that I've done the backstroke in the Potomac while fully kitted-up."

"And, bonus, you don't even need to towel off."

"Did you guys find the payload?" Stan said, bringing the seriousness of their mission back into focus with the look in his eyes.

Ben stepped up beside them. "It was just like you predicted. Three Russian MIRVs daisy-chained together with a common detonator."

"Man, I wish I could have seen it," Stan said, shaking his head. "Talk about a once-in-a-lifetime opportunity."

"That's twisted, Stan. You know that, right?" Adela said as the locking mechanism shifted and the hatch popped open after equalizing pressure with the warehouse.

Tyler shoved the steel door open and led his fellow operators out, not surprised to find Moody waiting right outside with Zee and Martin in tow.

"So . . . ?" Zee demanded.

"You said you found it?" Moody followed on more gently.

Tyler nodded.

"It was on board just like we predicted. What we didn't find were any terrorists to help us link the attack to its source."

"The boat was either on some sort of programmed autopilot or, perhaps more likely, was being piloted remotely from elsewhere."

"Interesting; no martyrs aboard," Moody said with a nod.

"The technology to bring the boat to the detonation site on autopilot or remotely is both cheap and easy," Marty pointed out.

"We didn't get a full search of the boat, but if someone was aboard you'd think they'd have been at the helm, so that's the likely explanation," Tyler agreed. The big problem now was that they had no clues to follow back to the mastermind behind the nuclear attack. "Can we trace the source of the warheads involved? I mean, nuclear bombs don't go missing without some sort of trail."

"We'll get the IC working on that straightaway," Moody said before turning to Adela and Ben. "Can you reproduce a diagram of what you saw?"

"Yeah, for sure," Adela said. "With Ben's help especially, I think we can give you an exact picture of what we saw—even some serial numbers, though they were in Cyrillic."

"Good," Moody said with a nod. "It's a start . . . let me know as soon as you've got the details sorted. I'll be in my office."

Tyler watched him go and then followed his teammates into the Reconstruct Room. After shedding their kits, Ben, Adela, and Stan joined Martin to work on reproducing the bomb configuration. Worthless in that capacity, Tyler headed straight for the coffee service in the back of the room. He rarely drank coffee after lunch, but for some reason, he felt more tired than usual and needed a pick-me-up.

"Here, let me help you with that," Zee said, walking up to him as he tried to figure out how to work an espresso machine he'd never seen before.

"Thanks," he said. He gave his teammate a tight smile. "Sorry you had to stay behind."

"Yeah," Zee said with a nod, but her eyes suggested she had no regrets.

Tyler watched his colleagues working at the table while sipping at his coffee. He wanted to feel complete relief—hell, it looked like they'd just stopped a nuclear attack on the nation's capital—but for some reason, he still felt uneasy. He looked over at Zee who seemed to be studying him closely.

"I think once we get the case file updated in the system and Moody routes our findings to wherever the hell he routes them, we should jump to the Omega Room tonight and see if we changed the outcome," Zee said.

"You wanna know if we stopped it?"

"Yeah, I do."

"Because of your parents?" he asked, the words spilling out before he could stop himself.

"Sure," she said, "and the other million or more people who would also die in the attack." Her expression, however, did not suggest she was offended.

"I didn't mean . . ."

She smiled and squeezed his arm.

"I know, Ty," she said.

He looked at his watch—just past 6:30 p.m. He looked at the team sketching out what they'd seen and realized he had little to offer for the next few minutes.

"I'll be back," he said, and Zee smiled.

"Calling Harper?" she asked.

He nodded, not sure why the admission felt weird. He had always been a full-on or all-off-mission kind of guy. But he really wanted to reconnect with his little girl.

He left the Pepper Grinder and literally jogged back to the Salt Shaker, then moments later was in his room, his personal cell phone pressed to his ear.

"Daddy!" Harper squealed with delight from the speaker, and his eyes rimmed with guilty tears. He could see her in his mind, her rolling curls of reddish hair bounding around blue eyes. They had no idea where in the family tree the red hair came from—with Nikki's jet-black hair and his "boring brown" as his ex used to joke. He'd made the obligatory jokes about checking the mailman's hair color, but he loved those curls. Then his thoughts turned immediately to the kids his dead teammates had left behind and he said a short silent prayer of thanks that he was here, despite the guilt that made him feel.

"Hey, Peanut! How are you!"

"Daddy, some of your friends got hurt real bad," Harper said.

He squeezed his eyes shut and tears spilled onto his cheeks.

"I know, Peanut. Riley's daddy was one of them. I'm so sorry."

"Daddy, did you get hurt?" Harper's voice was full of worry.

"No, baby. Daddy is just fine. And I'm not in the place where the war is anymore, so I'm safe." That was a lie of sorts, he supposed, but one that was innocent enough. "And I think I get to see you really soon, okay?"

"Yay!" she screamed and then her voice got softer as she shouted to Nikki. "Mommy, Daddy says he's gonna come and see me really soon!" He grimaced, remembering Nikki's warnings about getting up any false hopes in their daughter. "Promise, Daddy?"

"I do, Peanut. I don't know exactly when yet, but real soon, okay? And I'll call you a lot more this week—I promise that too, okay?"

"Okay."

He glanced at his watch. A few more minutes wouldn't hurt.

"Tell me what you did today at Grandma's house."

She did, and he closed his eyes, picturing the fun she described and wrestling with the overwhelming need to see her and hug her. He would give anything in the world to cuddle her to sleep . . ."

When she finished, he said, "That sounds so awesome, Peanut. Daddy's gonna go get some work done, but I'll talk to you tomorrow if I can and see you really soon."

"Okay, Daddy. Bye."

"I love you," he added, but the line had gone dead and he wasn't sure if she'd heard.

Tyler wiped the tears from his cheeks with his sleeve and then did a couple of quick stretches, rolling his hips clockwise, then counterclockwise. Then, he headed back to the Pepper Grinder to rejoin the team in the Reconstruct Room.

When he arrived, Moody was there talking with Zee.

"There you are," Moody said, smiling at him.

"Any developments?" he asked, looking from Moody to Zee.

"The yacht belongs to a Russian oligarch named Mikhail Smolensky. The most recent maritime AIS data is that it's moored at Gurney's Star Island Marina in Montauk," she said.

"And before that?"

"It departed Gdańsk three weeks ago. Stopped in Plymouth, crossed the Atlantic to St. John's, then made its way down the coast."

"Is the oligarch—what's his name . . . Smolensky—on it?"

"We don't think so, but his name is definitely going into HAL," Zee said.

"Obviously he's Russian, so that could explain a connection to the Russian military or an underground arms trafficking network."

"Hopefully our partner agencies can sort all that out over the next two weeks once we put them on the scent," Moody said. "As for us, Zee proposed jumping to check the future after we finish updating the Ares case file and I route the intel. I suggested Cheyenne Mountain, but she said that the consensus—and I guess I'm not surprised to hear it—would be for the team to jump back to the Omega Room."

"That makes the most sense to me too," he said, nodding to Zee.

"Keep in mind, if the intelligence we collected fails to alter the timeline, then a jump to the Omega Room will not give us any intel, and you'll have to make another jump to NORAD," Moody said and pressed his lips into a line.

"We know," Tyler said. He glanced at Adela, who'd been listening. She mouthed, *Thank you.* He smiled and gave her a nod.

"In that case, we don't need to send everybody," Moody said. "We can split the team and give some of you a rest."

Ben laughed. "Jumping in time ain't like jumping out of an airplane, boss. It's not tiring. You blink and it's over."

Moody hesitated a moment, and Tyler could see he was thinking about whether to split the team regardless. Before that could happen, Tyler said, "Assuming we did stop it, if we all jump we can get a head start on the next threat. Plus, even if NCTC stops the bomb, there weren't any terrorists on that boat. We still need to find the group responsible and figure out how, if this wasn't Russia, some assholes got their hands on Russian nuclear warheads."

Moody nodded. "Both good points. Okay, the team can jump. Are you sure you don't want to get a good night's sleep first and jump in the morning?"

"Hell no," Stan said. "I want another beer and pizza party if we stop this threat."

Moody grinned. "Beer and pizza in exchange for saving a million lives and stopping World War III . . . I think the President would be happy to cover that tab."

CHAPTER 28

HAMPTON INN VIRGINIA BEACH-OCEANFRONT SOUTH
VIRGINIA BEACH, VIRGINIA
1922 LOCAL TIME

Jun sat on the little balcony of his hotel room and stared at the moonlit Atlantic. The ocean-view rooms faced east, obviously, so no watching the sunset over the beach, but he didn't care. He liked smelling the salty sea breeze and hearing the sound of the waves breaking on the shore. Chengdu, where he'd grown up in China, was located over a thousand kilometers from the ocean. His parents had been poor, so as children he and Guo never traveled to a beach. Over the last several days, he'd had plenty of time to watch all kinds of families and children playing in the sand and surf.

It made him feel jealous and spiteful and cheated . . . cheated of an experience and of memories with his brother he wished he'd had. Should have had. None of that was Tyler Brooks's fault. Their childhood poverty and paternal abandonment happened two decades before his brother was murdered. There was no logical or sane reason to blame the American SEAL for such things, but Jun had decided to anyway. His heart had lumped all the pain, disappointment, and loss he'd experienced over the whole of his life and put it onto this one adversary. It just made it easier that way.

And when he killed the man's blameless wife and took his innocent daughter, Jun would be paying the world back for everything he'd been made to suffer.

He felt lucky that his desire for revenge, no matter how irrational, aligned with the mission of the men he worked with. They were convinced that so long as Tyler Brooks and the new American team were in play, they would continue to fail in their plan to bring about a new world order. Frankly, Jun cared little about this new power structure. He was a warrior, and though he'd chosen his new leadership carefully when he'd left China and taken his skill set on the road, in the end he cared very little for politics. He'd been bred in the Chinese military to view America as the enemy, and maybe they were, but for him it had always been more about finding a home—and a family—with his various combat teams. Bringing the world to the brink of a global nuclear holocaust seemed an insanely risky way for his new bosses to rise to power, but so be it.

And now, Hoffman's tasking intersected perfectly with his carnal desire to share his pain and suffering with United States Navy SEAL Chief Tyler Brooks.

He gave a little cough which made his neck and back hurt.

He was starting to believe he was unlikely to live long enough to see whether the master plan worked and the new world order came to be. He realized he might just be fine with that, with his brother gone . . .

Jun's satellite phone vibrated on the metal table next to his chair.

He answered it without checking the caller ID. Only one person in the world would call this number.

"Hello," he said.

"The next change event has happened," Hoffman said, his voice ripe with aggravation.

"Did they interfere again?"

"Yes. You have the green light for the operation. The recon team has determined the optimal window for your mission success is outside the woman's home as she's leaving for work in the morning. Precise chronology to follow in an encrypted message."

"Understood," Jun said. Then he asked something he'd never asked Hoffman before. "If Omega attempts an intervention, will you notify us?"

"Why would you ask such a question when the answer is obvious? If *you* do not prevail, then *I* do not prevail."

Jun considered telling Hoffman about his plan to use the daughter as bait to lure the American team into an abandoned warehouse. With the little girl and her mother chained to a girder in the middle of the warehouse floor and Jun's teammates positioned in hides along the perimeter, he would create an inescapable kill box. His desire to share details was hubris—or maybe just a passion to hear it said out loud. He intended for the American to watch his family die. He didn't think Hoffman would care one way or the other, so long as he killed Brooks and his team, but why take the risk? And . . . there was still the odd sense that informing the universe of his plan somehow made it harder to bring it into reality. That was madness of course, but still, why take that risk? He was pretty sure that *thinking* his plan didn't inform the universe of anything, but if he spoke it, especially to someone else, then might Time take notice?

"I've sent you reinforcements. They should arrive by midnight," Hoffman said. "Four shooters to augment your team. Do with them as you see fit. I will not hold you responsible for their safe return. They are competent gunmen, but they failed jump screening for various reasons. Consider them expendable."

"Thank you, Herr Hoffman," Jun said, surprised by this unexpected gift.

The line went dead.

With a smile on his face, Jun slid the little side table around to serve as a footrest and propped his feet up on it. Listening to the heartbeat of the ocean below, he closed his eyes and let his mind transport him to the warehouse, imagining the battle to come and savoring his sweet revenge.

CHAPTER 29

Tyler tipped his can of hazy IPA and took a long swig before lowering it from his lips. He'd not had this kind of beer before—M-43 it was called—but it tasted pretty good. Stan had complained that a hazy IPA was a summer beer and shouldn't be drunk in November, but Tyler thought that was bunk. As far as he was concerned, the only thing that determined when a beer should or shouldn't be drank wasn't the temperature outside, but rather the temperature of the stuff inside the can.

If it's cold, it's drinkable, he thought. *If it's warm, it's not.*

He scanned the room, taking in the familiar vibe of post-mission celebration he'd experienced many times before, and his entire team seemed very much in the moment.

"That hits the spot," he announced after a second swig of beer. "Ice-cold beer and pizza—there's nothing like it."

"Actually," Stan began, eliciting a collective but now good-natured groan from the room, "IPA should ideally be consumed at the temperature at which it's fermented—close to room temperature—whereas lagers are best consumed cold."

There was silence for a moment as Stan searched the room for a sympathetic face, then laughter as the entire team threw napkins, pizza crusts, and one empty red Solo cup his way. The Delta operator laughed along with them.

"All right, all right. I forgot you Neanderthals don't like to learn new things . . ."

This comment brought a fresh torrent of comedic abuse from everyone, which made Tyler grin and accept that all was right with the world.

Tonight's celebration of beer and pizza technically violated Tyler's "treat my body as a temple" policy that he lived by at the JSOC, but he wasn't such a lame ass that he wouldn't make exceptions to celebrate a win. And lately, strangely, he'd been finding his willpower more eroded than ever before—with his body craving coffee, junk food, and yes, even beer.

Weird, he thought, but he smiled and decided to let himself enjoy both the gluttony and his buzz while it lasted.

After all, they deserved it. The early evening jump to the Omega Room had been a tremendous win. Thanks to Alpha Team's intel, a future joint interagency task force led by NCTC had intercepted the nukes and stopped the attack before it could happen. Twenty-eight days from now, Washington, DC, was no longer a smoldering, post-apocalyptic hellscape.

Actually, it never was a smoldering, postapocalyptic hellscape, a superior sounding voice said in his mind, correcting his internal monologue, *because the future we observed had yet to happen.*

He shook his head.

Oh, dear God, Stan is in my head now.

"I'm hitting the cooler for a fresh beer. Can I get you one?" Ben said, pushing himself up from the sofa with the aid of the armrest. Tyler heard a *pop* and Ben grabbed his right shoulder with his left hand. "Ow, shit."

"What was that?" Tyler said with a laugh as he kicked his booted feet onto the makeshift coffee table and crossed them at the ankles.

"Ah, nothing," Ben said, waving it away. "I injured that shoulder a couple of years ago during an infil. Hollers at me now and again."

"You're gettin' old, dude," Tyler said as the medic fished another beer from the cooler beside the table.

"Nah," Ben said and curled his bicep. "I'm in my prime."

Tyler looked to where Stan was talking with Adela.

"Actually . . . that's not true . . ." Stan began, responding to something she'd said. Tyler watched her roll her eyes, but he also thought he saw the corners of her lips curl into something almost resembling a smile.

They were bonding—the team had finally gelled. . .

And the smile from Adela was reassuring. She'd powered through, but the memory of exploding the young airman in Cheyenne Mountain was surely still fresh for her.

With a smile on his own face, Tyler's gaze tracked to Zee and Martin, who were sitting by themselves at a card table, having a discussion that looked somewhat intense. They both wore serious expressions and neither one was drinking a beer. Tyler's smile faded as he watched, and his thoughts drifted back to the collective euphoria the team had experienced when they'd arrived in the Omega Room to find it powered up, with CNN and BBC streaming normal news on the TVs. They'd all cheered, and he distinctly remembered high-fiving Zee—but sometime after that, her mood had soured. He'd noticed it at the time but chalked it up to her aversion to traveling. Watching her now, he suspected it was something else.

She must have felt his eyes on her because she turned and met his gaze.

He raised an eyebrow in the universal "What's up?" face.

She shook her head and waved him over.

Tyler nodded and scooted forward on the sofa. As he pressed to his feet, his back twinged in the same spot as before. He winced and arched as his muscles, or maybe his spine, locked up for a split second.

"I heard that old man grunt," Ben said through a laugh, handing him a fresh beer. "Don't even try to deny it, bro."

Tyler gave Ben a half smile, took the beer, and made his way over to Zee and Martin at the card table.

"Talk to you outside?" she asked. "It's um"—she looked at Marty—"personal."

"Okay," he said and followed the two out of the room, down the long hall, and out to the courtyard between the Salt Shaker and the Pepper Grinder.

"Everything okay?" he asked, looking mostly at Marty, who shrugged.

"I wanted to get outside. I think they listen and record everything we say inside, Ty . . ."

"Okaaay," he dragged out, worried now.

"Tyler, do you remember the other day when Martin wrote a new subroutine for HAL so the program would automatically find and collate future data based on keywords and case-specific details?"

"Yeah, I remember. I thought that was brilliant, Marty." Tyler lifted his beer to the kid.

"Okay, well, here's the thing. When he was in the program he— You know what, why don't I just let him explain it," Zee said and turned to Marty.

Martin tucked a strand of his long dark hair behind his ear and, not making eye contact with Tyler, said, "While I was coding my new subroutine, I discovered another similar subroutine already present that aggregates data for manually entered keywords, but the results are not automatically displayed on any of the terminals in the Omega Room. With everything going on, I didn't really give it much thought, but now it's really bothering me."

"I don't understand. Explain what's bothering you."

"Well, the data is hidden. To access it you have to (a) know where to look and (b) know the password."

"Well, what's the point of that? We only have four minutes. Why hide it and make it password-protected?"

"Exactly my point," Martin said.

"Because it's future data that Moody doesn't want us to see," Zee said.

Tyler screwed up his face. "But it's future data, so if we don't look at it, nobody will know what it is. I guess I don't understand . . . Whoa, hold on—are you saying that Moody somehow has access to the Omega Room's future data here in the present?"

"No," Martin said, his voice a whisper now. "But he has access to it in the future. The data is collating in this subroutine . . ."

"How do we know it's Moody?"

"Who else would it be?" Marty said, tilting his head.

"Wait, we're the only ones who travel so where did he get the data?" Tyler said.

Martin and Zee looked at each other.

"Remember, Moody admitted on our first day that he's personally traveled to the future. Zee was of the opinion he said it to reassure us that time travel was safe, but I hacked into the jump logs and confirmed it's true. But while I was in there, I found something else . . . Moody has made one jump to the Omega Room since we arrived."

Hot anger surged in Tyler's chest, which Zee must have immediately picked up on. She laid her hand on his and gave it a brief squeeze.

"When did he jump?" Tyler asked through gritted teeth.

"At two in the morning, the night after the four of you jumped to the dark Omega Room and saw that DC had been nuked."

"I bet I can guess where he went—"

"He traveled to the Omega Room, same future date, but ten minutes after your jump," Zee said, confirming Tyler's hunch.

Tyler nodded, his anger ebbing a bit. "Okay, so he must have been double-checking we weren't fucking with him and that DC really had been nuked before he reported it to the President—a trust but verify sort of thing?"

"But that's not all," Zee said, "and this is the part where I need you to promise to take a deep breath and not lose your cool."

He felt his chest get tight at the comment and dreaded what was coming next. "I promise . . ."

"On our last jump, Martin accessed Moody's cache of hidden data, and the data being aggregated pertains to us."

Tyler exhaled through his nose and thought back to the conversation he'd had with Zee in his stateroom about the UNAUTH policy and Moody asking her to be his spy on the team. "That certainly adds some context to our conversation the other night."

Zee nodded, but the grave look on her face told him she wasn't finished.

"You saw something, didn't you?" Tyler asked. He looked at Martin, who wouldn't meet his eyes. "Something you weren't supposed to see. Something bad."

She reached out and took his hand again, but this time she didn't let go. "Ty, I don't know how to say this other than to just say it. In three days, Nikki and Harper are going to be targeted."

The comment knocked him senseless. "Targeted? What exactly do you mean by *targeted*?"

"There's a carjacking in Virginia Beach. Nikki and Harper are kidnapped."

Tyler stood stunned, unable to move or think or even breathe. Then, he charged toward the door to the Pepper Grinder, just as the rest of the team walked out of the Salt Shaker and into the courtyard.

"What're you guys up to out here?" Stan asked.

"I'm going to murder him for hiding this from us," Tyler barked, still stomping toward the door.

"Whoa, whoa, cowboy," Ben said, sprinting forward and intercepting Tyler with a hand to the chest. "What the hell is going on? Who's keeping stuff from us?"

"Tyler, there's a very good chance Moody doesn't even know about it yet," Zee called. "Remember, the Omega Room has been dark, and we only just changed the future."

Stan and Adela jogged over to where Tyler was fuming, pacing short steps back and forth.

"What's going on?" Stan asked.

"Tell them," Tyler said through gritted teeth. "They deserve to know."

Zee nodded and did just that, telling the others about the hidden future data files Martin had found while Tyler was forced to listen a second time to the news that his wife—*ex-wife*—and daughter were going to be kidnapped.

"Why the hell would Moody keep that from us?" Adela demanded. "We risked everything for this project, personally and professionally. What the fuck is he thinking?"

"It's the damn UNAUTH policy," Stan said. "Moody warned us that future knowledge pertaining to personnel matters was forbidden. Maybe this is him making good on that promise."

"We don't know definitively whether Moody planned to tell Tyler or not," Ben said. "I for one think Moody deserves the benefit of the doubt on the matter. What I'm more interested in knowing is who is targeting Ty's family and why."

"Well, his previous billet was at JSOC. Just weeks ago, he was a team leader at the Tier One. Every asshole terrorist in the world is searching for guys like Ty. It's certainly possible this is related to, or retaliation for, everything that went down during the Mali op," Stan said.

With his emotions out of control, Tyler hadn't thought about that.

Adela, who had become eerily calm, said, "I don't buy it."

"Why not?"

"Because terrorists in Mali don't have what it takes to pierce the JSOC veil. I know these groups. They're getting smarter, but they're not *that* smart. No way a bunch of jihadists in Africa hacked into the JSOC personnel records. The coincidence is too strong to ignore." She shifted her gaze to Martin and narrowed her eyes. "Martin, was the file you found on Tyler's family a duplicate record of the event?"

"What do you mean *duplicate record*?" Martin asked.

"I mean did this get flagged in the previous timeline and flagged again after our yacht intervention, or did it only get flagged by HAL after the jump onto the yacht?"

"It only appeared after," Martin said.

"Then, the future where Tyler's family is targeted only manifests *after* we stopped the attack on DC. There's no way that's random. I think whoever is responsible for planning the DC attack is going after Tyler's family as retribution," Adela said definitively.

"But the attack isn't thwarted by the NCTC joint task force for another two weeks," Ben said, and his eyes went wide with what looked like epiphany. "Shit . . . that means they know *when* and *where* we're traveling."

"Not necessary," Stan said. "If we're compromised from the inside, someone could leak our future findings to the enemy as we discover them. It's the future knowledge our adversary desperately wants. Once they have the same information as us, our advantage is lost, parity is reestablished, and the next chess move can be made."

"Exactly. It's basically the same intelligence/counterintelligence game the IC plays every day," Adela said. "Hell, the same game we've all been part of for years. We're trying to figure out the other guy's plans, they're trying to figure out ours, and both sides are trying to figure out what the other side knows and when and how they know it."

"If this task force is compromised and our identities have been leaked, then each and every one of us could be targeted," Tyler said.

"But we never leave the compound, except to travel to the future," Ben said.

"Which is exactly why Tyler's family had been targeted," Adela said. "This is a secure compound. To kill us they need a way to lure us out. Kidnapping the team leader's wife and daughter seems like a damn effective way to do just that."

"Or to blackmail him into cooperation or standing down . . ." Zee said, her gaze going to the middle distance for a second before snapping back. "Not that Ty would ever do that."

He nodded but wondered. What would he do to save his family? What would he not do to keep his baby girl safe from this trauma?

"So, what do we do?" Ben said.

"We confront Moody," Tyler said. "Then we haul ass and rescue my family."

CHAPTER 30

Moody kept his face neutral, his eyes sympathetic, and he let Tyler vent his anger, the rest of the team in a half circle behind him, arms crossed, except for Marty who had his hands in his pockets. They'd come as a group to confront him about his secret UNAUTH collection program. He'd anticipated this scenario when he'd given Martin Back clearance to write the new subroutine for HAL, but he'd only given this outcome one-in-five odds . . . a safe gamble when the alternative would be having to defend what would otherwise be an illogical denial to the rest of Omega Team. According to Martin's psychological profile, the boy genius—who had several markers indicative of Asperger's—was a rule follower. On a one-hundred-point scale, Martin rated a very low twenty-one for Risk Tolerance and fourteen for Anarchic Tendencies. Still, Moody knew better than to underestimate the impact that being part of a team—especially a dynamic team with a charismatic leader—could have.

Oh well, he thought to himself while Tyler read him the riot act.

That's the thing about people . . . just when I think I've got them all figured out, one goes off script and surprises me.

"Well, are you going to say something or not, Pat?" Tyler said, practically breathless.

Moody really hated being ambushed, but he had developed plenty of techniques to defuse situations like this over the years. Most of the time, angry people simply want to be heard and receive an apology for the perceived slight. He would start there.

"First off, let me just say that I hear you. All the points you've made are one hundred percent valid," he said, sweeping his gaze across the angry faces of the Omega team. "And second, I owe you an apology for breaching your trust . . ."

"I sense a *but* coming," Adela said behind crossed arms.

He gave her a tight smile. Always pragmatic and always to the point. She'd been the one to tell him her recruitment to the task force was a disappointment on the very first day.

He smiled. "You're right, there is a *but*. And to understand it, you have to put yourselves in my shoes as the program director. Without an UNAUTH policy, the potential for this program to go quickly off the rails is very real. The temptation for those with access to future information to seek answers about their own fate, and the fate of their loved ones, is tremendous. Our job is to safeguard the future of this nation—not to pursue personal agendas, enrichment, or harvest information to change the future for other ends."

"I see. It's not okay for us, but it's okay for you," Adela said with judgment.

"Martin, was my name included in the subroutine search pattern?" Moody said with heat, snapping his gaze from Adela to Martin.

"No," Martin said.

"Did you see any keywords or other search criteria that raised red flags about me seeking information for personal gain or an agenda outside the charter of this program?"

"No."

He looked at Adela, then swept his gaze across the team as he spoke.

"More than anyone in this task force, I understand the dangers and the power of future knowledge. As program director, it's my burden to bear and a weight that I, and I alone, volunteered to carry."

Tyler narrowed his eyes.

"How noble," the SEAL said, and Moody knew exactly what was coming next. "Then answer me this one final question: Were you planning to tell me about Nikki and Harper, or were you going to let them be taken, traumatized, and potentially murdered? I advise you to be honest because I'll know if you're lying."

Moody held Tyler's stare, and the answer he gave was the truth, never mind a few strategic omissions. "As you pointed out, I've only made one validation jump since your arrival, and it was to a dark, post-strike Omega Room. I didn't know about the future carjacking and kidnapping until just now, when you told me, but the moment I discovered it, yes, I would have told you."

"Are you going to stop me from intervening to save them?"

"Of course not, I'm not that heartless," Moody said, leaving out the part that preventing Tyler from doing so would fracture the team and certainly cost him a natural-born leader and gifted operator. He watched the muscles in Tyler's neck instantly relax at this statement.

"I need to move them somewhere safe," Tyler said, and Moody could see he was working out the plan in real time as he spoke. "Somewhere off-the-grid where the people we're up against can't find them. It needs to happen tonight so there's no time for our adversary to adjust their timeline."

"I can certainly help with that, I have contacts—"

"No," Tyler said, cutting him off. "Clearly, Omega is compromised. It could be a mole, an electronic breach, or, hell, maybe even both—but until we've found and neutralized the leak, I won't risk it. I'll take the lead on making sure my family is safe. The only people I trust are gathered in this room."

Based on Tyler's glare, Moody realized he was probably not included on that list.

A short-term stumbling block, but I can get the trust back . . .

"How long are you planning to be out of pocket? I can only afford you gone for a short time before it impacts our readiness," Moody said, as gently as possible.

"Not long. I just need to deliver Nikki and Harper to someone I trust who can handle the rest," Tyler said and turned to his teammates. "My plan is to kit up, take an up-armored Suburban, and leave in thirty. I can't order any of you guys to come, but I would certainly welcome all the backup I can get."

"Dude, of course I'm coming," Ben said and clapped a hand on the SEAL's shoulder.

"Count me in," Adela said.

"Me too," Stan and Zee said at the same time.

"I'm not sure how I'll be any help, but I'll go, if you want me to," Martin said.

Tyler fixed them with a tight-lipped smile. "Thanks, guys. That means everything to me."

"If I may offer an alternate plan for consideration," Moody said, testing the waters. "We could conduct a reconnaissance jump to observe the kidnapping event."

"That's a good idea," Adela said. "It would potentially allow us to ID the kidnappers. As soon as we show up tonight to relocate the girls, the future changes and we lose the opportunity. We'd need to do it now, before we intervene in the present."

"Absolutely not," Tyler said. "I'm not willing to put Nikki and Harper at risk so we can *maybe* ID the hit squad."

"Dude, I totally get it, but that's not what they're suggesting," Ben said. "We're not going to actually wait for the kidnapping to observe them, we're going to jump to the scene. That's three days from now, remember. We're going to change that timeline before it happens. Nikki and Harper are not going to be in any *actual* danger."

"No, I get what they're saying, but you guys don't get what *I'm* saying," Tyler said. "Why would I let my wife and daughter kidnapped in any timeline? It's sadistic and horrific."

"Tyler," Zee said and put a hand on his shoulder, "it's like the nuclear attack we just stopped. Once we intervene, it's never going to happen, but we have a chance to learn something important that could help us stop other future threats to our team and extended family of loved ones. What if these guys decide to target my parents next? See where I'm going with this?"

Moody loved how this was playing out. He'd floated the idea and now the others were doing the hard work of convincing Tyler for him. Six versus one was so much easier than one versus six.

"Fine," Tyler said with a grudging scowl, "but only because I think you're right about them picking a new target if Nikki and Harper are no longer an option."

"I know it's going to be hard to watch," Zee said, "but remember, it's not real."

Tyler nodded but didn't say anything else.

"Then it's decided," Moody said and got to his feet. "I'll mobilize the control room team while you guys kit up to jump. Let's shoot for a departure time of 2215."

Once everyone had left his office, Moody shut the door and locked it. He walked back to his desk and retrieved the encrypted satellite phone from his center desk drawer and dialed General Waltrip.

The general answered on the second ring. "It's after hours, Pat, is there a problem?"

"Yeah, I'd say there's a fucking problem," Moody said his blood pressure rising. "Omega is compromised . . ."

CHAPTER 31

THE FUTURE
VIRGINIA BEACH, VIRGINIA
0802 FUTURE TIME

Tyler blinked and he was standing on the sidewalk one block to the north and on the opposite side of the street from Nikki's house. Adela, who had landed close to Tyler, quickly oriented herself and fell in stride beside him, chatting away. They were dressed in sweatpants, zip-front hoodies, and cross-trainers—just a young couple out for a morning walk. Ben and Zee were supposed to be dropped in a mirror-image arrangement a block to the south, and Stan and Martin should have landed in the narrow side yard separating Nikki's house and her closest neighbor. For this mission, they would be three surveillance pairs, in three different locations, with three different angles to observe the event.

Hopefully, it was enough.

Tyler scanned the street in both directions, struggling to look like a casual couple out for a walk, and realized it may well have been a mistake for him to jump. Zee was right—even the thought of watching Harper cry in terror as they took her felt more than he could bear. He didn't have a photographic memory like the others, nor could he stop what was about to happen—not in the future anyway—so why put himself through the psychological trauma of watching it? But another part of him wanted to be here . . . wanted to see the evil bastards who would dare target his family. Also, as team leader for Omega's direct-action operators, the SEAL in him was incapable of sitting out a mission unless he was physically incapacitated or ordered to do so.

Trying to conduct traditional ISR during a jump was complicated and difficult. Normally for a situation like this, a team would position hours in advance either inside a building across the street or in an unmarked surveillance vehicle parked with an unobstructed vantage point of the scene. They'd have comms, cameras, a parabolic mike, and some sort of aerial surveillance, such as a dedicated satellite or drone. But Omega didn't have hours in the future to prep and position. They had four minutes, the clothes on their backs, and nothing but their eyes, ears, and minds to document what happened.

The rules of engagement of the op were simple and nonnegotiable. Moody had been explicit—*observation only.* Engaging the hit squad under any circumstance was not permitted. Consequently, none of the team was kitted-up. Everyone, even Marty this time, carried pistols concealed in shoulder holsters under their clothing, but only for self-defense. Tyler felt more anxious now than he remembered being for his first op as a newly minted SEAL, fresh out of SQT. His heart rate seemed uncharacteristically elevated, and he felt a dribble of cold sweat snake from his armpit over his ribs.

Keep it together, dude, he told himself. *It's no different than a bad dream. This is never going to happen.*

But was that really true? Because it *was* going to happen, in the future he now found himself in. In a minute he would see a very real Nikki and Harper taken by very real and very bad people.

He forced himself through a series of four-count tactical breathing to bring his pulse rate back down.

Fifty yards from the house, he saw the garage door begin to rumble open. The undersized garage was so full of junk—most of it his stuff undoubtedly—that there wasn't room for Nikki to park her white Nissan Rogue inside. So, she had it parked in the short driveway, nose out.

Just like I taught her. You never know when you might have to jam . . .

His heart melted as he watched Nikki lead Harper out of the garage. They held hands and Harper carried a little round backpack that looked like a panda bear. Her cute red curls bounced as she walked, and he thought how much longer her hair had grown. They used to worry her hair would *never* grow out, but that seemed to have changed. He heard his ex-wife giggle at something his daughter said, as she used her free hand to ruffle those curls.

As he continued to close range, he watched with no small amount of loving regret and divorced dad angst as Nikki opened the rear door and loaded Harper into her car seat. They appeared to have some playful ritual they did because both mother and daughter giggled as Nikki tickled Harper after she was strapped in and unable to squirm away.

In his peripheral vision, he saw Adela sneak a glance over her shoulder. At the same time, he registered the distinctive roar of heavy SUV tires on asphalt closing at high speed.

"Here they come," she said.

His watch chimed.

One minute . . .

Tyler reflexively reached to pull his pistol, but Adela stopped him. "Don't," she snapped, catching his right hand in midflight.

The compulsion to jerk his weapon and empty the magazine into the SUV tearing toward his family was so overpowering that it took every fiber of his being to resist. He wasn't sure which, but fate or God stayed his hand as a silver Ford Explorer ran over the curb and skidded to a hard stop directly in front of Nikki's Rogue, stopping so close that it blocked any chance of escape. The driver remained behind the wheel while two men leaped out of the back seat and assaulted the Nissan. He watched his wife—tough as nails—slam the door shut and move to lock it, but the bigger of the two men already had the rear door open and grabbed Harper while the other went for Nikki.

Time ground to a halt as Tyler watched the smaller man drag Nikki onto the driveway by her hair. She screamed, writhing and clutching his wrist to free herself. He kicked the back of her legs, sending her to her knees on the concrete in front of him.

Tyler felt Adela guiding him toward the shadows of the neighbor's front yard, angling for a better look at the faces of the men assaulting his family.

Then the screams of his baby girl reached him, and everything changed.

"Mommy, help me!" Harper cried.

The bearded man, who was carrying Harper like a loaf of bread tucked under his right arm, locked eyes with Tyler as he rounded the rear bumper of the Explorer.

I think I've seen that motherfucker . . .

He moved without conscious thought, the pistol in his hand reflexively, driven now as a protector rather than an operator. He surged forward, aiming carefully, barely aware of Adela yelling for him to stop. He squeezed the trigger. The kidnapper's head gave up a puff of gore before he fell, and Harper fell with him, still screaming. But she landed somehow on her feet and looked from the dead man to Tyler.

"Daddy?" Harper said, eyes flashing with recognition, and she ran toward him.

Gunfire erupted from the Explorer as the driver open fired. Tyler dropped low, still surging forward and looking for an angle on the shooter as he vectored to intercept and protect Harper.

Then he heard Adela shout, "Oh, shit!" from somewhere behind him and he knew.

He shifted his gaze from the Explore to where Nikki was being held hostage. Tyler locked eyes with the dark irises of the Asian man who raised a claw-shaped blade to his ex-wife's throat.

The man smiled.

Tyler's chest tightened and he watched helplessly as the man laughed, then stroked the blade from left to right, opening a gaping hole in the throat of the only woman Tyler had ever truly loved, painting a swath of crimson on her yellow sweater as her eyes widened in terror.

The killer pointed his blade directly at Tyler and smiled.

Tyler vomited bile into his mouth.

His watch chimed.

"Mommy, nooooo!" Harper screamed.

A flash and crack from the Ford told him that the driver was firing at him, but he kept his focus on the knife wielding killer. Nikki dropped, lifeless, to the pavement as he centered his iron sights on the man's chest and squeezed—

But the bullets ricocheted off the walls inside the Donut with deafening effect as the slugs he'd fired in the future returned to the present with velocity and a vengeance.

"Hit the deck," he barked, but everyone already had . . . except for Martin who was already crouched with his hands pressed over his ears. When the Donut fell silent, Tyler said, "Alpha, sitrep?"

"Two is freaked out, but uninjured," Zee called.

"Three is intact," Stan said.

"Four is intact, but all kinds of pissed off," Ben said. "What were you thinking?"

"He wasn't," Adela said as she reached up to feel her right ear. Then, after inspecting her bloody fingers, added, "Five is shot in the ear. Thanks a lot, Brooks."

He rushed to Adela, but he didn't hear Martin sound off. "Ben, check Marty."

"How bad is it?" Adela asked and turned her head so the injured ear faced Tyler.

"Lost a chunk about this big," he said and showed her the very end of his pinky finger.

"Six is intact, but he's not a happy camper," Ben called from where he knelt beside a trembling Martin.

Behind Tyler, the locking ring shifted and the door hissed.

"That was fucking stupid," Adela said, wagging a finger at him. "You're lucky none of us were killed by those assholes—or by you firing when we jumped."

"I know, I'm sorry," he said. "I didn't think about the round coming back with us."

"No, you didn't *think*, period," she said, glaring at him.

"You're right, I screwed up. It will never happen again," he said.

But his mind was churning with images of his daughter's terrified face and the sight of his ex-wife with her throat splayed open in front of their little girl. He squeezed his eyes shut and tears spilled onto his cheeks.

Adela's expression softened, and she put a hand on his shoulder. "But . . . if I'd been in your shoes, I imagine I would have done the exact same thing."

"I'm sorry about your ear."

"Could have been worse . . . Could have hit me between the eyes," she said with a shrug. Then the right corner of her mouth curled into a crooked grin. "Anyway, now every time I look in the mirror, I'll be reminded of what a dumbass you are."

Tyler chuckled, appreciating the hell out of Adela in that moment before his mood did a U-turn back to serious. "Did you get a good look at those guys from your vantage point?"

She nodded. "Oh yeah. If I could push Print and shit a Polaroid out of my ass right now, I would. But don't worry, I'll work with Ben and Marty on it. I'm sure there's some AI generator we can use to create images good enough to run through the facial rec libraries."

"Thanks, Adela."

"Of course."

What Tyler didn't tell her was that he thought he recognized one of the attackers. It had only been a split second, and the last time Tyler had been wearing NVGs, but the bearded dude who'd grabbed Harper looked like one of the shooters who'd ambushed his SEAL team in Mali. And then there was the dude who'd smiled and pointed his knife at Tyler—as if gloating and challenging Tyler specifically. Had the others seen it from their vantage point?

Now's not the time. I need to talk to Zee about it first . . .

"What the hell happened?" Moody asked, huffing as he yanked open the door and stepped into the Donut.

"Ty's wife was murdered and his daughter was being kidnapped, that's what happened," Stan said as he casually slipped his hand into his pocket, concealing the slugs Tyler had seen him collecting from the floor before Moody came in.

"We confirmed it happens. We saw who they were and how they did it," Zee said.

He glanced at Moody, who was staring at him.

What are you keeping from us, Moody? And why . . . ?

"Is there something else you'd like to share, Chief?" Moody asked. "Something that sheds light on why there was gunfire on an ISR op?"

"The attackers spotted us and opened fire," Zee said before Tyler could speak. "We returned fire to defend ourselves."

"I think this confirms our theory. The men who targeted my family are connected to the group behind the nuclear attack," Tyler said, the imagery of Nikki's murder and screams from his baby girl playing on a loop in his head. "That led to a"—he swallowed hard and begged the images to leave his brain—"change in the event."

"I have their faces," Adela said, tapping her temple. "So, we can begin our hunt."

"Okay," Moody said, seemingly satisfied. "Let's get to work."

Tyler shook his head. "First, we make sure Harper and Nikki are safe. I am not letting that happen to them again . . . or at all, or whatever. We go now."

"I agree," Zee said, giving him a look of real concern. "We need to secure Nikki and Harper *tonight* because the people that did this are highly trained, dangerous, and shouldn't be underestimated. The sooner we get Tyler's family safe, the better I'll feel."

CHAPTER 32

From the driver's seat, Tyler glanced in the rearview mirror at Harper and exhaled a sigh of relief. His daughter was safe and sound, buckled into her car seat, which he'd moved from Nikki's Rogue to the rear bench seat of the black Chevy Suburban. Incredible as it was, his kid had stayed asleep while Nikki had transferred her from her crib to the Suburban while Ben, Stan, and Adela kept guard. Now the three-year-old looked so peaceful and angelic as she slept, leaned over in the third row against the edge of her seat, holding her mom's hand, oblivious to the threat targeting her. In stark contrast, her kitted-up bodyguards—Stan and Ben—sat alert and vigilant in the middle row captain's chairs behind Tyler and Adela, who occupied the front passenger seat.

The vehicle Moody had given them for the task was the same up-armored SUV that had picked Tyler and Stan up from the airport on his first day at Task Force Omega—a day that felt like a lifetime ago but in real time had only been a few weeks. After the horrific reconnaissance jump, he'd phoned Nikki and warned her of a terrorist threat targeting members of his former JSOC unit. This was a fabrication he felt sure, but a believable one after the events in Mali and one she couldn't readily dismiss. To Nikki's credit, she'd agreed to the plan and followed his instructions to the letter—grabbing the go-bag he'd made for her while they'd been married and packing up the essentials for Harper. While they were en route, Tyler had put in a call to Commander Carroll, who'd sent a pair of SEALs to watch the house until Tyler and his crew could arrive. It was Carroll who saw the flaw in his tactical plan— a result of the emotions he fought after what he'd seen. Tyler doubted he would ever be the same after watching that man smile and splay his wife's throat open in front of their daughter . . .

Ex-wife . . .

"You don't think there may be surveillance on her house?" his former SEAL commander had asked. And, of course, they had to assume that to be the case; in fact, it seemed likely. A repeat call to Nikki had sent her to the base—one of the most secure military compounds on earth and one she still had access to with her dependent ID card. They'd entered the base and picked up Nikki and Harper at the Base Exchange.

He'd not yet asked Carroll for his next favor, but they were now en route to the SEAL commander's house in Cape Charles on the Delmarva Peninsula to do just that.

He shifted his gaze from Harper to Nikki, who sat in the back third row with Zee. She wore her roll-with-the-punches Navy-wife face, but she couldn't hide the worry in her eyes. In all the time they'd dated and been married, she'd faced plenty of difficult and stressful times, but never a direct threat to her and Harper. Zee, God bless her, was asking Nikki questions about Harper in a gallant attempt to keep Nikki's mind occupied and out of panic attack territory.

Zee had not left his ex-wife's side since they'd arrived, fielding questions and providing the confident reassurance he knew Nik needed.

He repositioned the rearview mirror. Two sets of headlights followed—one closing and the other well back in trail. He squinted, trying to identify the make and model of the closer vehicle, but its bright LED headlights made that impossible. Water stretched on either side as they crossed the midsection of Chesapeake Bay on America's longest bridge-tunnel system, connecting Hampton Roads metro to the Delmarva Peninsula. The four-lane divided highway with two separate mile-long tunnels, stretched seventeen and a half miles north–south and shaved hours off the alternative option, driving ninety-five miles the long way around on the inland side. Everything from cargo ships to destroyers, aircraft carriers, and submarines used the deep draft channel over the Bay Bridge-Tunnel when traveling to and from the Atlantic.

They'd passed through the first tunnel and were approaching the second. A quarter mile ahead, the two-lane northbound bridge highway necked down to a single lane into the bi-directional Chesapeake Channel tunnel. Given the hour, traffic was light in both directions, with only a few cars heading south toward Tidewater, plus the two behind them heading north.

Tyler passed a white VDOT pickup truck with its flashers on, parked on the shoulder between north- and southbound lanes at the mouth of the bridge. The road dipped as they descended, with the concrete retaining walls—holding back billions of gallons of water—rising on both sides of the road. When they entered, and his eyes adjusted from the dark of night to the orange glow of the tunnel lights, his Spidey Sense began to tingle . . .

He glanced at the rearview mirror again. This time, he saw nothing.

"What's the matter?" Adela asked from the front passenger seat beside him. "Does something have your antenna up?"

"There were two vehicles behind us on the bridge and the closer one was closing on us, but now I don't see him," he said, aware that he had eased off the gas. "He should have entered the tunnel by now."

"No exits on the bridge," she said.

"Exactly," he said, looking up in the rearview again, where only an empty, orange-lit tunnel stretched out behind them. "Did you see that VDOT service truck we passed?"

"Yeah . . ." she said.

Converging headlights ahead abruptly ended the conversation.

A white SUV heading the opposite direction in the southbound lane crossed the divider and lined up for a head-on collision. At the last second, Tyler jerked his wheel left, vectoring into the other lane, and slammed the brakes, narrowly dodging a fatal crash.

A grinding squeal filled the tunnel as the passenger side of their Suburban collided with the oncoming Ford. Like bumper cars, the impact sent Tyler into the left tunnel wall. Sparks flew and steel scraped concrete as he skidded along the wall. He fought to regain control, jerking the wheel right as their Suburban screeched to a stop, canted at a forty-five-degree angle across both lanes.

Harper, jarred from her slumber, wailed from her car seat behind him. He swiveled to scan his passengers. "Is everyone okay?"

Before anyone could answer, Stan shouted, "Get down!"

Tyler saw Zee put a hand on the back of Nikki's head and push her down as gunfire raked the rear window and walked up the passenger side. The rounds left a line of tiny starburst fractures, but the bullet-proof glass held. Stan kicked open his deformed door, which squealed in protest, and he jumped out on the far side of the shooters.

"Here," Adela said, passing Tyler his rifle, which she had been keeping for him in the footwell while he drove.

Tyler locked eyes with Ben, who was sandwiched between Harper and the door.

"With my life," Ben said before Tyler could even make his plea.

Tyler nodded and jumped out to join Stan for the battle to come. Adela climbed over the center console and fell in beside him.

"I count three shooters, all with long guns," Zee barked from inside the Suburban. She was looking out the rear window, providing intel just like she'd done for Tyler from the TOC on countless JSOC ops.

Stan crouched by the taillight, ready to engage from the rear corner of the Suburban. Adela was crouching behind the front wheel, sighting over the hood. This left Tyler the undesirable and lone remaining option: stepping up on the running board and firing over the roof.

Enemy gunfire rang out, as what sounded like two shooters strafed the Suburban from behind. At the end of the volley, Tyler popped up and scanned for targets. Sighting two figures moving down the tunnel in tactical crouches, he dropped his aim onto the shooter to the left and squeezed off two rounds. He saw the man's head jerk back as he crumpled to the ground. Tyler dropped low just as a fresh round of bullets kicked up sparks from the roof of their SUV, right where his head had been.

"Second pair on your right," Zee called.

"Got them," Stan said and opened fire.

Tyler dropped flat on the pavement, sighting underneath the Suburban.

Instead of a running pair of legs like he expected, his brain instantly registered one fallen body and the face and muzzle of a prone shooter who'd had the same idea. Tyler fired once, rolling right as he saw the flash from the enemy shooter's assault rifle. The attacker's round skipped off the pavement beside him and slammed into the tunnel wall behind. Tyler resighted and shot twice more, but his first round had landed. The killer's ruined head split open as he delivered two more.

"Two down," he called with a sideways glance at Stan, who was indexing and firing with mechanical precision. He reminded Tyler more of a robotic sentry unit than a man.

"Same," Stan called back, his rifle going silent after a final trigger pull.

"Fellas, looks like we got incoming from the north," Adela shouted. "Should I engage?"

"It could be civilians," Tyler shouted back.

"Could be, but they're not slowing down."

"Then let's give them something to think about and confirm," Tyler said.

"Switch with me," Stan shouted, already moving north in a crouch.

Tyler swapped places, taking a knee by the rear bumper and providing a burst of covering fire while Stan moved toward the front of their Suburban to do whatever it was he was planning.

"I got this," Stan said to Adela.

In Tyler's peripheral vision, he saw Adela scamper behind the open driver's door while Stan settled into a kneeling firing stance near the front bumper. Two gunshots echoed in the tunnel and Tyler heard the immediate squeal of rubber as the incoming vehicle lost control and skidded . . . undoubtedly from Stan blowing out both front tires with precision marksmanship.

"Dude, you're a fucking deadeye," Adela said.

To the south, Tyler heard the roar of an engine. He risked a glance around the bumper and saw the familiar face of the bearded shooter from both the Mali op and Nikki's driveway behind the wheel of the white Expedition. The look in the man's eyes told Tyler everything he needed to know:

Shit, he's going to ram us.

At the same time, fresh gunfire ripped down the tunnel from the north where a new green Ford SUV had arrived, its passenger-side windows rolled down and gunners inside. Tracers zipped past as Tyler and his teammates fired and moved, shifting from their unprotected side for cover.

"Back inside," Tyler shouted.

While Stan and Adela followed his order, Tyler aimed at the bearded operator's head through the windshield.

He squeezed the trigger, struggling to find his operator zen with the rage growing inside him, but in his optical sight, he saw the man drop below the dashboard a split second before the round punched a perfect hole through the windshield just above the steering wheel.

A second volley from the north ricocheted around Tyler and drove him back inside the armored Suburban. He slammed the door behind him and found himself face-to-face with his screaming daughter—her red-cheeked, tear-stained face framed by adorable light-red curls. He couldn't imagine what terror and confusion were running through her three-and-a-half-year-old mind, but maybe that was better than knowing what was coming next.

"Brace for impact!" Zee shouted from the rear seat.

Adela, who now occupied the driver's seat with Stan in the front passenger seat, shifted the transmission into Drive and pounded the accelerator. An instant before the white Ford Expedition made contact, the big Chevy catapulted into motion. Spinning the wheel, Adela changed the angle of impact from what would have been a solid rear right corner hit to a glancing blow on the left rear bumper. The Expedition bounced off their Suburban and slammed nose-first into the west tunnel wall while the Suburban fishtailed wildly to the right. Adela whipped the steering wheel, turning into the spin, and expertly wrangled control of the SUV. Adela was a total badass, clearly well trained in tactical driving.

A volley from shooters in the green SUV lit up the Suburban's windshield with fresh starbursts as Adela accelerated north, heading straight toward a gap between where the green SUV was stopped and the tunnel wall.

"What are you doing?" Nikki shouted from the back. "You're driving straight at them!".

"We're exfilling the fuck out of here," Adela shouted back.

As they drove past the green Explorer, Tyler locked eyes with the driver through the side passenger window. The man behind the wheel was the same Asian operator who'd grinned at Tyler as he opened Nikki's throat on the driveway . . . a future they were fighting like hell to prevent. Now this same man was here, in the present, targeting them in the middle of an intervention. In no universe or timeline could that be a coincidence. Tyler met the malice in the man's eyes and reflected his own hate back with equal intensity.

After slipping through the gap, he saw the rear tailgate of the green SUV pop open and an assaulter step out. Tyler attention shifted from the driver to the new threat, and what he saw made his breath catch as if he'd just been punched in the solar plexus. The black-clad operator held a tubular weapon with flared, bell-shaped ends that the depths of Tyler's brain identified as an NLAW anti-tank weapon. A flashbulb memory of Mali and the burning bodies of his SEAL teammates and their pickup truck filled Tyler's mind. The gruesome, horrific imagery paralyzed him—muting his voice, freezing his muscles, and leaving him powerless to do anything but watch as the long-haired assassin shouldered the rocket launcher and took aim.

The Suburban's bulletproof skin had saved them so far but was no match for such a weapon. As he shifted to aim his rifle, the killer's head suddenly snapped backward, the back of the man's skull blown out by a high-velocity round. Tyler spun around to see what had happened.

Stan happened.

The Green Beret and Tier One Delta Force operator was sitting on the windowsill of the front passenger door and had made a one-in-a-million, backward-facing kill shot over the roof of the Suburban while Adela opened range to the target.

"Bro, you weren't kidding when you said you were a killing machine," Ben said as Stan contorted himself back inside the SUV and into his seat. "I've never seen a shot like that."

Stan didn't say anything, just simply nodded and kept his gaze ahead.

"I think we're clear," Zee said. Tyler looked out the back window and didn't see either enemy vehicle—both of which were incapacitated—in pursuit.

"What the plan, Chief?" Adela said from the driver's seat. "We're heading north, but I don't know what might be at the exit."

"Haul ass out of this tunnel," he said. "We have no comms down here. Be ready for a possible blockade at the north exit. I think that VDOT truck was stolen, and they stopped traffic after we entered the tunnel. They might have used the same trick on the other end."

"Check," she said.

Nobody said a word as they barreled toward the exit. Even Harper had stopped crying and sat in what Tyler took for stunned silence. She looked at him and, for the first time since the battle started, recognition flashed in her eyes.

"Daddy?" she said.

He took her little hand in his and squeezed it gently. "Yeah, baby, it's me."

"What's happening, Daddy?"

"Some bad people were chasing us, but my friends and I are here to keep you and Mommy safe, okay?"

She nodded and gave him a brave smile. "I love you, Daddy."

"I love you too, Peanut."

"A hundred yards," Stan said.

Tyler glanced from Harper out the windshield and saw the rapidly approaching upsloping tunnel exit. He couldn't see the speedometer, but he guessed they were doing eighty-plus.

"Seat belts," Tyler said, and everyone quickly buckled up.

The Suburban angled up and blasted out of the tunnel like a missile out of an underground silo into the night. As the retaining walls fell away, Stan said, "Moment of truth, get ready . . ."

Adela kept on the gas as their SUV transitioned from the tunnel ramp to the widened northbound bridge double-lane highway. Tyler gripped his rifle tight, but no gunfire riddled their exterior, no rocket-powered grenade streaked toward them, and no roadblock was waiting to obstruct their path.

Tyler exhaled through pursed lips and looked back at Nikki, who was shaking uncontrollably.

Their eyes met.

"Is it over?" she asked, her voice barely above a whisper.

Tonight, they'd escaped with their lives, but if there was one thing he knew with certainty it was that the assassins targeting him and his family would try again.

"For now," he said with a solemn nod. "But I need you to give me your phone."

"My phone?"

"Yeah, your phone," he said. She fished her iPhone from her go-bag and handed it to him.

"I'm sorry for this," he said and tossed it out the window. "You're going to have to use a burner until this blows over. After that, I'll replace it with the newest model."

The shocked look on her face morphed into resignation as the reality of her situation sunk in. Then her eyes rimmed with tears.

"It'll all be okay," he said. "I just need a little time to sort it all out."

She nodded, and he watched his daughter unbuckle herself and scramble into his wife's lap. But, unlike the future he had witnessed on the jump, she was safe.

And Nikki was alive.

They'd stopped it. For now at least.

Time, once again, is both the problem and the solution. The alpha and the omega . . .

He'd wondered why Moody had code-named the task force and jump teams as he did, and now, in this dark and dangerous moment, it finally hit him.

CHAPTER 33

Jun stared down at Damien's lifeless body where it had fallen behind the green SUV. The Frenchman's unblinking eyes stared up with what looked like surprise to Jun. Surprise that the American had made an impossible shot? Surprise that this was the way his life had ended? Or was it surprise to discover whatever it was that souls discover in the moment of death? Whatever it was, Damien Rolle's last thought would forever remain a mystery.

Jun knelt, closed his friend's eyelids, and whispered, "You always made me laugh. I'm going to miss you. *Au revoir*, you crazy French guy."

"We gotta fucking go," Garth shouted from behind the wheel of the Ford Expedition which he'd just managed to start. "Right now, Jun!"

Jun looked up the tunnel, but the Americans were long gone. Fresh anger brewing, he ran to the white SUV and jumped into the passenger seat. Garth slammed on the gas and took off north.

"Maybe we can still catch them," Garth said.

Jun shook his head. "Unlikely, and even if we did, there's only two of us now. Plus, we're on the enemy's home soil, which puts us at a terrible disadvantage."

"Speak for yourself," Garth said. "This is my backyard."

"Not anymore, my friend," Jun said.

Garth didn't answer.

They sat in silence for a long moment. Then, in a sudden fit of fury, Jun pummeled the passenger-side dashboard with his gloved fists and screamed with all the rage and hate that was boiling over in his soul.

When he'd finished, Garth asked, "Feel better?"

"No."

"We're going to need to ditch this vehicle," the American said.

"Agreed."

"What about the dude we left behind in that VDOT truck?"

"Fuck him."

"What if he talks?" Garth said with a sideways glance.

The question made Jun laugh. "Who would believe him? And besides, he doesn't know shit."

"Good point . . ."

Knuckles throbbing, he pulled the sat phone from his left chest pocket and dialed Hoffman.

The German answered on the second ring. "Status?"

"Mission failed," Jun said.

The long silence told Jun everything he needed to know about his boss's reception of the news. Hoffman has sent him men, somehow managed to smuggle an NLAW anti-tank missile into the country, and fulfilled his promise to alert Jun of any future timeline changes by the Americans. He'd done all these things and still Jun had failed. A macabre grin spread across Jun's face as he considered asking the German if he should put a bullet in his own brain right now or if Hoffman would prefer to do it.

Finally, Hoffman spoke. "I am disappointed. How many on your team survived?"

"Two. Me and Garth."

Another long silence hung on the line before the German said, "Our mission, and therefore our long-term goals, will not come to fruition with Chief Brooks and his team in play. That is becoming more clear with each failure. We are running out of time to succeed in Washington, DC, so they must be stopped. Direct engagement is not working. It is time to try another way. Go to the safe house in Alexandria and await instruction while I position assets."

"*Ja*, Herr Hoffman," he said, and the line went dead.

"Head to the safe house?" Garth asked.

"Yes."

"Then what?"

"We wait . . ." he said, looking out the window at the water stretching away from the bridge, "and see what the future holds."

CHAPTER 34

"This is it," Tyler said, pointing to the modest two-story Dutch colonial with white shiplap siding, a covered front porch, and an American flag out front. The new adrenaline dump as he scanned the area, looking for people or vehicles that might seem out of place, chased away the bone-wearying fatigue he'd fought the last thirty minutes.

Adela nodded. She pulled along the curb instead of into the driveway and left the engine running.

"Do you want us to come with you?" Stan asked.

"How about you watch the back, and Ben, you keep an eye out front?" Tyler said.

They both nodded and exited the vehicle while Tyler leaned over and undid Harper's car seat restraints.

"Thank you, for everything," Nikki said to Zee. "I would have lost my mind if you hadn't stayed so calm and looked after me." She glanced up at Tyler and then at the other operators around the truck. "It's . . . it's different than . . ."

Zee smiled and simply said, "I know. For me too, Nikki. I'm an intel officer, so I know how you feel." He watched Zee take his ex-wife's hand. "I can walk you in, if you like."

"That would be nice, thank you."

Harper wrapped her arms around Tyler's neck as he lifted her out of her seat. She gripped him tight as he eased himself out of the SUV. He carried her around the front of the Suburban and toward the front porch where Commander Carroll stood, arms folded across his chest, in blue jeans and a long-sleeve black T-shirt. The SEAL commander was looking at the battle-scarred Chevy SUV with a dubious expression while his hand rested on the butt of a pistol he sported in a hip holster. Carroll was clearly not pleased that Tyler had brought the fight to his home—and that wasn't likely to change if Tyler couldn't give him the answers he wanted.

"This is my daughter, Harper," Tyler said to Carroll as he took the two steps leading up to the porch.

Carroll's expression softened and he gave a cutesy wave to the toddler. "Hi, Harper. I'm Uncle Maddox."

Harper looked away and buried her face in Tyler's neck.

Carroll's face hardened again. He just stared at Tyler, blocking the door.

"Oh, for Pete's sake, Dax, let them in," his wife, Angie, said as she opened the screen door behind him.

With an obedient grunt, Carroll swiveled ninety degrees to make room for Tyler to pass. Smiling at his old boss's wife, Tyler thanked Angie and stepped into the foyer. What sounded like a very big dog barked somewhere inside the house, but Tyler didn't hear the sound of paws and toenails on hardwood.

"That's Duke," Angie said. "We have him shut in the laundry room. It's just easier that way in the beginning with new people."

Tyler nodded, as Nikki and Zee walked in behind him. The Carroll house smelled like apple pie and hunting dog, an oddly comforting mix given the situation. Dax and Angie were only in their late thirties, but the house had a mature, generational feel to it—like Tyler's maternal grandparents' place.

"I'm Angie," she said, sticking out her hand to Nikki. "I think we met once at the family day at the command."

"I'm Nikki. I remember meeting you. And I'm so sorry about all this."

"You don't need to apologize. The unit is our family. We've got your six," Angie said. "We have the guest room made up for you and a Pack 'n Play for Harper. I held on to ours just in case we had any additional *unplanned* family members . . . if you know what I'm saying."

Nikki nodded and looked at Tyler expectantly. It was time to let Harper go. The last thing he wanted to do was to untangle himself from his daughter's bear hug, but he didn't have a choice.

"Harper, Daddy's got to pass you to Mommy now."

"No," Harper said, her face still pressed into the crook of his neck. "I want Daddy."

Tyler felt his throat tighten and his eyes turn wet.

"Harper," Nikki said. "You need to let go of Daddy and go back to bed. It's still night-night time."

"No," Harper repeated defiantly and squeezed Tyler tighter. Nikki looked at him with exhausted, exasperated eyes.

He solved the problem with butterfly kisses and a whispered promise of a cookie when Harper woke up. He kissed Harper's head, told her he loved her, and handed her off to his ex-wife. Zee, who'd been watching the exchange, fixed Tyler with a tender smile and a look he'd not seen from her before.

"You and I need to have a little chat, Chief," Carroll said, motioning for Tyler to follow him. Tyler trailed his former CSO into the kitchen where Carroll leaned against the counter.

"Damn, Brooks, you look rung out. No bullshit, dude, what the hell is going on? We got word through channels that you'd been targeted somehow, but typical spook bullshit—they gave no details."

"I've been targeted for sure, and the group behind it went after my family to get to me. We barely got Nik and Harper out alive," he said.

"I assume this is connected to the new spooky task force you left us for?" Carroll said with a good measure of judgment.

Tyler nodded.

"I figured as much, which begs the question: Why did you come to *me* with this instead of letting your new command handle it?"

"Because I don't trust them."

"What?"

"Also, Zee and I think they might be compromised."

Carroll let out a resigned groan that seemed to say *thanks for making this my problem* and *I told you so* simultaneously. "The thing is, you've now brought the fight to my doorstep and put *my* family and *my* kids in danger, but I don't have the luxury of being read in on the details. It's a shitty thing to do, brother."

"I know. But you're my only option. I can't trust anyone else to keep them safe while I hunt down the bastards responsible. I would never put your family in danger, so I don't intend for them to stay here . . ."

"We're a brotherhood, Tyler. We'll do what we need to keep them safe."

"I know that. But, to keep everyone safe until this gets unfucked, I have a different location in mind. A place that only a handful of people on this earth have visited, and half of whom are now dead."

"Go on," Carroll said.

"Do you remember that weekend when you, me, Keaton, and Lehmann went hunting but spent most of the time in the cabin drinking beer and playing Texas Hold'em instead?"

Carroll grinned. "I'd just given you your platoon. Miter was there too, before he got promoted and headed to Group Ten. And Keaton lost all his money, and to ante we made him bet his pants—which of course he lost—so he wandered around in his tighty-whiteys for the whole weekend . . . How could I forget?"

"I want you to take them there."

Carroll blew air threw pursed lips. "Okay."

"Are you sure?"

"I said *okay*, didn't I?"

"Thank you, Skipper. I mean it, thank you."

"How long do I need to keep them provisioned and hidden?"

"I don't know. It could be a while."

Carroll shook his head. "How long is a while, Brooks?"

"A couple . . . three weeks, maybe," he said. He expected Carroll to balk.

"Okay, I'll do it. Did you get rid of her phone already, I hope?"

Tyler nodded. "But I haven't had a chance to get her a burner, so if you could . . ."

"I'll take care of it. I'll take care of everything," Carroll said, shifting into SEAL commander mode now that he'd committed to the mission. "Clean your house, and let me worry about Nikki and Harper."

"Thank you."

"Stop saying *thank you* and go fix your shit, frogman."

"Yes, sir," Tyler said and exhaled. The hard part was over.

A knock on the doorframe to the kitchen turned both their heads. Zee was standing in the doorway. Carroll waved her in.

"Sir," she said with a nod.

"Been racking my brain whether I have you or this yahoo to thank for this mess. If memory serves, that spooky asshole recruited you first, and you recommended he poach Brooks? Am I right, Williams, or was it the other way around?"

"Guilty as charged," she said, raising her hand while bowing her head in a mea culpa.

Carroll, whose mood had returned to baseline, shook his head at both of them. "What the hell am I going to do with the two of you?"

"How about taking us back when this is all over?" Zee said. Tyler loved her for having the balls to say what he was thinking but couldn't articulate.

The SEAL commander rubbed his chin and lost the battle to suppress a smile. "Maybe," he said. "We'll see. But, in the meantime, I've had my eye on this real fancy lever-action Henry rifle. Something like that hanging over my mantel could go a long way as an apology for y'all's bullshit . . ."

Tyler chuckled. "We could probably work that out."

The O-6 Navy SEAL in command of the most lethal counterterrorism unit in the world gave a curt nod.

"Grass ain't usually greener, Chief," he said and gave his shoulder a squeeze.

"I see that, sir," Tyler said. "What the unit is doing is very important. But I sure as hell wish I were still kicking doors in with my team."

Carroll nodded.

"Be safe, brother."

CHAPTER 35

PROGRAM DIRECTOR'S OFFICE—WAREHOUSE A
0602 LOCAL TIME

Moody peeled the foil wrapper back and used his thumbnail to claw out two antacid tablets from the roll. Frowning, he popped them into his mouth and began to chew. He had heartburn this morning. He had heartburn all the time these days. He chased the antacid tablets with a slug of coffee—something his doctor had assured him was counterproductive. He sighed and buried his head in his hands. The wheels were literally falling off the bus and he wasn't sure if he could keep it together.

I don't know how much longer I can do this.

If only he had someone he could talk to. Someone he could unburden himself to. A pang of loneliness hit him like a punch to the solar plexus. God, he missed Holly. He missed her so fucking much. He'd been a better man when she was in his life. And a helluva better father . . .

A pity party isn't going to solve anything, the voice in his head chastised. *Man up, pull it together, and do what you need to do.*

He sat up and forced himself to take three slow, calming breaths—a trick Holly had shown him. He felt a little better.

A little stronger.

The world didn't know it, but it needed him.

And I will answer the call.

Whether motivated out of guilt, concern, or—God forbid—duty, he'd made a solo jump earlier this morning to check the future, and what he'd seen had taken him by surprise. He was not a man who was easily surprised these days.

Now that Martin had monkeyed with HAL and discovered Moody's private subroutine, he'd had no choice but to jump to Bravo site. From the beginning, he'd understood the importance of a secondary Omega Room, which is why he'd broken ground. But funding the construction from his own pocket, and the simple fact he couldn't be in two places at the same time, had made the build-out grindingly slow. Thankfully, at least the data feeds and servers were operational.

He thought through the problem. *I'm going to have to make another jump with a witness. I'll take Martin to the Omega Room, take one for the team, and spare the rest of Omega a jump. God knows they're going to need that with what's coming.*

The secure phone on his desk drew his gaze and he felt a pull—as if the man waiting for his call exerted a gravitational pull through the lines connecting them. The call had to be made; the question was: Did he tell the general everything now or dole out the bad news in bite-size, more easily digestible chunks?

Chunks are probably best, he decided. *Don't want to get fired before I can see this through.*

He reached for the secure phone, pressing number one on speed dial for the general.

"I assume this is an update on the attack inside the Chesapeake Bay Bridge-Tunnel?"

Moody shook his head in equal parts awe and irritation. The CI team at Dam Neck had buttoned up the scene as a complex traffic accident with fatalities, and no one outside the command and Omega knew about the attack.

But, of course, United States Air Force Brigadier General Travis fuck-ing Waltrip knows already . . .

"Yes, sir," he said. "I was calling to update you on the incident, but clearly you're—"

"Then update me," Waltrip said, cutting him off. "And while you're at it, might as well start at the beginning."

Moody took the next few minutes to read the general in how the team had discovered the UNAUTH subroutine in HAL, how HAL had flagged the murder–kidnapping event against Brooks's family, about the reconnaissance jump, and him approving the midnight extraction run to save Brooks's wife and daughter.

"Where is the team and Brooks family now?"

He sighed.

"The team is en route back to Omega, sir."

"And the family?"

"Well, Brooks used his own network and secured them somewhere secret. He didn't choose to read us in on the details."

"Smart man," the general said with a snort. "Quite the resourceful bunch you've recruited."

Moody gritted his teeth. "Yes, sir."

"I don't want the sanitized version, Pat. I want your no-bullshit assessment of what kind of threat we're up against."

"My assessment, sir, is that this incident confirms our worst fears. We're compromised. We have a leak at some level.

"What evidence have you collected to prove this, Pat?" He raised his eyebrows in surprise and thought a moment, but said nothing. He supposed they had no hard, concrete evidence. But if it walked like a duck . . .

"Well, sir, whoever this is seems to know our plays. And they now know at least one of our players. There seems to be someone out there a step ahead, and I don't know how that's possible without an adversary team doing the same thing. Whoever it is, they know who our operators are, when and where we're going to jump, and where our compound is located. We're behind the eight ball, General, and if we don't get ahead of this then we risk losing control."

There was a long, uncomfortable pause. For a moment, he thought the call might have even dropped. Then the general's voice returned.

"Have you ever wondered why I recruited you to lead Omega?" Waltrip asked.

Moody hesitated, thrown off balance by the question. What the hell difference did that make now?

Fine, I'll play along.

"I ask myself that question every day, sir," he said.

"Well, son, it's *not* because of your black site–management pedigree. There's tons of ex–station chiefs I could have recruited. It's *not* because of your pathological ability to manipulate people; I know dozens of politicians who fit that bill. Hell, it's not even because you're a closet friggin' genius who hides his Princeton physics bona fides from everyone. It's because, Pat, you're a true believer. It's because you understand at the most basic and fundamental level how this is a tool that can tip the scales in favor of preserving and safeguarding *our* way of life. And, because like me, you know if we don't prevail then our enemies will, and when that happens, the world is fucked."

"Agree one hundred percent, sir."

"Okay, then let's get ahead of this thing and make sure we're not all fucked, Pat. First order of business is to find the leak and plug it. You've either got a mole, a back door open somewhere in your network, or both. Lock down Omega. No one leaves. Shut down all voice and data traffic. Do whatever it takes to deprive the enemy of intelligence. Then, you flip the script and go from being the hunted to the hunter . . . But you already know all this, don't you?"

"Yes, sir."

"Then why the fuck aren't you doing it!"

Moody took a long, slow breath.

Because I just figured it out today, you pompous asshole, he thought, but did not say. "I suppose I was lost on how best to get ahead of them."

"Well, get unlost, son. I'm keeping this development between you and me for now. No reason to spook our bosses, Pat. When the President calls me with tasking, I need Omega ready to go."

"Yes, sir. We will be," Moody said, a bit surprised that Waltrip would keep something this important from the President. Further evidence that, when it came to time travel, the buck stopped with Waltrip.

"Not to add gas to the fire, but any updates on the other issue— operator sustainability?" the general asked.

"We're making good progress on that front, sir," he lied, jotting a note to schedule a meeting with Dr. Donahue. "I'm sure we'll have it licked before it becomes a problem."

"Keep me in the loop on both fronts, Pat. I want daily updates."

There was a click, and the general was gone.

Moody replaced the receiver and stared at the wall while his mind got to work on triaging the problems. The general was right, the first order of business was plugging the leak. Omega operated with a lean staff already, and he'd handpicked almost everyone. As far as low-hanging fruit, not a single person came to mind who fit the bill as a traitor.

And there was another possible explanation—one too terrifying to consider just yet.

One Waltrip had warned him might happen.

He ran a hand through what was left of his hair.

"I don't have time for a fucking mole hunt," he grumbled as he pressed the speakerphone button on his desk and called Jimmy in the control room.

The senior jump technician, like Moody, kept a stateroom on the compound. He'd been up since 5 a.m., when Moody had woken him for the unscheduled jump. Jimmy was the only person on the planet whom Moody trusted unconditionally. Moody had bought that trust by violating the UNAUTH policy and saving Jimmy from a future fatal car accident—and also by paying for Jimmy's kids' college in the present. On top of that, Jimmy was—as Waltrip might say—a true believer.

Jimmy answered after the first ring. "Hey, boss, what's up?"

"Plot a jump to the Omega Room. Two to travel," he said.

"Sure thing. Who's going with you?"

"Martin."

"Future date?"

"Fourteen days," he said.

"Roger that," Jimmy said. "Anything else?"

"No," Moody said, but before he hung up added, "Oh, and Jimmy . . ."

"Yeah, boss?"

"Thank you."

"For what?" Jimmy said, sounding confused.

"For the long hours. For the stress. For the time away from your family . . ." he said, feeling uncharacteristically magnanimous.

"Oh, you're welcome," Jimmy said, and after a beat added. "I'll always have your back, Pat. I hope you know that."

"I do, and thank you," he said. "I'm going to go wake up Martin. I'll see you in a few minutes."

"I'll have the Donut warmed up and ready when you do."

Moody ended the call, stretched his back, and pressed to his feet.

On the way out, he glanced at the framed picture of Albert Einstein on his wall. Shaking a fist at the world's most famous physicist, he said, "Damn you . . . This is all your fault, you know that, right?"

CHAPTER 36

Zee noticed that the closer they got to the compound, the more tense Tyler's jaw looked. By the time they arrived, she was worried he might explode from all the pent-up anxiety, uncertainty, and angry thoughts undoubtedly running around in his head. She empathized with his family concerns, but Nikki and Harper were safe with Commander Carroll and there were other pressing matters that they needed to discuss with the team. She'd given Tyler the drive back to broach the subject himself, but he hadn't. Now they were running out of time. It looked like he needed a nudge to do it, so she literally reached over the seat and did just that.

He turned to look at her where she sat alone in the third-row seat. "What's up?"

"I was thinking now might be a good time to talk about some of the stuff we probably need to brief the others about before we get back to the compound," she said in a quiet voice.

He exhaled. "I'm feeling pretty spun up at the moment. Maybe it would be better if you took the lead."

"Sure," she replied with a nod. Then, talking loud enough to be heard from the back and over the music that they'd been listening to to decompress, she said, "Hey guys, there's something important that Tyler and I need to talk to you about."

"I already know what it is," Stan said from the front passenger seat.

"Okay, then by all means, Stan, since you're such a genius, why don't you lead the discussion?" Tyler snapped.

Zee put a hand on his shoulder.

"Sorry, dude, I didn't mean to steal your thunder," Stan said from the front passenger seat looking back at Tyler.

"It's fine," he said. "I'm not in a good headspace right now. Go on, Stan, what were you going to say?"

"What I was going to say is that I recognized one of the dudes in the tunnel from the carjacking ISR jump," Stan said. "The dude who grabbed Harper was the driver of the white Expedition."

"I recognized him too. And the guy who knifed Nikki on the driveway was the driver of the green SUV," Adela added from the driver's seat.

Zee looked at Tyler and asked the unspoken question with her eyes. It was time to finally have the difficult conversation with the others they'd been putting off.

He nodded. "Go ahead. You tell them . . ."

Zee took a deep breath and told them the theory that *their* Alpha team was not the first team to operate at the compound, sharing all of her and Tyler's observations and insights on the matter.

"Holy shit," Ben said, shaking his head when she finished.

"If what you're saying is true, then what happened to the last Alpha team?" Stan said, "Moreover, why keep it from us? Why scrub their existence?"

"Maybe they were killed in direct action," Adela offered.

"Then why not tell us?" Stan pressed.

"Maybe they died on a jump. Maybe something mechanically happened with the TFR that killed them, and Moody didn't want to scare us," Ben said.

"That's exactly my point. We don't know what we don't know, and that, in my experience, makes it dangerous to speculate," Stan said.

"As an intelligence officer, I can speak with authority when I say that compartmentalizing information is standard protocol when it comes to task forces like this," Zee said, finding herself playing devil's advocate for some strange reason. "And keeping secrets is often necessary for mission success. The term 'need to know' was invented for a reason."

"But it's not helpful either. I've worked with plenty of task forces downrange," Stan said, his tone sharp. "And I've been on the receiving end of the shitstorm that happens when vital information is kept from the operators serving on the pointy tip of the spear."

"Look, I'm not defending it. I'm just saying that, like Ben said, it doesn't mean Moody's a traitor," Zee said.

"No one said he was a traitor," Tyler came back. "My gut tells me Moody is a patriot, but maybe a patriot who skews toward an 'ends justify the means' approach to running his shop. And if that means we can't trust him to tell us the whole truth, it makes our work more dangerous and us as a team less effective."

To Zee's surprise, Adela spoke up next. "First of all, let me start off by saying I agree with everything Zee said. Running a deep, dark task force is complicated, and the decision about what to compartmentalize and what not to is never black and white. The truth is always colored in shades of gray. Second, I've thought Moody was sus from day one. Obviously, having been 'a Moody' myself for the past two decades, I know how to spot one of my kindreds. And third, I need to let you in on a little secret of my own. After Martin found Moody's hidden cache of UNAUTH files on the Omega Room servers, I decided to give Marty some spooky tasking—which he agreed to do."

"What kind of spooky tasking?" Tyler asked.

"To cybersnoop in *all* the task-force servers and see if he could dig up any more hidden files pertaining to this program that Moody has kept from us," she said. "Also, while you guys were working out the plan with Carroll, I called a buddy of mine at DIA and asked him to dig up anything he could on Moody for me."

"You mean just now, when we were at the house?" Zee asked.

Adela nodded.

"Wow, I never thought I'd say this, but I feel a strong compulsion to hug me a spook," Ben said, earning a much-needed laugh from everyone.

"So, we weren't the only ones with suspicions about the history of the program. Sounds like we're all on the same page," Zee said, feeling like a hundred-pound pack had just been lifted off her shoulders.

"What did your contact at DIA share about Moody?" Stan asked.

"Nothing yet. But he'll get back with whatever he finds."

"I'm glad we're talking about this, guys," Tyler said when Adela finished. "We need to be on the same page as we decide how to manage this."

"I say we just kick his ass," Stan said.

Zee couldn't tell but thought the Delta operator might just be serious.

"*That* would definitely undermine our cause," Adela said, making eye contact with Zee in the rearview mirror with a *God help me* look in her eyes. "Mind games, managing people, and digging up secrets is what I do for a living. A confrontation with Moody is inevitable, but kicking his ass is off the table, Stan."

Stan grumbled something under his breath, but Zee could see he was already calming down.

"There's something else," Tyler said and looked at Zee. "I think the bearded dude on the hit squad is one of the guys who ambushed us in Mali."

Zee's heart skipped a beat at this revelation. "Are you serious?"

Ty nodded.

Stan swiveled in his seat to look back at Ty. "Wait—in Mali? But the incident in Mali happened *before* you joined Omega."

"Correct," Ty said, and he recounted the events of the *out of thin air* ambush that happened during the counterterror op in Africa.

His words came out unfiltered and raw—part stream-of-consciousness part diatribe as he dove deep down the bunny hole while everyone listened without interruption. While he talked, Zee wondered if this was the missing puzzle piece to explain the bizarre series of events that night which had haunted her ever since.

"Whoa, whoa, whoa, hold on . . . Are you saying that the hit team is a jump team like us?" Ben said, his voice incredulous. "I thought we were talking about a mole leaking our tasking and future knowledge to the bad guys, but this is something else entirely."

"Yeah, I guess that's what I'm proposing," Ty said, scrubbing his face with his hands.

"Unlikely," Stan said. "Even if someone stole Omega tech, it would take time to get the technology reverse engineered and working. We only started jumping weeks ago."

"Maybe *we* stole it from someone else and we're the ones trying to play catch-up," Adela said, flipping the paradigm. "When it comes to innovation and tech, we're not always first, even though we tell the world we are."

"Let's dig into this theory and see if we can stress test it based on what we know about time travel," Stan said and turned to Tyler. "The Mali incident happened in your present, which means the bearded operator would've had to have jumped from your past."

Tyler nodded. "Okay . . ."

"How did the bearded operator kill your teammate?"

"With a headshot," Tyler said.

"But that's not possible because the laws of time travel prevent it," Stan said.

"Stan's right," Ben said. "Anything that gets changed in the future is supposed to reset."

Zee watched Tyler shut his eyes and rub his temples as he tried to work through the strange logic and rules of time travel as they understood them. When he opened his eyes again, Tyler said, "But the op happened in my present."

"That's right," Stan said, "and more importantly it was your teammate's present, and the injury didn't reset. As you told the story, Stick died and he stayed dead after the shooters vanished."

Tyler suddenly looked pale. "Are you saying the rules are wrong, that we *can* change the future?"

"No, because we saw Nikki die in the future, and that incident clearly reset because she was alive when we exfilled her tonight."

"Also, when you fired those rounds at the dude on the driveway, the same rounds came back with us to the present," Ben added.

"So, what the fuck are you saying?" Tyler asked, with a screwed-up look on his face. "That these guys found a way to break the rules?"

"No," Stan said. "I'm saying that the laws of physics and time travel cannot be broken. They can't be cheated. As you explained it, the op was a violent, kinetic, and traumatic affair. You took losses, Ty, hard losses. The fog of war is real. Are you *positive* the bearded operator you saw in the tunnel and during the kidnapping is the same guy you saw in Mali?"

"I don't have an eidetic memory," Tyler grumbled. "I wish I did, but I don't."

"So, you're not sure?"

"I'm not sure," Tyler said, his voice beyond weary.

"Look," Stan said, "it's natural to want to force a convenient explanation that ties up all loose ends, but time travel into the past is impossible. And for this same hit squad to have targeted you in Mali that would mean not only is there another TFR out there with a team jumping, but that they were targeting you in the past before Moody recruited you to Omega. Ockham's Razor says the hypothesis requiring the fewest assumptions is the most likely one, and in this case the simplest hypothesis is that bearded operator you saw in the tunnel reminds you of the bearded terrorist you battled in Mali. Just sayin', most terrorist fighters have beards."

Zee felt herself deflate, but Stan was right. They'd become so paranoid they were seeing conspiracies everywhere now.

"So, you think we're the only jumpers and my family being targeted can be fully explained by a mole in Omega?" Tyler said.

"If the mole is sharing future knowledge with the enemy as we obtain it, then yes. Like I said before, if they learn what we learn as we learn it, then we don't have an advantage. If both parties have the same future knowledge, neither one can stay one step ahead for long. It's why the future keeps changing with every move either one of us makes."

"Then our next move is obvious. We have to plug the leak at Omega," Tyler said.

"Agreed," Stan said and was about to say something else, but Adela cut him off.

"We're here," Adela said as she eased to a stop at the front gate. After flashing their IDs, the chain-link roller gate slid open, and Adela piloted the pockmarked Suburban through the open garage door into the Pepper Grinder. She could see Moody standing on the warehouse floor, with Martin at his side, waiting for them.

Moody wore a grave expression, and Martin looked shaken.

Moody waited until the entire team was assembled before he spoke. "After learning of the hit on you guys in the tunnel, Martin and I jumped to the Omega Room. We were trying to back you up and find any future intel in case the hit squad tried again . . ."

Zee felt her chest go tight as she waited for the punch line.

"Go on," Tyler said, crossing his arms over his broad chest.

"And the Omega Room was dark. We opened the emergency hatch, took a look, and saw DC in ruins once again," he said, his voice like sandpaper on wood. "It appears that our adversary has found a way to reclaim the future. Once again, it is your job to figure out how and when they do it and change the narrative back."

Zee stared at him, her heart sinking.

It's just like Stan said. Whatever we do, we can't maintain the advantage for long. We're right back where we started—with a nuclear attack on DC that we have to stop.

Only now, the stakes were much, much higher because Omega was compromised, their families were being targeted, and a hit squad was hunting them. And if they failed to find and stop the mastermind behind it, the bad guys would keep prevailing—killing millions and everyone she cared about.

PART III

"The distinction between the past, present, and future is only a stubbornly persistent illusion."

–Albert Einstein

CHAPTER 37

THE RECONSTRUCT ROOM

THE PEPPER GRINDER—WAREHOUSE B

FIVE DAYS LATER

1022 LOCAL TIME

Zee tried squinting and massaging the eyelid, but her left eye wouldn't stop twitching. Never in her life had her eye twitched before, but for the last couple days, it had been happening on and off like crazy.

It's the crappy sleep I'm getting, she told herself, *and the stress of the job.*

The jumps were blurring together and felt like one long ass day, but with nothing to show for it. All the jumps were intel gathering. They needed something to prosecute, something that might give them insight into who and what they were up against.

They were running out of time, and they all knew it. The stress of that, combined with the frenetic pace and the fear for their families if someone other than Tyler had been ID'd—no wonder they were all frazzled and irritable.

But it wasn't just the stress of the job that had her eye twitching. There was something else, something causing her great anxiety—and she wasn't sure how much longer she could keep it hidden. She hated, absolutely loathed, being inside the Donut. With her claustrophobia screaming at her that there was no air and the walls were going to swallow her up, it got worse with every single jump.

In her peripheral vision, she saw Adela walking toward her.

"Zee, I think I've got our next—" Adela started to say but then stopped midsentence when she noticed Zee's eyelid dancing the jitterbug. "Whoa, *that* must be annoying."

"Yeah, it's been happening off and on for a couple days. I think I'm just tired and overcaffeinated," she said. "I'm sure it's nothing."

"Well, actually," Stan said, chiming in from where he was standing at the high-top worktable, "while hemifacial spasms are generally benign, in rare cases they can be a precursor symptom to an underlying nervous system disorder like Bell's palsy, multiple sclerosis, Parkinson's disease, or even Tourette's."

"She's twenty-eight, Stan," Adela said and fixed him with her *I'm annoyed at you* stare. "I'm pretty sure she doesn't have any of those things."

"And here I thought she was flirting with me all this time," Martin said with an awkward chuckle. "I've never had a girl wink at me so persistently before."

The three of them turned to the wunderkind and all burst out laughing.

"Look at that, Marty made a joke," Adela said.

"And a damn good one at that," Stan added.

Zee grinned at Martin—whose cheeks had gone rosy—and blew him a kiss, which made his cheeks turn an even darker shade of red. Then, she turned to Adela. "So, you wanted to talk to me about something?"

"Yeah, can you follow me over to the whiteboard?" Adela asked.

"Sure," Zee said and hopped off her stool.

The bad news Moody had sprung on them when they returned from saving Tyler's family had thrown the team into crisis mode. Confronting him about any other secrets he might be hiding was forced to take a back seat to once again trying to stop DC from getting nuked. In response, Moody had ordered that they completely compartmentalize their reconstructs with only jump team members involved. He had also implemented a total lockdown on the compound—confiscating mobile phones, prohibiting personal internet access, screening all communications, and confining all personnel to campus. They were also convinced that the entity responsible for attacking DC and the entity directing the hit squad must be one and the same. There wasn't a single bit of noise from the conventional IC channels to even suggest a nation-state player was behind the attack. Whoever the bad guys were, they were pros, operated off-the-grid, and left no fingerprints. And despite Ben, Adela, and Marty's best efforts to create CGI faces of the men using their eidetic memories, they'd not been able to positively ID either the Asian hit man or the bearded operator.

The bad guys, it would seem, were ghosts. And if they didn't find them soon, then DC was going to burn.

"Whatcha got?" Zee asked Adela, hoping finally for some good news.

"On our last jump to NORAD, Ben and Martin identified a new detonation location inside ground zero," Adela said, *ground zero* having become their shorthand term for the roughly two-square-mile area where the bombers seemed to want the nukes to go off for maximum effect. "I marked it here on the satellite image."

Zee stepped up to the giant whiteboard with a screen dedicated to showing the bird's-eye view of ground zero. She double tapped to zoom the image and get data on the location Adela had marked.

"Water Park Towers Apartments," she said, reading the annotation that appeared next to a crescent-shaped building on the west side of the green space between Crystal City and the airport, and directly adjacent to the Crystal City train station. "Damn, it's huge. If we have to search every room . . . we'll run out of time."

"I know," Adela said. "That was my concern too, but then Ben pointed out that preblast imagery showed construction work being carried out on the rooftop. I just got off the phone with the property's maintenance manager; he told me they are conducting a major over-haul of the building's rooftop AC and air handling system. Wanna guess when the work is scheduled to start?"

"D-Day?"

"Bingo. The imagery Ben reviewed shows crews and equipment on the rooftop the day before. Ben said it wouldn't be uncommon for a contractor to want to prep and start moving materials in advance. They have a roof crane that would allow them to lift a payload with the mass we're estimating. It could easily be hidden in a construction container or disguised in a housing of some sort. Also, Stan made an interesting supporting point, which is that detonating the nuke from the top of a thirteen-story building increases the damage quotient compared to a detonation at ground level."

"Strong work, Adela," Zee said. "Let's brief Tyler and Moody and plan a jump."

CHAPTER 38

Staring down at her salad bowl, Zee hunted through the lettuce with her plastic fork for a piece of grilled chicken. Her body felt like it desperately needed protein, so she ate way more meat than typical these days. The novelty of time travel had completely worn off, and now it was just a job. A stressful, difficult job, but there was something else needling her subconscious. She couldn't quite articulate it, but it was like her body didn't want her to go. The feeling was different and distinct from her claustrophobia, which she was still battling every time she stepped inside the Donut. This was more . . . *visceral*. Like how she felt whenever she looked at tuna salad, a reaction from having suffered a terrible bout of food poisoning from the stuff in high school. Just the thought of traveling was almost nauseating.

"That's exactly how I eat salad," Tyler said with a chuckle, leaning in from the seat next to her. "Pick out the tasty things and leave all the green stuff in the bowl."

"It's weird," she said. "Lately, I feel depleted, you know? Like my body needs meat or something."

"Welcome to every day of a SEAL's life," he said with a boyish grin, checking his watch. "Well, probably need to finish up. We're jumping in fifteen."

She speared what appeared to be the last piece of grilled chicken and popped it into her mouth. "Let's go . . ."

Fifteen minutes later, hydrated and injected with antioxidants, she followed her teammates into the Pepper Grinder. After completing the ritual of kissing her fingertips and pressing them to the Father of Time Travel shrine—something even Adela did now before every jump—she grudgingly stepped into the Donut and took her position on her stupid X taped on the floor. Marty was sitting this jump out as usual. There'd been no time to get him tactically proficient, and his time was better spent working on a new data-sifting algorithm for the NSA's cellular voice traffic analysis to help identify the men who'd gone after Tyler's family. NSA had intercepted a call from an encrypted phone within minutes of the tunnel incident that looked promising.

For this op, the team dressed as law enforcement officers and jumped with badges and sidearms, so they had the authority and firepower they needed to search for any potential threat quickly and safely. They generally jumped "under the radar" but with the likelihood of encountering workers—who might, in fact, be part of the terror network planning the attack, the subterfuge of posing as law enforcement might give them an edge—if even for a moment. Compliance often accompanied a badge and a gun.

To Zee, the air in the Donut felt leaden and suffocating, just like her mood. She decided she wasn't the only one feeling this way, because even Ben and Stan were quiet. She glanced at Tyler, who was in prejump mode with a face that looked like it could have been chiseled from stone. He'd lost weight since they came to Omega, which accentuated his jaw despite the beard he was growing.

"Omega Team is set and ready to travel," Tyler said without bothering to get a verbal from each team member.

"Spinning up. Good luck and Godspeed," Moody said, and the intercom went quiet.

She synchronized her watch timer, a practice she'd taken to after a previous jump when Tyler had, absentmindedly forgotten to press his timer button. She figured it was probably not a bad idea to back him up. He was under tremendous stress, and she knew not being able to check on Nikki and Harper—not knowing if they were safe and doing okay—must be weighing heavily on him.

And me too, she thought. She liked Harper, and admired Nikki's courage under fire. She had always been in awe of the strength it took to be the wife—or now coparent—of an elite Navy SEAL. With all she was forced to bear, Nikki was amazing.

Zee heard the field coming up and got that familiar tingle on the back of her neck and forearms as her hair stood up. On the zero beat, her heart skipped and they traveled.

She blinked and the inside of the Donut was replaced by the roof-top of the Water Park Towers Apartments in Crystal City. Squinting in the sun, she scanned the vacant rooftop, turning a complete circle. The rooftop had three structures on it—mirror-image HVAC systems on the north and south ends and a block-shaped structure in the middle that housed the elevator and stairwell for rooftop access. Moody and the control room techs had done a perfect job landing Omega Team out of the way on the south side of the roof to prevent unintended collisions with interfering matter—including people.

This landing had been flawless, but to her dismay, the scene on arrival did not match the imagery. In the satellite surveillance, there had been a crane loading equipment and five workers milling about in the area between the central structure and the north HVAC unit, but this rooftop did not match the predetonation imagery.

"What the hell?" Stan said with a screwed-up look on his face. "Where is everybody?"

"And where's the crane?" Ben said.

"Are we sure we jumped to the right time?" Adela asked.

"Maybe Control screwed up and sent us early," Tyler said.

"I'm going to check out the north side where the crane was supposed to be," Ben said, but as soon as he set off in a jog, he stumbled.

"Are you okay, Ben?" Zee asked, extending a hand to help her teammate up from a kneeling position.

"My knee just gave out while I was running," Ben said with surprise. He straightened it, and she heard an audible pop which made him grimace. Then, with a goofy grin, he was up and moving again. "All good now."

But are you?

"Spread out and see what we can find," Tyler growled. "Maybe they changed plans and the weapons are concealed differently. We only have a few minutes. Adela with me . . ."

Zee moved swiftly with Ben, Tyler partnered with Adela, and Stan shifted toward a corner on his own, quickly searching. To Zee, this was feeling like a dry hole, and she felt anger growing in her chest. Someone *had* to be leaking information. They must have a mole, right? How else could this future have changed without their adversaries being alerted? But how? Moody had the complex locked down tight with no communications gear and every bit of computer traffic tightly regulated—and no doubt being scoured by his internal CI. Her understanding was that no data currently flowed in or out of Omega.

So how could they have known? We planned this entire jump after the lockdown. Unless . . .

The germ of an idea got sidelined by a strange sound, and she looked around, locking eyes with Tyler who approached her, shaking his head grimly.

"Nothing," he said, then seemed to hear the sound as well, scanning suddenly around.

Zee turned in a slow circle, searching for the source of the buzzing sound, like a bumble bee circling her head.

"Anybody else hear that?" Adela said.

"Yeah," Stan said, "but I don't see what's making—"

"It's a drone," Ty said, pointing to a quadcopter in an ascending hover ten meters away, just above the eastern edge of the rooftop.

"Guys, there's nobody over here," Ben called, "and no boxes or crates that could be holding the warheads. It's just us."

"Roger that," Tyler said, eyes locked on the drone.

"Hey, what the hell is that?" Ben asked, seeing what Tyler stared at.

"What's it doing?" Zee said, feeling her pulse rate picking up.

"Filming us . . ."

Tyler pulled his pistol and, with machinelike precision, put two rounds into the chassis of the thing, sending it spiraling down and out of view.

Stan shook his head. "That's not good."

"You think?" Adela said, hands on hips.

"Damn it. They knew we were—" Zee stopped midsentence, interrupted by a new buzzing, only this time at their nine o'clock on the other side of the building.

"We've got another one," Stan said, pointing west.

Zee squinted, bringing it into better focus, and noticed something different about this drone. "Guys, what's the bulge on the underside?"

"That's a payload," Adela said with dreadful certainty. "That's a kamikaze drone. Either we shoot it down or we die."

Tyler squared his stance and brought his pistol up to dispatch this drone like he had the last. But this time, as he squeezed off rounds from his SFX9, the drone juked in midair, conducting evasive maneuvers.

"Stay still, you fucker," Stan yelled as he took a kneeling stance and joined Ty in trying to down the acrobatic quadcopter.

"Guys, we've got another one incoming!" Ben shouted. Fresh gunfire erupted from Ben and Adela to Zee's right as another quadcopter zoomed toward the rooftop.

Zee glanced at the countdown timer on her watch. "Eighteen seconds," she called, but that didn't matter if they got blown up in the interim.

The whine of the quadcopters' rotors jumped an octave as they synchronized and abruptly accelerated into vertical climbs, shrinking from view.

"What's happening?" Stan called.

"I think they're leaving," Ben said.

That's not what's happening, Zee realized as her stomach turned to lead.

"No, they're going to dive-bomb us," Ty shouted, reading her mind. He sprinted to the roof access central structure and tried the door handle. "It's locked."

Zee scanned the rooftop. They had nowhere to go and nowhere to shelter from a vertical attack. If the drones detonated their payloads—probably fragmentation explosives of some sort—five meters above their heads, the outcome would be catastrophic. Everyone would take massive damage.

"Spread out," Tyler barked, which, mathematically speaking, was the optimal strategy. "Maximize distance between each other."

One of the advantages of working with supersmart people who also happened to be tactically trained was that nobody had to waste time on explanations. With this crew, everyone got it. Zee took off in a sprint toward the southwest corner, and her teammates scattered on diverging vectors. As she ran, she heard another rotor pitch change as the drones commenced the dive-bomb.

"Incoming!" Stan shouted.

A split second later, the rooftop sounded like a firing range as her teammates emptied their magazines at the incoming drones, but the quadcopters descended in unpredictable corkscrew maneuvers, juking left and right while spiraling, making themselves nearly impossible targets.

Zee glanced at her countdown timer and an insane idea came to her:

Eleven stories at eleven feet per story puts the roof at 121 feet high, falling at 32 feet per second squared until terminal velocity . . . about two and half seconds.

"In nine seconds, we jump," she shouted and climbed onto the edge of the stubby wall that surrounded the top of the building. "On my mark . . ."

"Are you fucking nuts?" Stan yelled, but he said it while climbing onto the ledge himself.

If her watch's countdown timer was off by even a fraction of a second, the fall would be fatal. If the drones detonated before they jumped, the explosion would be fatal. The window for their survival was impossibly narrow, but her gut told her this was the only way. Her plan would work, so long as today was *not* the day when Moody's engineers figured out how to maintain the flux vortex for longer than four minutes, extending their stay in the future.

"Do it," Tyler shouted from his corner with a fatalistic grin. "See you on the flip side, Zee."

When her timer hit two seconds, she shouted, "Jump!"

The world went silent as she stepped off the roof. She heard herself gasp and then the sound of wind whipping past her ears. She'd stepped out of plenty of airplanes during jump school, but for those leaps of faith, she'd always had a parachute strapped to her back. A morbid dread washed over her as she realized what she'd done. The ground was coming up fast. Really fast. Too fast.

Shit, I screwed up.

The drones exploded somewhere above her.

Her watch chimed.

Her heart skipped a beat.

She hit the floor of the Donut with a *thud* followed by the *chink, chink, chink* of the brass they'd fired.

"Are you fuckin' kidding me!" Ben said and followed it with a whoop.

She looked from Ben to Stan, who was laughing hysterically, then to Adela, and finally at Tyler.

They locked eyes and all Ty could do was shake his head and laugh.

"Omega, Control—sitrep. What was that landing? Are you guys okay?" Moody's voice asked over the loudspeaker.

"Omega, status," Tyler said, pressing to his feet with a groan. They sounded off in order. Collectively, they were bruised and battered, but nobody had broken bones or dislocated joints.

"Looks like Omega is intact . . . but we are *definitely* not okay. We just got targeted by assassin drones. This time they knew exactly when and where we were jumping."

The door lock disengaged, and Zee watched Stan push the door open, then step aside for her with a tight smile. As she exited, Moody sprinted toward them from the bottom of the control balcony's steel steps.

"What happened?"

"They were waiting for us is what happened," Tyler growled, his voice raw and furious. "We still have a fucking leak, Pat."

CHAPTER 39

"Guys, guys, guys," Tyler said, silencing the din at the high-top workta-ble where they were all gathered and practically shouting at each other. "Can we please just talk one at a time? Zee, I think you were trying to say something when everyone started piling on."

"Thank you. What I was trying to say is what just happened indi-cates a noteworthy and significant tactical shift by our adversary. Between our last NORAD jump and this recon jump, the timeline changed," Zee said.

"She's right," Stan said. "This goes beyond a hit planned and executed in the present—this was a countermove in the *future*."

An uncomfortable quiet hung in the air until a silent consensus was reached and they turned to look at Moody as a group.

"Why are you all staring at me?" Moody said.

"Because someone leaked our jump coordinates and the exact future time window to the enemy," Tyler said. "And they did it over fucking lunch."

"How could the bad guys prep an op that fast?" Ben asked.

"Are you kidding me, Ben?" Adela said, her voice oozing with derision. "We've been doing this for a month."

"The mole had an hour to send the message before our jump, but the bad guys had eleven days to prep the intervention in the present," Stan said, clapping Ben on the shoulder.

Ben's cheeks went crimson. "Oh yeah, I'm sorry. Dealing with some brain fog today."

"It's all right, bro. We're all exhausted," Tyler said with a tight smile before turning back to Moody. "Pat, you've gotta do something. The lockdown and all the other safeguards you've implemented obviously aren't working."

"How many people knew about this jump?" Adela said before Moody could answer.

"Jimmy, Becca, me, and the six of you," Moody said. "I kept it small. That's it."

"Then we have our list of suspects," Tyler said and turned to Adela. "I think it's time we narrow the list, don't you?"

Adela gave him a knowing look and nodded.

"Guys, come on—what are you implying? That we waterboard everyone until we get a confession," Zee said with a shocked look on her face.

"If that's what it takes, then yes," Tyler said, his anger getting the better of him before saying, "I'm sorry. I don't know what's wrong with me. I didn't mean that."

"Before we turn on each other and this devolves into an Omega witch hunt," Moody said in his trademark *we're all friends here* demeanor, "I can tell you that I was with Jimmy and Becca the entire time after you guys briefed me. That was a new jump, and they worked like maniacs from the minute I gave the coordinates and time window to when we warmed up the Donut. There wasn't time for them to sneak away and make a call or send a message."

"And the six of us were together that entire period too," Adela said. "So, it couldn't have been one of us."

An uncomfortable silence hung in the air until, at last, Martin spoke.

"I might have another theory," the boy genius said. "What if the jump computer itself is the problem?"

"What do you mean?" Moody asked.

"If I wanted to know what an adversary jump team was doing, but not jeopardize my asset or risk regular communication, I would infect the jump computer with a Trojan horse. A simple exploit that runs in the background is all it would take. When new jump coordinates are entered, it would transmit the data."

"But we've run virus scans on all the computers and servers. I've restricted outgoing traffic, and on top of that, everything exported gets screened," Moody said. "Wouldn't our cyber team notice it?"

"The data packet would be incredibly small and easy to bury in authorized traffic."

"Give me a specific example of authorized traffic that could be exploited," Moody said.

"Sure, we're constantly generating case files and queries for partner agencies to spur interventions in the future," Martin said. "We forced two interventions this week already."

"Yes, but I—and I alone—route those files, and I didn't send one during the window of opportunity. What else could it be?"

Martin thought for a moment, then said, "Well, HAL is routing data and queries back and forth between here and the Omega Room 24-7. The instant the jump computer scheduled the jump, HAL would be alerted and start flagging any and all potentially relevant information or news associated with the jump coordinates and the future time window. Remember, HAL exists in two places at once—here and the Omega Room—and it's constantly synchronizing files."

"Fuck," Moody said through gritted teeth. "I didn't consider the Omega Room."

"Out of sight, out of mind," Tyler said.

"Yeah, and also I think of it as a future asset, but that's a mistake because its computers are running here and now in the present. Martin, could the Trojan be on one of the computers in the Omega Room instead of the jump computer?"

"Yes," Martin said. "And that would also explain why your virus scans have come up clean."

"And it would explain the enemy's operating pattern we've seen to date as well as this change in tactics," Zee added.

"Can you elaborate on that, please?" Moody said, looking at her.

"Think about it, we've not been jumping to the Omega Room. We've been jumping to Cheyenne Mountain. The bad guys can't possibly know what we discovered in the NORAD SCIF until we actively start entering data into HAL and generating an intervention package. Also, the other thing we always do is free jump to ground zero to validate the bomb detonation location and collect as much intel on the scene as possible. After we foiled the last two attempts, they must have figured out what we were doing."

"Marty and Zee, you're both brilliant," Tyler said. "They connected the dots, identified our operational pattern, and instead of moving the nuke again, this time they set a trap on our validation jump."

Moody steepled his fingers and said, "This is very strong work, team. Until I can confirm this, I'm not willing to take any chances. I'm going to secure power to the Omega Room. We'll continue jumping to the NORAD and ground zero locations for intelligence collection while I work on trying to stand up a temporary Omega Room somewhere. For every free jump going forward, until we've confirmed the origin of the leak, we should assume you could be walking into a trap. It's possible we're wrong and the Trojan is not in the Omega Room's computers but somewhere else."

"Agreed," Tyler said and turned to Martin. "Marty, does that sound reasonable to you?"

Martin nodded. "It's safer than trying to remote in and risking infecting the computers here. If the Omega Room hardware is offline, the Trojan can't relay our jump coordinates or other findings. Keep in mind, I was just proposing a hypothetical. It doesn't mean there's not a more complicated or comprehensive exploit installed here that the scans have missed."

"We understand," Tyler said, "but it sounds like you're onto something."

"I agree with everything you guys said, but we can't take our eye off the ball for long. Yes, they swapped the nukes on the roof for a drone attack, but knowing these guys, they're not going to give up," Ben said. "They're going to move it somewhere else and try again."

"You're right, which means we return to Cheyenne Mountain for a new twenty-eight-day look back," Tyler said, then flashed Adela a wry grin. "Besides, it's been a couple of days, and I think Adela is probably missing her boyfriend, Sergeant Bloom."

CHAPTER 40

"That's right, shut the Omega Room down completely—the data servers, HAL, everything," Moody said, talking to Jimmy over the speakerphone from his office. "It's the only way to be one hundred percent sure. And nobody is to restore power without my express permission, is that clear?"

"Crystal clear," Jimmy said. "I hope you're right about this. The idea of us being compromised from within has been bothering me."

"Me too, Jimmy. Me too."

"Anything else?"

"Alpha is going to jump this afternoon to the NORAD SCIF, but don't enter anything into the jump computer until right before go time."

"No problem. The calcs are done for that one. All we have to do is pick the time and hit Enter. But, if the bad guys are grabbing the info from the future, what difference will that make?"

Moody pursed his lips. He'd thought of that too, but if ever there was a time for belt and suspenders . . .

"I get that, but we don't know for sure that's what's happening, so let's cover all our bases, okay?"

"Yeah, sure," Jimmy said. "What time to you want to plan for?"

"Fifteen hundred hours."

"Roger that. I'll message you when the Omega Room is offline."

"Thanks, Jimmy.

"Easy day."

Moody hung up the phone and actually managed a smile.

Easy day? Brooks's SEAL speak is rubbing off on everyone in this place, it seems.

A timid knock vibrated his office door in the frame, interrupting his concentration.

He hated how there was a gap in the striker plate that allowed the latch to rattle—metal on metal—even when his door was shut. Every time someone walked past in the hall, it clattered. This was a half-billion-dollar facility, for Christ's sake, and they couldn't hang a door properly.

"Come in," he said and put on a smile when he saw who it was. "Doctor Donahue, how are you?"

Inside, however, he sighed and rolled his eyes. Claire was brilliant. Claire was beyond hardworking. And she seemed completely committed to solving the problem assigned to her. But she could be *so* annoying, and his head was already about to explode. There were two types of people he simply didn't have patience for: bleeding hearts and car salesmen, and Donahue was the former. But maybe he was finally going to get some good news in this otherwise shit-fest of a day.

"I'm well, Director Moody. I came by for our 1130 meeting, but you were with the team."

"Ah, that's right, I'm sorry about missing that. Something urgent came up," he said, gesturing toward the chair opposite his desk. "Have a seat, please."

"Is everything all right with the team?" she asked, remaining standing.

"Not entirely, but medically they seem to be just fine. We have multiple tactical and mission-oriented issues—the details of which are not your concern—but they're adding to the team's stress right now. Consequently, the jump schedule will continue to be aggressive for the foreseeable future."

She frowned at this last statement and hugged the tablet computer she was holding tight to her chest. "All the more reason you need to review the latest scans and blood work."

"Absolutely. How are our intrepid travelers doing?" he asked. Her face suggested this wasn't going to be the good news he was hoping for.

"Honestly, not so great," she said, leaned over his desk, and handed him the tablet. "I have some concerns. The revised protocol is not as effective at mitigating cellular degradation as we'd hoped. Everything that happened to the previous team is happening again, only at a slower rate."

Moody sighed.

"They seem to be holding up pretty well—better than the last team, it seems."

"Maybe on the outside," she said through a sigh. "But the scans and blood work tell a different story. For example, take a look at this lumbar scan I took of Chief Brooks. You can see two bulging discs, reduced joint space, signs of early arthritis, and what appears to be a microfracture here in L3. The image is particularly troublesome."

"What do you mean?" he asked, playing dumb as he swiped through the scans.

"You're joking, right?" she said. "Tyler is twenty-eight, but he has the spine of a sixty-year-old man."

"It doesn't look *that* bad," he said.

"With all due respect, you're not a doctor. Making medical diagnoses and managing care is what you hired me to do."

He handed back the tablet without bothering to look at the rest of the scans and results she'd prepared for him. "How's the girl, Zee, doing?"

"Better than the men. Her telomeres appear to be aging at half the rate of the others."

"I told you we needed a woman in the program to run as a comp," he said. "And what about Adela?"

"Also faring better than the men," Donahue said, "but not as stable as Zee. I'd like to collect a bone marrow sample from each of the team. The rapid cell production in the marrow will give me a much more accurate snapshot of their nucleotide and mitochondrial health."

Moody grimaced and shook his head. They needed answers and Donahue might well be the one to find them, but the timing was terrible. In the middle of all that was going on, he could hardly suggest to the team that they needed bone marrow biopsies. They were operators, not idiots, and they were already paranoid enough.

"It'll have to wait until we're out of our current crisis, Claire. We can't raise a big ol' red flag right now," he said.

"Over the past week, Stan has cornered several members of the medical staff to ask probing questions. Are you aware of this development?"

He nodded. "I am. So tell me, what are you going to do about it?"

"I . . . I assumed . . ." she stammered.

"You assumed I would intervene, didn't you?"

"Um, yes. You always have in the past."

"Well, not this time," he said with a smug smile. "As chief medical officer, this is something *you* need to manage going forward. I want you to have one-on-one meetings with any member of the jump team who requests it. I want you to answer their questions and put their minds at ease."

"But how can I put their minds at ease and answer their questions truthfully?"

He leaned back and studied her, choosing his words carefully now. He needed Donahue on board, and he simply couldn't risk unmasking the problem to the team right now. Stan would possibly never jump again. Ben would be far less effective. They needed to be laser focused . . .

"Claire, I know I've tasked you with a nearly impossible mission. And you have handled it beautifully so far. With an operational, covert ops unit, there is so much we have to consider. I hate keeping this from them because I care about each and every member of this team. They've become like a family to me," he said and added a gentle tremor in his voice to suggest the emotion he thought she needed to hear, "but they also have a job to do . . ."

"You want me to lie to them?" she asked with a pained look on her face. "Is that what you're saying?"

He shook his head.

"No, no," he said. "I don't want you to lie to them. But I *need* you to keep the truth to yourself a little longer. What you need to understand is that any distraction—and this knowledge would be an incredible, debilitating distraction—can take them off their game. And in the high-stakes world they live and operate in, keeping focus is the difference between life and death. I wish I could magically hit the Pause button and give you all the time you need to finish your research, but unfortunately, I don't have that luxury. Omega is a counterterrorism task force, and we need to complete our current tasking or millions of innocent people could die. I wish I could tell you more . . ."

He watched her face and knew he had her. She sighed.

"I understand, but . . ."

He rose and walked around the desk, giving her a sad, empathetic smile.

"I know how hard this is for you. And it's hard for me too, but until they finish their tasking, the best thing we can do for them is keep their minds in the game. Once they stop this threat, we'll do a stand down, read them in on your progress, and get all the samples you need. Okay?"

"Okay," she said through a sigh. "I just hate this . . ."

He felt relief as he kicked this particular can of worms down the road. The team already didn't trust him and learning that he'd kept *this* from them would be the straw that broke the proverbial camel's back. That day was inevitable, but it didn't need to be today.

"I know, me too," he said. "Is there anything else on your mind?"

"There is something else," she said, her expression brightening. "I've started working on a new treatment protocol with the potential to not only stop the accelerated aging caused by the jumps but possibly even reverse it—"

"Wait, reverse it?" Moody said, caught off guard by this astounding discovery. "Claire, that's amazing. How does it work?"

"Based on the work of David Sinclair at Harvard, I've been using epigenetic reprogramming to reset the cellular software, so to speak, which causes the cell to essentially reboot and repair the damage to the telomeres. Our rodent test group is showing reverse aging, which suggests the same mechanism is possible with humans. But Alpha Team is degrading quickly. I heard what you said, but if we could just slow down the pace of the jumps a little until I can catch up. If I just had more time—"

"Unfortunately, Claire, time is the one thing we don't have," he said, cutting her off. "I know people talk in this facility and share details about our mission and intelligence we've collected that they shouldn't. Even though your operational clearance is restricted, I suspect you're not completely oblivious to what we do here, are you?"

She hesitated a beat, then nodded. "I do hear *things*, from time to time."

"Good. So, you know we're trying to prevent World War III and it's proving to be more challenging than we anticipated. There's nothing I'd love more than to slow the tempo. I myself have even had to jump a few times to augment the team."

"I noticed that from the logs," she said.

"My point is, Claire, that I need you to work harder. Faster. Better. The reality is that people with the skill sets *and* eidetic memories of these operators are exceedingly rare. I don't have a B-team waiting on standby. If this team can't save the world, nobody can. If I could ask the terrorists to go on holiday so you can have more time, I would, but sadly that's not the world we live in. Evil doesn't take time off, Doctor."

His words seemed to have the desired impact. She nodded and, with what sounded like renewed purpose and conviction, said, "We'll double our efforts. I'll run the lab day and night if I have to. I may need more sequencers."

"Whatever you need, I'll get it," he said.

"Thank you," she said, turning to leave.

"And, Claire," he called, smiling when she turned back to him. "Thank you. I know how stressful this is, but I want you to know how much I appreciate you and your team. And most importantly, I don't want you to think I don't take your Hippocratic oath seriously. I know how much you care. We're all focused on the same mission—saving lives. You're looking out for your patients, and I'm trying to safeguard millions of innocents. Omega's success all hinges on everyone being able to do their jobs at the highest level."

Her answer was a cautious smile.

"Anyway, I just want you to know how much I personally appreciate your dedication. If anyone can find the answer to reversing cellular degradation, it's you."

"We'll get there," she said with a nod. "I promise."

"I know you will, Claire."

And then she left, closing the door behind her.

As soon as she was gone, he exhaled through pursed lips. It seemed things were much worse than he'd hoped. He really did like this crew. They were motivated, effective, and had gelled as a team. It wasn't easy to find experienced tactical operators with eidetic memories—he didn't even have four viable candidates to recruit in their place.

"Fuck," he murmured, pressing a closed fist against his sternum as an upswell of hot acid scalded his esophagus.

She's right, though, he thought as he reached for his Tums. *I've got to find a way to reduce the number of jumps but still retain the same effectiveness. If we don't slow down, it's game over.*

"Think, think, think . . ." he murmured and looked at the framed photo of Einstein on his wall. "What would you do?"

The most complex problems often have the simplest solutions.

He smiled and then popped to his feet. "Bravo site," he said with a nod to Einstein.

How had he not thought of this already? The Bravo site was still only partially completed, but it could still be made operational and might be more effective than jumping to NORAD. The Bravo site would potentially mean one jump for every two the team was doing now. Instead of jumping to NORAD and ground zero, they could jump only to the Bravo site twenty-eight days out. As long as he could route the same satellite imagery they accessed at NORAD to the Bravo site, the team could ID detonation locations and enter intervention packages here.

"They don't have to validate every predetonation set of coordinates," he said, pacing his office. "We know the warheads these assholes are using. So long as NCTC keeps thwarting each attack in the window leading up to D-Day, we can stay ahead of them."

It was a good plan. A very good plan . . . except . . .

Except, I'll be giving up my ace in the hole. And I don't know if I'm willing to do that.

He sighed.

Unfortunately, I don't really have a choice. I'm out of options.

CHAPTER 41

DIE URSACHE SAFE HOUSE
ALEXANDRIA, VIRGINIA
1400 LOCAL TIME

Jun resisted the compulsion to leave the room as Garth installed the frag-explosive payload on the quadcopter drone which was turned upside down on the dining-room table. From outward appearances, the slow-talking, tobacco-chewing American mercenary did not seem like the type of person anyone would want working on high-tech drones, electronic detonators, or explosives. But as was so often the case, appearances could be deceiving. When Jun had asked him if he knew what he was doing, Garth flashed him a toothy tobacco-stained grin and said something about this not being his first rodeo. Jun didn't know anything about rodeos, but as he watched Garth work, he figured it out. The man appeared to know exactly what he was doing, and his work seemed to be both methodical and meticulous.

When he'd finished and the drone had *not* blown them up, Garth leaned back in his chair, looked at Jun, and asked, "Who's your huckleberry now?"

As with most of Garth's slang, Jun didn't understand the literal meaning, only the inferred one. When he'd learned English in China, they'd not provided any instruction on idioms from the American South, which was where Garth claimed to be from. Idioms and slang were the most difficult part of learning a language. Jun didn't ask Garth to explain what it meant to be a *huckleberry*, but it was clear his colleague was simply looking for praise.

"Good work," Jun said and gave Garth a thumbs-up.

"You thought I was gonna blow us up?"

Jun nodded. "Yes."

"Ye of little faith." When Jun didn't smile or react, Garth said, "You're upset. Did I do somethin' wrong?"

"No. You do everything very well. I am frustrated with this safe house, with Hoffman, with everything about this situation . . ."

"Yeah, man, I get it."

"But it does not seem to bother you?"

"You mean the not knowing how things are going to turn out?"

"Exactly!" Jun said and threw his hands up in aggravation. "Hoffman tells us to do this . . . do that . . . and then he changes his mind. I made a good plan to kidnap the SEAL's daughter and set a trap for the Omega team. The plan worked. We killed all of them. Hoffman told me this. But then, this is not what happens."

"That's cuz they changed the future, Jun."

"I know, so then we attack them in the tunnel and Damien dies. Why would Hoffman let us do this if he knew it would be a failure?"

"Because either he didn't know the outcome, or the Omega team changed the future until they got the outcome they wanted. That's the thing, Jun, the future ain't set in stone. All that has to happen is for one person to do one thing they weren't supposed to, and it all goes to hell. Trust me, I bet they're thinking the same damn thing as us."

Jun swatted the comment away as if it were a buzzing mosquito.

"You don't believe me?"

"I don't know what I believe anymore," he said through a sigh and pulled out a chair to sit next to Garth at the table. "Take this drone, for example. Hoffman has a plan for us to attack the Americans in the future at a specific time and place. By creating it we have set that plan in motion."

"That's right."

"So shouldn't he be able to send a jump recon team to the event and see if it works?"

"Yeah, that's what he does. He burns up recon teams like nobody's business," Garth said, then grimaced as he straightened his right knee with a grinding *pop*. "Fuck. I'm glad I'm not traveling no more. My knees can't take it."

"I have arthritis in my hands and feet. They are always hurting," Jun said. Then, in a moment of trust, he decided to cross the line that they'd all silently but implicitly agreed not to cross. "I'm going to be honest with you. My brother and I joined *Die Ursache* for the money."

Garth chuckled. "We all did, dude."

"I thought I was signing on to be a paramilitary contractor, not a terrorist."

At this comment, Garth's face hardened. "Yeah, me too."

"But this is your home, your country. How can you . . . I don't know . . . let Hoffman bomb Washington, DC?"

Garth shook his head. "I'm on the fence about that one. I love my country, but the people running it—not so much. A little house-cleaning would do the nation good. It's like when someone gets cancer, the doctors gotta use poison for the treatment. Sometimes, to cure a patient, you have to damn near kill 'em first."

Jun nodded. "Do you think Hoffman is the brain behind *Die Ursache?*"

"Nah, he's middle management."

"Then who do you think is in charge?"

"Probably some crazy billionaire. They're all nuts, if you ask me. Just because you invent some piece of code in your mom's basement and get rich doesn't mean you get to rule the world, but that's what they all think."

"Garth, you don't look like a philosopher, but that is what you are."

The American chuckled. "Hell no, I'm just a bitter, broke-ass door-kicker that couldn't get hired anymore."

"Until Hoffman found you . . ." Jun said.

Just then, the sat phone in his pocket rang. He retrieved it and showed Garth the caller ID.

"Speak of the devil," Garth said and dribbled tobacco juice over his lower lip into a water bottle.

Jun accepted the call and held it to his ear.

"Change of plans," Hoffman said without greeting or preamble. "Jun, you will return to our base of operations. Your colleague will stay in theater."

"Something has changed, hasn't it?"

"*Ja*, something has changed," Hoffman said but did not elaborate.

"I want the American dead by my own hand," Jun said, his voice more growl than speech.

"I know. I'm going to give you that chance."

"And what about my colleague?"

"His next operation is not your concern. Transfer custody of this phone to him. Your travel instructions will follow electronically."

Jun was about to protest but the line went dead. He stared at the phone for a long moment, considering calling back. But even if Hoffman picked up—which he likely wouldn't—the German would not change his mind. *Die Ursache* was a dictatorship and Hoffman was the dictator. Shaking his head, Jun reached out and slapped the phone into Garth's upturned paw.

The American fixed him with what Jun could tell was a tight-lipped grin, although he couldn't see it beneath Garth's shaggy beard and mustache.

"Looks like our paths have just hit a fork in the road," Garth said.

Jun nodded because this particular American slang he actually knew. "I respect you, Garth," he said and stuck out his hand.

"You too, brother. You're a helluva operator," the American said and shook it. "Good luck avenging your brother, Jun. I'm sure I'll see you on the flip side—or, if not, I guess I'll see you in Valhalla."

CHAPTER 42

THE CHOW HALL

THE SALT SHAKER—WAREHOUSE A

TWO DAYS LATER

1231 LOCAL TIME

Tyler took a sip of sweet tea, which he normally loved, but today somehow tasted stale and flavorless. Staring into the cup, he stirred it with a spoon and watched the little vortex swirling in the center.

"I feel like I'm in that movie *Groundhog Day*," Ben said across from him. "You know, like we wake up and do the same thing we did the day before. We find the nuke, we stop the nuke, and tomorrow we have to do it all over again."

Tyler nodded. Ben's comment perfectly captured how he was feeling too. They'd done five jumps in twenty-four hours and thwarted two more detonations—one where the payload had been loaded in the back of a truck, the other in a train car. Playing Whack-A-Nuke wasn't fun anymore—if it ever had been.

"You're so right, Ben," Tyler said.

"Yeah, except none of us are as funny as Bill Murray, and we never get to see Punxsutawney Phil on any of our jumps," Stan said.

"Punxsutawney who?" Zee asked, looking up from her salad with a perplexed expression. "What in the world are you guys talking about?"

"Are you kidding me? You've never seen *Groundhog Day*?" Stan said.

"She wasn't even born when that movie was made," Adela said, shaking her head.

"Neither was I, but I've seen it," Ben said. "It's a classic."

"That's because you're both old men trapped in young men's bodies. You know that?" Adela came back.

Speaking of feeling like an old man trapped in a young man's body . . .

Tyler arched his back, hoping for a nice, tension-relieving pop, but instead got a stinger that shot down his leg and made him wince. Damn, he felt wrung out—had for a while. He'd chalked it up to exhaustion—both physical and emotional—from the stress, poor sleep, and operational tempo. But how did that explain his weight loss, lethargy, and joint pain? Both of his shoulders not only hurt, but they creaked and cracked when he moved, and his left ankle had throbbed so bad he'd caught himself limping a bit on the walk into lunch.

He looked at the weary crew seated with him around the table. Truth was the whole team looked like shit—pallid and worn. Not just worn, they looked—

"What the fuck?" Stan said, snapping Tyler from his thoughts.

"Dude, what happened? Are you okay?" Tyler said, squinting at the Delta operator who was cupping his hand over his mouth.

Stan bowed his head and spit something out. He stared at it with wide eyes. "That's my tooth. I just broke my friggin' tooth in half."

"Did you hit a bone?" Ben asked.

"It's a chicken tender. They're boneless," Stan said, staring in disbelief at the chunk of tooth he was holding between thumb and forefinger.

Tyler looked around the table, staring at his teammates one at a time and really studying them: Stan had always been lean, but these days he was looking downright gaunt. Ben had been stout like a linebacker when he showed up at Omega, but now he looked more like a wide receiver. Plus, his hairline looked like it was receding. Adela had pronounced crow's-feet outside her eyes and age spots on her hands where three weeks ago there'd been neither. Marty didn't seem to have changed much, but he was barely in his twenties when they'd started. Zee's left eye was always twitching these days and—

Holy shit, is that a gray streak in Zee's hair?

"What?" Ben said, catching Tyler studying them.

"How are you feeling, Ben?"

Ben smiled, his cheeks creasing with laugh lines. "Like shit, to be honest. I think I'm just worn out."

"When were you last downrange?"

"About six months ago—five maybe."

"Was the op tempo more or less than this?"

Ben chuckled. "Way more. We were conducting raids in a not-to-be-named country south of the Horn of Africa. Out almost every night for hours. These four-minute jumps ain't nothing."

"And did you ever feel this run-down? Maybe toward the end of the tour?"

Ben stared at him, his lips pursing and his brow furrowing with deep worry lines. "No," he said. "Not ever."

Tyler looked at Zee. "Zee, do you color your hair?"

"What?" she said, laughing and feigning incredulity.

"That's a helluva thing to ask a lady, bro," Adela said.

"I'm not screwing around, guys. Zee, you have some gray streaks in your hair today that I didn't notice yesterday."

"What?" Zee said. She picked up a butter knife and held it to catch her reflection. "Oh my God, you're right . . ."

Tyler pursed his lips and said, "Guys, I should have noticed before, but we've been so damn busy. I could tell everyone was worn out, but this is something else. I think traveling is making us sick."

"Not sick . . . it's *aging* us," Ben said.

"The scans, the blood draws, the antioxidant injections . . ." Marty said, nodding.

Then Stan slammed a closed fist on the table. "They've known from the beginning and been lying to us."

Anger flared in Tyler's chest, and he looked at Adela. "Remember our conversation in the Suburban after dropping off Nikki and Harper?"

"Of course," Adela said.

"I wanted to confront that sonuvabitch about his lies and omissions, and you said you wanted to investigate and ask around. Well, what have you found?"

"Not much," she said and lowered her voice. "Moody is former CIA, but we never crossed paths when I was there. My guy told me Moody was Special Activities Division and ran a couple of critical black sites. Supposedly, he has a rep for being smart, loyal, and discrete, but that's all I got."

"None of that is surprising or particularly helpful," Tyler said, irritated. "What about finding hidden files or evidence of a previous team that operated here before us?"

Marty shook his head.

"I hacked into the data files and there's nothing pertaining to a previous team. Either Moody did a meticulous job purging his dirty laundry or on that point he was telling the truth. I meant to tell you that, but we've been so—"

"Busy, I know. He keeps us very busy, and I can't help but wonder if that's by design." Tyler stood, noticing the ache in his back and how stiff his knees felt. "Let's go."

The team formed around Tyler as he headed for the door, Zee catching up.

"Where are we going?" she asked, pulling at his sleeve.

"To confront Moody," Tyler said, "and have a conversation that's long overdue."

Tyler marched the team to Moody's office where he opened the door without knocking.

Moody looked up from his desk, surprised.

But . . . not.

"By all means, come in everyone," Moody said, with his good-natured, aw-shucks charm. "What's going on?"

"You tell us, Pat," Tyler said, barely able to stop himself from leaping over Moody's desk and punching the bastard. "Look at us, Pat. Look at what is happening to our bodies . . ."

"I can see you're upset," Moody said, and he leaned back in his chair, making a silly little steeple with his fingers.

"The Donut is slowly killing us and you knew. You fucking knew, and you didn't tell us!" Stan snapped.

"Listen, guys, I know you've been working harder than ever . . ."

"Enough with the bullshit," Tyler barked, startling himself with the venom in his voice.

Moody nodded, then leaned forward into their hate and judgment, like a black hole consuming all of it and only growing stronger. "Did you really think that it would come without a cost?"

"That *what* would come without a cost?" Zee asked, stepping up next to Tyler.

"The power to play God," Moody said. "Because that's what future knowledge is . . . It's omnipotence."

The potency of the words caused gooseflesh to stand up on Tyler's forearms. The simple truth of the matter was that he'd not considered any such thing. He'd taken time travel at face value—four minutes was four minutes whether he spent it in the present or the future. But that was Moody's fault, wasn't it? His mind went back to their first day and Moody's PowerPoint presentation. There'd been a lot of fuss around the limits of time travel—how long they could stay, how far they could travel, and that time travel was limited to the future—but nothing had been said about a physical toll.

"We have an incredible team of experts here," Moody said, softening again. "They are close to finding a fix for this. Once they do . . ."

"What's the ratio?" Stan asked. "The future time to aging ratio? Four minutes in the future costs us how much time in the present?"

"It's a nonlinear function," Moody said.

"Approximate the slope," Marty insisted, crossing his thin arms on his chest like the operator he stood beside.

Tyler sucked at math, but he got the gist of what the two brainiacs were talking about. And he knew one thing for sure: despite the good ol' boy persona, Moody was a brainiac. He just happened to be a gifted actor too.

"A month per minute . . ."

Collectively shell-shocked, no one said anything.

"But like I said, it's nonlinear. The accumulated effects seem to amplify the rate of degradation over time."

"You're a monster," Adela said, her voice quiet and tremulous. "A calculating, heartless monster."

"No," Moody said, and his gaze went to the middle distance. "I'm not. I'm a soldier, just like each of you—following orders, making difficult choices, and sacrificing my present to safeguard the future lives and safety of my countrymen and countrywomen."

"A month per minute," Tyler muttered, his brain unable to move past this unfathomable figure. "We've unknowingly given you the best years of our life—and for what?"

"For what?" Moody sputtered, incredulous. "To save millions of lives. To save the capital of the United States. To stop World War III and nuclear Armageddon. What the six of you have done is both noble and exceptional."

"But you didn't give us a choice," Zee said. "You should have told us the price and let us decide if we were willing to pay it."

"She's right," Tyler said. "That's how it is with Special Operations. We brief on the risks and benefits of every mission. We know the rules before we go outside the wire."

Moody's lip curled. "Funny. The only thing I ever hear operators talking about is how the spooks fucked them over with faulty intel. You go outside the wire on every mission with imperfect information. You've operated without a crystal ball your entire career, Chief."

"So that makes what you did to us okay?"

"No," Moody said, "but if I'd told you the truth, would any of you have accepted my offer? Would we be in a position to stop the worst attack on American soil in history?"

No one answered.

Moody sighed. "I know it's no consolation, but it wasn't supposed to be this way. We were never supposed to get *here*. The plan was for you to jump once a week to the twenty-eight-day limit, and we'd prosecute the threats in the present. Meanwhile, Dr. Donahue would be working on a treatment to mitigate the effects. She's close to the cure, guys," he said and held up his fingers in a pinch with a half-inch gap between them. "This fucking close. But then the DC attack happened, and the leak. Now we believe that these assholes may have stolen our technology, and this is where we're at."

"We're not the first team, are we?" Tyler said, asking the question that had been needling him for weeks.

"No," Moody said without missing a beat.

"What happened to them?" Zee asked.

"They died during an intervention."

"In the future or the present?"

"The present," Moody said. "Counterterrorism op gone bad."

"Did you let them get degraded like us?" Ben asked.

"I did."

"I want to put a bullet in your brain right now," Stan said, "but . . ."

"But you can't, can you?" Moody said. "Because you'd do the same damn thing if you were in my shoes. Isn't that right, Stan?"

Stan didn't say anything, but that was an answer in and of itself.

"How does it happen? Biologically speaking, what is the mechanism of degradation?" Ben asked, changing subjects to the thing a combat medic would be most interested in.

"Telomeres."

Ben nodded. "Part of our DNA sequence?"

"Actually," Stan said, and it took all of Tyler's willpower to not knock out another of his teammate's teeth, "that's not exactly true. Telomeres are a simple repeating sequence at the ends of every chromosome. They're like a cap on the ends of the strand, not a part of the DNA sequence. They protect our genes from fraying, becoming entangled, or bonding with loose nucleotides. Think of them as a fail-safe to keep the chromosomes pure and intact to do what they're coded to do."

Moody nodded.

"So, the flux vortex in the Donut damages our telomeres?" Ben asked.

"Yes," Moody said.

"How does that make us age?" Tyler asked.

"Telomeres function as a sort of clock for the chromosomes in a cell. What I mean is that they limit the life span of a cell line. The telomeres are simple sequences that start out long, like furry tails on both ends of the chromosome," Stan said. "But each time the cell divides, the telomeres become shorter and shorter—except in stem cells, sperm cells, and egg cells, where the simple sequences can be reconstituted to keep them long indefinitely. In adult cells, when the telomeres eventually become too short, the cell stops dividing and is disposed of. So, over time, our reserve of healthy, dividing cells decreases, our tissues become less healthy, and our organs don't function as well . . ."

"Aging," Adela said.

"Correct," Moody said. "The system is designed to protect us from mutations and cancers growing out of control by limiting their life span."

"It sounds like we're screwed," Ben said. "I mean, even if we stop jumping, once the telomeres shorten its game over. Whatever damage has been done is ours to keep. You've cut twenty years or more off our lives."

"Not necessarily," Moody said and looked from Ben to Tyler. "Dr. Donahue believes she's close to a breakthrough that can reverse the process."

"Bullshit," Adela scoffed. "Reversing aging? The holy grail of modern medicine that billions of dollars and thousands of the world's smartest medical minds have been unable to achieve? You want us to believe that Claire Donahue figured it out? This is just another one of your many lies to manipulate us."

"I deserve that, but what I'm telling you is the truth. We can all take a field trip to the research lab right now, if you like. I'll tell Donahue to make all her data and findings available for review. You can decide for yourselves."

"When were you going to tell us, Pat?" Tyler asked, studying the man carefully.

"Yesterday," Moody said, not missing a beat.

Tyler screwed up his face. "What the hell is that supposed to mean?"

Moody shook his head. "It means I've been planning on telling you for a while, but every time I was about to, something else would happen that made the need to keep jumping the priority. Also, if you haven't noticed, I'm a fucking coward."

"Sounds about right," Adela said.

"Now what?" Ben said, looking at Tyler and getting to the heart of the matter. "Do we quit or do we keep going?"

Tyler let out a long, rattling sigh, then swept his gaze across the faces of the finest, albeit insanely eclectic, team ever assembled. He knew his answer but wanted them to know they had a choice.

"As much as I want to walk away, I can't. Not until we've permanently stopped the attack on DC and found the bastards responsible. But this is a decision each of you is going to have to make for yourself. No bullshit, guys. Volunteers only, and absolutely no shame in passing. We take it one jump at a time, stop the attack, then stand down."

"Why not just take what we know and get back to our roots—stop this the old-fashioned way in the present? Hell, dude, we've been stopping the bad guys since long before this asshole invited us to his party," Ben said with an evil-eyed glare at Moody. "Zee is a brilliant analyst, Marty's a cyber genius, Adela is a spooky shooter, and the rest of us—despite being older and stiffer—are still badass operators."

The rest of the team stared at Tyler, waiting to be led. "This is way more than any of us volunteered for, so stand down now if its best for you until we get a treatment perfected. But show of hands, who's willing to jump, just a few more times, to stop World War III?"

Six hands shot up in the air without hesitation.

Tyler turned to Moody, meeting the man's stare with his own hard gaze, crossing his arms again on his chest.

"You can see now that you should have trusted us," he said to Moody.

Moody nodded. "For what it's worth, I am sorry, guys. More than you know. Every one of you deserves better. And you're right—it should have been your choice to make."

"You're damn right," Ben said.

"You just get Donahue to fix this," Tyler said, pointing a finger at Moody. "We'll take care of saving the world."

Tyler spun on a heel and headed for the door, his team forming in on him as he did. He held it open for them, and before following the last in line out, he turned to Moody one last time.

"We've all risked our lives countless times in our careers to protect our country and her interests," he said. "That's our job. Now do yours and get this shit fixed. And make sure that Omega is worthy of the sacrifice these people are making."

Moody gave him a tight smile and nod.

Tyler walked out, slamming the door behind him.

CHAPTER 43

Tyler felt the whoosh, blinked, and he was standing with his teammates in a medium-sized square room.

The spook-master had come to them with a plan to cut their number of jumps in half, but Moody had refused to give the location, telling them that, for safety and OPSEC, only he and Jimmy knew the details. Tyler could appreciate keeping the circle small, but he found the unspoken implication—that Moody still didn't trust them—insulting.

OPSEC is the priority, he reminded himself. *We can't afford another ambush. If we get killed in the future, it's game over.*

The left wall had a door and two windows that looked out into what appeared to be a pine forest. The center of the room where they landed was, thankfully, vacant and devoid of furniture. The facing wall reminded Tyler of the Omega Room, with multiple workstation terminals and a half dozen TVs streaming cable and world news programs.

"Looks thrown together," Ben said as he trotted to one of the open terminals.

"At least Moody didn't lie about that," Stan said as he did the same.

"While you guys do your thing, I'm going to look around," Tyler said, feeling an unexpected compulsion to conduct a little future recon of his own.

"Good idea," Zee said as she picked a pair of headphones.

In the past, Tyler might have felt guilty about leaving the team, but not today. His operator's sixth sense told him he needed to check this place out, so that's what he was going to do. He drew his pistol, pressed the lever handle on the door, and stepped outside.

The first thing he noticed was how crisp and clean the air felt. The temperature here had to be at least fifteen degrees cooler than in Virginia. A few patches of snow survived in shady spots between the trees and against the side of the building, which he quickly deduced was the north-facing facade. Out of habit, he brought his pistol up and advanced stealthily to the western corner of the simple, single-story, steel-sided structure. After a three-count pause, he cleared it, scanning left into the blind side for threats, before turning a complete circle. Finding nothing of concern, he lowered his pistol to a relaxed carry and assessed his surroundings. It reminded Ty of his brother Nate's detached garage where Nate spent all his free time restoring classic cars.

The other two buildings in this patchy grass clearing were much older—a quaint New England farmhouse and a traditional gable barn.

Bravo site my ass. I bet this is Moody's property . . .

Something about the idea felt right. Moody never talked about a family or where he was from, and since Tyler's first day at the spice factory, the man had not left the compound. It would make sense and help explain why the dude had been so cagey about revealing the jump location . . . This was Moody's private land.

Tyler checked his watch.

Time remaining: 2:32

Like an invisible string, curiosity pulled him toward the barn.

The wood siding had once been painted white, but almost all the paint had worn off and the exposed cedar was so weathered it had a gray-blue tint. The barn entrance faced him, the inside hidden by a pair of large heavy doors. His booted feet carried him silently over the slick, snow-covered grass. At the doors, he scanned for threats a second time and then listened for any signs of activity inside the barn. Hearing nothing, he grabbed the left handle and pulled. At first, the stout wooden door refused to budge, but when he put a little more muscle into it, the door grudgingly yielded to his will and swung open on creaking hinges.

"What the . . ." he murmured as he stepped into the dark, cavernous space.

Electrical control cabinets lined the south wall. Heavy black power cables snaked from the cabinets, across the dirt floor, and disappeared under a tarp, which covered a dome-shaped structure in the middle of the center bay. Movement to the right stole his attention, and he swept his Wilson Combat SFX9 along the row of horse stalls lining the north wall. A single horse, a tall Bay with shiny black points, whinnied and stomped a hoof at him.

"Aren't you a handsome boy?" Tyler said, lowering his pistol and smiling at the horse.

Then, behind him, someone cocked a gun.

Still holding his pistol, Tyler slowly raised his hands over his head. "Don't shoot . . . I'm going to turn around very slowly."

The would-be shooter didn't say anything, but he could hear nervous breathing.

"It's okay. I'm not here to hurt you," he said, his voice calm and polite.

He turned to face a girl, sixteen he guessed, pointing an over/under double-barreled shotgun at him. She was putting on a brave face, but her hands trembled, the barrel swinging gently, still pointed at his head.

"You're not allowed in the barn," she said, trying to sound tough but the fear cutting through. "You weren't supposed to leave the workshop."

"I'm sorry about that. I didn't know the rules," he said with an easy smile. "I'm just going to put my gun down so that you can put yours down too. How's that sound?"

She nodded, but kept the shaking muzzle on him, with her finger on the trigger.

Slowly, Tyler lowered himself in a squat and set his pistol on the ground. When he stood back up, his left hip cracked audibly. He winced involuntarily at the stinger in his joint but forced his expression back to *good ol' boy* friendly.

"My name is Tyler. What's yours?"

She opened her mouth to answer him, but she caught herself and shot daggers at him with her eyes.

"Not supposed to say."

"That's fine, we don't have to talk. I'm going to be leaving in a moment anyway," he said but decided to keep trying. "Is this your dad's place? He probably messaged you a couple of weeks ago and asked for you not to go into the workshop. Am I right about that?"

She took a step back and looked even more nervous than she did before. "He said you understood the rules. I'm not supposed to talk to you, period."

Tyler's gaze dropped to the chest of the navy-blue hoodie she wore. Baby-blue font spelled out MAINE and a cartoonish black bear growled ferociously. "Is that where you go to school, the University of Maine? It's a great campus, I hear."

A flash of guilty anger washed across her face at the mistake.

Gotcha . . . We're in Maine.

His watch chimed.

Thirty seconds.

She glanced at his wrist.

"Just a timer," he said. "That's all."

Suddenly, tears rimmed her eyes. She swallowed hard and said, "Screw the rules . . . I have to know."

"You have to know what?"

"If he's okay. I haven't heard from him since the attack. Do you know if . . . if my dad's alive?" she stammered.

Tyler's stomach sank at the question for so many reasons. His watch chimed a second time.

"Tyler, dude, where are you?" Stan called from across the yard. "Ten seconds, bro."

He ignored Stan and said, "I'm sorry, sweetie, I can't answer that question."

"Because you don't know or because you won't tell me?" she asked with angst in her voice.

"Because I don't know . . ."

He felt the whoosh, blinked, and he was standing on his mark inside the Donut.

"Well?" Tyler asked, scanning the solemn faces of his teammates.

"They moved it again," Zee said as she made a beeline to the door. "This time it's on a plane . . ."

CHAPTER 44

Zee knew that something strange had happened on Tyler's "walkabout" at the Bravo site, but now was not the time to ask him. Moody would be joining them any second, and Tyler would read them in as soon as the opportunity presented itself. That was okay with her; she could wait.

But not too long . . .

And therein lay the bitter irony of the job.

Task Force Omega was a thief. Every trip Zee made to safeguard other people's futures robbed her of her own. These days her mind kept coming back to a quote that Stan had taped to his stateroom door:

> *"I look to the future because that's where*
> *I'm going to spend the rest of my life."*
> *—George Burns*

Her future was disappearing at a disturbing pace, and there was nothing she could do to get the stolen time back. Her heart held hope that Dr. Donahue would find a cure to reverse the aging effects, but her head told her that the whole thing was propaganda dreamed up by Moody to manipulate them. Hell, she wouldn't be surprised if Claire Donahue wasn't even a real doctor. The woman was probably some actress Moody hired. The thought made Zee chuckle. These days, looking for morbid humor in her dreadful situation seemed to be the only salve for her scorched heart.

Everyone on the team viewed Moody's withholding of the cellular effects of travel as an uncategorical betrayal of their trust and military principles. The man was Machiavellian, but there was nothing to be done about it now. Collectively, they'd made their decision to put their own health second to the lives and safety of their fellow Americans. It was the same commitment they'd each made when they'd chosen a life of military service and, in the case of Adela and Marty, government service. The only difference was time. Now, her life had been depleted in big chunks— months instead of minutes—and the toll felt more tangible as she and her teammates raced heedlessly toward their biological expiration date.

Moody walked into the room. She couldn't read his face as he joined them at the standing worktable.

"All right, let's rock and roll, people," Tyler said. "Where is ground zero this time?"

Ben turned to Martin and the two men shared a tense look. "The nukes are aboard United Airlines Flight 351 out of Reagan. They detonate at 1,621 feet in the air, moments after takeoff."

"By exploding at altitude, the damage is worse than detonating on the ground. It's the same reason the MIRVs on missiles are programmed to explode over a target instead of crashing into it. This time, the destruction is worse than all the previous attempts we've foiled," Marty said.

"But that's not the only bad news," Adela said. "They moved the timetable up dramatically. D-Day is tomorrow. We have less than twenty-four hours to stop this attack."

No one said anything at first as they contemplated her words. They'd become so accustomed to having second, third, and fourth chances. But this was a bridge they'd never had to cross before.

"That might not be enough time for our partner agencies to intervene," Zee said.

"But if we know the exact airplane, we can ground the aircraft before it arrives at Reagan. I'm not worried about that as much as the fact that our adversary is upping the ante and accelerating the timeline," Moody said.

"Guys," Zee said, her voice sounding even more weary than she felt, "we need to be realistic. I know I said this morning that I'm all in, and I still am, but our strategy is unsustainable. What if the bad guys know about the effects of time travel? I think what we're seeing is both strategic and tactical. They're not going to give us a break. They're going to jump us to death—literally."

"She's right," Ben said, shaking his head. "I hate to say it but she's right."

"But what other choice do we have?" Stan said.

Zee's mind went to her parents, and the thought of her mom's tender smile almost stopped her from saying what she was about to propose but the words came out anyway. "We don't jump. We intercept the payload in the present and disarm the bomb."

"Too risky," Ben said. "If we fail, the bomb goes off with no chance to try again."

"But is it?" Tyler said, coming to her defense. "Think about it. What Zee is proposing is nothing more than what we all used to do before we joined Moody's time-traveling circus. When I was a SEAL at JSOC, we never had second chances. We didn't get do-overs, and we operated only in the present. We had one shot on every mission and that was it. If you failed, innocent people died. If you succeeded, they didn't. This is no different."

"I would normally agree, but if D-Day is tomorrow, that means the payload has almost certainly been smuggled into the country. The second they see us coming, they'll remote detonate. It doesn't matter if the crate is in DC or Miami, Houston or LA, or even en route somewhere between. Wherever it goes off, it affects millions," Stan said.

Zee deflated. Stan's argument was compelling. Remote detonation was a very real possibility.

"This sucks," she murmured. "If only we could jump onto the plane and disarm the bomb at the very last second before it goes off. That way they couldn't try again."

"But the future resets, so it wouldn't work," Adela said.

"I know," she said through a sigh.

"But does it always?" Tyler asked and turned to Moody. "You lied about everything else; I wouldn't be surprised if you lied about that too."

Moody jerked back a little at the comment. "I deserve that, but the rules of time travel are not something I can control or compartmentalize. You've experienced time travel firsthand. Changes made by travelers in the future reset when they return to present. That's how it works. Period."

"There might be a second option to consider," Martin said with an odd, almost wincing expression on his face.

"What second option is that?" Moody asked.

"Theoretically speaking, there is a specific set of conditions when an action taken in the future could, hypothetically, take hold in the present."

"How?"

"Einstein once famously said, 'The distinction between the past, present, and future is only a stubbornly persistent illusion.' I think Einstein was speaking both metaphorically and literally," Marty said. He walked over to one of the digital whiteboards covered with case notes from their last intervention. He gestured to the scribble and turned to Zee. "May I?"

"By all means," she said.

He tapped the trash bin icon in the bottom left corner and, like magic, the virtual canvas cleared. Then, he picked up a stylus and drew two timeline diagrams on the board, labeling them CASE 1 and CASE 2.

"Case One depicts our typical jump into, what for illustrative purposes, we will call the *distant* future. I know it's not that distant, but it's more than four minutes into the future which, not coincidentally, is the same duration as our loiter time when we jump. I'm going to label the loiter period as Jump Time," he said, pointing with the stylus while he spoke. "Let's say, for example, we decide to jump ten minutes into the future. If I label the present as zero minutes, then our landing point is zero plus ten minutes in the future, or simply plus ten. With a Jump Time of four minutes, we remain in the future until time hits plus fourteen, then we will return home. Meanwhile, time is advancing in the present. Like Becca's riverboat example, the present is moving into the future at a velocity of one minute per minute. So, when we return home, we're not returning to the moment we left, we return to where the present is now. We don't gain any minutes. We don't lose any minutes. Time is conserved. We return to the present four minutes later than we departed. Is everyone with me?"

"We know all this stuff, Marty," Stan said.

"*Some* of us," Ben said. "This is actually quite helpful for me."

"Me too," Tyler said with a chuckle.

"Case Two, however, depicts a jump into what I will call the *near* future, which we shall define as any time between the present and the present plus four minutes. We've never done a jump of this kind, nor have we even discussed it," Martin said, glancing nervously at Moody.

"For good reason," Moody said. "What's the point of jumping three minutes into the future? Nothing has changed enough to warrant it."

"Is that the only reason?" Martin asked, eyeing the director.

"What are you implying here, Marty?" Moody said with an edge to his voice.

"I'm just wondering if, during testing, the science team or any of the test pilots ever jumped into the near future."

Moody scratched his neck. "No. It was discussed and the consensus was that attempting to do so could be . . . problematic."

"As in *break the universe* problematic or *we're not sure what would happen so let's not do that* problematic?" Stan asked.

"More the latter but with a dollop of the former," Moody admitted. "Martin, please continue."

In the first example, Martin had drawn an arrow jumping ten minutes into what he'd call the *distant* future. Now, Zee watched as he drew an arrow jumping only two minutes into the *near* future.

"If we jump into the near future, something different happens than before. Our jump time is still four minutes, with us loitering in the future from plus two to plus six minutes, but when we try to return, we see that the present has caught up to and overlapped our jump time by two minutes."

"So what?" Adela said, "We simply return to the present, which is at the plus-four-minute mark."

"That's right, but there's a problem with this overlapping two-minute period," Martin said. He shaded the area, then wrote the words *Spooky Time* over it.

Tyler stared at the drawing Martin had sketched:

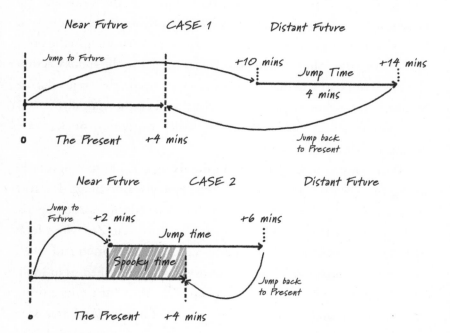

Zee expected Stan to say something, but when no one spoke, she decided to float the idea that had come to her.

"Okay, I'll try. Let's say I jump two minutes into the future, and the rest of you stay here in the present. From your point of view, I would disappear. But from my point of view, I would arrive two minutes into your future. I hang out with you for four minutes and, during that time, let's say we talk about the World Series. Then, at six minutes I'd disappear and travel back to the present, but the present would have advanced four minutes. I can't go back to the time I left from because that's in the past now. But there also can't be two of me in the same place at the same time, so future me disappears when I arrive back at the present at plus four minutes." She closed her eyes a moment trying to work it out, "God, this is so weird to think about. Okay, so for you guys, the second two minutes would reset the instant I return, but the first two minutes of our conversation about the World Series *can't* reset because it's now in the past. Did I get it right?"

"Yes, you captured the dilemma of spooky time perfectly," Martin said, grinning. "Time has no choice but to confound the future and the present in such a case. It can't rob you of any of your time, or rob us of ours, so it must integrate the first half of your jump time into the present for the period they overlapped. This is similar to the spooky action observed with particles that are quantum entangled. The events during spooky time become entangled as well . . . at least theoretically."

"Whoa," Adela said, and the awestruck expression on her face matched what Zee was feeling too.

Tyler popped to his feet, practically flying off the stool he'd been sitting on. "Marty, you're genius! This explains everything. I wasn't crazy. It wasn't the fog of war. I knew I recognized the bearded operator from the tunnel and the kidnapping." He turned to Zee with a look that made her heart practically melt—a look of vindication and relief, victory and resignation. "It wasn't terrorists who ambushed us in Mali, it *was* a jump team. You didn't screw up, Zee. You didn't miss a thing because those assholes literally *did* appear out of thin air. And they were targeting me, which means they must have had future knowledge. Not from a Trojan horse installed in the Omega Room servers, not from a mole on this task force, but from the friggin' future. Stick's death didn't violate the rules of time travel. The reason it didn't reset is because of this spooky time anomaly Marty just figured out."

Zee shuddered with emotional release as tears rimmed her eyes. All the angst and fear she'd been keeping bottled up released at once, as if someone had opened a pressure relief valve in her soul. She smiled at Ty and he smiled back, and they shared a moment of unspoken communion. Despite everything that had happened—all the adversity and uncertainty the universe had thrown at them—they had persevered, and they'd done it together.

She took his hand and gave it a quick squeeze, and he squeezed back.

"Also, I think it's worth pointing out that this jump we just made was to the Bravo site. The Omega Room and HAL are shut down," Adela said. "And still, the future we observed on the jump was changed. That's the confirmation we were looking for. Tyler's right. We're not compromised."

"Holy shit, guys, that means we're not the only ones with Omega tech. We're not the only jumpers," Ben said, stating the obvious as the final puzzle piece clicked into place for all of them.

In unison, everyone turned to look at Moody who immediately threw his hands up.

"I swear to God, guys, I'm learning this at the same time as you," Moody said, sweeping his gaze across the group. "Scout's honor."

"What about spooky time jumps? Have you ever attempted them?" Tyler asked, his voice a hard line. "And don't fucking lie to us."

"No, I swear," Moody said, and for once Zee believed him. "We're in uncharted territory, guys, on both fronts . . ."

A heavy silence settled on the room as they each took a moment to contemplate the implications of this double paradigm shift: one, that they were battling a foe with the same capabilities and future knowledge as Omega, and two, that the near future could be changed.

Moody and Tyler broke the silence at the same time, talking over each other.

"You first, Chief," Moody said, and Zee took note that he yielded the floor to Tyler.

Tyler nodded. "What I was going to say is that starting right now, take everything you thought you knew and throw it out the window. This is a new game with new rules. We thought we were one step ahead of our adversary, but we were wrong. This whole time we've been one step behind. I don't know about you, but that makes me feel a whole helluva lot better about our performance. And it also makes me feel a whole helluva lot more confident about our odds going forward. They still have the advantage because they know who we are, and we don't know jack shit about them . . . But that's okay because I know this team, and this team can do anything. We may be underdogs in this match, but we're going to adapt and overcome. First things first, we're going to take care of business and stop this bomb. But after, we're going to take the fight to their house and give them a taste of their own medicine. Hooyah?"

"Hooyah!" the team shouted.

Zee felt gooseflesh standing up on her skin from Tyler's inspiring words and confidence.

"I agree with everything Chief said," Moody added. "In addition to leveraging our resources here, now that we know there is another team out there with our tech, I can task other resources in the IC to help us identify this shadow Omega group. We weren't looking for that because we thought we were the only ones. In the meantime, as Tyler said, our first priority has to be stopping the nuke from arriving on that plane. Let's start working that plan."

"Thanks to Marty, I have an idea about that," Tyler said. "We take a page from the enemy's playbook. We do to them what they tried to do to me in Mali."

"Go on," Moody said. "Tell us what you're thinking, Chief?"

"Well, we know exactly when and where the bomb goes off. Four minutes before it detonates, we jump one second into the future. Based on Marty's logic, that gives us three minutes and fifty-nine seconds of spooky time to disarm the warheads. Anything we change during that time doesn't reset. We can jump directly into the cargo compartment of the plane, which means they won't see us coming, they won't have reason to remote detonate, and they won't be able to try again if we succeed."

"But what if we fail?" Adela pressed. "We're only jumping one second into the future. That doesn't leave any time for a second try."

"No, it doesn't," Moody said.

"I'm not going to pretend I understand any of this, but I think it's our best shot," Tyler said. "Like Zee pointed out earlier, if we don't man up and take our shot now, they're just going to jump us to death."

"I'm in," Ben said.

"Me too," Adela said.

Martin nodded.

All eyes settled on Stan, who had yet to respond.

"Sure, why not," he said, and the serious scowl he was wearing transformed into a Cheshire grin that showed off his half-missing tooth. "Now all we have to do is calculate how to jump into the cargo hold of a moving airplane and learn to disarm—in under three minutes and fifty-nine seconds—three Russian warheads daisy-chained together in less than twenty-four hours. I'm so glad Moody recruited me. Where else do you get to swim in the disgusting Potomac, materialize into Space Force sergeants, have your teeth fall out, and get blown up by nuclear bombs? It's so fun."

CHAPTER 45

DIE URSACHE UNDERGROUND COMPOUND

SZCZECIN, POLAND

D-DAY

THIRTY MINUTES BEFORE NUCLEAR DETONATION

Avenge your brother . . .

They were *not* the last words his father had spoken to him all those years ago, but they were the words he heard now, playing in a loop in his mind over and over again. As he lay in his rack, looking up at the bottom of the empty bunk above him, it occurred to him that from the day Guo had been born until the day the American SEAL killed him, not a single moment had passed where Jun hadn't spent time with his little brother. As children, they slept in the same bed, attended the same school, and played the same sports. As men, they'd gone through basic training together, advanced through the ranks simultaneously, and served in all the same regiments . . .

The universe had had countless opportunities to cleave their paths or catapult them into different life trajectories, but that had not happened. Fate had kept them together through everything until Hoffman separated them for the Mali op. Epiphany struck Jun like a lightning bolt, and he jerked into a sitting position with violent realization.

It's because he separated us in time. Time was our bond. Only once it was broken did Guo become vulnerable. How could I have been so stupid?

"I should have defied Hoffman," he muttered, tears rimming his eyes. *I should have made it clear. Separating us was not an option.*

The past weeks living without his brother had been the most hollow and forlorn time of his existence. Tears snowballed into sobs that racked his body . . . sobs powered by guilt, regret, and self-loathing.

Had I gone on that jump, Guo would either be alive or we both would be dead . . . either preferable to this hell.

After the bonfire in his chest had burned up all the emotional fuel inside him, his breathing stilled, his heart rate slowed, and a cold, detached focus enveloped him.

It's time, he realized. *Time to rejoin my brother.*

Jun sat up and swung his legs off the mattress. He quickly threw on a T-shirt, laced up his tactical boots, and grabbed his kit from the hook beside his bed. Then, he went looking for Hoffman. It didn't take him long to find the German, a man whom Jun had only ever seen in one of three locations: his office, the control room, or the field reactor chamber.

"Herr Hoffman," he said, marching up to the man who was looking at a monitor in the control room. "I want to guard the bomb."

"What are you talking about?" Hoffman asked, looking at Jun over top of his reading glasses.

"Use the time machine. Transport me to coordinates that will place me inside the plane, directly next to the bomb. Send me three minutes and fifty seconds early."

Hoffman snorted a little laugh, although he did not smile. Jun could not ever remember seeing the man smile. "But this will create an overlap. You will be on the plane when it detonates. You will die in the future ten seconds before your return trip. What you are proposing is suicide."

"I know," Jun said, "but it is what I want . . . to see my brother again."

"Garth is expecting your squad to augment the other mission we have planned."

"Send my squad without me. Kaspar can lead the op. Use me to guard the bomb."

"Why would I do this?"

"Because I know the American SEAL will try to jump into the plane and stop the bomb. Send me to stop him."

"Our last reconnaissance jump showed the bomb detonating," Hoffman said.

Jun shook his head. "I know this man. He's a patriot. He'll die before he lets a bomb go off in the capital. You have to trust me. He has a plan."

The German looked almost moved by his request. "Without your brother, you no longer wish to live?"

Jun nodded.

Hoffman stared at him for a long moment, then said, "Very well. You are nearing the end of your useful contract life anyway. What do you want me to do with your earnings?"

"Wire all of it into my mother's bank account in China."

Hoffman stuck out his hand and Jun shook it. "I will see it done."

"*Danke*," Jun said, thanking the man in his native German.

"*Viel Glück*, Lin Jun," Hoffman said, and the negotiation was complete.

Jun turned to set off for the armory to prepare for the mission. The environment would be tight, so he needed to outfit himself for close-quarters combat. *Very close quarters.*

He took two steps but abruptly stopped and turned back to Hoffman. "I have a question—something that I've been wondering for a long time, but never asked."

"What is your question?" the German said.

"What is the point of this operation? Are you secret Nazis, trying to get revenge or something?"

Hoffman looked offended for an instant then his expression became almost contemplative. "Since you've volunteered to martyr yourself, I will tell you. Our patron has a vision—a vision of one world, united under a single banner. American industrial-political hegemony has shaped the world for too long. The age of the nation-state is over. The age of illumination is about to begin."

Jun nodded.

Just as I thought . . . Nazis.

And with that, he walked away and headed into the central corridor. As his footsteps echoed down the passage, for a fleeting moment he swore he heard a second set . . . as if his brother were walking beside him. This made him smile, and he looked up.

I will see you very soon, little brother. I'm sorry I've made you wait so long . . .

CHAPTER 46

THE DONUT

THE PEPPER GRINDER——WAREHOUSE B

D-DAY

SIX MINUTES BEFORE DETONATION

1229 LOCAL TIME

"Did everyone pay homage to Lopez?" Tyler said, only half joking as they passed the shrine to the Father of Time Travel en route to the Donut.

"We sure did," Stan said. "And Adela even gave him an actual kiss."

"Really?" Tyler said, flashing her a crooked grin.

Adela raised her eyebrows at him. "What can I say? That little guy is growing on me."

This exchange resulted in a tension-breaking laugh from everyone, including Marty—who'd shocked everyone by insisting on coming to help with the disarming sequence. If not for the wunderkind and his ridiculous brain, they never would have conceived of this plan. Tyler would be grateful to have Marty there for any technical roadblocks that might come up.

Tyler's knees ached and his back complained loudly as he stooped to enter the open hatch leading into the Donut. But all his aches and pains were nothing compared to the overwhelming anxiety and uncertainty that simmered just under the surface. They were about to attempt the most dangerous, complicated future intervention he could possibly imagine—jumping into the cargo hold of an airplane taxiing for takeoff and loaded with three nuclear warheads. If Jimmy's jump calculations were off, they could blow a hole in the skin of the airplane, or critical hydraulic lines, or even land outside the plane on the tarmac, which would result in a mission failure. If Stan and Martin weren't able to disarm the Russian warheads in time, or if they accidentally detonated them, then they'd be vaporized.

In the Teams, they liked to say that a good leader was "sometimes mistaken, but never in doubt." The adage meant that a team's survival often depended on the rapid-fire decisions of an operator who led with a mindset of self-confidence and certitude. Both tactically and strategically, exploiting the strange temporal entanglement Marty had dubbed *spooky time* was the right call. It would allow them to essentially teleport into position and affect change in the near future that would not reset. If it worked, this new application of time travel was potentially even more powerful than jumps into the distant future.

If we're not vaporized, he thought with a grim smile, *we can brainstorm ways to use this loophole to great tactical advantage.*

He gripped his rifle tightly as he formed up and pressed into the backs of his teammates. They made a tight circle, back-to-back, all crouching near the ground to minimize their footprint for insertion into the cargo hold of the jet. They would be working in a space with just a four-foot ceiling.

"This is crazy," Ben mumbled from his right.

"Marty, I sure hope you're right about spooky time," Adela said.

"I'm right," the boy genius said, with more confidence in his voice than Tyler had ever heard before. Instantly, Tyler relaxed.

Sometimes mistaken, but never in doubt, Tyler thought with a chuckle. *Maybe there's a little bit of SEAL hidden in Martin, beneath all those layers of nerd.*

Moody's voice echoed over the Donut's loudspeaker. "I just want to say, you are the bravest men and women I've ever known. Good luck and Godspeed. Standby to travel in five . . . four . . . three . . . two . . ."

On the zero beat, Tyler pressed the timer on his watch.

He felt the whoosh, and they traveled—

Multiple suitcases exploded, spraying pieces of clothing and toiletries all over the inside of the cargo hold when they landed.

"Shit," Adela said, both rattled and pissed off.

Stan had told them not to expect luggage in the forward cargo area, but apparently there had been overflow from the aft compartment. Tyler forced his mind to ignore the molecularly displaced luggage and focus instead on their objective. Unfortunately, the thong-style underwear now hanging from the end of his custom short-barrel assault rifle did momentarily distract him, as he scanned the cargo hold for threats.

While his eyes looked for enemy shooters, his other senses performed a situational assessment. Beneath his booted feet, he felt the gentle shudder of an airliner rolling over the tarmac. He heard the continuous thrum of the jet's twin engines cycling to provide only enough thrust to taxi. His nose smelled perfume and mouthwash, but not hydraulic fluid. With precision that was nothing short of a miracle, Jimmy had done it and jumped them, perfectly positioned, into the jet's cargo hold.

"Clear," he barked, flinging the undies off his muzzle before slinging his rifle. "Let's get to it, Alpha. We have nukes to disarm."

The team hustled past Tyler into the forward cargo compartment where a large wooden crate, of similar size to the one they'd found on the yacht, was secured to the deck with tie-down straps. Stan, Ben, Martin, Adela, and Zee got to work cutting the straps and trying to pry the heavy lid off with KA-Bar Bridge Breacher tools they'd brought for the op.

Tyler was about to lend a hand when he felt a whoosh of air behind him. He whirled as a black-clad operator holding a bowie knife materialized a mere three feet away, confirming what his subconscious had known for weeks.

"Jumper!" Tyler shouted, locking eyes with the adversary staring back at him—a face he recognized from the recon jump to Virginia Beach. A flashbulb memory of this man opening Nikki's throat filled his mind's eye.

The enemy jumper raised his knife, pointed the blade at Tyler, and smirked.

"You," Tyler growled.

Somebody called something to him—Ben, his subconscious registered—but the message was filtered as irrelevant as Tyler shifted into battle mode. Adrenaline flooded his bloodstream as the primitive and primal mechanisms took control in preparation for mortal combat. He pulled the KA-Bar Tanto from his kit and shifted into a low, wide crouch.

"Keep working on the bomb; I got this guy," he called, eschewing help because the team needed every member to get the crate opened and the nuke disarmed in the limited time they had.

The SEAL inside Tyler told him to be methodical and not rush the kill; a mistake would give his opponent an opening to capitalize on. Ultimately, it probably wouldn't matter—knife fights between skilled warriors usually ended badly for both parties.

As he advanced in the cramped compartment, the jet abruptly turned, sending everyone careening left and Tyler slamming into the port bulkhead. At the same time, the engines spooled up, roaring loudly in the unpressurized, uninsulated compartment. It was at this exact moment that Tyler's adversary attacked. The Asian operator's first strike—a straight thrust to center mass—slammed into Tyler's vest. If not for the ballistic plate inside, the man's six-inch blade would have pierced Tyler's heart and killed him instantly.

Operating at reflex speed and guided entirely by muscle memory, Tyler thrust up at a forty-five-degree angle, aiming to ram his blade into the V of the fighter's jawbone. His attacker barely shifted clear of the lethal strike, but not without cost. The cutting point of Tyler's Tanto blade opened a deep groove from the left rear corner of the man's jaw and split his ear in half. Maybe the warrior didn't feel the gash, or maybe he was just that good, but Tyler's attack didn't buy him any time because the retaliatory strike came a millisecond later.

The Asian man executed a second straight thrust, this time targeting the inside of Tyler's left bicep, exposed from where he steadied himself against the bulkhead. Red-hot fire flared in his upper arm as the blade penetrated the muscle and came out the other side. An electric stinger shot down his left arm into his hand and, for an instant, he thought all his fingertips had exploded. Maybe because the blade severed nerves, or maybe in response to the pain, Tyler's left arm turned to jelly and gave out. Without his bracing, he fell to his side.

His adversary capitalized, punching Tyler in the side of the head as he fell. The blow momentarily stunned the SEAL. In his peripheral vision, he saw a flash of movement. The operator in him knew the movement was a kill strike coming toward the exposed side of his neck. Years of close-quarters combat training set his body in motion. He rolled clear, and the enemy fighter's bowie knife slammed into the aluminum cargo deck behind Tyler's head with a metallic ping.

Lying prone beneath his attacker, Tyler drove his Tanto blade deep into the man's groin crease and the femoral artery just below. He corkscrewed his wrist and yanked the blade free and blood sprayed out of the wound, up the wall, and onto the low ceiling as the man rolled over, grunting in pain. Tyler capitalized on the moment for a second strike, and he stabbed again, thrusting the blade underneath the skirt of the fighter's vest and upward into the abdomen. He swiveled the blade left and right, looking to sever the aorta and end the battle once and for all.

Tyler looked up and saw the shocked expression on the man's face as his brain played catch-up to the wounds his body had received. The killer dropped his bowie knife, and his eyes glazed as he stared at his own blood dripping down from the ceiling. Tyler felt the blood from his fallen foe chase down his right hand and forearm as he sheathed the knife and got to his knees.

The clock is ticking . . .

"Stan, where are we?" he barked and tried to raise his left wrist to check the time remaining on his watch.

The arm ignored the command to curl.

When Stan didn't answer, Tyler looked over to see his teammates working inside the massive wooden crate, the lid now off. He shifted his attention back to the dying operator and looked down at the man.

"Who do you work for?"

The jumper flashed him a bloodstained grin and muttered something in a foreign language—Korean maybe.

"Are you North Korean?"

The dying man ignored the question and lifted his right hand as if reaching for the ceiling.

"Are you MSS?" Tyler shouted, this time referring to China's clandestine operations entity, the Ministry of State Security.

"There you are, brother . . . We are reunited at last," the dying warrior said, this time in English. Tyler watched the man smile, then his outstretched arm dropped and his eyes went to glass.

"Damn it." Tyler sighed and started checking pockets on the man's kit for any clues as to who he might work for.

"Dude, you're losing a ton of blood from that arm," Ben said. The combat medic fell in beside him and grabbed Ty's wrist. "Let me take a look at that."

"Help Stan, or we all die." Tyler nodded at the warheads.

"Roger that," Ben said and scrambled to assist the rest of Alpha Team.

A wave of wooziness made Tyler sway, and he realized Ben was right. He pulled his blowout kit from a thigh pocket and worked, one-handed, to get a tourniquet on his left arm.

"How are we doing?" he shouted, seeing that the crate top was off and his five teammates were throwing packing foam out right and left.

"Do you want the good news or the bad news?" Stan said, looking over with wide eyes.

"The good news," he shouted before grabbing hold of one end of the tourniquet with his teeth and pulling the other with his good hand to tighten it.

"The nukes are in the crate," Stan said.

"What's the bad news?"

"The wiring detonator configuration is different from what we saw on the yacht," Adela said, beating Stan to the punch.

Shit . . .

"Can you still disarm them?"

"We're sure as hell going to try," Stan said.

Tyler used his right hand to lift his left wrist and check the time remaining: 02:43

There's still time . . .

He went back to emptying the dead killer's kit and pockets while his teammates worked the bomb. The pile of expected tactical items grew in lockstep with his frustration. Light, flash-bangs, extra mags, paracord, blowout kit, signal mirror, small Kershaw folder, pills in a bag with no label . . . then he found something.

"What if we cut the wires between the three warheads? Will that help?" Ben asked.

"No," Martin and Stan said in unison. Then, Stan added, "Looks like they were expecting us this time. They've added a tamper wire. Cut it and all warheads instantly go boom."

"Then what do we do?" Ben asked, real panic in his voice.

"I'm working on that," Martin said, leaning into the closest crate to the end. "I need light!"

Zee clicked on her flashlight and shined it into the crate.

"What do you think this green wire does?" Stan asked.

"I don't know," Martin said, "but it's definitely not the tamper wire because that one is gray and runs parallel to the trigger wire right there."

"We need to open the detonator housing," Stan said. "Screwdriver!"

Ben slapped a Phillips-head into Stan's outstretched palm.

"Wait!" Martin said and grabbed Stan's wrist just as he reached into the crate. "I think that green wire is a tamper wire too—"

"For the housing cover?" Stan asked.

"Yeah," Martin said.

"Fuck!" Stan shouted. "What do we do . . ."

While Stan and Martin worked, Tyler unfolded a photograph he'd found in the dead jumper's vest. Four men were staring at the camera, all kitted-up in full battle rattle. Tyler recognized three of the four faces: the dead guy he'd just killed, the bearded operator, the operator with the NLAW rocket launcher that Stan had killed with the *immaculate headshot in the tunnel,* and another Asian dude who was a spitting image of the dead assassin.

"That's your brother, huh?" Tyler said, turning the picture to show it to the dead guy. That's when, on the back, he saw the handwritten words *Die Ursache* and the date. "This was taken three months ago."

He flipped the picture back over and noted how much younger and healthier they looked in the picture than when he'd seen them on the recent jumps.

They're aging just like us.

Prompted by the picture to feel the press of time, he turned his wrist and announced, "Two minutes."

He knew they heard him, but Stan and Martin just kept working without responding.

"I have an idea. We strip the tamper wire insulation back, wire a five-volt battery in line, then we can snip it and open the housing," Martin said, talking so quick he sounded like his voice was on fast-forward.

"Are you sure the tamper circuit triggers on voltage-off and not voltage-on?" Stan asked.

"Has to be loss of signal or snipping the wire wouldn't trigger the bomb."

"Good point," Stan said, talking while he worked.

Tyler could see sweat beading on Stan's forehead. Marty's face had gone completely ashen.

"Work faster," Marty said.

"I'm trying; you ever tried to strip a wire that's connected?" Stan said, his head completely inside the crate now. "Marty, is the battery ready?"

"Yeah," Martin said, clutching a small watch-sized battery with tiny leads. "Shit, where should I ground it?"

"Somewhere near the tamper wire."

"There's nothing I can use."

"Then tape it to the housing."

"I think the housing is aluminum."

"Shit, I think you're right," Stan said. "The bracket. The bracket is steel. Use the bracket."

"Good, but I need more wire . . ."

Tyler watched Martin pull a piece of loose wire from a chest pocket and twist it onto one of the tiny battery leads.

"Ben, get a screwdriver ready. Adela, you too," Stan said, his voice borderline frantic. "As soon as I say *go*, start unscrewing the four screws in the corners of the detonator housing, got it?"

"Got it," Ben and Adela said together.

"Okay, Marty, ready for the splice . . . Yep, yep, that's it . . . one more wrap . . . Okay, looks good . . . I'm gonna cut . . ."

Tyler cringed, closed his eyes, and wondered what it would feel like to be vaporized by a nuclear bomb.

"Please God, let this work . . ." Stan said. "Fuck yeah, it worked. Hallelujah! Ben, Adela—go!"

The plane's engines roared and the fuselage began to rattle and shake.

They were taking off, the acceleration forcing them all to brace as g-forces pulled them toward the rear of the compartment. Stan grabbed Adela by her belt to keep her from falling headfirst into the crate as the nose of the aircraft came up. The jet noise was deafening now, and the cargo deck rattled beneath Tyler's boots. A moment later they were airborne, and the rattling stopped. A loud mechanical noise sounded as the landing gear cycled up.

"Shit, I dropped my screwdriver . . ." Ben said, leaning far into the crate.

"Use mine," Zee said and handed him a replacement.

Tyler checked his watch. "One minute," he said softly.

"Faster, guys," Stan said.

"One screw out," Ben said, "starting the second."

"Done," Adela said and stepped clear of the crate.

"Almost there . . . Last one out," Ben said, moving so Marty and Stan could work.

Tyler glanced at his wrist again, and his chest tightened.

00:49 . . . We're not going to make it.

"You got this, Marty, plenty of time," Stan said. "Remember the sequence: white, red, white, black."

Marty's feet weren't even on the deck anymore. His body looked like a see-saw, his waist supported by the lip of the crate as he leaned in. "Zee, move the light to the right . . . sorry, I mean the left . . . Yeah, that's the spot . . . They added a wire, Stan, I don't know what it is."

Stan's torso disappeared into the crate. "It goes to . . . this thing. Shit, they added a remote detonator."

"What do we?" Marty said, terror in his voice.

Tyler resisted the urge to glance at his wrist, but his internal clock knew they were coming up on thirty seconds. A heartbeat later his watch chimed.

"Um . . . we ignore it. Just cut the four leads in order. Do it now. White, red, white, black."

"My hands are shaking so bad I can't get the wires in the jaws," Marty said.

"Let me help, I'll guide the wires. White first—cut. Good. Next, red—cut. Good . . ."

Tyler closed his eyes and let out a long, slow breath. In nineteen seconds, they would either be back at the spice factory or they would be dead. Either a million people would die from a nuclear blast or they would go about their days never having any idea what almost happened. If they failed, war was certain to follow. Even with the Pentagon and White House destroyed, even without Task Force Omega, he knew USSTRATCOM would discover who attacked us and retaliate. Nuclear war, the very thing the world had somehow avoided for eighty years, would happen.

A strange and resigned fatalism engulfed him.

Maybe we aren't supposed to mess around with time. What if things just happen—good and bad—and it's not for us to decide? Maybe we aren't supposed to play God . . .

Stan's voice echoed as they continued to work the problem. "White next . . ."

Tyler glanced at his wrist: *0:10 . . . 0:09 . . . 0:08*

"Cut . . . good. Last cut is black . . ."

He looked up, his subconscious wishing he had brought a picture of Harper. The beautiful face of his little girl should really be the last thing he saw.

"That's the wrong wire, Stan," Martin said.

"Shit, you're right, it's this one. Hurry, cut it!"

"The timer stopped!" Ben shouted with wonder and triumph in his voice. "You did it!"

"Hooah!" Stan screamed, leaned backward, and threw his hands up to heaven. "We did it! We fucking did it."

Three . . . two . . . one . . .

Tyler felt his ears pop with the pressure change, he blinked, and he was sitting on the floor of the Donut with his five teammates huddled around him, all of them smiling, laughing, and crying.

CHAPTER 47

THE DONUT

THE PEPPER GRINDER——WAREHOUSE B

Tyler got to his feet, but it wasn't easy.

His knees ached with stiffness, his back screamed in protest, a jolt of pain was shooting down his left leg, and his left arm had gone completely numb. But it didn't matter, because they'd won. They'd stopped the nuke, killed the bastard hunting his family, and gotten their first, solid clue about their adversary.

A strange emotion washed over him, something he'd not felt in a very long time. Hope . . . Hope that with this win they'd finally, and once and for all, put an end to the maddening cycle of thwarting and resetting the nuclear attack on DC. Hope for a secure future where Harper could grow up without living in fear or the need to go into hiding ever again. Hope that they could stop jumping and that Dr. Donahue would have time to finish her work on a treatment to reverse the aging effects from traveling.

He closed his eyes and pictured his little girl's smiling face while he scooped her up in his arms for a hug. The special moment evaporated, however, when his brain registered that the photograph he'd been holding was no longer clutched between his fingers. He opened his eyes, looked down, and confirmed that, yes, the item had not come back to the present with him.

"Stan, I need you to memorize something before I forget it," he said. "*Die Ursache*—spelled D-i-e U-r-s-a-c-h-e."

"That's German," Stan said. "It means *The Cause*."

"Oh . . . that was easy," Tyler said and, with a grunt, twisted at the waist to stretch out his back. A strange quiet filled the Donut, and it dawned on Tyler that Moody hadn't welcomed them home or asked for a sitrep. He looked up at the speaker. "Moody, we're back. We did it. We stopped the bomb!"

No answer came.

A fresh wave of dizziness washed over Tyler, followed immediately by the all-too-familiar, powerful wave of déjà vu. He teetered and a strong hand steadied him.

"Hey, boss, I need to take a look at that arm," Ben said from where he'd taken up position at Tyler's side.

"Dude, the déjà vu is bad." Tyler pressed his hands to his temples. "We just got back, right?"

"Yeah, man. We did it," Ben said.

"Moody, open the friggin' door!" Zee hollered, pounding with her right hand against the metal hatch while cradling her rib cage with her left hand at the spot where she'd broken a rib weeks ago. She turned to Tyler, her eyes wide, and he noticed a new, heavy streak of gray hair framing her face. "How come they're not opening the door?" she asked in a strange, almost childlike voice.

"Ben, as soon as we get out of here, I'll let you fix my arm," Tyler said to the combat medic, then walked over to Zee. "Let me take a look."

Zee stepped aside, and Tyler peered out through the door's porthole window. He couldn't see much, just the far wall and a bit of the metal stairs if he strained to the right, the two-inch thick ballistic glass distorting the view.

"Control, we're Mike Charlie—mission complete. Will you please let us out of here?" he shouted. When nothing happened, a wave of uncertainty hit him. He turned to Stan and Adela. "You don't think the nuke went off after we traveled, do you? It was only a one-second future overlap. They couldn't have somehow . . . I mean, that's not possible, is it?"

"No, I don't think so," Stan said, but his face went pale. He looked at Martin. "Unless they remote detonated it. We didn't remove the remote detonator."

"No, but we cut the control wires. Even if they send the remote detonate signal, it comes in upstream to the logic board. We cut the output wires that send the signal to the warheads," Martin said.

"You're sure?"

"Yes, I'm positive," Martin said.

"I need to get out of here. Now!" Zee said, her voice a tight strain of panic. She'd yet to come out and admit it, but Tyler knew she battled claustrophobia, and it was clawing at her now.

"Time to use the emergency egress procedure," Stan said, stepping up to an access panel beside the hatch. "Let's get the hell out of here."

While Stan pulled the pin with a red tag that locked the yellow manual override lever in place, Tyler's mind ran through what-if scenarios. What if Martin was wrong, and the bad guys did somehow remotely detonate the nuke? Or what if they had been wrong about spooky time? What if everything they'd just done didn't stick? What if the future reset, like always, and the enemy had outfoxed them? If the nuke had gone off, it would explain why this place was . . .

Wait a second.

"Wait!" Tyler shouted, and Stan's hand froze on the handle a split second before pulling it. "Something happened here. Whatever it was, we need to be smart—and ready. We do this like a tactical breach—like we're hitting an enemy stronghold. Two by two with me and Ben out first and clearing left; Stan and Adela clear right; and Marty and Zee at the back."

"He's right," Adela said. "Something is definitely wrong here."

"Boss, you only got one working arm," Ben said. "Maybe Deadeye Stan and Adela should go first, and you and I go second?"

Tyler wanted to argue and point out that a Tier One SEAL with one arm could shoot better than 99 percent of people with two arms, but Ben did have a point. And, thanks to the blood loss and the fact he now had the body of a sixty-year-old man, he wasn't anywhere near the operator he'd been a month ago.

"Fair point," he said and took a step back.

The team assembled in three two-man sticks by the door, weapons gripped in gloved hands. Tyler looked back at Marty and watched a bead of sweat trickle down his temple.

"You're good, Marty. Just follow our lead and stay in tight behind us, okay?"

The boy genius nodded.

"And don't shoot a teammate in the back," Stan added.

"And if you see a bad guy, just put the red dot center mass and squeeze the trigger. No different than on the range or in the kill house," Ben chimed in.

If only that were true . . .

Tyler looked over at Stan, raised his rifle to a forty-five-degree angle, and nodded his head in a three-count cadence. On *go*, Ben pulled the lever, metal *thunked*, and the magnetic locking ring disengaged. The door cracked open. Ben gave it a shove, and Stan and Adela exited the Donut into the warehouse, moving swiftly in combat crouches, rifles up, breaking to the left. Tyler and Ben breached behind them, moving right. Holding his weapon in his right hand and his useless left arm against his side, Tyler swept the holographic sight across the right side of the cavernous warehouse, then surged forward.

Ahead, two dead bodies—both in bloodstained white lab coats— lay sprawled at the foot of the metal stairs that led to the control mezzanine.

"Oh my God," Zee muttered from behind him. "We've been hit."

"Whoever did this is still here. We were only gone four minutes," Tyler said.

Reflexively, Tyler tried to chop his left hand forward, but it hung limply at his side, refusing to move. So, he used his voice instead.

"Three, Five—clear medical and the lab spaces below. We'll clear Control and the second floor."

"Check," Stan said as he and Adela quickstepped toward the door under the mezzanine that led to medical and Donahue's lab.

Ben breached the stairs, scanning as he ascended. Tyler followed, his boots pounding the metal treads right behind his teammate. At the top, Ben cleared left and Tyler cleared right.

"Clear," Ben said.

Tyler scanned the right half of the mezzanine, his mind focused on looking for threats—like shooters, booby traps, or bombs—but his heart broke at the carnage he couldn't help but see. Three of the corpses still sat in their chairs, slumped over their workstations in pools of blood and brains. A fourth, Becca, lay supine on the floor, a crimson hole in the center of her forehead and her lifeless eyes staring up at nothing.

"Clear," he said, his voice cracking.

"Where's Moody?" Martin said, his voice a weak whisper. Tyler looked over to find the kid standing at the top of the staircase, his eyes wide, mouth open, and rifle hanging uselessly by the strap. "Moody should be here, and so should Jimmy."

A low moan pricked Tyler's ear and he spun in the direction of the noise.

"It's coming from the hall," Ben said. He dropped into a combat crouch and advanced on the door that separated the mezzanine from the hall where the staff offices, SCIF, and conference rooms were located.

Tyler looked back at Zee. She stood with Martin, but at least had her rifle up and ready. "Stay here and watch our six," he told her.

She nodded.

"Go," Tyler said, turning back to Ben. The AFSOC shooter breached the hallway and Tyler followed, falling in behind Ben.

Once in the hall, they found the source of the moaning. Jimmy sat propped against the wall fifteen feet away. A swath of blood streaked the linoleum tile floor and led back to the mezzanine, from where he'd apparently dragged himself. The rest of the corridor appeared to be empty. Ben advanced in a combat crouch and stepped over Jimmy's legs as he moved to clear the offices and conference rooms beyond.

Tyler took a knee beside the badly wounded engineer he'd come to both like and respect. "Jimmy, what happened here? Who did this?"

Jimmy looked at him, coughed weakly, and said, "We got hit . . . Black-ops team . . ."

"Where's Moody?" he asked, looking down the hall to check on Ben.

"I think . . . I think they took him . . . Tyler, am I going to die?"

Tyler scanned Jimmy's torso and saw that he'd taken at least three rounds—two to the chest and one to the gut.

"No, just hang in there, buddy," he said with a forced smile. "Ben's a combat medic. He'll get you patched up real good."

"Liar," Jimmy said with a blood-tinged grin.

Tyler noticed the engineer's breath was growing shallow, raspy, and weak. His complexion matched the white-gray tile floor. "Hang in there for me, okay?"

Jimmy nodded weakly, but said, "Tyler . . . memorize what I say."

"You know I'm the only guy on the team without an eidetic memory," Tyler said, desperately wanting Ben to come back.

Jimmy weakly pawed at his chest pocket where Tyler saw a fine point Sharpie.

Oh, thank God . . .

He pulled the pen, removed the cap with his teeth, and got ready to write.

"45.143 north . . . 69.146 west," Jimmy said, with barely enough strength to get the words out.

Tyler scribbled the coordinates on the back of his useless left hand. "Jimmy, what's important about this location?"

But the engineer was gone.

"Damn it," he said, reaching over to gently close the man's eyelids.

Ben came jogging back. "All clear down the hall. Is he . . . ?"

"Gone," Tyler said and grunted as he got to his feet.

"What did he say?"

"Doesn't know who hit them. Thinks the guys that did this took Moody. And he gave me lat-long coordinates before he died."

Ben shook his head. "Shit."

"We should clear the rest of the compound—there's still the Salt Shaker and the Poblano."

"Agreed. But, dude, we gotta get blood flow back in your arm or you're going to lose it."

"All right, work fast," Tyler said, and Ben did, loosening the tourniquet, cutting Tyler's sleeve away, then quickly packing and wrapping the biceps. "That should do it for now."

Pins and needles assaulted Tyler's left arm from his elbow to his fingertips, but he tried to ignore them as he fell in behind Ben and headed back to the mezzanine.

When they arrived, Martin pointed to an open panel below one of the terminals. "They took the SSDs from the jump computer."

"Which will give them what?" Tyler asked, but he thought he knew the answer.

"Every location and time we jumped," Martin said grimly.

"That's not good," Ben said.

"No, it's not," Tyler mumbled.

"Medical and the labs are clear. It's a bloodbath," Stan called from below. "And they definitely knew what they were doing. Looks like they raided the research lab."

"What about Dr. Donahue?" Zee asked grimly, maybe matching Tyler's own selfish concern about the fate of the cure.

"Missing," Stan called out with a tight voice.

A sudden burst of gunfire, unsuppressed, came from somewhere below. Tyler crouched instinctively behind the control panel as a scream of pain—Adela's scream—echoed below. He popped up, sweeping his holographic sight across the warehouse floor, his elevated position giving him excellent sight lines. His red dot quickly found a target—a shooter clad head to toe in black, wearing a face mask, and aiming a short-barreled assault rifle as he emerged from behind the Donut. Tyler squeezed the trigger just as Stan fired from below—both rounds hitting the insurgent simultaneously. The shooter crumpled and his machine gun clattered on the polished cement.

Another black-clad figure appeared, moving to flank Stan from the other side of the Donut, but Tyler sighted and dropped the assaulter with a headshot.

"I thought we were clear," he shouted.

"Me too," Stan hollered. "Where the hell did they come from?"

Sudden commotion behind him caused Tyler to spin and, impossibly, he saw Ben grappling with yet another masked, black-clad shooter who'd just emerged from the hallway. A second gunman followed in trail, rifle up and aiming at Tyler.

Shit . . .

Sparks erupted as someone strafed the doorway, and Tyler watched the trailing fighter jerk once as he stumbled backward, his rifle firing but the round going wide. Tyler put his own red dot onto the man's cloth-covered temple and squeezed twice as the assaulter stumbled into the doorframe. Blood and brains painted a modern art mural on the hallway wall behind him and the black-clad breacher collapsed in a heap. Tyler heard a crunch of bone giving way and turned to see Ben land two more blows on the shattered jaw of the man he was grappling. Ben then crouched—taking himself out of the line of fire—so Tyler could drill two rounds through the back of the assaulter's head. The shooter pitched forward, dead, onto the steel grate floor of the mezzanine with a resounding *clang*.

Tyler advanced on the doorframe and sighted down the hallway, looking for more attackers, aware that the tingling in his left hand had transitioned to burning pain. As he scanned the hallway over his rifle, he wiggled his fingers and they felt like they moved.

Finding no new threats, he glanced over his shoulder at Martin.

"You saved my life, Marty. Well done . . ."

Martin, who was trembling, simply nodded as tears spilled onto his cheeks.

"Adela's hit," Stan shouted from below.

"We'll cover here," Tyler said and locked eyes with Ben. "Go."

Ben charged down the metal stairs to the lower level to work on Adela.

"Zee, switch with me," Tyler said, wanting to give himself the flexibility to provide cover from the mezzanine if another ambush happened.

"Roger that," she said and took a kneeling stance at the doorway.

"Sitrep?" he called down to the rest of the team as he moved to the rail, and only then noticed that he held his rifle now with both hands—his left arm mobility at least partially restored with the blood flow.

"She took a single round through her left thigh, but lateral of the bone," Ben called up. "No arterial bleeding that I see and no expanding hematoma. Nine-millimeter wound, I think. Nonurgent for now."

"I'm fine," Adela said.

"Let me dress it," Ben insisted.

"There's a black satchel beside the Donut," Martin said, standing at the railing next to Tyler and pointing at TFR. "It could be explosives!"

"Good eyes, Marty," he said, then yelled down, "Stan, did you hear that?"

"I heard," Stan called.

"If it is a bomb, it might not be armed," Martin said. "He dropped the bag when you shot him. I think this second squad came to destroy the reactor and the control room."

Stan jogged to the satchel, inspected it, and hollered up, "Marty's right. Bunch of C4 bricks but they didn't get a chance to set the charges."

Tyler nodded and wondered how many more infiltrators were roaming the compound. If he'd had a large team he'd split them, clear the parking lot, then the Poblano and the Salt Shaker. But they were only six—three now really, with Marty and Zee nonoperators and Adela hobbled.

"I'm in the fight," Adela called from below, as if reading his mind.

He watched her stand, then move shockingly quick to the bottom of the stairs with Ben and Stan.

Tyler took a knee beside a downed gunman. "Listen up, guys. Quickly check these assholes for clues. Then, we sweep the parking lot, and after that, we clear the rest of the compound and look for survivors." But as he reached for the dead man's kit, the body, the rifle, and even the blood spatter were gone.

No shimmer, no flash of light, just gone—as if they'd never been there.

Jumpers.

"Well, that explains how they got the drop on us," he muttered.

"They're jumpers," Zee said, her voice a tight chord. "Just like the guy you fought on the plane."

"Well, they've got a few less jumpers now," Tyler said with some satisfaction. "Those assholes just arrived dead in their own Donut, wherever the hell that is."

"It was a timed operation," Stan shouted. "Fifty bucks says they used a primary team operating in the present for the hit, timing the compound breach to happen while we were gone. Then, they pop jumpers in as a secondary mop up crew to murder us on our return and destroy the control room and Donut."

"Guys, if Stan's right, there's still a chance we can catch the primary team on-site before they exfil," Ben shouted.

"Front lot, now," Tyler barked, knowing in his gut that Stan was right. "There could be shooters guarding the door, so clear your corners, people."

"And stay frosty," Adela added. "They could still have a QRF stationed nearby."

Tyler descended the metal stairs at a run and joined Ben and Stan as they sprinted toward the north end of the warehouse and the exit next to the large roll-up garage door, which was shut.

"I'll cover from the doorway," Adela said, limping only slightly as she caught up to them.

He nodded and said, "On my count—three . . . two . . . one . . ."

On *go* Tyler pressed the beater bar and swung the door outward. Ben charged left, Stan went right, and Tyler surged up the middle.

"By the gate!" he shouted, spotting a green Ford SUV heading for the main entrance.

Clearly, the enemy had dual motives for this mission—snatch Omega's leadership and kill the engineers and technicians, then finish off the program by killing the jump team and blowing up the

Donut. If Moody and Donahue were in that SUV, he couldn't risk killing them.

Aiming for the SUV's tires, Tyler flipped his selector to three-round-burst with his thumb and squeezed the trigger multiple times. The vehicle slewed to the right, fishtailed wildly, then recovered and rocketed through the gate and onto Route 40. In his peripheral vision, he saw a black Ford—same make and model—already speeding south on the two-lane highway and a third vehicle even farther away.

Stan raised his rifle, sighted through its optical scope, and took aim—ready to deal death and vengeance from a quarter mile.

Tyler stopped him. "Hold fire. We don't know which vehicle Moody and Donahue are in."

"That last green Ford had the same plates as the one that attacked us in the tunnel," Stan said as he lowered his rifle. "And guess what else . . . That same bearded operator was driving."

Tyler gritted his teeth in frustration and shook his head as the magnitude of their losses hit home.

Task Force Omega was finished. Tyler realized they had no idea who Moody reported to—if there even was anyone. They were on their own with no one they could be sure had their back. They could always turn to his brothers at the Tier One, but other than overwhelming firepower to keep them alive, what could they offer? Omega was deep, deep black. And that meant they were on their own.

"We're totally fucked, guys."

"We did save the Donut," Ben said, ever the eternal optimist.

"Yeah, but there's nobody left to operate it," Tyler said. "And we have no idea who to contact or who we can trust. Our chain of command stopped at Moody."

"Then we need to find Moody," Ben said. "It's that simple."

"We should probably bug out," Stan said. "We don't want to be here when the police and the feds show up."

The rattle of the roll-up garage door behind them drew the gaze of all three men. As the metal door came up, the nose of Task Force

Omega's other, non-battle-scarred Chevy Suburban came into view with Zee behind the wheel. They watched Adela hobble over and climb into the back seat.

"Looks like the girls are of the same mind as the boys," Ben said.

"We need to hurry," Tyler said. "Someone is coming, and we have no idea who they'll be or if we can trust them."

"In case you're wondering," Martin said as he climbed into the third-row seating. "We stopped the nuke. I checked media."

"Thanks, Marty," Tyler said, looking at the midday, sunlit Maryland countryside out the window. It was good news, but not enough to brighten their moods. "But what keeps them from trying again?"

"Well, we need to get word to the feds that the disarmed nukes are on the plane. It can't have been easy to secure them so what are the odds they have more warheads?" Ben said.

"Who knows?" Tyler wondered aloud as he climbed into the front passenger seat. "But we sure as hell need to find out."

"There'll be plenty of material evidence with the nukes in custody," Adela said. "They'll trace the source and with that, hopefully, follow it to our adversary."

Tyler nodded, unconvinced. There were a lot of unknowns and even more uncertainties. But, for now at least, these weren't the problems of what was left of Omega Team. For now, they needed to find a place to rest. His job now was to keep the team safe, make sure Nikki and Harper were secure, and then figure out how to find Moody and Donahue—the two people who held the future of Omega in their hands in more ways than one.

Until then, without knowing who to trust, they would stick together and lay low.

He turned and looked at Zee in profile while she drove. She had that new streak of gray hair tucked behind her right ear. It didn't matter. She looked regal. Not in a royal sense, but in a powerful, unbreakable way.

"Where are we going, by the way?" she asked with an awkward smile as he stared at her.

Tyler turned his attention to the touchscreen infotainment computer in the center dashboard and pulled up the navigation app. Then, looking at the back of his hand, he entered the coordinates Jimmy had given him.

"North," he said while the system found the location and calculated their route. "We're going to Maine."

EPILOGUE

Margot Moody sat in her dad's large leather reading chair, fretting.

She had her knees tucked inside her oversized baby-blue U of Maine sweatshirt, her UGG slippers on, and a stocking cap pulled down over her ears. The house was cold but finally starting to warm up. Radiator heat took a while. She'd fired up the boiler the way her dad had taught her. He'd made her do it seven times while he'd watched. Practicing something seven times was apparently some sort of magic number for memorizing stuff.

It had certainly worked for her, and she wasn't a mechanical type of person.

The antique wall clock—the kind that ticked every second with the swing of a little pendulum—was driving her crazy. When clocks made noise, time was impossible to ignore.

I'm going to smash it, she thought with gritted teeth, then sighed and shook her head. *No, you can't. He loves that stupid clock. Just take it down and put it in the basement.*

She checked her phone for what must have been the twentieth

time that day to see if her dad had responded yet. And like the nineteen previous times, the last message in the thread was the one she'd sent yesterday informing him she'd arrived safe and sound at the farmhouse.

But she hadn't actually typed those words. She'd used a code word: GRYFFINDOR.

Just like he'd used a code word to tell her to leave school immediately and head straight home: HOGWARTS.

The instruction had arrived via text message while she'd been in chemistry class. The instant she read it, she walked out of the lecture, grabbed her go-bag from her dorm room, and hopped in her Bronco. Sixteen minutes. That's how long it had taken her to get on the road. She wasn't like other kids who didn't take their parents—or any adults for that matter—seriously. When it came to safety, Margot Moody didn't fuck around. She knew who her dad was and what he did for a living.

Well, sort of.

After Mom died, he'd "read her in" that he worked for the CIA. He told her that he loved her more than his job, more than his country, more than he loved himself. He told her that she was the single most important thing in his life and that he cherished her. Not in a fake, obligatory way, but in a real, no-bullshit, what-matters-in-life kind of way. She'd been fourteen at the time, and she'd desperately needed to hear that because her mom had always been her rock while her dad was deployed overseas. He'd held her tight, and they'd both cried, and he'd promised her that he would quit his job.

And, to her surprise, he'd kept that promise. A month later he bought the farmhouse and they moved. At first, she'd been furious about the move from Virginia to Maine, but when she saw the stable and the horses . . . well, screw Virginia.

They'd had four good years together on the farm. He'd become her best friend.

Then the summer after her freshman year at U of Maine, a man in uniform showed up at the property in a black government SUV. She knew he was high-ranking because he had stars on his shoulders, a driver, and an assistant. After he left, her dad told her that the man was a general and that he was sorry, but he had to return to work. Hopefully, after one year, he would retire for good. But something had happened, something he wouldn't talk to her about. With his new job, he had secrets he didn't trust her to keep.

That stung.

Then other weird stuff started to happen.

Like that massive machine he was hiding in the barn . . .

Feeling antsy, she climbed out of the chair and walked to her bedroom to get her favorite cozy camp blanket from the foot of her bed. That's when she saw it—an envelope propped against her pillow with her name written on it in her dad's handwriting. With nervous fingers, she tore open the sealed flap and pulled out the folded, hand-written note. She read it once, twice, three times . . .

But not one word of it made sense.

"I don't understand what the hell you're talking about, Dad," she muttered. "And who the hell are Zee and Tyler?"

A shiver snaked down her spine.

"You're supposed to be here by now." She shook the paper. "Where the hell are you, Dad? You're scaring me . . ."

The sound of truck tires on the gravel drive outside made her heart leap with hope.

"Oh, thank God," she said and ran out of her bedroom into the living room to peer out the front window. The vehicle coming down the drive wasn't her dad's truck, but a black unmarked SUV. The elation and relief she felt a mere second ago evaporated and was replaced by panic.

"Shit," she said. She ran to the hall closet, which did double duty as a gun locker.

She flung the door open and hesitated, unsure whether to grab a rifle or shotgun. Going with her gut, she settled on her dad's over/under Benelli, the gun she was most familiar with. She pulled it from the rack, slid the unlocking lever, cracked the breech, and checked for cartridges in the upper and lower barrels. Finding it loaded, she swung the barrels up until they locked into the receiver. Next, she grabbed a box of shells, stuffed them in the front pouch of her hoodie, and flicked off the safety with her thumb. Her hands shook, but she forced herself to take a deep breath and blow it out hard.

Be brave; you can do this.

She jogged back to the window and looked out. The SUV had stopped fifteen yards from the house. The front driver and passenger doors opened. A woman stepped out of the driver's side and a man climbed from the passenger seat. They were dressed like military soldiers, but in unmarked clothes—like Dad used to wear—and both had pistols in hip holsters. The guy had his left arm in a sling.

"Shit, what do I do?" she muttered. She felt like she was about to hyperventilate.

The two strangers looked at each other, nodded, and started walking toward the porch. She scanned their faces and body language. They looked relaxed, not angry or menacing, and neither of them had drawn their weapons or put their hands on their pistol grips.

That's a good sign.

From a distance, they both looked fairly young—late twenties or early thirties—but as they walked closer, she realized she was wrong. They were *much* older than that, but in a weird way—as if CGI had been used to make their young faces look old. And they walked like older people, like how a retired Olympic athlete might walk years after their prime. How could somebody look young and old at the same time?

What's going on here?

Before they reached the porch, she flung open the front door and stepped out with the Benelli leveled at the guy's chest.

"Whoa, hey . . ." he said as he raised his hands, and the woman did the same. "It's okay. We're not here to hurt you."

"I don't know you, and I want you off my property right now," she said, her eyes flicking back and forth between them.

"I can definitely appreciate that. But I promise we're here to help you." The man spoke in a strong voice, confident and even. "What's your name?"

Margot didn't answer. She wasn't *that* stupid.

"I don't need any help," she said, but it was the biggest lie of her life.

"We're friends of your dad's," the woman said, speaking up for the first time, "and he sent us to check on you."

"You know my dad?" Margot asked but took a half step back for some reason.

"Yeah, we work with him in Maryland."

"What's his name?"

"Pat Moody," the guy said. When she didn't react, he hedged, "At least, that's the name we know him by. In our business, people often use fake names. Pat Moody might not be a name you're familiar with, but that's what he asked us to call him."

Patrick Moody *was* her dad's name, but that didn't mean she could trust these people. She swallowed and considered the very likely scenario that she was being manipulated. That's what people who worked for the military and CIA did for a living, right?

"Is my dad okay?" Margot felt herself lower the shotgun slightly, her need for answers overwhelming her want for security.

Her uninvited guests looked at each other and shared a silent thought.

"We're not sure," the woman said, and Margot believed her. "Your dad's gone missing, and we came here to make sure you were safe but also to see if he may have told you something that could give us a clue to finding him."

Margot decided she wasn't telling them anything. "You're making me very scared and nervous now. Please leave. I don't want to have to shoot you."

"Okay," the man said and took a step backward. "If that's what you want, we'll respect your wishes."

"But we will stay in the area for a little while in case you change your mind," the woman said. "I'm going to reach into my pocket and get a mobile phone which I'm going to set down at my feet. Okay? Don't shoot me."

Margot nodded and watched the woman do just that.

"We programmed our numbers into speed dial," the woman continued. "I'm Zee, and this is Tyler. Tyler is number one, and my phone is
number two. All three phones are burners, so nobody can track us."

Margot saw Tyler's gaze tick to the barn, and she realized instantly
that he knew about the thing inside.

They're here for the machine.

She raised the shotgun again, but then something the woman said
screamed for her brain's attention and her eyes went wide.

"We're leaving now," Zee said. "If you get scared or need our help,
or if other people with guns come and threaten or try to take you, call
us and we'll rush back."

"Wait! What did you say your names were again?" she asked, lowering the shotgun and pointing it at the deck of the porch.

"I'm Zee, and this is Tyler," the woman said and exchanged a look
with her partner.

Those were the names in Dad's note . . .

Margot looked back and forth between them, checking their
old-young eyes for signs of deceit. Maybe it was desperate hope, but
she trusted what she saw. Then she noticed the bloodstained bandages
on Tyler's left arm.

"My dad told me you might come."

Zee's lips pressed into a soft smile and she looked at Tyler again before
glancing back to Margot. "What I'm about to say is not meant to scare
you. Obviously, you're a very brave girl who can take care of herself, but
you're not safe here. Eventually, the bad guys are going to find out about
this place and come looking. We have a few other teammates in the Suburban—people you will really like, I promise. We can help protect you, but
to do that, you're going to have to take a leap of faith and trust us."

Margot considered for a long moment. Something in the woman's
eyes told her she could trust Zee. She said a silent prayer that it wasn't
just her terror making her grasp at straws. But she'd always been a
pretty good judge of character and had good intuition about people.
Hopefully, she wasn't wrong this time. If they said the right things,
maybe they could help her figure out just what in the hell Dad was

trying to tell her in his cryptic note.

"Okay, but if you want to stay, and if you want me to trust you, then you need to answer my questions truthfully and *read me in* fully to what's going on." She threw in that bit of lingo so they'd know she wasn't clueless. "I know I look young, but I'm not a kid. I'm nineteen . . . and my name is Margot, by the way."

Zee fixed her with a kind and knowing smile. "And I know I *look* old, but I promise you, I'm not much older than you are. We've got a lot to talk about, Margot, and the clock is ticking."

"And if you agree to share your time with us," Tyler said, stepping next to Zee, "we promise to share some of ours with you—and help find your dad."

"Okay," she said. "First, we talk out here. Then, if I like what I hear, I can show you something."

Tyler raised an eyebrow. "And what's that?"

"A very strange note my dad left that I think was meant for you . . ."

ACKNOWLEDGMENTS

Thank you to our amazing team at the Blackstone Publishing family for helping and guiding us on our storytelling journey. *Family* is the first word that comes to mind when we think of Blackstone, and we are truly blessed to have a publisher that embraces the very team and mission-before-self ethos that defines who we are and our approach to business and storytelling.

Thanks always to our wonderful wives and amazing kids who stand with and beside us for every new story we write.

And thank you, our readers, for kitting up and going outside the wire with us. Again . . .

GLOSSARY

AFSOC Air Force Special Operations Command

AIS Automatic Identification System

AQIZ Fictional terrorist organization

ATP Adenosine Triphosphate (the source of energy use and storage at the cellular level)

CI Counterintelligence

comp Shorthand for *comparison*

CONUS Continental United States

CSO Combat Systems Officer

DARPA Defense Advanced Research Projects Agency

DIA Defense Intelligence Agency

DoD Department of Defense

EGA Eagle, Globe, and Anchor (current emblem of US Marine Corps)

EMF Electromagnetic Field

exfil Exfiltrate

HM1 Hospital corpsman first class

HRT Hostage Rescue Team

HUMINT Human Intelligence

HVT High-Value Target

IC Intelligence Community

ICBM Intercontinental Ballistic Missile

infil Infiltrate

IR Infrared

ISR Intelligence, Surveillance, and Reconnaissance

JSOC Joint Special Operations Command

Lima Charlie Shorthand for *loud and clear*

Mike Charlie Shorthand for *mission complete*

MIRV Multiple Independently Targetable Reentry Vehicles

NCO Noncommissioned Officer

NCTC National Counterterrorism Center

NLAW Next-generation Light Anti-Tank Weapon

NOC Nonofficial Cover

NORAD North American Aerospace Defense Command

NSA National Security Agency

NSW Naval Special Warfare

NVGs Night-Vision Goggles

ODNI Office of the Director of National Intelligence

OGA Other Government Agency

op Operation

OPSEC Operational Security

PCA Patient-Controlled Analgesia

QRF Quick-Reaction Force

RPG Rocket-Propelled Grenade

SCIF Sensitive Compartmental Information Facility

SDV SEAL Delivery Vehicle (crewed submersible and swimmer delivery
    vehicle used in underwater missions)

sitrep Situation report

SOF Special Operations Forces

SQT SEAL Qualification Training

SSD Solid-State Drive

TFR Transdimensional Field Reactor (a.k.a. the Donut)

TOC Tactical Operations Center

TS Top Secret

TS/SCI Top Secret/Sensitive Compartmental Information (highest level security clearance)

UNAUTH Unauthorized information from the future (about future events)

UPS Uninterruptible Power System

USSTRATCOM United States Strategic Command